P
The Beth Getty Mystery Series

"From its evocative opening to its breathtaking finish, Karen Neary Smithson blends a bit of Irish culture with a dead-on description of Venice, Italy in *Death Unmasked*, while telling an engrossing thriller about a woman seeking justice for a murdered friend. Sibèal "Beth" Getty's 'sixth sense' gives her a unique quality in the world of female sleuths."

—**Debbi Mack,** *New York Times* **bestselling author of the Sam McRae Mysteries and** *Damaged Goods*

"Smithson weaves murder, intrigue, and Venetian history into her latest novel, *Death Unmasked*. Everyone's hiding secrets. Love affairs turn into obsessions. Hidden identities reveal past mistakes. The novel is ripe with description and double-dealing, and a mystery full of so many twists and turns it will have readers guessing until the very end.

—**R. Lanier Clemons, author of the Jonelle Sweet Mystery Series**

Death in Disguise is a brilliantly written mystery that pulls the reader head-first into the pages with an eclectic array of well-drawn characters. The story unfolds at a rapid pace and builds intrigue and suspense. The ending will blow you away!

—**Kim Hamilton, author of** *Accidental Lawyer* **and the Accidental Lawyer Short Read Series**

Death in Disguise had me hooked from the first page. With a varied cast of characters, and one twist after another, fasten your seat belts for a thrilling ride!

—**Shawn Reilly Simmons, author of the Red Carpet Catering Mysteries**

Death in Disguise is everything I could ever want in a mind-boggling mystery. I was pulled in from the beginning and amazed by the ending, which I never saw coming. Murder, romance, deception, infidelity [and] celebrity characters fill the pages of a very exciting book. I really loved *Death in Disguise*. Please, do not pass this one up but put it at the top of your reading list.

—**Trudy LoPreto for** *Readers' Favorite*

Death in Disguise is a gripping mystery that had me addicted from the first page.

—Laura M. Snider, author of *Witches' Quarters*

Death in Disguise is full of action and suspense, with a great twisty ending that will take you for a loop.

—Jennifer Haskin, author of the Freedom Flight Trilogy

Sweet and well-meaning Betty Getty is an unlikely hero in *Death in Disguise*, a Hollywood 'whodunnit' that has all the ingredients for a great mystery: fame, money, murder, intrigue, and a touch of the Irish.

—m. m. burke, author of *Gymrat*

Smithson has a unique writing style that turns up the volume with over-the-top characters, detailed descriptions, and lots of emotional ups and downs. *Death in Disguise* will hook readers and brings them along on a wild ride into the private back rooms of Hollywood glitterati, the backstretch of the horse racing biz, and the secret rooms of some very dark characters.

—L.R. Trovillion, author of the Maryland Equestrian Series

An exciting and thrilling murder mystery, *Death in Disguise* is sure to send chills of fear down the spine of the stoutest reader, and often uses the reader's momentum to steer them to a place where anyone can kill.

—*InD'tale Magazine*

Death is Disguise is definitely well worth the read even if you're not a mystery reader. My favorite part was the protagonist's intuitive nature. If you enjoy mysteries, you'll love this book.

—Kathryn Ramsperger, author of *The Shores of Our Souls*

Death Unmasked

A BETH GETTY MYSTERY
BOOK 2

KAREN NEARY SMITHSON

Relax. Read.Repeat.

DEATH UNMASKED (A Beth Getty Mystery, Book 2)
By Karen Neary Smithson
Published by TouchPoint Press
Brookland, AR 72417
www.touchpointpress.com

ISBN: 978-1-952816-52-9

Editor: Kimberly Coghlan
Cover Design: Colbie Myles
Cover Photo Credit: Karen Neary
Author Photo Credit: Pierre Parker

Connect with the author
https://www.karennearysmithsonbooks.com/

First Edition

Printed in the United States of America.

In memory of my dearest friend and
fellow author Karen Smithson Esibill

Cast of Characters

SIBEAL "BETH" GETTY: An Irish-born fashion model who believes her sixth-sense, *fey*, guides her in solving crimes.

SHANE DALTON: Former Los Angeles homicide detective and Beth's husband.

DEIDRE da PARMA: Beth's life-long friend residing in Venice.

JACOPO da PARMA: Deidre's wealthy husband and owner of La Serenissima Travel Bureau.

DANIELE MARINELLO: The Chief Superintendent under whose jurisdiction the murder cases fall.

DR. ELENA BAROZZI: Pediatrician and budding love interest of Marinello.

CHIARA BAROZZI: Fifteen-year-old "boy-crazy" daughter of Elena. She is mourning the death of her father killed in Afghanistan while working as part of an international medical team.

LIDIA FELONI: Personal assistant to Jacopo and is running away from her past.

ORIANA FELONI: Studious and mature fifteen-year-old daughter of Lidia. Worried about her mother's well-being and is best friends with Chiara.

BERNARDINO "DINO" MORO: One of Venice's top tour guides.

LIA RENNER: Mysterious first wife of the canal victim.

NICOLE SHELBY: Current wife of the canal victim who would benefit from his death.

LORENZO CARAVELLO: Admitted to committing murder to impress a young lady.

FATHER BUSTATO: Pastor of San Silvestro Church and Lidia's confessor.

CARMEL McKENNA: Deidre's mother who encouraged Beth to follow her dreams.

SATINA: The da Parma housekeeper.

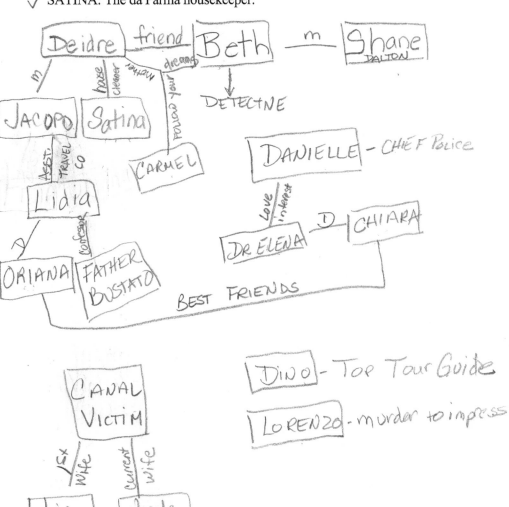

Chapter One

LOUD CLAPS ECHOED in the pitch-dark alleyway as he heaved the dray forward. The jarring strikes of the wooden wheels created a thumping rhythm that quieted the anxiety that only an hour earlier had him doubting his mission. With his back curved and a resolute grip on the cart's broken shaft, he trudged along the ancient pavement. After maneuvering around a tight corner, he froze as a halo of white light spilled across the narrow lane, diminishing the obscurity of the night. He glanced at the rusted lantern hanging on a stucco wall veined with cracks and damp with moisture. A vexing instant of hesitation faded as he tugged the cart harder and risked being seen as he moved onward. The illumination gave way to a welcomed darkness, and once again, he became a creeping specter under the starless sky.

He had discovered the vegetable cart by accident, with its generous bed and oversized wheels in a pile of debris waiting to be broken up as refuse and transported to Porto Marghera for recycling. Hardly believing his luck, he'd walked around the ramshackle wagon and decided it would be perfect. But noticing that the cart had once been handsomely painted with a great flourish of engaging colors, a pang of sorrow seized him, seeing that it stood derelict, deemed nothing more than an antiquated relic to be discarded.

It's like everything else in Venice, he thought as the smell of rotting vegetation drifting from a canal filled his nostrils. He sighed, tugging the cart harder and clinging to a thin hope that his beloved city still reigned as a financial and maritime power—the jewel of the Adriatic. Though he tried

1

to deny Venice's decline, he knew better. *A thousand years ago, but not today.* He grimaced as the shaft dug into his shoulder. *Now she's only a curiosity for day-trippers or starry-eyed honeymooners.*

The minutes passed slowly as he plodded through the shadowy labyrinth of intersecting alleys. He tried to ignore the burn of his straining muscles and the overwhelming sense of claustrophobia as the towering buildings loomed around him like the walls of a cage. At every corner, he stopped, looked around, and tugged down on the wide visor of his leather scally cap, needlessly shielding his face in the dark. Perspiration sopped his forehead and drenched his hair. Not bothering to blot away the moisture, he maintained his pace, trapped in a tunnel-like vision, focused on reaching his destination.

A smile pulled at the corners of his mouth when he spied the intended spot a few meters away. A burst of adrenalin energized his spent body and with renewed vigor, he lurched the rickety wagon onward for the final few steps.

He dropped the staves and flexed his stiff fingers. With his back to the short, sturdy footbridge, which spanned a narrow canal, he untied the kerchief wrapped around his neck and swiped his face. He stuck the bandanna into a side pocket, brushing his hand against the knife sheltered there.

After a couple of deep breaths, he crouched on the rutted stone lane and glanced at the cart's bed, filled with a half dozen wooden crates. The cartons held a variety of vegetables: red peppers, Portobello mushrooms, green zucchini, ripe tomatoes, and a coveted hundred-gram truffle. *When I'm finished here, I'll drop the vegetables off at the Convent of Santa Angela de Merici. The nuns will praise me ceaselessly for my generosity.* A full-fledged smile shot across his face.

He checked the illuminated dial of his watch, and the time surprised him. *No need to rush*, he thought, as he freed a package of cigarettes from his black T-shirt pocket. He tapped one out and stuck it between his lips. The flick of the lighter penetrated the gloomy darkness and, for a second, chased the shadows from his face. He sucked hard then slowly released the smoke. After another deep drag, he stared at the cigarette's glowing butt, a pinpoint of light, and crushed it into the pavement.

He stood and stretched his arms, working out the kinks binding his overspent muscles. After a quick glance at the canal's dark ribbon of water, he moved to the cart, yanked off the vegetable crates, and stacked them onto the walkway.

A plastic tarp covered one last item in the wagon. With a quick flick of his wrist, the sheet crumpled to the ground. Potent disgust seized him as the rising odor of the decaying corpse assaulted his nostrils. He gulped a mouthful of air. Though he hadn't been the one to kill the unsuspecting dupe, exhilaration pumped through him as he spied the dried blood, no more than a black splotch in the darkness, caking the dead man's shirt. *No, he assured himself, I had to keep my hands clean of the actual killing, but disposing the body...* His lips curled recalling how he had worked out every detail of the ambush and murder. Even so, he wished he'd been the one to have strangled him and plunged the knife into the bastard's chest.

He grabbed the corpse's ankles and pulled the stiffened legs until he eased half of the body over the wagon's ragged edge. As it dangled precariously, he retrieved the final, masterful touch from the rear of the bed. He tore the wrapped parcel open, crumpled the paper into the cart, and lifted the *Bauta*. In the misty atmosphere, the mask's pure white surface gleamed, and the two eye slits, no more than sooted hallows, fused with the darkness.

Quick steps led him back to the corpse. He held the mask over the once handsome face, now grotesquely twisted with the mouth ajar as if gasping for air. The decision to leave the eyes open was easy since he liked the frozen look of fear. He reached into his back pocket and withdrew his cellphone, clicked it on, and placed it face down on the cart's bed. He hoped to God that the light wouldn't attract anyone's attention as he lifted the bottle of adhesive and squeezed out the thick liquid along the mask's inner edge. He finished before the cellphone light went out. Firmly pressing the mask onto the ashen face, the instant bond would be waterproof. Though it wouldn't serve any purpose, he reached behind the covered face and fastened the mask's two black ribbons together. Satisfied, he pulled the body further off the cart.

Warily, he looked once again at the buildings lining the narrow street. Even if someone peered out of one of those windows, he told himself, it's

3

too dark for anyone to recognize me. Nevertheless, he pulled the cap lower on his brow and turned back to the cart.

He grabbed one of the lifeless arms and positioned the body so he could grip it. He held his breath and slid the body free from the bed, dragging it to the foot of the bridge, and up the handful of steps. A mixture of anxiety and elation spurred him on as he eased the corpse on top of the bridge's stone balustrade. He needed to catch his breath, but a jolt of sudden triumph triggered him to shove the body into the canal. A splash shattered the stillness of the night as the body landed face up in the murky water.

He turned to the crates littering the ground. Lifting them two at a time, it took only moments to hoist them into the wagon. Then, he remembered. "*Porca Vacca!*" he cursed under his breath.

He retraced his steps and faced the canal. The mask, a symbol of the glory and downfall of the ancient city, had become obscured beneath the water. He reached into his back pocket and tugged loose the billfold that he'd removed from the body hours ago. *A shame*, he thought, *to dispose of such a fine, leather wallet but…* He shrugged then removed the stack of bills and stuffed the euros into his jeans. "*Ciao, idiota,*" he spat at the submerged body. Relief surged through him as he tossed the wallet into the water.

He left the bridge knowing the nuns were early risers and would only be too eager to accept his gift of charity.

Chapter Two

THE GENTLE SWAYING of the airport *vaporetto* gliding across the expansive lagoon eased Sibéal "Beth" Getty's frazzled nerves. *It's the Irish in me,* she mused, *preventing me from telling my Shane I'm still a wee bit shaken. After all, I did ignore his demands to keep my nose out of his homicide investigation.* Even so, she never would've traded the near-deadly escapade of hunting down a phantom murderer in the Hollywood Hills for anything—even if it had been akin to a reeling roller-coaster ride, a mixture of heart pulsing excitement, and penetrating dread. A touch of a smile crossed her face but faded when a sharp twinge shot through her shoulder. The wound hadn't quite healed, but nothing was going to stop Beth from focusing all her energy on their long-awaited honeymoon.

She snuggled deeper into the bucket seat and leaned her head against her husband's shoulder. She'd met Shane Dalton by happenstance in a Los Angeles courthouse where she was to testify in a drunk driving accident that almost took her life. Though they'd been married for nearly a year, they hadn't been able to get away for a honeymoon. Until now.

Shane had surprised her last week with the resignation of his post as a homicide detective in the Los Angeles County Sheriff's Department. But, after a month away from the job, Beth hoped he'd come to his senses and realize that he ate, drank, and slept police work—it's what made him face each day with purpose—and though he had his heart set on obtaining his contractor's license, she doubted that would offer him the same sense of satisfaction.

The gentle rocking motion lulled her into a much-needed calmness as the grind of travel slipped away. They were only minutes from their destination—Venice—a treasure trove of art and architecture, meandering waterways and footbridges, pageantry and upscale shops, candlelight restaurants, and strands of music floating in the air.

That's what this vacation is all about—rest, rejuvenation, and romance—mostly romance.

The sound of her mobile phone jangled from somewhere inside her oversized tote bag. She rummaged around in the bag and located the phone wedged between a paperback novel and her wallet. Checking the screen, she rolled her eyes upward seeing the caller's name. Skye. The drama of the previous two months had swirled around Skye Andrews, the movie star, and her good friend. With her romantic getaway about to begin, she had no time to gab with Skye. She dropped the mobile back into her bag.

Shane turned away from the row of windows lining the sleek waterbus. "Who's calling? Everyone knows we're on our honeymoon."

"Skye."

"Don't tell me she's going to be a pest while we're in Venice?" Irritation laced his voice.

"Of course not. She was probably wondering if we arrived safe and sound. I can't blame her with recent events." Beth gulped a mouthful of sea air. "No worries, darlin'. Skye can respect our privacy if need be."

"It'd be a first then."

Beth reached for his hand and squeezed it. She wasn't about to let anything or anyone, Skye included, interfere with their honeymoon. "Forget about Skye. Look."

Golden domes with shining spires rose from a soft iridescence where the fusing of wave and sky converged, fanciful as a dream, fashioning a seemingly magical landscape. In reality, they faced Venice at sunset.

"Every time I approach this skyline, it's as if all my cares fall away. I feel incredibly free. As if I can finally breathe," Beth said.

"I can see why," Shane mumbled then cleared his throat. "It's hard to believe that I'm going to be in the most romantic city on Earth with the most beautiful girl in the world."

She smiled recognizing her husband's rising enthusiasm.

"I can't wait to see Palladio's masterpieces." He faced her. "There's the two churches in Venice and a number of villas in the countryside."

Besides law enforcement, architecture was Shane's passion, making it another reason to honeymoon in Venice. Palladio, the Renaissance master, ranked high on his scale of architects, and this part of Italy displayed his finest works. Shane droned on about Palladio's influence on English, then American architecture as she gazed across the rushing water toward the beguiling city steadily coming closer with each passing moment.

"...his designs were drawn from extensive research of Vitruvius, the first-century Roman architect," Shane spoke with calm knowledge of the subject, but obvious animation colored his words. "The popularity of Palladio's style extends back to his four books of—"

"There'll be plenty of time to discuss Palladio and his tremendous influence on *all* of western architecture, but now my dear, look; we're here."

The waterbus lumbered toward a dock flanked by *pali*, wooden posts, painted white with a black spiral like a barbershop pole. Within minutes, their luggage in hand, they were once again on terra firma. Beth took the lead as she headed toward the largest and most beautiful square in all of Venice, the Piazza San Marco.

In the golden dusk, the monumental buildings they skirted around shimmered in the reflected light that bounced off the lagoon. She pointed out the main structures as they paused a moment in the elongated shadow of the immense bell tower. The *campanile* stood like a sentinel guarding the expansive piazza.

Though the gentle June breeze was warm, a sudden chill wrapped its icy fingers around her. She tried to fight the sensation of apprehension but knew it'd be useless since her sixth-sense, her *fey,* was a gift she had no control over. Whether it be a blessing or a curse, her *fey* was a persistent harbinger of adversity, and that was the last thing she wanted during her honeymoon.

"Please not now," she murmured.

Shane turned his attention away from the bell tower. "Did you say something, Betty Getty?"

She couldn't help but smile when he used his pet name for her. "'Tis nothing, Shane. Just an odd sensation. My *fey*—"

"Not that again."

7

"After everything that's happened, you can't still be denying the veracity of my *fey*?"

"You know I don't believe in that hocus-pocus stuff. I deal in facts. Evidence. But I gotta hand it to you Beth; you've got the best gut instincts of any cop I've ever known."

She swallowed her protests and pulled on her rollaboard suitcase. "Once we're settled in the hotel, why don't we come back here? I'm thinking it'd be a grand spot to relax with a glass of wine." She pointed to a cluster of tables and chairs that flanked a café.

"Sounds like a plan." He reached for the two over-sized suitcases he'd set down. "How much further to the hotel?"

"We're nearly there." She motioned with a diagonal thrust of her arm across the piazza, tugged on her rollaboard's handle, and forced the wheels to turn over the ancient volcanic stone pavement. "I was disappointed that the family sold the hotel. Now it has new owners, a new name, and has been totally redecorated. I'm afraid it's lost some of its charm."

"As long as it's got a bed and a shower, I'm satisfied."

"I want every minute of our honeymoon to be perfect," Beth said.

"How could it be anything but amazing? We're standing in the center of the 'Most Serene Republic'." He quickened his pace, and Beth kept up with him. "Look, it's only for one night. I hate living out of a suitcase, but by tomorrow this time, we'll be settled into the apartment."

"Deirdre outdid herself finding us a flat on such short notice." Beth had turned to her dearest friend and now a Venetian resident, Deirdre da Parma, to help plan the trip. "Especially since she's up to her eyeballs with work. It's almost the end of the school term."

"Doesn't she teach math?"

"English."

"I don't why I thought it was math. I guess, maybe it's because she reminds me of my high school geometry teacher. Down to earth—though I suspect she was a brainiac—but fair, even-tempered, and pretty with a sprinkling of freckles on her nose ... with an uncanny sense of humor—she was a lot like your best bud, Deirdre."

"So, you had a crush on your teacher." She shot him a quick smile. "Math never was one of Deirdre's strongpoints. I think it's a good thing that her husband takes care of all the finances. But, she's a lovely teacher. Her students adore her."

"I'm not surprised. She's so warm and friendly—a great gal." He stopped at the edge of the massive square and slowly turned around taking in its grandeur. "I'm eager to explore all of Venice's six neighborhoods."

"The first neighborhood on your list will have to be the Castello district since that's where our flat is located," Beth said. "Only steps away from all of the major attractions. Even though this is a small city, it's still easy to get lost. I know that from experience."

"No worries. After a couple days of exploring, I'll know Venice like the palm of my hand." He gestured toward an ice cream shop. "Hey, I hear the *gelati* is to die for. You want some?"

She stopped at the entrance leading into a narrow lane. "Maybe later. After we're settled in our room. Take a look," she said pointing to a cream-colored rectangle with two lines of words posted on the side of the gelato shop. "Calle is a street that runs between two sets of buildings. So the name of this street is Calle Dei Fabbri. And the line posted above it is the name of the bridge, Ponte dei Dai. The Bridge of the Gods. The name probably evolved from the word *Dadi*. Dice. A very popular game six hundred years ago. Anyway, the hotel is on the other side of the bridge."

They headed under the arched portico and moved through a short tunnel flanked by a couple of brightly lit shops. Not pausing to glance at the array of glittering items behind the stores' plate-glass windows, they climbed the bridge's two sets of six stairs.

"I had no idea the hotel was so close to the heart of Venice." Shane stopped on the bridge and released the two suitcases. "I guess the city is full of these canals." He rested against the railing and faced her.

"They're everywhere." She let go of the rollaboard, leaned a bit over the railing, and stared into the channel.

He kissed her cheek.

She tilted her head toward him when something caught her eye. "What's that?" She crouched down to get nearer to the canal and peered through the bottom section of the wrought iron railing. "Looks like a carnival mask." She pointed to the ghostly papiér mâché mask in the watery darkness below.

"That's unusual?" He looked into the canal. "Wait a minute. Damn, it's too dark. I need a light."

She stood and fished out the mini-flashlight she kept in her bag for perusing menus in dimly-lighted restaurants. Though it was tiny, the beam was strong and easily illuminated the mask.

"What the..." Shane grabbed the flashlight from her and held it closer to the water.

Though submerged, the mask was secured to the face of a body, bobbing beneath the water.

Chapter Three

"MAMMA," CHIARA CALLED as she threw open the door and ran down the main hall, leading toward the kitchen. "A terrible thing has happened."

Elena Barozzi lifted her eyes from the asparagus she was slicing for the evening meal. "Calm down," she said resuming her task. "Everything it seems is an unfolding drama to you." She glanced beyond her daughter. "Where's Oriana?"

Chiara looked over her shoulder and fluffed her wavy, shoulder-length, ebony hair. Not seeing her friend, she retraced her steps. Oriana Feloni, her eyes shut, stood slumped against the wall of the wide corridor. Chiara noticed her friend's cheeks looked wet. "What's wrong?"

Oriana shook her head. "Nothing. Really, I'm fine." She offered a small smile. "What's for dinner? Smells good."

Chiara shrugged. "Probably fish and risotto with vegetables. My mamma uses just the right amount of spices. Anyway, I'm not buying into any excuses; you're staying for dinner." She grabbed Oriana's arm and tugged her in the direction of the kitchen.

"Chiara, stop," Oriana said raising her voice. "I have to go home."

"My mother asked for you. Come on."

Dutifully, Oriana stepped next to Chiara and entered the kitchen. The bouquet of sunflowers on the countertop, simmering pots, and mound of vegetables offered a dose of hospitality, as did Elena's welcoming smile.

"Here she is, Mamma." Chiara beamed.

Elena motioned to one of the stools flanking the work island's quartz countertop.

"*Grazie*," Oriana murmured and pulled out the stool.

"Now, what's this terrible thing you're so excited about?"

11

"A body floating in the canal at the *Ponte dei Dai*." Chiara glanced at her friend. "Godfather Daniele is in charge, giving orders, and securing the area." She paused to gauge the expression on her mother's face. Only the narrowing of her dark eyes and the appearance of a crease between her eyebrows betrayed her growing interest. "You should go there. Now. Oriana agrees with me."

"Is that so, Oriana?"

"I should go home. My mother will be worried." Oriana sprang from the stool. "*Buona sera, Dottoressa* Barozzi." She hurried out of the room before either one of them could protest.

Chiara rolled her eyes upward. "You would think Oriana is the mother, the way she fusses over Signora Feloni." She reached into the supple leather purse strapped across her chest and pulled out a hair clip, twisted her thick locks, and secured them off her neck. "Please Mamma, come with me to the canal. It's so exciting compared to how boring it usually is around here. Please."

"The risotto is about finished and so is the fish. Go wash up and then set the table."

"We'll miss everything," Chiara protested as she stepped out of the kitchen. She stomped to the bathroom, turned on the spigot, and lathered her hands. After a quick rinse, she bounded back to the kitchen. "Can't we eat later?"

"Are you sure there's a body in the canal?" Irritation ticked Elena's usually moderate voice. "Did you see it?"

Chiara shrugged. "Oriana saw it. I'd just caught a glimpse of Antonio and tried to reach him, but the crowd was thick, and then a large group of tourists marched by blocking everything. By the time I reached Antonio, the police were clearing everyone away."

"Antonio. Well, I'm not surprised it was a boy who diverted your attention."

Chiara offered her mother her best pleading expression. She had practiced it often enough in her bedroom mirror, and it usually did the trick.

"If the police shooed everyone away, why go back and let our dinner get cold?"

"What if the dead person is someone we know? That would be terrible." The thought scared Chiara for a second, but then she remembered a group of onlookers had been talking about a murdered tourist. "Anyway, everyone knows you're friends with Chief Superintendent Marinello. Plus, you're a doctor. They may need you to examine the body."

"A pediatrician to examine a corpse?" Elena raised her neatly arched eyebrows.

Chiara couldn't keep the corners of her lips from inching upward. "Please."

"Oh, alright. But if this is about seeing Antonio—I've told you he's much too old for you—he's eighteen and soon to be off on military duty."

"The *Guardia Costiera*." She corrected her mother under her breath but then thought it best to be agreeable. "You're right, Mamma. Antonio is almost a man." She jogged toward the front door.

THOUGH DARKNESS HAD overtaken the sky, it took Elena only a moment to single him out from the crowd. Daniele Marinello had been her husband's best friend, and he'd been a rock when her husband was killed as a member of an international medical team working in Afghanistan. Though she'd always considered him confident with keen insight and innate intelligence, his sense of empathy helped her manage during that hellish blur.

Elena stood by the line of round, linen-covered tables and wicker armchairs, nestled against the restaurant's façade adjacent to the murder scene. She watched as Daniele exercised calm control and easily handled what could've been total chaos. The crowd Chiara had described had thinned, and only a couple of uniformed police officers hovered around him—and thankfully, no sign of Antonio.

With measured steps, she walked closer and stopped near the footbridge where tape cordoned off the crime scene. Chiara rushed next to her mother and leaned over the iron railing abutting the bridge, peering into the murky water. Elena sensed her daughter's disappointment. She slipped her arm around Chiara's waist and joined in the futile search for a waterlogged corpse.

"*Buona sera, Dottoressa Barozzi.*" Marinello smiled at Elena before shifting his sight to Chiara. He nodded at the gloomy-faced girl. "I think a gelato will erase that frown from your pretty face." He stuck his hands into his pocket and withdrew a couple of coins.

Chiara reached for the money but stopped and looked at her mother with questioning eyes. Elena couldn't hide her amusement. "Go. Get a gelato."

After thanking him, Chiara hurried away.

"To what do I owe this unexpected pleasure?" Marinello shot her a warm smile.

She threw out her hands as if exasperated. "Your goddaughter swore there was a body in the canal. She wouldn't give me a moment's peace until she dragged me down here." She glanced at the officers. "Ah, something did happen."

He nodded.

"A body in the canal?"

He nodded again.

"How?"

"That's what we're attempting to find out. An American couple discovered the body. It was probably dumped further down the canal but wound up here since it got caught onto a rusted old stake used to repair the bridge years ago." He shook his head. "It's obviously a murder."

Elena pursed her lips and studied his face in the light cast from the shops and cafes lining the street. "With the state of the economy, are you sure it wasn't suicide?"

"*Sgozzare*," he said with a violent thrust of his index finger across his neck. "The odd thing is the victim's face was concealed by a *Bauta*. The mask was actually glued on. A macabre sense of the dramatic, I'd say."

She widened her eyes. "How horrifying. Won't that make it difficult to identify the victim? You don't think he's someone we know?"

"What the hell is going on?"

Both of them turned toward the man approaching them.

"Oh, Jacopo. It's just awful," Elena said as she pecked his cheeks and he hers.

"I arrived home from a business trip not even an hour ago and find Venice in an uproar. Rumors are buzzing throughout the city. So, what's the real story, Chief Superintendent?" Jacopo da Parma stretched his opened palm in Marinello's direction.

"It's not that uncommon." Marinello shook his hand.

"Murder in Venice?" Jacopo asked.

Marinello squinted. "The incident is being called a murder?"

"Isn't it?" Jacopo raised his thick eyebrows. "Won't be good for business."

"You think a murder will keep the tourists away? Cruise ships turning around and throngs of Europeans on holiday to go to where ... Poland?" Elena paused. "You have nothing to worry about, Jacopo. The Tourist Bureau won't suffer."

"Neither will your innumerable tours." All three of them focused on the tall, strapping fellow that edged toward their little group. "Thankfully," he added with a grin.

"Dino." Marinello slapped the man's muscular back. "So, he's keeping you busy." He jutted his chin in Jacopo's direction.

"Tour after tour after tour. But, I'm not complaining. It pays the bills, after all." Bernardino Moro took a step closer to Elena. "How is the most beautiful doctor in all of Venice this evening?"

"A bit perplexed about this tragic turn of events. I pray to God it's no one we know."

"Ah." Bernardino stroked his chin. "Probably a tourist."

"How did you come up with that?" Marinello asked.

Bernardino shrugged. "Pure logic. After all, one doesn't have to murder Venetians to do away with them. They're fleeing of their own accord."

Jacopo narrowed his eyes. "Well, good riddance to them. If they can't appreciate the wonder of all of this," he said as if trying to encompass the entire narrow street, "they can go straight to hell."

"I believe they're venturing only as far as the mainland, Jacopo," Bernardino said.

Elena noticed the mischievous glint in Bernardino's dark eyes. "Don't taut him, Dino. I admire Jacopo. The way he loves his city. It's refreshing."

Bernardino glanced at Jacopo who stood ramrod straight with arms folded. "He loves it alright. It's made him a pile of money."

"Don't forget I'm the one who sets up all of your tours," Jacopo said between clenched teeth.

"It's a bit ironic that our city's past enables our future," Marinello said with a wisp of sadness touching his voice.

"Well, my immediate future includes dinner. Would you like to join me?" Bernardino extended his arm toward Elena.

"Thanks for the offer," she said with a shake of her head.

"Another time then," Bernardino said with a shrug. "Good night."

Marinello nodded, and Jacopo frowned as Bernardino moved toward the nearby restaurant.

"That guy—"

"Excuse me," Marinello interrupted Jacopo and turned his back to them.

Elena watched Marinello walk toward a man she didn't recognize. She wondered if he could be the one who made the gruesome discovery. She sized the stranger up in a split-second—obviously handsome—tall, blond, and tanned. But his eyes held her attention—steely blue and piercing—in the beams cast from the police spot-lights.

"Elena?"

"Oh, sorry Jacopo." She paused a second. "There's something I want to discuss with you. I'm concerned about Signora Feloni—Lidia."

"No wonder Lidia has headaches. That jerk." Jacopo flicked his chin at Bernardino who'd made himself comfortable at one of the restaurant's outside tables. "He's always at the office bugging her. If he wasn't my best tour guide, I'd fire his ass." He paused a second and looked at Elena. "Excuse me for my bout of temper, but Bernardino Moro fires me up."

"Dino's a charmer. But, harmless. I'm sure Lidia sees right through him."

"You're probably right. After all, the only thing that captures Lidia's attention is her daughter."

"That's what I wanted to talk with you about. Her daughter is Chiara's best friend. Oriana seems unduly upset about her mother."

"Lidia called out sick today. Another headache. But I'm not surprised that Oriana is worried. Lidia slips into bouts of deep depression. And though she doesn't share a lot of personal stuff, she comes across as a bit preoccupied. Like something is, I don't know, troubling her? Even so, Lidia is one of my most efficient workers. That's why I promoted her to be my personal assistant." Jacopo draped his arm around Elena's shoulders. "How about a glass of wine? I'm sure we can come up with something more pleasant to discuss besides my assistant's health issues."

Elena shook her head. "I have my hands full with..." She jutted her chin in the direction of Chiara approaching—with Antonio at her side.

Chapter Four

ORIANA FELONI TOOK THE long route home as she darted along murky alleys and skirted between gaily-lit restaurants and pastel-painted hotels lining *Riva dei Vin*. Her home was on the other side of the Rialto Bridge in the San Polo *sestiere,* the district separated from San Marco by the Grand Canal. Centuries ago, the building stood as a gracious *palazzo*, but now, all vestiges of its regal past had been lost, with its reconfiguration into small, nondescript apartments. She lingered on the bridge and looked into its dark, choppy water.

Her mother's instability had her on edge. Oriana wondered if the old routine was about to repeat itself. First, her mother would quit her job, then whisk them off to a new town and another cramped apartment. She'd have to adjust to a new school and attempt to make friends—those newly-formed relationships wouldn't last long—since after a handful of months they'd be moving again, and the process would start over.

Before that would happen, she'd no longer be Oriana Feloni. Her mother would come up with a new surname. There had been so many—Moretti, Gallo, Rossi, Parisi, Sanna—and a few she didn't remember. When she was a little girl, her mother had made it into a game; she'd recite a list of names and allow Oriana to select one. The last time had been different. Oriana had just turned twelve, and instead of choosing a name, she'd asked a question. "Why?" Her mother hadn't answered.

That had been the norm until they moved to Venice. They'd resided in the old, drafty apartment for over three years, longer than she could ever remember living in one location.

She'd believed her mamma had finally found a place to call home. But now Oriana had a sinking suspicion that was about to change.

18

Her mother's behavior had shifted radically, so much so, Oriana feared something was seriously wrong. Her mother always had lunch waiting when she returned home from school and spent time with her during *riposo* before heading back to the Travel Bureau. But that had stopped weeks ago. Her mother's explanation seemed haphazard when she haltingly explained that the start of the travel season had increased her workload and she'd have to remain late into the night at her job. The past three summers had been hectic, but she'd never missed a single lunchtime. And she could count the evenings on one hand that her mother had returned home for dinner—another red flag—her mamma had offered a flimsy explanation that the sisters of Santa Angela de Merici had become so much more dependent on her assistance. Oriana wasn't buying into her mother's excuses.

She turned away from the canal and plodded down the bridge's wide ramp behind a couple who stopped every few steps and looked around as if enthralled by the bridge's lights reflecting on the water. *Tourists.* Although she could've raced around the couple and the others milling around on the bridge she crept along remembering the last time her mother had slipped into a depression. It seemed to last months, and even *Carnevale* hadn't snapped her out of it. Reaching the end of the bridge she paused a second and glanced at the expanse of water.

She doesn't seem depressed ... just not behaving like Mamma.

Oriana resumed walking. With each step, a deepening sensation of trepidation coursed through her. *Mamma will be home*, she buoyed herself, but the niggling in the back of her mind told her otherwise. She reached into her jean pocket and grasped her cellphone. *If anyone can help Mamma, it's Signore da Parma. He's been so kind, lending her money with no pressure to pay it back.* She looked at the phone's screen and realized she didn't know his number.

The time glowing from the cellphone startled her—nearly nine o'clock. She picked up her pace and neared Campo San Silvestro. The imposing church, for which the square was named, blended with the night shadows and stood dark and deserted.

She raced up the church's short flight of steps and pulled on the wooden doors, intent on offering a prayer for her mother in front of the tabernacle. But they didn't budge. She turned away, sunk onto the top step, and buried her face in her hands.

A few moments passed when her cellphone sounded. She wanted it to be her mother calling, in a panic, wondering where she was, but glancing at the screen, she saw Chiara's name. She let the call go to voicemail. The sound of her friend's excited voice babbling on about some tidbit regarding Antonio or any of the boys who'd caught her attention would be too much. Instead, she ran her fingers along the edge of the smooth, stone stair knowing she'd have to go home but dreading the thought of entering the empty apartment.

Oriana stuffed the phone back into her pocket. She suspected that earlier Chiara had only wanted to return to Piazza San Marco to meet up with Antonio and somehow talk her mother into inviting him back to their house for dinner. Chiara hadn't the slightest interest in the crime that had been committed.

But the grisly scene at the *Ponte dei Dai* had shaken her. Not in the horrifying way of unexpectedly seeing a dead body, but in an unsettling fascination that frightened her. She had squeezed between the onlookers and worked her way to the canal's iron railing. Taking in the scene, she'd been mesmerized as the police boat with its blue light flashing, swayed in the canal as a couple of men in wet suits splashed into the waterway. Unlike those around her who murmured and gasped when the body was released from its watery shroud, she only narrowed her eyes hoping to see the victim's face. It took only seconds to realize that she'd be denied that opportunity since it was covered with a *Bauta*. But when the dead man's arm dropped, she caught her breath. She'd recognized the simple heart-shaped tattoo inked above the man's wrist that encircled a name—Gemma. Seeing the tattoo had caused an inexplicable sense of warmth and security to flood through her. The sensation lasted only a moment, and by the time the body had been hoisted into the small skiff, the strange feeling had vanished.

Hidden in the darkness cast by the church, she squeezed her eyes shut trying to remember why the tattoo seemed familiar. *Gemma is not that unusual of a name. I must've seen a tattoo like that before.* She opened her eyes and glanced at the night sky as if the answer was written among the few visible stars. She shook her head, stood, and headed down the steps for home.

Chapter Five

NEAR THE DOORWAY OF Hotel Leone, Shane studied the man in charge of the investigation. Though the officer spoke in a quiet tone, he'd been unable to disguise the intensity charging his every motion. Dressed in civilian clothing, Shane suspected the cop had been called away from home. *Probably left the comfort of family to meet the unmistakable stench of death. Thank God, I don't have to deal with that anymore,* he told himself, as he continued to watch. He couldn't help but be impressed by how smoothly the officer handled the men in his charge. When the cop stopped for a few moments to talk to a couple of locals, his manner relaxed, but his intensity remained unchanged. Then their eyes met.

Shane noticed the confidence in his stride as the officer moved closer.

"Signore, I am Chief Superintendent Daniele Marinello." He reached out his hand. "I understand that you discovered the body?"

Shane was surprised that the chief wasn't taller. *Five-nine tops,* he thought, as he shook the officer's outstretched hand. "Shane Dalton," he said withdrawing from the quick, strong clasp. "Actually, it was my wife who spotted it first—the Carnival mask—and then the body."

"The poor signora. Must be a terrific shock. Has she taken herself to bed?"

Shane couldn't help but smile. "Bed? No." He shook his head. "Of course, it's a terrible tragedy. My wife, Beth, is anxious to find out what happened. She couldn't bear to stand around waiting to meet with you, so she decided to unpack and freshen up a bit. I expect she'll be here in a few minutes."

From the corner of his eye, Shane noticed a uniformed cop hurry toward them. Marinello raised his hand in Shane's direction as if asking for a moment to confer with his officer. The two men spoke softly as

Marinello took the plastic evidence bag. Knowing it would be proper to look away, Shane couldn't help but to eye the bag. Marinello glanced at it briefly, turned it over, and then handed it back to the officer. Smudged with gunk, Shane easily identified the item. A wallet. *The victim's wallet?*

Marinello turned his attention back to Shane. "I have a few questions. Perhaps we can meet at the station—"

"I'll tell you everything I know right now," Shane said. "My wife and I had just disembarked from the airport *vaporetto,* and were making our way to the hotel." He motioned toward the building behind him. "I paused on the bridge, and my wife looked into the canal. That's when she saw the mask. Realizing it was attached to a body, we entered the hotel and asked the concierge to call the police."

"You didn't recognize the victim?"

"Recognize him? He was submerged in four feet of water. His face covered by a mask. Anyway, we hardly know anyone in Venice. I'm sure, even if I had a good look him, I wouldn't know him from John Doe."

Marinello nodded with his lips pressed tight. "You are from New York?"

"California."

"Ah." Marinello tapped his square jaw a couple of times. "That's all I need for now. If you and your wife can stop by the station tomorrow, I have some forms for you to..." He moved his hand as if writing. Shane nodded as Marinello withdrew a card from his pocket and handed it to him. "Do not let this unfortunate incident color your impression of Venice. It is a rare occurrence; I assure you."

Shane noticed Marinello's eyes shift and his face soften. He realized the officer had spotted Beth as she stepped next to him. "This is Chief Superintendent Marinello. He's in charge of the investigation. My wife, Beth Getty."

"*Non ci siamo visti prima?*" Marinello said taking her hand. "Ah." He shook his head. "Haven't we seen each other before?"

"I'm afraid we haven't, *Commissario Capo*. I certainly would've remembered."

"I'm sure I've seen you," Marinello said squeezing her hand before releasing it. "I rarely forget a face." He pursed his lips and remained silent for a couple seconds. "You speak Italian?"

"Not fluently." She offered him a half-smile.

Marinello paused a moment as a stream of air escaped his lips. "Madam, as I told your husband, don't let this," he said gesturing toward the canal, "spoil your vacation."

"Spoil it? Oh no, *Commissario Capo*. It's added an unexpected layer of intrigue, though not what we expected at the start of our honeymoon."

"Ah, Venice is an ideal spot for romance." Marinello reclaimed his impassive expression.

"But the image of that poor man in the canal will be hard to forget. I was wondering about the significance of the mask."

Marinello's eyes narrowed.

"I've been thinking," Beth continued. "Could organized crime be responsible for the murder? The problem with that is the M.O. doesn't seem like a typical execution, does it?"

Marinello opened his mouth as if to comment, but then he looked at Shane with a bewildered expression. "Please, erase this unfortunate incident from your mind. Venice offers so much beauty. Architecture, food, music—from the treasures of the Gallerie dell' Accademia to a day at the beach— there are many things to see and—"

"Shane has told you he's a homicide detective."

"Former homicide detective," Shane snapped.

Beth waved her hand as if swatting away his words. "I was wondering *Commissario Capo* ... Perhaps, Shane could be of some assistance. He's an amazing detective and could offer some suggestions on how to handle the investigation. After all, the buzz in the hotel is that the murdered man was an American tourist."

Marinello crossed his arms against his chest. "I assure you, Madam, the Venetian State Police is capable of handling our own affairs."

"I didn't mean to insinuate—"

"On that note, we'll leave you to your investigation." Shane grabbed Beth's hand.

Without a word, Marinello turned away from them.

Shane hurried Beth down the narrow lane away from the crime scene and, no doubt, a perplexed Chief Superintendent Marinello.

"WHAT WERE YOU thinking, Beth?"

The anger lacing his words was loud and clear. Obviously, it'd been a bad idea to try to reignite Shane's interest in police work by offering his services to Marinello.

"Took a loss from my senses, I suppose," Beth lied but immediately felt a pang of conscience. She couldn't remember how many times she'd promised herself not to lie to Shane, and then so easily slipped into breaking her resolve. "You are the most talented detective in all of Los Angeles. I'm proud of you and I want everyone to know including *Commissario Capo* Marinello. Thought you might be able to offer him a wee bit of your expertise."

"Well, Betty Getty, those days are behind me for good."

"If you're sure—"

"I'm as sure as you are about not prancing down any more runways. You knew when it was the right time to drop out of modeling, and I know the time has come for me to leave the department."

Beth sucked in her lower lip.

They walked a few steps in silence.

"I'm heartbroken for the victim. And his family. What they must be going through now, that is, if they even know he's dead. I didn't mean to put you on the spot. It's just that your knowledge of solving the most horrific murders..."

Shane stopped walking and looked into Beth's face. Most of it was covered in shadow. "Don't worry, *mo ghrá*; this isn't Marinello's first rodeo." He brushed her cheek with his lips but stopped short of the jagged scar that all but ended her modeling career. "Come on," he said, taking her arm.

As they entered the square, soft beams of light illuminating the golden façade of St. Mark's Basilica caused it to shimmer under the night sky as lively strains of a romantic waltz filled the air. Before she could comment on the music, Shane grasped her waist and drew her close, then swept her around in circles edging them further into the grand piazza. She laughed as the plaza twirled into a blur of glimmering light and shadow.

"What's this music?" he whispered into her ear.

"Strauss?"

"The strains of it will always remind me of you. Of our time in Venice."

The music ended. Beth took his hand and led him to an array of tables lined in front of the six-piece ensemble, sheltered under a silvery canopy jutting into the square. She paused until noticing a vacant table a few rows in and gestured toward it. Shane hurried ahead, pulled out a rattan chair, and leaned close to her ear. "I want to speak to one of those musicians."

She sat and watched the wait staff weave between the tables holding large platters filled with drinks, plates of olives, and puff pastry canapes. Crisp, white linen covered the tiny tables, while the four chairs that formed each seating arrangement left little space for navigating. She caught a glimpse of Shane as the cellist handed him a napkin and followed his zigzagged route around the crowded café. When he made his way back, she noticed a glint of excitement in his eyes.

"I've got it. The name of that waltz." Shane pulled out a chair, plopped into it, and placed the napkin with a long German word scrawled across it in front of her. He stumbled as he pronounced the word, "Hoffnungsstrahlen."

Beth screwed up her nose as if trying to recall something.

"My high school German is a little rusty, but I think it means something like rays of hope." He paused a second. "Composed by Joseph Lanner."

"Rays of hope," she said as if to herself. "Lovely sentiment. Beautiful waltz."

"I have endless rays of hope for us. One is a honeymoon with no drama." He reached for her hand and squeezed it.

"It has started with a bit of commotion, but from this point forward, I think it's going to be like a beautiful dream."

"As long as the dream doesn't turn into a nightmare, I'll be happy." Shane rubbed his thumb against his dimpled chin and focused on a spot above her shoulder.

"Speaking of nightmares, I don't believe for one second it was a coincidence," she said.

He pulled his attention away from the back of a waiter. "Huh?"

"Coincidence. That we arrived here the precise moment to discover a body in a canal."

"Somebody was bound to find it. Just happened to be us."

Beth waved away his words. "What's really bugging me is the mask. Why a carnival mask in June?"

"Your *fey* on the blink or something?"

"I'm serious, Shane."

"Your curiosity has gotten you into trouble more than once, Betty Getty."

"That might be true but—"

"The murder victim has nothing to do with us. It up to the authorities to deal with it."

"But *Commissario Capo*, the Chief Superintendent—"

"Look, Beth, I've been around cops a long time, and my gut is telling me that Marinello is the analytical type. He'll leave no stone unturned and check out every possible angle."

"Marinello," she said allowing the syllables of the Chief Superintendent's name to roll off her tongue. "He is a rather attractive man. In a typical continental way."

"Is that so?"

"He must be a bit vain though, the way his clothes fit so perfectly. They must be hand-tailored to accentuate his athletic figure. But *Janey Mac* did you see those dark, dreamy eyes—"

"Talking like that on our honeymoon." Shane sighed, rolled his eyes towards the heavens, and shook his head before offering her a wink. "Marinello may look like a modern-day Apollo, but from my perspective, it's a different picture altogether. I watched him handle his subordinates with complete authority, and those dreamy eyes you referred to are as cutting as a knife's blade. Nothing gets by him. I'd stake my reputation on that. During the recovery process, I caught a glimpse of his face when he saw the corpse; the change in his expression was minor, just the slightest tightening of his lips. It made me think he'd recognized the victim. Not by his face, of course, maybe his clothing or the tattoo on his wrist."

"Tattoo?"

"An identifier that would be noted on a missing person's report."

"Right." She nodded. "I'm still a bit confused. Why didn't the killer dump the body into the middle of the lagoon and let it wash out into the Adriatic?"

"I think the perp wanted the body to be found. If not, why did he bother to attach the mask to the face and dispose of it into a narrow canal? Most canals are usually between ten to fifteen feet deep, but the one where we found the body has at least a six-foot buildup of mud and gunk. That's why we were able to make out the body submerged only under a few feet of water. From what I understand, cleaning the canals is going to continue next fall."

Beth squinted wondering how Shane knew so much about Venetian canals.

Before she could ask, he said, "I'd say the body was in the water no more than a day or two."

A waiter whizzed by them and distracted Beth for a moment. "How do you know that?"

"When the body was recovered, there wasn't any obvious damage besides evidence of immersion. Wrinkly skin. Absolutely no skin separation from the fingers or any detachment. Of course, that takes at least a week. Maybe Marinello will find something in the guy's wallet."

"Wallet?"

"It was floating downstream but was fished out of the canal. Of course, Marinello and his officer were speaking in Italian. The only word I picked up sounded like whoa-toe. Whatever the hell that means."

Beth cupped her chin in her hand and pursed her lips. "*Vuoto*. It means empty." She paused a moment. "A canal. A corpse. A carnival mask. Now an empty wallet," she said ticking each item off on her fingers.

"Interesting as it is, Beth, it's none of our business."

"If you say so, but I'd sure like to know the whole story."

The ensemble started playing another waltz. Shane tapped his fingers against the tabletop. "We've been waiting over ten minutes. Let's get out of here."

"This is Italy, Shane. It's *La Dolce Vita,* not the rat race. You're supposed to take in the atmosphere. After all, this is the most beautiful drawing room in all of Europe."

"You're right, of course." He twisted his neck to take in the view of the square. "There sure isn't anything like this at home. The architecture is amazing. The marble facades, symmetrical arches, and such precise details—it's mind-blowing."

Instead of glancing at the grandeur of the piazza, she looked at Shane's face lit with excitement. She wanted nothing more than to sit in St. Mark's

Square until the last strains of music ceased and the place became deserted. Then they'd be alone to face the splendor of Venice as the first light of day filled the morning sky.

A waiter impeccably dressed in a white dinner jacket and black bow tie approached them. "*Buona sera.*"

"*Due vetri di vino bianco, per favore,*" Beth said.

After a curt nod, the waiter darted away.

"I didn't realize that you're fluent in Italian."

"I wouldn't go that far. When I lived in Milan for nearly four years, I picked up some of the local lingo."

"Ah, yes. Your time as a runway model for the famed House of Affinito, which led to your superstar status."

She couldn't help but discern the sarcasm lacing his words. She still wondered why Shane was jealous of her success as a fashion model and her subsequent career in print ads and as the television spokesperson for Noelle cosmetics.

"Anyway, tomorrow we'll have our morning *cuppa* over there," she said, waving in the direction of the square, "at Caffè Florian. It's the oldest coffee house in Europe."

"That so?"

"It was established nearly three hundred years ago. Though it was completely controversial back then, women were welcomed as guests."

Shane nodded absently, and Beth wondered if he was listening to her. Perhaps the body in the canal held his interest more than he was letting on.

"When Casanova escaped from "The Leads," she said, jutting her chin toward the Doge' Palace, "not from the dank, stinky dungeon, but a prison on the top floor reserved for inmates of higher status, he stopped at Florian's for a cup of coffee before escaping to Paris."

"Sounds like a legend to me."

"I don't know. Casanova seemed to have luck on his side. More so than the poor lad in the canal."

The waiter reappeared holding a silver tray with two flutes of white wine. He placed them on the table and hurried away.

"I can't get that *Bauta* out of my mind," she said.

"*Bauta?*"

"The carnival mask."

Shane raised his glass, but before taking a sip, he put it down. "How do you know what kind of mask was on the dead guy?"

"I did a photoshoot here once during *Carnevale*. You know, the Carnival of Venice. I was amazed by the elaborate costumes and the beautiful masks people wore during the festivities. So, I spent some time learning a little background. As I recall, the *Bauta* mask was popular in the 18th Century and worn mostly by men. Imagine them," she said flinging her arm out as if trying to encompass the square, "walking here with their faces covered by the white, mouthless masks, wearing tricorn hats, and black capes in an attempt to ensure anonymity."

"Why would they want to be anonymous?"

"Gave them confidence," she said.

"Confidence?"

"To cross the bounds of civilized behavior. Allowed them to be comfortable at the gaming houses as well as in the copious brothels that filled Venice."

Shane slumped back in his chair and took a few sips of wine.

Strains of another waltz began to fill the air, but Beth didn't think he was listening.

"Maybe the mask doesn't have anything to do with the victim, but more a statement about the perp," he said. "If the purpose of the mask is to hide one's identity, maybe he switched it around."

"Switched it around?" Beth knit her brows.

"Instead of the murderer hiding his face, he masks the victim's face."

"Why would he do that?" She pressed her lips together as if irritated as a touch of amusement flicked across Shane's face. "Unless..." She inhaled deeply. "Unless the killer is boasting that he doesn't need to conceal his face because he's clever enough to get away with murder." She smiled. "Masking the victim's face could be a taunt. A tease. No, a mockery targeting at the heart of Venice itself. A malicious charade, so." She shook her head.

"Could be," he said with a shrug. "Anyway, it's Marinello's problem." He downed the remainder of his wine.

"I'll be sure to say a decade tonight for the soul of the poor murdered man." Beth lifted her glass and took a sip.

Shane brushed the top of her hand with his. Their eyes met for a couple of seconds. Drawn into his gray-blue irises, she read the intensity of his love for her.

The spell was broken when he stifled a yawn and stood. He reached into his pocket, flipped open his wallet, and removed a couple of bills. He dropped the euros onto the table. "I'm beat. Feels as if I've done a double shift."

"Staying awake will prevent jet lag." She stood and grasped his hand.

They crossed the square and entered the lane that led to the hotel. The police tape was gone from the footbridge. Shane paused a moment glancing at the murky canal. Then, without a word, he placed his hand under Beth's elbow and ushered her through the hotel's automatic door. After stopping at the concierge desk to pick up the room key, he took the steps up to their floor two at a time while the large, brass key stuck out of the back pocket of his trousers. Following close behind, Beth grabbed the key and scooted in front of him, unlocked the door, and flung it open. They entered the neatly-appointed room, and Beth dropped her leather tote bag on top of a low dresser. She faced Shane who'd sunk onto the edge of the bed.

"I swear Betty Getty, I can't keep my eyes open."

She sat next to him. "You don't want jet lag, do you?"

"At this point, I don't care."

She kissed his cheek and then began to unbutton his shirt. Her fingertips stroked his developed pecs. "You really want to sleep now?" She deposited a row of feather-light kisses down his breastbone.

He placed his fingers under her chin and lifted her face. "Maybe not this minute." He eased her down across the bed and kissed her firmly on the lips. "Though it hasn't been proven, this might be another cure for jet lag. I think it'd be wise to test out the theory," he murmured unzipping his trousers.

"You've read my mind," she said tugging off his shirt. "And I thought I was the one with the sixth sense."

Chapter Six

LIDIA FELONI HUMMED AS she walked along the shadowy, deserted street toward her apartment. She'd stayed longer at the convent than planned. *But how could I leave*, she thought remembering how the happy news had brightened the sisters' faces with joy. And the questions—they wanted to know every detail—especially if there was going to be a wedding.

She slowed at the little footbridge and smiled. How could all of this have happened in just a few short weeks? But miraculously, it had. He had forgiven her. And even hinted about them getting back together. They'd be a family after a decade of being separated. *Separated.* The word he'd used. But he was being kind because broken to shreds would've been more accurate.

Lidia dropped onto the bridge's middle step. She buried her face in her hands and willed herself to forget, but her mind refused. She released her hands and pressed them to her chest.

"How could I have been so stupid?" She spoke as if expecting an answer from the ancient stucco buildings towering on either side of her. She'd confessed, the night he arrived in Venice, that this long, horrible ordeal had been her fault. Then, as if the albatross had been lifted from her neck, he'd absolved her from the burden of her sin. "He forgave me," she whispered. *Ten years of hell are behind me.*

With a sigh, she stopped fighting the memories. They couldn't crush her spirit any longer. She looked up at the clouds scudding across the black velvet sky and allowed herself to remember. Somehow, she'd managed to take care of Oriana and earn her bachelor's degree in civil engineering. She was in the midst of sending out resumes and going for interviews when the worst depression she'd ever experienced hit. The medication wasn't working. Her marriage was crumbling. But she was too blind to see her world crashing at her feet.

Eventually, she'd stopped caring and left Oriana to basically fend for herself. That awful day was perhaps inevitable. A puppy—Oriana's puppy—and a ball. It had rolled into the street, and without looking, the four-year-old dashed after the wayward rainbow-striped sphere. The driver of the compact pick-up slammed his brakes, and though he tried to avoid hitting the little girl ... Lidia squeezed her eyes shut not wanting to remember, but she knew there wasn't another choice—face it now and then tuck it away forever. The ear-splitting wail of the siren resounded in her ears, making her dizzy as she glanced outside. Fear seized her as she clutched her dressing gown and ran barefooted into the street. She forced her way through the small group of spectators, dropped to her knees, and clutched her battered daughter. Oriana fluttered her eyes opened and whispered, "Mamma," as if she was trying to comfort her derelict mother. At that moment, somewhere in her muddled mind, Lidia realized that she didn't deserve to be Oriana's mother—that surely, she'd lose custody of her daughter forever.

After the accident, she'd forced herself to take the pills. But, it was too little too late. Her husband had started divorce proceedings and was seeking full custody of her precious Oriana. Overwhelmed, depressed, and scared, Lidia didn't know what to do.

Her closest friend, Bernardino Moro, had kidded about absconding with Oriana to Italy, their homeland. She was certain that he'd only been jesting, but somewhere in her confused brain, his words rang true. If she returned home to Italy, everything would turn out fine. She'd be a proper mother, and Oriana would grow up healthy and happy in her care. Then one afternoon, the opportunity she'd been anxiously awaiting arose, and they'd been running ever since.

"Until," she whispered the word with a smile. "Until I came to my senses." It had happened so quickly—contacting him, his arrival in Venice, their reconciliation—and now plans to reunite as a family. He'd begged her to let him meet with Oriana, but she wanted to prepare their daughter for the shock of learning that her papà hadn't abandoned his only daughter ... that had been a lie she'd concocted to squelch Oriana's longing for her father.

She lowered her gaze, pressed her hands together, and offered a sincere prayer that Oriana would find it in her heart to forgive her after learning the truth that her papà had been searching for over a decade for her.

Lidia stood, climbed up the steps, and crossed the bridge. *Tomorrow,* she decided, *I'll tell Oriana the whole story.* She glanced at her watch. It was nearly eleven. She hurried her steps, certain that Oriana would be up, pacing, worried about her.

Chapter Seven

SHANE TOOK A SIP OF CAPPUCCINO as they sat in a shady swatch in front of Caffè Florian. An hour earlier, he and Beth consumed a typical continental breakfast at the hotel. Unsatisfied with the skimpy offering of hard rolls and berries, he'd commented that the orange juice tasted like weak-flavored water. Beth had ignored his comment.

"Look at this, Shane." Beth tapped the headline of the front page of the morning edition of the *Il Gazzettino*.

He stared at the unrecognizable words. "Do you know what it says?"

"Murder in Venice." She glanced down at the page. "My Italian is a bit rusty..."

He reached into his back pocket and handed her an Italian phrasebook.

She shot him a smile. "Thanks, but..." She glanced back at the article. "It says that the victim has a heart-shaped tattoo outlining the name, Gemma. Maybe he's Italian after all."

She read a couple of sentences out loud first in Italian and then translated them into English. Impressed by her ability with the language, he wondered what other talents Beth possessed that he was unaware of... *Can she fly a plane, swim in syncopation, knit?*

"Wait a minute. What's this?" She shot Shane a wide-eyed, quizzical expression. "The reporter interviewed you?"

"I wouldn't call it an interview. He just asked how I found the body. I'm sure you noticed; I gave you all the credit since you couldn't do it for yourself. You were still in the hotel room unpacking."

"Hmm." She glanced back at the page.

"Then the reporter educated me on the canals of Venice—how many, how deep, and how often they should be cleaned."

"I was wondering why you knew so much about the canals," she mumbled as she resumed reading the article. "Well, there's no mention about the significance of the mask." She folded the paper in half.

"That reminds me. Marinello wants us to stop by the police station to fill out some paperwork."

"Does he now?" She paused a second. "Maybe he'll have uncovered more details about the murder, but I doubt he'll share it with us." She let out a sigh and lifted her coffee and took a swallow.

"You're right," Shane said. "He won't share any information from an ongoing homicide investigation with two tourists from California. I'll bet my bottom dollar on that. Anyway, I think you need to take the advice of the *Commissario*— whatever you call him—and forget about the body in the canal. After all, we're sitting at the famed Florian's in St. Mark's Square, sipping coffee. It's freaking amazing." He raised his cup but then replaced it on the saucer. "You know, the only thing that spoils this place are those." He motioned to a kit of pigeons pecking at some scraps of bread that had been dropped onto the ground beyond them. "They're nothing more than flying rats."

"A few years ago, the city outlawed vendors from selling bird feed in St. Mark's. The number of them has been reduced. But, I suspect tourists still like having their pictures snapped with the birds eating out of their hands. So, they feed them just about anything from French fries to pizza."

"Damn nuisance."

"The city officials agree with you. If you're caught feeding pigeons there's a hefty fee. Seven hundred euros."

"Whoa! That's almost eight hundred dollars." He shook his head. "I think the city should close down the square for a day and have a pigeon shoot."

Beth's jaw dropped.

"Just kidding, Betty Getty. But they are a damn nuisance."

Beth motioned beyond him. "There she is." She jumped up and raced toward a woman dressed in a conservative gray skirt suit with the strap of an oversized briefcase crossing her chest.

The two embraced, hooked their arms together, and approached the table. Unsure how to greet his wife's closest friend, he stood and reached for Deirdre de Parma's hand, but then moved closer and embraced her. She, in return, brushed his cheeks with a light kiss.

"It's grand seeing you again, Shane Dalton." Deirdre took a couple of backward steps. "Fine looking as ever. Sibéal outdid herself latching on to you."

"I'm the lucky one," Shane said.

"Can't argue with you on that, so," Deirdre said. "You two were made for each other."

Shane pulled out a chair for her. When he'd first met Deirdre at their wedding rehearsal dinner, he was surprised that Beth's childhood friend from Ireland wasn't a bit fair, but instead had chestnut-colored hair and shining brown eyes. The first word that sprung to his mind when he thought of Deirdre was vivacious. Her bubbly, outgoing personality easily caused one to forget that her five-foot-four frame was overburdened by at least thirty pounds.

Deirdre plopped onto the chair without ceremony. Almost instantaneously, the waiter appeared. To Shane's ears, Deirdre ordered something that sounded like tea. As the waiter hurried away she said, "It's about time you two finally decided to honeymoon. I'm thrilled you chose my adopted home."

"I couldn't come up with a more romantic place if I tried. Gondola rides in the moonlight, music, wine, meandering canals." Beth paused a moment. "I take it, you've heard the news." She patted the folded newspaper lying on the table.

"Horrible." Deirdre shook her head. "'Tis hard to believe something like that happened here."

"Murder is universal," Shane said under his breath. "Anyway, there's nothing much new about the case in the paper."

"I know you're a homicide detective Shane, but—"

"Apparently, murder follows me wherever I go."

Deirdre frowned but then a glimmer of understanding seemed to fill her eyes. "Good Lord, don't tell me, you're the tourist couple who found the body?"

He nodded.

"What a way to begin a honeymoon," Deirdre said.

"Was a bit unsettling," Beth said. "'Twas creepy seeing that carnival mask. It seemed to gleam in the water."

Deirdre shook her head. "Best to put the whole horrid experience behind you. Once you're settled into the flat, why don't you spend the afternoon at the Lido? Looks like it's shaping up into a beautiful day. Besides, what could be more relaxing than sun, sand, and surf?"

The waiter returned with a silver pot and an assortment of tiny pastries artfully arranged on a two-tier serving tray. He placed a cup and saucer in front of Deirdre and poured the steaming liquid into the delicate cup edged in gold filigree. She took a sip of the mint herbal tea.

"Ahh, that's good. I've been rushing so this morning, getting the girls off to school, and me ready for work, I didn't have time for a *cuppa*."

"How are the twins? Getting big, I suspect." Beth reached for the mini *focaccia Veneziana* and bit into the pillowy pastry studded with almonds and pearlized sugar.

"They'll be seven in September; can you believe it?"

"*Janey Mac*, going on seven?" Beth pressed a linen napkin against her lips then took a quick sip of cappuccino.

"Where does the time go, Sibéal—oh, I mean Beth—I keep forgetting."

Shane offered an upturned hand in Deirdre's direction. "Why don't you call her Betty Getty? I do."

"You don't?" Deirdre's eyes widened.

"Now don't be paying him no mind, *me ould flower*," Beth said with a wink. No need for you to call me Beth. To you and *me da* I'll always be Sibéal, so."

Deirdre reached for Beth's hand and squeezed it. "Let me tell you about the flat. It's newly renovated, bright and airy, and overlooks the *compo*—a charming park— and it's just darling. Only about five minutes from here."

"Sounds lovely," Beth said.

"The apartment does have all the necessities?" Shane asked.

"Not everything in Venice is centuries old. The flat is fresh and modern. No worries, Shane," Deirdre said. "The air conditioning will be turned on in a few days."

He raised his eyebrows.

"In Venice, June sixth is the day the units are allowed to be turned on. Other than that, the flat has a cute kitchenette with a Majolica tile floor, a spacious living area, and a darling bedroom with a king-sized bed. It's in a quiet neighborhood convenient to everything. The boat stop is right outside the front door." She lifted an apricot pastry and took a bite then glanced at her watch. "Goodness, the time. I've got to run."

"Hectic time for a teacher," Beth said.

"You can say that again. Final assessments, year-end grades, and mountains of paperwork. Even so, I can't help but be a bit melancholic at the end of the school term." Deirdre placed the half-eaten pastry onto her saucer. "Sibéal, you know how sentimental I am. Hate to say goodbye to my students."

Shane noticed how Deirdre's face had darkened. An instant later, a beaming smile chased away the clouds.

"Why don't you come to our home next Friday night?" Deirdre asked. "What could be better than an authentic homemade Venetian dinner? And Jacopo is looking forward to meeting you, Shane." She stood and reached for her briefcase strap looped on the rattan chair's armrest. "Ah, I almost forgot ... where is my brain these days?" She stuck her hand into her skirt pocket and removed a slip of paper and a key. "The flat's address. I'm sure you'll love it." She stooped over and kissed Beth's cheek then reached for Shane's outstretched hand.

"Next Friday sounds lovely," Beth said.

A moment later, Deirdre was out of sight as she mingled within the crowd of day-trippers congregating in the square.

"Isn't she wonderful?" Beth selected a flakey, honey-coated sweet from the tray. "When we were kids, it was like we were joined at the hips. We did everything together. When I landed the modeling job in Milan, Deirdre insisted on accompanying me, and her ma gave both of us her blessing. Deirdre always seemed to be touched with a bit of wanderlust. She was looking for an adventure."

"How did she wind up in Venice?" Shane asked eyeing the last couple of pastries. He selected one and took a bite.

"She came along on the photoshoot I told you about."

He wiped away a smattering of honey from his fingertips then dropped the napkin on top of the table. "Photoshoot?"

"In Venice during Carnival."

"Oh, that photoshoot." He raised his cup and drained it.

"Deirdre was captivated and decided to stay. Almost immediately, she found a job as an English tutor and governess to a Venetian family who happened to be Jacopo's cousins. That's how they met. After a whirlwind of a courtship, they married. At first, I was a bit concerned. Jacopo is fifteen years older than Deirdre. I thought the age difference might cause a problem, but they seem to get along well enough."

Shane only half listened. The check the waiter had dropped onto the table had his full attention.

"I've got a great idea," Beth said

"Oh?" He still stared at the slip of paper doing his best to calculate euros into dollars.

"Let's stop by La Serenissima Travel Bureau and say hello to Jacopo. He's got a fantastic business since he's monopolized the market. Most every tour is set up through his office."

He didn't answer her but continued to stare at the check. "Maybe I'm not converting euros and dollars right. But according to my calculations, we've spent over fifty dollars for two cups of coffee, a cup of tea, and a few pastries."

"Florian's is one of the most expensive cafés in all of Venice. So, you're probably right.

But darling, consider the view," she said sweeping her arm in front of her, "not to mention the orchestra."

He glared at the canopied entrance. "They're not playing now."

"See. You've already saved six euros."

With a grin, he shook his head and dropped the crisp bills plus a couple of coins onto the table. An instant later, the waiter breezed by and scooped up the money.

"Come on; the Tourist Bureau is just on the other side of the square." She jumped away from the table and hurried into the piazza. After snatching the final pastry and popping it in his mouth, it took Shane only a couple of seconds to catch up. He took Beth's arm, and they threaded their way through the jammed-packed square. She stopped and pulled out her mobile. "I want a picture," she said.

"Here? With all these people?"

"Not of you, darlin'." She poked her chin in the direction of a little boy. His dimples deepened, and his eyes sparkled with delight as one pigeon rested on his shoulder and another pecked corn from his hand.

"I would've believed that you'd frown on something so blatantly lawless as feeding those pests."

She shrugged then snapped the button on her phone and dropped it back into her tote bag.

"Damn flying rats," he muttered as Beth hurried beneath a marble arch.

He pulled open the glass door stenciled with gold letters: *La Serenissima Travel Bureau.* They entered the compact main room and stopped in front of a tall counter that served as a partition between the customer and workspace. Shane tapped the granite countertop as he looked at a flaxen-haired woman seated at a desk staring at a computer screen.

"*Mi scusi,*" Beth said.

The woman glanced in their direction, removed her glasses, and stood. "*Mi dispiace,*" she apologized. "*Posso esserle utile?*"

"*Sí, grazie. Parli inglese?*"

The woman nodded. "How can I help? Would you like to book a tour of the city or purchase tickets for a glass blowing demonstration? Those are two of our most popular options."

"Thanks, but no. Actually, we stopped by to see Signore da Parma. I'm Beth Getty."

"Ah, Ms. Getty. One moment." With a nod, she turned away and disappeared behind a closed door.

Shane moved next to a kiosk displaying an array of glossy rack cards. He fingered the cleft in his chin as he focused on the colorful leaflets. He pulled one free that advertised classic gondola rides and slipped it into his pocket.

"Did you see this?" Beth handed him a card featuring a Renaissance villa.

"Villa Saraceno," he said. "Look." He pointed at the photo. "They offer rooms for overnight guests. That would be amazing."

"I've booked us a two-day stay there."

"What?" He kissed her squarely on the lips. The leaflet fluttered to the floor as he lifted and spun her around.

"An early anniversary gift," she managed to say through soft peals of laughter.

The door flew open, and Shane deposited Beth back onto the floor.

"Sibéal, *mia cara amica*." Jacopo grasped her hands and kissed her cheeks. "I am so pleased to see you. *Bella donna*."

"You haven't changed a bit," Beth said with a smile.

Shane took in the man's appearance. Short, well-built, jet black hair ... he looked familiar. He squinted trying to place him.

"Jacopo, this is my husband, Shane Dalton."

"You are a very lucky man." Jacopo stepped back and folded his arms. "I must say, I think you're lucky too, Sibéal." He reached for Shane's hand and offered a firm handshake. "Have you moved into the *appartmento* yet?"

"We wanted to stop by and say hello first," Beth said.

Shane glanced away and spied Jacopo's assistant behind the counter busying herself by straightening papers on a table. She worked so quietly that he was a bit surprised that she was still in the room. Physically, the woman was the opposite of Jacopo—tall, slender, and fair—her eyes a cornflower blue.

"Tonight we must dine in the best restaurant in town." Jacopo's booming voice regained Shane's attention.

"That'd be lovely. But tonight," she said stealing a glance at Shane, "I think we want to settle into our new place."

"Of course. Of course. Another night then."

"Deirdre has invited us over to your *palazzo* next Friday for dinner."

"I'm not surprised." A smile touched Jacopo's lips. "When the two of you are ready to sightsee, let me know. I offer fabulous tours that I'm certain you will enjoy."

"Pleasure meeting you," Shane said wrapping his arm around Beth's waist.

"Jacopo," Beth said, "there was quite a lot of excitement when we arrived last night."

"You mean the murder." He waved his hand in front of his face. "These things happen everywhere. Sadly, even in Venice."

"We discovered the body."

"*Santa Maria, Madre di Dio*. How terrible. No question about it. You

41

must go on a tour and free your minds from such a shocking sight. Lidia."

The woman approached him.

"This is Lidia Feloni, my personal assistant. She will arrange an amazing tour for you. Even though I gave it up years ago, I will take you personally. Anywhere you want to go—Murano, Burano, Torcello, even to Ravenna or Padua."

"How kind," Beth said. "But I've already booked a tour through your office. A quick trip throughout the Veneto. If I'm not mistaken, Lidia arranged the itinerary for us."

Lidia nodded handing Jacopo a sheet of paper.

"I see. You leave this Thursday and return next Wednesday. Wonderful—wonderful. I'm sure you'll have a splendid time. *Buon viaggio!*"

"Ciao," Beth said as Shane hurried her out of the office and into the warm Venetian light.

Chapter Eight

ONCE THE DOOR CLOSED BEHIND them, Jacopo turned and faced Lidia Feloni. "Those two are newlyweds. It's obvious how much in love they are."

Lidia walked back behind the counter, sat at her desk, and began typing on the computer. She had a couple of itineraries to compile and didn't want to waste time chit-chatting with Jacopo.

"Love is something you don't want to think about," he continued. "You want to escape from the mere possibility of it."

She glanced away from the computer and noticed him leaning against the counter with his arms crossed. "I'm not afraid of love and its possibilities. But, at this point, I need to focus on my daughter and my job." She pointed at the computer screen.

He stepped closer. "I can't stop thinking about you. Ever since that kiss."

"Kiss?" She jumped up and moved away from the desk. "I'm sorry if you misunderstood, but that kiss, well, that was just an expression of gratitude for your financial assistance. How else would I've been able to pay Oriana's tuition?"

"Gratitude, eh?"

"Yes. I'm very thankful—"

"Your eyes tell me more than your words."

"You're imagining way too much. It was just a kiss, Jacopo. Forget about it, alright."

"I think you're scared. Afraid to trust your heart."

"Have you forgotten that you're married?"

"How can I?" He ran his fingertips through his thick, dark hair. "I've been kidding myself, but it's about time to face facts. My marriage isn't working out. Deirdre isn't able to give me what I need."

"Maybe you should talk to your priest ... or ... or a marriage counselor."

"That would be useless." His voice went low almost to a whisper. "But if you were my lover, this horrid marriage would be, I think, manageable. At least for a few more months."

She inhaled sharply.

"I've shocked you." He reached out to her but didn't make contact. "From the first time I saw you, I fell a little bit in love with you. You're the most beautiful woman I've ever known."

Lidia chewed her lip. She'd heard this line many times before, and it turned her stomach. She hated being judged by her outward appearance. She'd been told innumerable times that she could've been a stand-in for Marilyn Monroe if she'd been an adult during her grandmother's era. But all she'd ever wanted was to be loved for who she was—not what she looked like.

"You're making me uncomfortable." She took a few steps toward her desk. "I have work—"

"Look, I didn't mean to come across so strong. But please, don't shut me out. Allow me to unburden my heart. Tell you how I feel."

"I'd rather you didn't." She turned her back to him.

"I want you to understand."

The intensity of his voice frightened her. Lidia never imagined that Jacopo da Parma, her employer for God's sake, would cross the professional line. She silently cursed, overcome with regret for accepting the monetary advance. If she could do it all over—there were many things Lidia wished she could do over—*just add this to the list*, she thought, trying to block out his voice.

"Are you listening to me?"

She walked to her desk, lifted her water bottle, and took a long swallow. "I'll repay the loan soon." She hated the thought of asking Bernardino Moro for the money. But what choice did she have with Jacopo holding it over her head in exchange for sex? But then, she thought relaxing, if everything turns out the way she hoped ... but she hadn't heard from *him* since yesterday morning. Maybe *he* had changed his mind.

"This isn't about money. After all, what're 3000 euros? Pocket change."

Jacopo's words interrupted her thoughts. She shook her head, realizing she'd have to swallow her pride and ask Dino since that other thing might not work out after all.

"I have feelings for you. Deep feelings."

Lidia raised her eyebrows and crossed her arms. *Feelings my culo*, she thought. *Always, it's only about sex.*

"Deirdre is level-headed—reasonable—and realizes I need my freedom when it comes to *amore*." He paused a second. "After all, you certainly wouldn't be my first lover, but hopefully my last."

"You equate sex with love?" She didn't wait for an answer. "I find it hard to believe that your wife's attitude is so cavalier about your extramarital exploits. A good woman like Deirdre," she said flinging her arm in the air, "but if you don't respect her, what about your daughters? One day, they'll find out." She looked at him directly in the eyes. "I want no part of that."

A smile touched his face. "I've suspected for some time now that you feel the same way about me."

"What? Are you kidding me?"

"If you'd surrender to your desires, I guarantee you won't give a damn about what my girls think." He stepped closer to her.

She backed away. "Believe me, I don't—"

"Either way, I will be ending my marriage. As I said, things aren't working out. Divorce is the only avenue left for me. And then, my dear, I'll be in the market for a new wife. You'd be perfect."

Lidia raised her hand, gesturing him to stop. She couldn't stomach another word. "You've admitted to having lovers. Adultery won't earn you an annulment. If you marry again, it will be a sin."

"Indeed, that's true," he said with a shake of his head. "You've been spending too much time with those Ursuline nuns. What do they know about passion? Of love between a man and woman? Nothing. They imagine themselves as immaculate brides of Christ," he spat the words. "Don't allow them to pollute your mind with inane thoughts of piety and repentance. What's important is the here and now. Not some pie in the sky myth of eternal bliss."

She turned away.

He laid a hand on her shoulder and whispered into her ear. "Everyone loves Deirdre ... she's kind, smart, friendly ... but the sad reality is, I made a mistake marrying her. I need more."

"More?" She faced him.

"After the twins were born, she let herself go. Gained weight. Even though I'm not attracted to her anymore, that's not the problem. Her life revolves around her job, volunteer work, running the house. Not me."

"And with a new wife who also has responsibilities besides catering to your needs ... things will be different? You'll stop cheating and be a faithful husband?"

"If that wife is you."

Her head began to pound. "Please, Jacopo. Stop."

"I want to be upfront with you. Let you understand how I feel—"

"I'm in love with someone else." She blurted out the words without thinking. The moment they slipped through her lips, she wanted to retrieve them.

"Dammit. Don't tell me it's Bernardino Moro."

"Dino? No." A band of tension tightened around her forehead.

"It's obvious he's in love with you."

"Don't be ridiculous."

"Well, whoever he is, please reconsider. I can offer you the world. No more scrimping and missing meals to pay for Oriana's education." He traced his index finger along the curve of her cheek and across her full lips.

Lidia yanked her face away. She didn't know whether to believe the sincerity of Jacopo's words or if this was just a ploy to trick her into having sex. Pressure squeezed her temples making it impossible for her to think clearly. "I have work to do." She stepped closer to her desk.

"I promise you, Lidia. I'll never disappoint you. And I'll treat Oriana as one of my own. Every second of every day, I promise, I'll cherish you."

The door flew open, and Bernardino Moro stepped inside holding a colorful bouquet of wildflowers.

"Speaking of the devil," Jacopo muttered. "What brings you here, Dino?"

"What do you think?" He raised the bouquet in Jacopo's direction. "These damn well aren't for you." He headed toward Lidia.

She attempted a smile, but Jacopo's words were still flying through her brain.

"My dearest, even though these flowers pale in your presence, please accept this small token of my esteem and affection." He offered Lidia a gallant half-bow.

Jacopo rolled his eyes. "That's a mouthful of fancy language for a bunch of flowers that couldn't have cost more than two euros."

Lidia focused on Bernardino's warm eyes and easy smile. Some of the tension began to drain away. "Ignore Jacopo. They're beautiful. But, you shouldn't have." She walked around the counter, grasped the cellophane-wrapped bouquet, and inhaled the fragrant scent. "I was about to discard the last bunch you gave me." She gestured to the wilting daisies on her desk then glanced at Jacopo. He seemed to be fuming with his arms folded against his chest and a scowl plastered across his face.

"Then I arrived just in the nick of time." Bernardino checked his watch. "Can I interest you in a cup of coffee? Certainly, Jacopo isn't such a strict taskmaster that he doesn't offer you a mid-morning break."

"Don't you have a tour at the top of the hour?" Jacopo barked.

"Of the basilica. But, there's plenty of time—"

"Stop harassing my assistant." Jacopo pointed at Lidia.

"Harassing?" Bernardino's brow furrowed. "I'd hardly call it harassing."

"You've interrupted an important discussion about some changes to our office procedures."

How easy he lies, Lidia thought noticing the anger smoldering in Jacopo's dark eyes.

"So, you've given her the flowers, now leave."

"*Va bene*, Jacopo. Calm down. I'm leaving." Bernardino turned away but then glanced over his shoulder at Lidia. "We're still on for tonight?"

She glanced from Bernardino to Jacopo. The pain in her head hammered at full force. "I'm not feeling..." She rubbed her throbbing temple.

"Now look what you've done," Jacopo said.

"Dino had nothing to do with it. Just one of my bad headaches." Though she tried to admonish Jacopo, her words came out in a whisper.

Bernardino took the flowers from Lidia, laid them on the counter, and steered her to a chair. "It'll only take me a couple of minutes to run to the drug store and pick up some aspirin."

She rested on the chair's edge. "That's sweet of you, but I have a prescription. Once I take it, I'll be fine."

"Let me get it for you. Where is it?"

"Please, don't trouble yourself."

Lidia hadn't noticed that Jacopo had left them until he handed her a glass of water and two tablets. She kept a few spare pills in her desk in case she'd forget to bring her prescription to work. Jacopo was aware of that and had sprung into action. She lifted her chin and offered him a tiny smile. "Thanks."

"Well, now that things are under control, I better get going. Don't want to keep my group waiting. See you at eight." Bernardino exited the office with a bounce in his step.

Lidia swallowed the pills and handed Jacopo the empty glass.

"I don't understand why you give him the time of day."

The last thing she wanted was to argue any more with Jacopo. "We're friends."

The door opened, and two young men stepped inside. Lidia stood and hurried to the counter. "May I help you?"

"We're interested in renting a boat."

Lidia nodded. "No problem. I'll be happy to assist you." She exhaled with relief, noticing that Jacopo had retreated into his office. "A speedboat?" she questioned with a smile.

Chapter Nine

WITH HER HANDS FULL, Lidia pushed the apartment door open with her hip. Lengthening shadows filled the small, airless living room, and a sense of total abandonment caused her sliver of hope to collapse. No word from the two people she cared most about.

She placed the paper bag containing their dinner and her leather shoulder bag on an end table. With quick strides, she moved from one shuttered window to the next and opened them. A puff of air drifting across the canal ruffled her hair. After one deep breath, she turned her back to the view of the sky, golden with streaks of pink, as the sun neared the horizon. The loneliness of the room intensified, and she realized that calling her daughter's name would be useless. She clicked on a lamp, clutched the paper bag, and hurried into the narrow galley kitchen. A glance at the clock confirmed her fear.

Something isn't right. It's after seven, and Oriana isn't home from school?

Lidia rushed back to the living area, opened her purse, and fished out her cellphone. She tapped the screen as the door opened. Oriana stood there with her backpack in hand. The drabness of the worn settee, its beige cushions stained and lumpy set against a wall decorated with faded paper seemed to brighten with Oriana's presence.

"You're home," Oriana said lifting her pack to her shoulder. "If I'd known you were here ... I'm sorry I'm late. I was with Chiara and lost track of time." She attempted a smile, but only one side of her mouth inched upward, leaving her with a lopsided guise.

"I've been neglecting you." Lidia glanced away from her daughter for a split-second. "But," she paused brightening, "I've been busy the past couple of weeks working on a special surprise. It's actually rather wonderful."

"Really? What?"

Lidia wanted to reach out and stroke her daughter's cheek and smooth back the loose strains of hair that had spilled onto her forehead. Instead, she placed her cellphone on an end table. "Wash up for dinner first."

Oriana sighed before heading toward the edge of the room.

"I picked up your favorite. *Pasta con le Vongole*," she called as Oriana disappeared into the narrow corridor leading to her bedroom.

Back in the kitchen, Lidia reached into a cabinet and removed two plates. She placed them on the table and noticed a news article that had been ripped from the paper. Without thinking, she crumpled the flimsy piece of newsprint, but then realized that maybe Oriana had meant to save it. She smoothed the bit of paper and glanced at the heading. *Body Found in Canal*. She squinted, but without her glasses, the fine print blurred into a fuzzy jumble. With a shrug, she placed the article out of harm's way on the adjacent countertop and reached for the Styrofoam boxes containing their dinner.

"Oriana," she called slicing a fresh loaf of crusty bread. Grabbing a handful of utensils from a drawer that stuck when the air was humid, she finished setting the table, scooped the pasta onto the plates, and filled the glasses—Oriana's with mineral water and hers with a table red.

Oriana entered the kitchen. She'd changed out of her school clothes and had slipped into an oversized t-shirt and a pair of soft, faded jeans.

"I hope you're hungry."

Oriana sat down, unfolded the napkin next to her plate, and dropped it onto her lap. "I'm curious about your news but..." She lifted her fork, but only moved the linguine around on the plate.

Something's bothering her. Lidia frowned. *After a long day at school, she'd normally be chatting about how she aced a test, an interesting event from one of her classes, or Chiara's latest crush, between quick gulps of food. She's always been comfortable sharing her problems. We have no secrets between us, well, except the secret of all secrets*, she thought, taking a sip of wine. "Are you worried about the exams?"

Oriana put down her fork. "Exams? Oh, no." She shook her head. "Chiara and I were studying chemistry all afternoon. I'll do fine. Both of us will, actually. That's if Chiara can keep her mind off Antonio and about a half dozen other boys she thinks she's in love with."

"That one is boy-crazy. But, as pretty as you are, there must be plenty of boys trying to catch your eye."

Oriana twisted a forkful of pasta into her spoon. "A couple, I guess." She offered her mother a sheepish smile. "But, they're so silly and immature. Anyway, right now maintaining my grades is what matters most. So that I'm accepted into university."

"That, I'm sure, won't be a problem," Lidia said scooping a clam free from its shell. "Even as a little girl you were inquisitive wanting to know how everything works. It's no wonder you want to follow in my footsteps and study engineering."

"Or archeology." Oriana raised her fork but returned it to her plate. "I haven't made up my mind yet."

"You're a lot like your papà. Smart, determined, but also kind and ... forgiving."

A quizzical look crossed Oriana's face. Lidia wasn't sure if it was confusion or skepticism.

They sat in silence for a few minutes focused on eating their rapidly cooling dinner. Oriana broke off a piece of bread and mopped up a pool of garlic sauce. She looked up from her nearly empty plate. "I almost forgot. The surprise?"

"Ahh." Lidia lifted the glass to her lips and emptied it. "It has to do with your papà."

Oriana drew her brows together. Lidia sensed the storm brewing in her daughter's eyes. "You shouldn't be angry at him."

"He doesn't care about me. If he did, I would've heard from him at least once during the past ten ... almost eleven years." Oriana lifted the cellphone from its spot next to her plate and shook it. "But nothing. Not a word."

"Your papà wanted to contact you. He misses you so much." Lidia felt her daughter's eyes bore into her.

"You know this because?"

"We've been having long conversations... about you and me... us, actually. What it would be like if we could be a family again."

"What? I mean how ... when did you talk—"

"He wants you to spend the summer with him in California. That's the surprise."

Oriana shot to her feet. "That doesn't make sense."

51

"Both of us made some bad choices. But your papà and I have worked out our differences. Before we make more permanent plans, he wants to get to know you."

"What if I don't want to?"

Lidia hadn't expected opposition. "Don't blame Papà. I've kept you away from him for too long. It was wrong of me, so don't make him suffer for my mistake." She looked away from Oriana. "He's anxious... excited... thrilled about the possibility of seeing his little girl again. He's already bought you an airline ticket."

"But, but..." she sputtered then flung her hands wide open.

"It would break his heart if you refused him." *I broke it the first time by stealing you away. Please God, don't let Oriana do the same thing.*

Oriana sat back down. She lifted her glass and stared into it. "I don't remember him." She placed the glass back on the table and looked at Lidia. "When I was a little girl, I used to dream of Papà walking into our house and holding me ... telling me that I was his princess ... that he loved me more than anything in the world. But, I gave up on that dream years ago. Now, this. It's almost too much to hope for." She took a quick sip from the water glass. "But..." Oriana hesitated. "I don't want to go by myself. I want you to be with me."

Lidia pushed her plate aside and folded her hands on the scuffed wooden tabletop. "I don't belong at this homecoming. Even if I wanted to, I can't leave Venice during the heart of the busy season."

"I'll be alone."

"Alone? You have grandparents and cousins, aunts and uncles, and two half-brothers you've never met. They're all eager to see you. Most importantly, you need to be with your papà. To make up for so much lost time." Lidia reached for her daughter's hand. It felt unusually cool.

Oriana pulled her hand free. "I still don't understand why Papà left us. Leaving you no choice but to return to Italy. The weird thing is that when you talk about him, you describe him as the most charming, handsome, and amazing man in the world. It doesn't make sense." Her eyes pleaded for an explanation.

Lidia lowered her eyes. *I can't tell her the truth now.* "Your American family can hardly wait to see you again. It's going to be so exciting."

52

"What horrible thing did Papà do that broke apart our family?"

The breath caught in the back of her throat as she searched for an answer. "Your father will explain everything." Lidia closed her eyes, sensing a flush of unexpected tears. *Once she finds out the whole story, I pray to God she forgives me.* She rose and raced to her bedroom.

Lidia leaned against the closed bedroom door with her mind in an uproar. The thought had never crossed her mind that Oriana might choose her father—over her—once she knows the facts. *That won't happen*, she reassured herself. *No. I won't let it happen. After all, we're going to be a family again.*

She took a deep, cleansing breath and headed to the window. After staring at the shutters for a minute, she pulled them open and looked outside at the derelict courtyard. Weeds poked through the crevices of fractured stone pavers, and peeling, moldy stucco walls revealed their ancient brick bones. A stray cat, black as night, slinked across the dilapidated square in search of prey. The air, wet with humidity, clung like a thick blanket while neglected laundry strung between the buildings cast elongated shadows in the dusky light. She stared at the deserted *piazzetta* until the last remnant of illumination surrendered to darkness.

As she turned away from the window, she remembered her get-together with Dino. She clicked on a light and checked her watch. Half-past eight. Though she didn't want to stand him up, she felt like all the energy had been sucked out of her. *But*, she debated, *a close, nonjudgmental friend might be exactly what I need.* She slipped into her favorite dress: sleeveless, cotton, and soft pink—bushed her hair, and refreshed her lipstick.

THE THOUGHT OF STUDYING was out of the question. Oriana leaned against a mound of pillows propped next to the iron headboard and squeezed her eyes shut. She was still a bit baffled sensing her mother hadn't told her the whole story, but could hardly believe she was going to be reunited with her papà. *How many times have I prayed for this to happen? And now ...* A smile spread across her face.

She tried to remember something, anything, about her early life in California. Nothing came to mind—except for one image that she wasn't quite sure was a memory or the trace of a dream; perhaps it was a bit of both. She'd been crawling around her giant sandbox digging holes with a red plastic shovel when she felt his strong hands encircle her waist—he lifted and spun her around—both of them laughing. Oriana let out a sigh. She'd forgotten his face. *If Mamma only had a photo of him, I might be able to remember....*

She reached for her chemistry book but dropped her hand and brushed her cellphone. Lifting it, she pressed the speed dial and waited for Chiara to answer.

"*Pronto.*" Her friend's voice filled her ear.

"Guess where I'm spending the summer?"

"Here." A tinge of suspicion touched Chiara's voice.

"No."

"We made plans."

"This is better," Oriana said.

"Better than the beach, the sun, the boys. I doubt it." Chiara paused. "Alright, tell me."

"I just got a great idea. Maybe you can come with me."

"I don't even know where you're going. But if you think I'd leave Antonio. No way."

"You might change your mind once I tell you."

"I doubt it. Come on, Oriana; quit stalling. Tell me already."

"*Va bene*, okay. I'm going to California. To see my papà." Not hearing a reply, Oriana thought she'd lost the connection. "Chiara," she spoke louder into the phone.

"We bonded over not having fathers. All this time I thought your papà was out of the picture. Now you're going to visit him; good for you, but that's never going to happen for me. I have to go."

"Wait," Oriana said but realized Chiara had already hung up.

She sucked in a mouthful of air then slowly blew it out. *What was I thinking? Though she doesn't show it, Chiara is still mourning the loss of her papà. She tries to act like nothing's wrong, flirting with boys, studying as if her life depends on it.... Trying to block out the reality that her papà is dead. I did the same thing. My papà could've been dead for all I knew. But now, everything is different. Wonderful. Amazing.*

She reached for her English workbook. Flipping it open, she glanced at a long list of vocabulary words. *Top priority*, she thought, *practicing my English pronunciation. I don't want my papà wondering what I'm saying.*

She looked away from the book as the sharp sound of a quick knock filled the room. She glanced at the door, which opened slowly until her mother's form filled the threshold.

"I'm going out for a little while," Lidia said.

Oriana wasn't surprised. *The Sisters of Santa Angela de Merici. Again.*

"Do you need this?" Lidia lifted the crinkled newspaper article. "I almost threw it in the trash."

Oriana closed her workbook. "Not really. It's an article about the murder."

"Terrible," Lidia said under her breath as she turned away.

"I saw it."

"What?" Lidia spun around and stepped into the small bedroom.

"I was with Chiara when the body was recovered."

Lidia dropped onto the bed. "Why didn't you tell me?"

"I didn't see you last night. You must've stayed late at the convent."

Not answering, Lidia grasped Oriana's hand and squeezed it. "It must've been horrible."

Oriana shrugged. "There were a lot of people around. Though I tried, I couldn't see his face. It was covered by a *Bauta*."

"A mask? That seems strange. I've been so busy at work; I haven't heard many details. Of course, last night the sisters prayed for his soul."

"There was something about the dead man..." Oriana looked into her mother's face and noticed that worry had caused lines to form on her brow. "When I saw the tattoo on his wrist—"

"Tattoo?"

"A name inside a heart. I don't know how it'd be possible, but that tattoo seemed familiar, like, oh, I don't know, but I got a strange feeling, no, more like a warm feeling when I saw it. Anyway, look, it's all there." Oriana motioned to the crinkled paper in her mother's hand.

"I don't have my glasses. You read it."

Oriana scanned the article. "Here it is. 'The only distinguishing mark is a tattoo above the victim's wrist—a heart encircling the name, Gemma.'"

Lidia's hand flew to her mouth.

"You know who he is." Oriana dropped the article onto her lap. "You saw him at the Travel Bureau."

Lidia shook her head.

"But your reaction—"

"It's ... horrible ... that someone was murdered here," Lidia said.

"I found the whole thing kind of interesting ... but puzzling. That tattoo—"

"Tattoos are very popular. You could've seen one like that almost anywhere. Put it out of your mind." She kissed Oriana's forehead.

"Yes, Mamma." Oriana reached for her notebook. "But there's a good chance you did see the man with the tattoo. At school, I heard that he was a tourist. American. He may have stopped by the Travel Bureau—"

"I told you, I didn't." Lidia paused a second. "Don't let seeing that awful sight distract you. Forget it. Focus on your studies."

"I've tried. But I can't seem to. Even when I'm in the middle of doing something, like today's exam, that heart tattoo comes back into my mind. I can't shake it."

Lidia turned away from Oriana. "Everything will be alright. I promise." She glanced over her shoulder and offered a tiny smile before closing the door behind her.

Oriana stared at the closed door. Her mother's reaction startled her. It wasn't her words, but the way her hand shook and the color seemed to drain away from her face. She shrugged.

"Who can understand parents," she whispered then smiled. "Soon I'll have another parent—my papà—who will probably be just as perplexing as Mamma."

LIDIA MOVED AWAY from the bedroom. After a few steps, she leaned against the wall and swallowed a mouthful of air but couldn't hold back the rush of tears. After a few seconds, she stumbled down the corridor into the living room, sunk to her knees, and pounded the floor with her fists. She silenced the wails demanding to escape so that only a tortured whimpering seeped between her clenched teeth.

She wiped her tear-soaked face with her trembling hands. "Dear God," she whispered. "Please don't let this be true." She pulled herself upward, grabbed her purse off the settee, and fled the apartment.

Chapter Ten

BERNARDINO PLACED THE highball glass on the table and rose when he spied Lidia entering the small bar. He'd almost given up. But since she hadn't texted him, he decided to relax as the minutes ticked away, nursing his *Americano* cocktail. He thought it an appropriate drink after reading the latest update on the canal murder.

"Lidia." He gestured toward her.

She nodded and skirted around the edge of the bar. She hesitated a moment before approaching the table.

Even in the dim light, he could tell something was wrong. It was evident in her walk—shoulders slumped, head bowed, her step tentative. As she inched closer, he saw that her eyes were puffy. It could mean only one thing. She knew.

He pulled out a chair, and Lidia dropped into it.

"Amato." He raised his glass in the direction of the bartender. "*Due.*"

They sat in silence until Amato brought the two cocktails to the table.

"The alcohol will help you cope. Drink up." Bernardino took a glass and handed it to her.

Lidia barely took a sip then replaced the drink on the worn, scuffed table.

"How did you find out?" he asked.

She didn't answer but only stared at the red liquid filling the glass. He wanted to shake Lidia free of her malaise, tell her she should be thanking her lucky stars, but instead, he did nothing but wait for her response.

"My daughter was at the bridge when they fished his body out of the canal. She saw the tattoo. Oriana had no idea that she was looking at her father's corpse." She raised the glass and swallowed. "I should've known something terrible had happened. Jonathan hadn't contacted me for two days."

57

Bernardino leaned back in the chair and crossed his arms. "Unlike you, I'm glad that bastard is dead." He cursed under his breath, realizing, a moment too late, that his unsympathetic comment sounded crass, perhaps even heartless. "What I mean is that after the way he treated you, I'm relieved he's finally out of your life. For good." He reached for her hand resting on the table and squeezed it.

"I thought things had changed. But, even now, you still hate him?"

That's an understatement, he thought with a nod.

"But Dino, I was the one who stole Oriana away from *him*. If my conscience hadn't finally gotten the best of me, right now, he'd be searching for her."

"Then, I guess, he'd still be alive and kicking, living the high life in LA."

"Oh my God," she gasped. "I'm the reason he's dead. If he hadn't come to Venice..." She squeezed her eyes shut.

"Don't blame yourself." He released her hand, moved his chair, and sat next to her. Their shoulders touched. "There are multitudes of people who have good reasons to want him dead. He defended hardened criminals for God's sake. Any one of those slimeballs he didn't keep out of jail could've done this. Or at least put out a hit on him."

She flashed her eyes open. "In Venice?"

Bernardino brushed a stray curl off his forehead. "I spent more than enough time with him over the past what ... four weeks? Hell. That was long enough for Jonathan to make an enemy or two."

She shook her head. "You hardly saw him during his visit here. Anyway, the dinner we had together was wonderful. I thought you two patched up your differences. You seemed to be friends again."

"That was a bit of expert acting on both our parts ... for your benefit." He noticed her lip tremble. "I know you wanted everything to work out, especially for Oriana. But in the end, I think it would've been a disaster. I know him. Really know him. After being his so-called friend for years, I've come to the conclusion that he doesn't respect women. Look at his current wife—"

"I don't want to hear about her. I've always considered Jonathan to be my husband. Even though he'd married again to that ... that Nicole person."

"I don't know what he told you about her, but she tried her damnedest to keep the family together. Of course, the money was a motivating factor—Nicole is very fond of money—but unfortunately, she still loved him ... a little bit anyway." He took a swallow of his drink. "She used to confide in me about the affairs with other women and how he buried himself in his work. Never had much time for her or his sons."

"Jonathan told me it was a mistake on his part to remarry. He spent years searching, but all the women he met left him feeling empty—that only one woman could make him happy—me." She blinked her eyes, but a stray tear slid down her cheek.

"And you believed that?"

"That's why I didn't tell you the most wonderfully unbelievable news. I knew how you'd react—"

"Didn't tell me what?" He frowned.

"We reconciled." Lidia looked at her hand resting on the table as if inspecting her neatly shaped nails. "He was going to divorce Nicole and petition for an annulment. Then we would renew our vows and be a family again."

Bernardino blew out a stream of air. "Really? You bought that line? I'd bet my last cent that once he got Oriana back to LA, you were never going to hear from him again. Well, unless he pressed charges against you for kidnapping."

"How can you be cynical at a time like this? After the way he died. And you two used to be so close." She shook her head.

"College was a long time ago." He raised his glass and emptied it.

"I never did understand why the two of you had a falling out."

"It really doesn't matter now." A streak of anger flashed through him as he recalled the volatile scene when he and Lidia's then-fiancé had almost come to blows. "Back then, both of us were a couple of damn hotheads."

"It was because of me, wasn't it?"

Bernardino shrugged. "I didn't think he was treating you right. All he seemed to care about was himself. You were just one of his many possessions." He paused a second. "That's the way it looked to me, and I told him so."

She offered him a weak smile. "You've been wonderful keeping my secret all these years."

"Hey, it was my idea. Remember?" When he'd first mentioned the plan of Lidia running away with her daughter, he realized she thought he was kidding. Though it took a while, she eventually came around to his way of thinking. Before she took off, he had promised that one day they'd meet again in Italy. And thanks to the fates, it had played out exactly as he'd hoped.

"I was desperate. I would've done anything to keep my daughter." She lifted her glass but then set it down. "We've all made mistakes. So, stop judging him."

"If a leopard could change his spots, I'd agree with you. But, that ex-husband of yours ... winding up dead in a canal served him right." *Justice, pure and simple*, he thought as he again reached for Lidia's hand. "Let me walk you home."

Lidia raised her glass, emptied it, and jumped up. She swayed. He grabbed her shoulders and steadied her.

"You okay?"

"Must've gotten up too fast."

He wrapped a strong arm around her waist. "I've got you now. Just lean against me."

"I feel as if I've been leaning on you forever, my friend."

She's finally free, he thought as his lips curled into a smile.

Chapter Eleven

BETH WALKED WITH SHANE toward the *loggia*, the covered porch, which attached the Villa Saraceno to the original building that housed the guestrooms. Twilight's fingers crept slowly and cloaked the brilliance of splattered reds, streamers of deep violets, and patches of rusty gold that painted the sky as elongated shadows crossed their path. She grabbed Shane's arm and couldn't disguise the delight filling her voice, "I should be dead tired after all we did today, but instead, I feel alive. Energized."

He leaned in close to her and tapped the notebook tucked into his breast pocket. "Even though this little excursion ends tomorrow, I've plenty of notes, not to mention a zillion photos, to remind me of all the impressive structures we've seen. Staying at this place," he said stretching his hand toward the villa, "has been amazing. Too bad it has to end so soon."

She shot a glance in his direction, surprised to hear the note of disappointment coloring his voice. *It's his honeymoon too*, she thought, *and if being at the Villa Saraceno makes him happy...* "I think it'd be lovely to spend the rest of our trip here, at the villa; it's so serene and peaceful."

Shane's brow shot upward, though he didn't comment.

"Let's contact Landmark Trust and check on availability. We might have to switch rooms but—"

"I was hoping to take a side trip to Milan. I'd love to see the catwalk you strutted on that ignited your brilliant career," he said.

"Really?"

"Why not?" He led her to a bench situated behind the loggia's row of sturdy Doric columns and sunk onto its wooden surface. Beth took in the vast yard surrounded by a wall of conifers and wondered why there wasn't a garden, but only a neat lawn, which had turned golden due to the summer sun. The grouping of potted plants situated between the columns didn't offer much appeal since the green leaves were small and stubby. She sat next to him.

"Venice is enchanting, but being here is so peaceful. Lovely, actually," she murmured.

"And no murders." He squeezed her hand.

"It's settled then. We'll extend our stay, if not here, then in Vicenza." She started to rise, but Shane pulled her back and wrapped his arms around her. She wanted to rest in his embrace and breathe deeply of the cool country air, but a surge of regret swept through her. An impulsive act from earlier in the day replayed in her mind and troubled her. She had no choice but to tell Shane. But how? *He'll be effin' and blindin' to high heaven, and it'll be my own stupid fault.* She swallowed hard. "Shane." Her voice sounded barely louder than a whisper. "When the caretaker—"

"Mario?"

"Right. When Mario took me into town this afternoon, I heard some news."

"Oh." He relaxed his hold on her.

She moved away and kept her sight focused on the pavement under her feet. "It turns out that the canal victim was from Los Angeles."

"Hmmm." He reached for her, but she jumped up, pivoted, and faced him.

"Promise me you won't act the maggot?"

"Act the what?"

"Just stay calm and listen to what I have to tell you." She paused a moment. "I called Gavin."

"Collins? Why would you contact my partner—former partner? Collins and I have—"

"When I learned that the victim was from home, I thought Gavin might have some information."

"And how does any of that concern you?" His voice sounded strained.

"I can't believe you're not the least bit interested. That poor, hapless victim could be a neighbor, friend, colleague—but even if he's a stranger—I'm heartbroken for his family. I thought if Gavin knew something, maybe I could contact the poor soul's family. Offer condolences and assure them that he was treated with respect at the end."

He released a stream of air like a soft whistle. "Of course you'd want to do that. Your heart is so good. Not jaded like mine. I'm a damn idiot suspecting you of ... of, of what I don't know. I don't deserve you."

She wanted to kick herself. How many times had she vowed to stop lying to Shane? But how could she tell him the truth—that she's just plain fascinated by this murder?

He stood next to her. "Forgive me," he said wrapping his arms around her.

She squeezed her eyes shut for a moment then pulled back a little. He released her. "There's nothing to be asking forgiveness for, darlin' boy." She hated herself at that moment. Before he could say a word, she reached for his hand and began walking toward their guestroom.

"You could forgive me for being an unromantic blockhead." He reached into his back pocket and pulled out the heavy room key.

She couldn't prevent the corners of her mouth from inching upward even though she was the one in need of forgiving. "I wouldn't say you're unromantic. But a blockhead, well..."

He grabbed her by the wrists, pulled her close, and covered her mouth with his. His kiss was insistent, demanding, but she tore away and jogged toward the entrance, leading into the building. It took him only seconds to catch up. He stuck the key into the lock, twisted, and shoved the door open. Scooping her up, he carried Beth to the bed and landed her there. A moment later, he covered her body with his as his mouth sought her silky smooth skin. His kisses made her forget her transgression.

BETH WOKE UP WITH a smile on her face. Shane, sprawled out next to her, was still asleep. She tried not to stir as she scooted up and leaned against the dense feather pillows resting against the wooden headboard. The spacious room gave the impression of a primeval farmhouse with its stone floor and heavy beams crossing the ceiling. The simple furniture would have looked familiar, she believed, to eighteenth-century eyes. The room did possess three modern conveniences: a tiny refrigerator, a telephone, and a bath.

"Hey." Shane's hand brushed against her thigh. He turned over and planted a kiss on her cheek then stretched his arms above his head. "What time is it?"

She glanced at her watch. "Nine thirty-seven."

"We should think about dinner."

"After that huge lunch, I'm not very hungry. But earlier, in town at that little grocery, I picked up a few things." Beth wiggled off the bed, slipped into her dressing gown, and padded to the refrigerator. She squatted on her heels, reached inside the fridge, and pulled out a slab of Parmigiano-Reggiano cheese. Standing, she reached into a slender cabinet and withdrew a jar of honey, a tin of biscotti, and a couple of paper plates. "Darlin'," she said over her shoulder and noticed he'd slipped back into his clothes, "could you pour us some grappa?"

While Shane poured the pomace brandy into small, tulip-shaped glasses, she drizzled honey over a couple of the anise-flavored cookies and capped each with a flake of cheese. She handed Shane a plate with her creation.

After a bite and a sip of the Grappa Bianca, he nodded his head in admiration.

"I'll make you another one," she said. As drips of slow-flowing honey trickled from the jar, her mobile sounded. She set the container down, licked her sticky fingers, and grabbed the phone from a low dresser.

Tapping the screen, she noticed Shane had picked up where she'd left off and was now slicing the cheese.

"Hi, Deirdre," she said into the phone. "We're having a grand time. Couldn't be lovelier. Tomorrow we're off to see Palladio's masterpiece, the Villa Barbaro at Maser. You know, it ticked Palladio off the way everyone was gushing compliments in Veronese's direction for his murals and ignoring the genius of the architecture." She plopped down into a chair with a woven rush seat and focused on Deirdre's words.

With a biscotti-filled plate and a fresh glass of grappa, Shane settled back on the bed. Beth glanced at him and realized that he wasn't paying attention to her conversation. She squeezed her lips tightly to hold back her excitement as she listened to Deirdre's animated voice. Her knowledge that the canal victim was American paled to the bombshell Deirdre shared.

"Wow," Beth said. "That's fantastic news." She listened intently for a few more moments frowning. "Dinner Friday?" Beth said a bit peeved at herself for forgetting all about the invitation. "I was going to ring you since we've changed our plans to include a side trip to Milan. I hate to disappoint..."

Beth realized Deirdre was trying to sound upbeat, but her effort had failed miserably. A somber tone filled her words, stitched together with a tread of foreboding.

"Try not to fret, Deirdre. I'll run it by Shane. Talk to you soon." Beth tapped the screen and ended the call.

"That was a short conversation," Shane spoke around a mouthful of biscuit.

She moved to the bed. "The news is buzzing all around Venice. They've made an arrest."

His face remained impassive, and she noticed only the slight narrowing of his eyes.

"Deirdre said the suspect, Lorenzo Caravello, admitted to a robbery gone bad. He turned himself in to the authorities this afternoon."

Shane raised the glass to his lips but then lowered it. She imagined the wheels turning around in his brain. The little gray cells at work.

"Apparently, he's a clever pickpocket artist who possesses a silver tongue," she said.

"There's a big leap from petty theft to murder." Shane downed the remainder of his drink. "Nah. I don't think so. Unless this Caravello fellow had a personal beef with the victim."

She shrugged. "I'm just relieved that the *Commissario Capo* caught the murderer. Although Jacopo spent half his life acting like a big brother to this Caravello character, Jacopo felt sorry for him and has been keeping an eye on him since he was a wee lad. He worked hard to keep Lorenzo out of trouble and always held fast to a sliver of hope that the young man would get his act together. That's why, according to Deirdre, Jacopo is sick with worry. But in a way, Deirdre is relieved because she's always thought that *boyo* was rotten to the core." She flicked a loose strand of auburn hair behind her ear.

"Hmmm. The connection between the suspect and your friend is a bit intriguing. Kind of brings this whole murder around in a full circle. We find the body and your best friend's husband winds up being the suspect's long-time mentor."

"Venice is a small place. I guess it's not too surprising."

"Nothing surprises me when it comes to murder."

"Though I had my doubts, you pegged Marinello perfectly. You've believed all along that he's a crackerjack detective," Beth said.

"He is. That's why I think there's more to the story. How many pickpockets slink around Venice armed with a knife, super glue, and a carnival mask?"

"Hmmm." She pursed her lips while Shane fingered his dimpled chin. *I knew it*, she decided; *he's thinking like a detective, and deep down, I bet, he still wants to be one.* A smile crossed her face but lingered only a second.

"Oh well, it's Marinello's problem," he said.

She didn't know how to suggest that they should return to Venice. After all, she all but begged Shane to consider spending the remainder of their honeymoon in the Veneto. She lifted her cup of grappa and downed it. "Deirdre is worried that Jacopo may spiral downward into depression over Lorenzo's arrest. She was hoping we'd be keeping our dinner date with them on Friday."

"I thought it was settled that we're going to spend a few more days at the villa."

"Deirdre would feel so much better if we were around to help distract Jacopo. You know, to help brighten his mood a bit and divert him from dwelling on Lorenzo's arrest."

He shrugged. "I'll think about it."

Deciding not to press the subject, she opted to change the topic of conversation. "Wouldn't it be lovely to take a picnic lunch with us tomorrow? We could find a romantic spot and—"

"Okay," Shane interrupted, "sounds like a plan." He raked his fingers through his unruly hair, eased off the bed, and kissed her cheek. "I think I'll go outside for a few minutes. Get a breath of air."

"If you happen to see Mario, head the other way; otherwise, he'll talk your ear off. He's a nice enough lad but..." She shrugged.

"Will do."

With the door closed securely behind him, Beth discarded the used paper plates and put away the package of biscotti, honey, and cheese. Lifting the nearly empty bottle of brandy, she drained the remnant into her glass. A wave of exhaustion overcame her, so intense, that instead of drinking the clear, aromatic liquid, she decided to prepare for bed.

After brushing her teeth, she slipped into an ivory silk chemise. Stepping away from the bathroom, she paused halfway to the bed. A shiver ran through her. "My *fey*. Something's happened." She closed her eyes and strained to hear the message, but nothing surfaced.

Giving up, she folded her arms, crossed the room, and stood by the opened window. She peered into the darkness and searched for a glimpse of Shane. Not seeing him, her eyes traveled beyond the endless fields and made out the faint outline of a mountain against the clear night sky. It reminded her of the giant, Fionn mac Cumhaill, standing amid the Causeway. A wave of longing for Ireland rolled through her. She sighed and turned away from the window.

Taking slow steps, she stopped at the marquetry inlaid chest at the foot of the bed, opened it, and pulled out a down comforter. After spreading it across the bed, she crawled between the sheets and pulled on the duvet until she was able to tuck it around her bare shoulders. *Shane will, no doubt, pull the cover off, but then, I'll have his body to keep me warm and cozy.* She murmured one Ave, closed her eyes, and drifted off.

"Beth." A note of insistence filled Shane's voice.

She flickered her eyes open.

"You gotta hear this news."

She blinked the sleep away and struggled into a sitting position.

"Collins called while I was walking on the grounds."

Now fully awake, Beth opened her eyes wide but kept her lips closed.

"He thinks it's an omen that we found the body in the canal. Some kinda supernatural sign that I'm supposed to continue on as a homicide detective." He sat on the bed's edge.

"Really?" Beth shifted closer to him.

"Or not." Shane shook his head. "That's Collins for you."

"Well, my *fey* is telling me—"

"Do you want to hear what Collins had to say?" He raised his eyebrows.

She sucked in a quick breath. "News about the body in the canal?"

He nodded slowly, exaggerating the motion.

"Go on with yourself, so," she said tossing off the comforter.

He pulled the notepad from his pocket, flipped a few pages, and glanced at it. "About an hour ago, a woman called the station about her missing husband. He's been in Venice for over a month and kept daily contact with her until last week. She notified the Venetian State Police, but they haven't offered any info so that's why she contacted Collins—to see if he'd be able to intercede on her behalf."

"A homicide detective? Interesting that she thinks her husband is what ... dead? Maybe he just decided to leave her. But, you know what? Earlier my *fey* alerted me that..." Beth squeezed her lips together as Shane looked away from the pad and rolled his eyes toward the ceiling.

"Anyway," he continued, "the woman told Collins that her husband's first wife, an Italian woman named..." He ran his finger down the lined page. "Lia Renner had abducted their child before their divorce had been finalized—and disappeared over ten years ago. But in a turn of events, this past April, the ex-wife contacted him. That's what brought him to Venice in the first place."

"But Shane, how could this Lia Renner stay hidden for years? Especially with a child in tow."

"Must've been some kinda breakdown between the FBI and Interpol. Or she really knows how to cover her tracks."

"Oh?"

"You know, she probably didn't stay in one place very long and, no doubt had a list of aliases as long as my arm. Could've even changed her appearance surgically."

Beth wrinkled her nose.

"But get this. The missing man's wife, um, one Nicole Shelby, did say that her husband has a heart-shaped tattoo with the name Gemma above his wrist."

"What?" She paused a second. "Then he's the one—"

"Yup," he said with a nod. "The body in the canal was once Jonathan Shelby."

Chapter Twelve

LIDIA STARED AT THE CEILING cloaked in darkness, eager to block out the haunting dream that had roused her from a fitful sleep. The dream, more like a nightmare, teemed with sinister masked phantoms and bodies floating face-up in murky canals. She plumped the pillow, turned on her right side then her left, and waited for sleep that never came. Giving up after an hour, she opened her eyes as a ribbon of sunlight crossed her bed.

Throwing back the tangled sheet, she slipped off the mattress and padded to her wardrobe. She flung the door open and began freeing clothes from their hangers and tossed them on the bed. With determined steps, she moved to the haphazard pile, lifted a blouse, and folded it. She reached for the next item, stopped, and dropped her hand.

"I hate this," she said under her breath, "uprooting Oriana from her home again." A bolt of anger shot through her. Then she remembered. Oriana won't be going with her. *She'll be on a flight to California next week.*

Lidia couldn't shake the overwhelming guilt that she was somehow responsible for Jonathan's death. He'd traveled to Venice specifically because of her and the promise of being reunited with his daughter. Even though now it was impossible for Jonathan to know his own daughter, she wasn't going to deprive the American aunts and uncles, and especially Oriana's grandparents, that pleasure. *It's their right*, she'd decided, even though the devastation of losing her daughter caused her chest to tighten and her throat go dry. *After what I've done, I don't deserve to be her mother.* The thought that Oriana would be loved and cared for did little to soothe her breaking heart.

She grabbed her blonde tresses, twisted the hair into a knot, and secured the bun with a clip she'd snatched from the nightstand. With quick steps she paced across the small room not wanting to believe the fact that Jonathan had been murdered. *Is he dead because of me?* The question rung inside her head, over and over, like the deafening peal of a never-ending alarm bell. She'd spent most of the night refusing to relinquish the possibility of reuniting her family. But now she couldn't deny the fact that her chance of redemption had evaporated like the early morning mist.

That's why it's so important for Oriana to be with her family in California. To aid in absolving my sins and for them to give my daughter the life she deserves—the privileged life she was born into—the life I stole away from her.

She stopped next to the pile of clothing. Jonathan had reassured her that the statute of limitations had run out on the kidnapping charge. But Lidia feared it wouldn't take the police long to connect the dots—and possibly come to a devastatingly wrong conclusion—that she had murdered her ex-husband to keep Oriana for herself. She clutched her throbbing head.

"Mamma," Oriana called through the closed door.

Lidia inhaled sharply, rushed to the door, and cracked it open.

"I wanted to make sure you're awake." Oriana stood dressed and ready to leave the apartment for her private science school.

Lidia widened the door a few inches and smoothed the front of Oriana's simple white blouse. A blue paisley print bandana was tied beneath the shirt's flat collar. "I'm sure you'll do perfect on your geometry exam."

Oriana kissed her mother's cheek. "That was yesterday," she said with a smile. "Chemistry today."

"It'll be a snap for you, my little scholar."

Oriana's smile faded as she glanced down at her sandaled feet. "Have you talked to Papà?"

"Umm. Not yet. No."

"I was wondering if..." Oriana paused a moment. "I was telling Chiara about visiting Papà. She misses her father so much. Unlike me, she'll never get the chance to see him again."

Lidia sucked in a mouthful of air.

"Do you think he would mind if Chiara were to come along with me to California?" Oriana asked softly.

"I don't think he'd mind, but—"

"Oh Mamma, Chiara will be thrilled." She grabbed Lidia's hand, squeezed it, and then ran down the short hallway.

The sound of the apartment door slamming felt like a slap. Lidia raced to the bed and grabbed the dress lying on top of the pile. A tangle of thoughts tumbled around her brain, but one thing was certain: she needed to plan a strategy. Immediately.

She slipped into the smartly-cut summer frock. As she pulled up the back zipper, she froze, realizing that she wouldn't be able to depend on Dino for help. No matter how much he'd try to shield her from the looming allegation. Supportive words from Dino and even Jacopo, a pillar of the community, would be useless on her behalf.

"Father Busato will know what to do." A fleeting image of her kindly confessor swept through her mind. *He'll be able to shed light and direction,* she decided with a dash of hope. *If not, I'll be exiled from Venice forever.*

Chapter Thirteen

LIDIA STEPPED INTO LA SERENISSIMA Travel Bureau, struggling to come up with some kind of plan, but her overtaxed mind refused to work. Father Busato had been absent from morning Mass, which led her to discover that he was on the mainland for a funeral. Not able to speak with the priest spiked her anxiety, and during the short *vaporetto* ride to work, she'd begun to hyperventilate. Not that anyone on the crowded waterbus noticed as she forced herself to take deep breaths and exhale slowly through her nose. During the panic attack, she regretted her move to Venice. Settling down in the lagoon city had been Dino's suggestion—and where had that landed her—as a probable suspect in a murder investigation. Her insight warned that he'd beg her to stay in Venice and fight any accusations. But she lacked the strength. Or she wondered was it the desire for her sins to remain hidden away from the harsh criticism of an unyielding public.

Now in the secure surroundings of her office, the familiar pressure behind her eyes, caused by the stress she couldn't shake, guaranteed the onset of a migraine. An image of Jonathan swept through her mind, and a rush of overwhelming anguish paralyzed her. *This won't do,* she chided herself, realizing that to maintain her freedom she'd have to banish all thoughts of him. Because if she surrendered to her emotions, it'd be impossible to devise a successful plan. She'd have to stay focused, clear-minded, and determined even if the long fearful years of evading law-enforcement had completely drained her. But now the stakes were much higher and she wondered if she could pull off this final escape on her own. She'd vacillated about asking Jacopo for advice not sure if he could be trusted with her secret.

Lidia stepped behind the counter and headed toward her desk. She noticed Rosa, her coworker, looking through a pile of invoices. Jacopo's office door stood shut.

"*Buongiorno.*" Rosa glanced at her and then her watch. "Ah, Lidia. Finally made it in, eh? Well, it's a good thing—"

"Has Signore da Parma arrived?"

Rosa jerked her chin over her shoulder and gestured toward his office. "I'm not so sure I'd go in there if I were you."

Lidia raised her eyebrows.

"In a foul mood. Came in growling." Rosa lifted one of the little custard-filled pastry balls from a napkin placed next to her computer. She popped the *bigné* into her mouth. "It's possible he and the signora had another row." She licked the remnants of chocolate frosting from her fingertips and shrugged.

"I'll have to take my chances," Lidia said.

"If you're smart, don't ask for the day off."

Lidia shot her a quizzical look.

"Tourists have been traipsing in here all morning. I haven't had a chance to work on an itinerary Signore da Parma wanted an hour ago. Well, that's really your forte, isn't it? I still don't understand why *he* thinks a bookkeeper could plan travel arrangements—"

She stopped listening to Rosa's complaints as she freed a water bottle from her tote bag. *I doubt that Jacopo will be shocked when I tell him the truth. He might even think kidnapping Oriana was a justified act. After all, he's very devoted to his daughters. Hmmm. Jacopo just might be the perfect person to help me.* But then she remembered his unwanted advances and his crazy talk of them being married. Not knowing what to do, she tried to block out Rosa's droning but the woman's words rattled in her ears making it impossible to think.

The entry chime sounded, and a very fair, blond couple entered the office. She dropped the bottle and shoulder bag onto her desk and grabbed her reading glasses. With her best customer service voice, she greeted the couple. Within a few minutes, she'd answered all their questions regarding local glass-blowing demonstrations. She handed them two admission tickets, and they thanked her with beaming smiles. For an instant, the worries that plagued her evaporated. But as soon as the door slammed behind the tourists, Lidia's chest tightened, and her breath caught in the back of her throat. Not knowing what else to do, she headed toward Jacopo's office.

"Good luck," Rosa said lifting another cream puff.

Lidia rapped on the door then opened it. Not waiting for his permission to enter, she stepped inside the roomy office and moved in Jacopo's direction. Hunched behind his massive mahogany desk with a cigarette clamped between his lips, he sat reading the morning newspaper. She faced him, unsure of what to expect.

He glanced up and removed the smoldering cigarette from between his lips. "Lidia." He pointed to one of his guest chairs and she sat on the edge of its leather seat. Before she could utter a word, he tossed the paper in her direction. "Can you believe this?" He crushed the cigarette into a blocky, glass ashtray.

"What?"

"You haven't heard?" Not waiting for her response, he said, "Lorenzo Caravello has been arrested for the murder."

"Lorenzo?"

"The kid is a pickpocket, not some cold-blooded killer." He slammed his fist on the desk. "How the hell Marinello ever..."

Lidia lifted the reading glasses attached to the chain around her neck and positioned them on her face. She skimmed the front-page article in a frantic search for the answer as to why ... why in God's name did Lorenzo kill Jonathan. Whatever his motive, it wasn't spelled out among the printed words. "It says Lorenzo admitted to the murder. That he turned himself in."

"*Mio Dio*," he said slapping the mahogany desk's shiny surface. "You know Lorenzo. Does he strike you as a murderer?"

"I don't know him, not really, only to say hello to when he drops by the office to see you."

"Believe me, he didn't do it."

"He's admitted to the murder." She couldn't stop herself from visualizing Jonathan's handsome face, his warm eyes, bright smile. She gritted her teeth.

"It's a high-profile case. People are scared. Demanding the killer be apprehended. So, what do they do? Arrest Lorenzo. But it's a known fact that plenty of people admit to crimes they didn't commit—after hours of constant and brutal interrogation." He paused a couple of seconds. "Unless he did something really stupid."

Lidia was barely listening. A deep hatred for Lorenzo Caravello was growing inside her. "Stupid? Isn't murdering a total stranger stupid enough?"

"I told you. He couldn't have done it. But, sometimes, I swear, he doesn't have the good sense that God gave a gnat. The other night, I saw him giving the Barozzi girl the eye."

"Chiara?" Lidia frowned. "She's only fifteen. Lorenzo must be at least twenty—"

"Two. And an idiot. Lorenzo told me he was planning to impress Chiara big time. He said the girl is turned on by bad boys."

She wanted to protest but instead looked at her folded hands pressed into her lap.

"I told him Chiara is out of his league. After all, she's educated and comes from a wealthy, prominent family. God only knows if he took my advice. But if he didn't..." Jacopo sighed loudly. "I wouldn't be a damned bit surprised if the *polizia* bullied him into admitting to the crime just because he wanted to impress a girl." He shook his head. "I know first-hand the power of money. Maybe Elena Barozzi didn't like Lorenzo's attempt of romance aimed at her daughter and slipped Marinello a thick stack of euros to take care of it." He stroked his chin beneath a day's worth of stubble. "No. No, that's not it. A bribe wouldn't be necessary. I understand those two are now a couple. So, maybe arresting Lorenzo was just a way to placate his girlfriend."

Lidia didn't buy into Jacopo's blather that Lorenzo had been framed. She didn't like Lorenzo—his swagger or the way he ogled her—his eyes always lingering on her breasts. Even though he was a physical specimen of great beauty, a sense of unease filled her whenever he entered the office. The first time she'd met Lorenzo, her intuition had signaled that the young man possessed a cold, dark heart. Now her suspicion had been confirmed.

"I've no choice but to confront Marinello regarding this joke of an arrest. Once I've had my say, hopefully, he'll be released. Immediately." Jacopo's words tumbled in a long stream as if he'd forgotten to breathe.

She slid the newspaper back in his direction. "I've never understood why you're such a good friend with a petty thief."

"I have a long history with that boy." He selected a fresh cigarette from the gold case on his desk. "I've known Lorenzo since he was seven. Unwanted, he was tossed from one home to another. Finally, he wound up with a maiden aunt who pitied the poor kid. But she couldn't control him, and he ran wild. I was a young man then wanting to make a difference. So, I took him under my wing, but I guess it was too late for Lorenzo to change." He leaned back in the plush swivel chair and lit the cigarette. "But murder? No. Never." Jacopo waved his hand around, slicing the air while a thread of smoke drifted in front of his face. As if remembering the cigarette, he crushed it out without having taken a single puff.

"So, you really think that Lorenzo was arrested because he was flirting with a girl he wanted to impress? A young schoolgirl who ties her hair back in pig-tails and has stuffed animals on her pillow."

"Come on now. You make it sound like she's a *bambina*. Chiara is over the age of consent. She could have relations with me if she wanted to, and it'd be perfectly legal."

For an instant, she detected a lustful gleam that brightened his eyes. It turned her stomach.

"You can't really blame Lorenzo for being attracted to such a girl. She's a feisty little beauty."

Lidia had heard enough. "If Lorenzo didn't commit the murder, who do you think killed the ... the tourist?"

He shrugged. "I doubt it was on account of a few euros. Not the way his throat was slit. *Vendetta*," he said under his breath.

Lidia removed her glasses as a wave of dizziness washed over her. She tucked her chin toward her chest and rubbed her forehead.

"What's wrong? Not another headache."

"It's nothing," she lied, raising her head. "If you're going to plead Lorenzo's case to the Chief Superintendent, I imagine, there's no time to waste."

"Of course, you're right as usual." He stood and walked around the desk. He stopped in front of her. "There's something important I have to discuss with you first."

Pressure wrapped around her head like the tightening of a vise. Lidia reached into her dress' slit of a pocket and curled her fingers around her prescription bottle. She looked up at him and realized his attitude had changed. His face was relaxed, his mouth almost smiling, as if he'd forgotten all about Lorenzo.

"I've come to a decision." He grasped her hand and motioned her to stand.

Lidia too had come to a decision. Though he was rich and influential, she wouldn't be depending on Jacopo for help. *How could she trust someone who would defend a criminal who very well might have murdered her Jonathan?*

"I'm going to tell Deirdre I want a divorce. Tonight. I love you too much to ever consider asking you to be my mistress. Not only is it disrespectful it's ... cheap. You deserve so much better."

She pulled her hand away from him.

"If I was divorced—"

"Fine," Lidia spat. "Divorce your wife. But not on my account."

"We belong together."

"You must be out of your mind to even consider divorcing a woman like Deirdre. She's one of the kindest women I've ever known. Generous. Intelligent. Compassionate. Oriana and I arrived in Venice with nothing. We were little more than refugees. But did Deirdre judge us? No. She met us with opened arms in the church shelter and found us a home and a job for me, working for you. How dare you toss her away like a piece of trash because of your rampant, unbridled lust. She doesn't deserve to be treated that way."

"You're right. Deirdre is amazing. She's quite the dutiful wife. She cooks, takes care of the girls, loves me, but she hasn't been able to give me the one thing I want above anything else. Not that it's entirely her fault."

She narrowed her eyes.

"A son."

"You're blaming her for that?" Lidia fled to the door. She gripped the handle, but then spun around. "What do you think I am, some kind of broodmare? So what happens if we get married and in a couple of years, I don't produce a son? You divorce me too?"

"Never. You're beautiful and fit. You could give me ten sons."

"I'm a lot older than your child bride."

"That's a reason to start immediately." He moved closer to her.

Lidia turned away, pulled open the door, and stepped out of the office. She knew what she had to do.

Chapter Fourteen

JACOPO HAD EVERY INTENTION of demanding a divorce from Deirdre the moment he entered the house. His heels clicked against the entrance *loggia's* marble and red porphyry surface as he dropped the day's mail onto a gilded antique table. The letter on top was stamped Ireland, and upon a closer look, he noticed it was from Deirdre's mother. He sucked in a mouthful of air and steeled himself, preparing to face his wife.

The majestic house had been in Jacopo's family for centuries, handed down from first son to first son. Over time, it had fallen into near ruin, but his great-great-grandfather, Alvise da Parma, who'd died nearly a hundred years before Jacopo was born, had pumped a fortune into the building to bring it back to its former fifteenth-century magnificence. About ten years ago, Jacopo had installed a renovation of his own by upgrading the wiring and electrical panel. And once again when Deirdre had insisted on a modern, updated kitchen.

Every time he entered the *palazzo*, pride washed over him, delighted by its high coffered ceilings, shiny parquet floors, and printed damask wall coverings. The sheer curtains had been pulled back, and sunlight flooded through the floor-to-ceiling windows at the end of the *portego,* the grand hall. Though sparsely furnished, the walls of the *portego* told the history of the house. The frieze located below elaborate cornices displayed portraits of his ancestors spanning back centuries. The space below the long row of portraits boasted murals of mythological scenes, but Jacopo's crowning joy was the Tiepolo depicting Apollo pursuing Daphne with her fingers turning into branches of a laurel tree.

The *portego*, more like a living room of passage, opened to the main rooms and functioned as a celebratory space for receptions and galas.

Jacopo took a few steps down the hall but stopped to glance through the six-foot-wide doorway into the main salon. He smiled drinking in the ornate room, glittering in its richness like the interior of a jewelry box.

He resumed walking, certain that Deidre would be busy in the kitchen. She loved cooking just as much as eating. Even before they married, she'd nixed his suggestion of hiring a chef to prepare their meals. Though, she harbored no objections to employing a cleaning team comprised of an interfering older lady, her three daughters, plus a daughter-in-law. Jacopo didn't know their work schedule, which led to fireworks whenever one of them showed up in his study with a feather duster in hand. He'd instructed Deirdre to keep them out of his sanctuary, his bit of private space, within the massive house. To his chagrin, Deirdre had ignored his pleas due to her unnatural obsession with cleanliness. And because of that, his slice of privacy routinely suffered the indignity of pails of water and mops, wax and polish, and the gossip of uneducated housemaids.

Standing outside the kitchen door, he cringed at the sound of clanking pans and clattering dishes. But the most offensive noise was Deirdre's voice as she croaked out an Irish ditty, the melody tuneless as the fractured notes rang piercingly shrill. He covered his ears, not only to block out her caterwauling but to organize his thoughts. Though the demand for a divorce would seem to appear out of nowhere, he wanted to lessen the blow. Somehow. The harder he thought, the more his head pounded.

He dropped his hands, glanced along the *portego,* and frowned. Usually, he couldn't get further than a few steps into the house without his girls running into his arms. This certainly wasn't going to be a typical evening: Deirdre singing at the top of her lungs, the girls nowhere to be seen, and he about to shatter all their lives.

Just spit it out. No apologies. No sing and dance routine. Just the God's honest truth. Jacopo grabbed the knobby brass handle as purpose pumped through him. He flung the kitchen door open.

Deirdre faced the stove, fussing over a cast-iron skillet. He said her name loud enough to be heard over her singing and the sizzling on the burner. She glanced over her shoulder and greeted him with a radiant smile. "The girls have already eaten. They're upstairs playing. Our dinner is just about ready. They'll be here in a few minutes."

"Who'll be here?" Jacopo asked in English. It had been their habit for Deidre to speak in Italian and for him to answer in English. It helped strengthen their ability to speak both of their second languages. They spoke the same way with their children.

"The Daltons. Sibéal and Shane. Don't tell me you forgot?"

He grimaced then massaged his right temple with two thick fingers.

Deirdre pursed her lips. "Stressful day?"

He shrugged. "I spoke with Marinello—"

"Not good?" She grabbed a tea towel and wiped her hands. "I thought Lorenzo was turning his life around after you got him a job in the market." She paused a second. "I know your heart must be breaking but, truth be told, I'm not really surprised. It's a shame about that boy, but honestly, he's just, well, a bad seed."

Jacopo felt heat rise to his cheeks. He wanted to lash out. Tell Deirdre he was leaving her for a beautiful woman, but couldn't find the words. "You and the whole world might give up on Lorenzo, but I never will."

She moved next to him and patted his arm. "Of course, you won't. He's like a son to you."

"Marinello wouldn't even listen. Said it was none of my business. How can Lorenzo not be my business? I'm worried sick."

"Look. I've made all your favorites." Deidre walked him to the stove.

"I'm in no mood for company. It's not too late to bow out, is it?"

She sighed. "I can't think of a single time during the eight years we've been married that there hasn't been a crisis swirling around Lorenzo. It's time to cut the apron strings. He's not that little boy who touched your heart all those years ago. He's a grown man, and he got himself into this mess. It's not up to you to bail him out."

He shrugged. "I know you're right but..."

"A delicious dinner and an evening with friends is bound to ease away your stress. Anyway, you've always been fond of Sibéal. She could always bring out the most charming side of you." She kissed his cheek.

"Dinner does smell amazing." He lifted a lid from a simmering pot. "Ummm. Garlic sauce with clams."

"And eggplant parmesan, asparagus, and those potatoes you like so much. Not to mention your favorite canapés." She nodded to the baking sheet on the work island. "I know how much you enjoy putting together a salad. Would you mind?"

Jacopo glanced at the vegetables lying on top of the ebony granite countertop. He pulled a knife free from the block and dutifully chopped the tomatoes, mushrooms, peppers, and onions.

As he combined all the veggies onto a bed of lettuce, the doorbell sounded.

Deirdre untied her apron, dropped it on top of the work island, and sprang from the kitchen. He lingered and gave the salad a few good tosses. Satisfied, he retraced his steps along the *portego,* but instead of walking to the main salon, he stopped short and entered his study that opened into his bed-chamber.

Jacopo undressed, stepped into the shower, and willed the pelting water to ease the tightness knotting his muscles. He didn't rush as he lathered his body and inhaled the citrus fragrance of the lemon-bergamot soap. Though the jet of water comforted him like a soothing balm, his mind wouldn't release the building frustration ensuing from his foiled plans. He dried his skin, wrapped a striped Turkish towel around his waist, and stepped onto the cool marble floor.

He exhaled loudly, unable to shake away the heavy sense of dread that loomed over him. It wasn't just the issue with Deirdre that occupied his thoughts. After all, he told himself, *I'll set her up in a nice apartment and allow ample visitation with the girls. She'll have nothing to complain about.* But the thought of Lorenzo made his blood pressure spike. A string of obscenities flew between his lips as he cursed the young man for being so stupid. The undeniable fact was that Lorenzo's problem was now his.

He yanked open his wardrobe and selected an aqua linen shirt and a pair of khakis. After dressing, he slipped his bare feet into a pair of Gucci beige drivers. He stole a quick glance in the free-standing mirror, swiped his fingertips through his damp hair, and exited the room.

Jacopo found them seated in the T-shaped salon. A flash of anger sparked. *Deirdre should've taken them to the grand salon.* He tapped down his annoyance as he stood in the doorway with arms folded. His eyes immediately fell on Beth. Her lavender sundress emphasized her lithe figure and sun-kissed skin, while her luxuriant auburn hair swept up in a loose knot accentuated her face. He swallowed hard as a slow tingle ran along his backbone. *That precious face.* It had adorned magazine covers, posters, and billboards and undoubtedly had caused unrestrained desire to cross even the most pious of men's minds. Even the scar that crossed her cheek didn't mar her beauty but instead lent a sense of authenticity to Sibéal's impossible perfection.

His eyes flittered to Deirdre. Where Beth possessed angelic sublimity, Deidre appeared but a shadow; ordinary, dumpy ... repulsive. He'd married Deidre not because of her beauty, but because her back was straight, her hips wide, and though her face was plain, it lacked guile and radiated amiability. A perfect specimen for childbearing. *How in God's name had it gone so wrong?*

"Here he is." Deirdre's bubbly voice ripped away his thoughts.

He uncrossed his arms and pasted a wide smile on his face. "A very pleasant evening, my friends." He strode toward the cluster of couches and chairs where they were seated. "I hope you're hungry because Deirdre has prepared a delectable feast." The words flowed without effort. "How were your travels in the Veneto?"

"Lovely," Beth said standing, "but how could we stay away? Deirdre told us about the situation with Lorenzo."

Livid with rage, an explosion of fury surged through Jacopo. He couldn't fathom why Deirdre had told these *outsiders* about Lorenzo. He wanted to shout that it was none of their damn business, but instead, he lowered his head and stared at the rug's pattern beneath his feet.

"How are you holding up?" Beth moved next to him, grabbed his hand, and squeezed it.

Jacopo raised his head and hoped the fire in his eyes wouldn't give him away. "Much better now that you're here."

She kissed his cheek. "I'm so sorry. Deirdre explained that you took Lorenzo under your wing and treated him like a son. And now, he's betrayed your trust in him."

He steered Beth back to her spot on the couch and offered Shane a curt nod. Without a word, Shane stood and extended his hand. Jacopo gripped it firmer than usual and pumped hard. He found a sliver of enjoyment by squeezing the hand of a big-shot LA detective. He flashed a satisfied smile as Shane reclaimed his seat.

"The charges have to be trumped up. I realize that Lorenzo is no saint." Jacopo remained standing. He liked the advantage of towering over them. "But murder? No. Never."

Deirdre shook her head. "You're living in a dream world when it comes to Lorenzo. You make up excuse after excuse for his bad behavior. I'd wish you'd just accept the fact that there's a deep-seated defect in that *boyo*."

Jacopo waved the air in front of his face as if swatting away her words. "That damn Chief Superintendent, Marinello, has deaf ears. I did everything but fall to my knees in supplication, begging him to listen to reason. But would he? Hell, no."

"Well, you already know that we discovered the body." Shane gestured from himself to Beth. "My gut reaction regarding Marinello is that he's a thorough investigator. Isn't it true that murder is a rare occurrence in Venice?"

Jacopo nodded.

"Instantly then..." Shane snapped his fingers. "The canal murder becomes a high-profile case. Add to that the media coverage sensationalizing it, and Marinello probably feels like he's in a pressure cooker. But, charging a known pickpocket for murder seems a bit hinky."

Jacopo frowned.

"The arrest doesn't make sense," Shane said. "Unless there's a motive that we're unaware of ... such as the two men crossed paths, which led to an altercation and rising tempers that spiraled out of control. But, that still doesn't explain the carnival mask."

"But Shane," Deirdre said. "Lorenzo confessed."

"False confessions occur on a regular basis in case law," Shane said. "Sometimes coercion is involved. Other times, the confession is sacrificial to divert attention away from the actual person who committed the crime, you know, like a mother taking the blame for her child. And sometimes, it's just for the attention. The canal murder is surely getting a lot of that." He looked directly at Jacopo. "Is Lorenzo the type that craves attention?"

Jacopo shrugged. "God knows why he confessed. If only I could speak to him."

"The smart thing is to let the Chief Superintendent do his job," Shane said. "If Lorenzo is innocent, Marinello will know soon enough."

"We may not be a hundred percent sure about the identity of the killer, but we've discovered some interesting details about the murdered man," Beth said.

Jacopo detected a note of excitement touching her words. He narrowed his eyes in concentration, knowing that Beth tended to speak fast, making it hard for him to pick up every word.

"His name is Jonathan Shelby, and he's from Los Angeles," Beth said. "His trip to Venice had something to do with his daughter being abducted by his first wife over ten years ago. His current wife had been frantic with worry, but now, the poor woman is mourning his death. It's such a terrible tragedy."

Jacopo sunk into an eighteenth century Rococo armchair, his hand flying to his temple. "You know all this—"

"Because of the tattoo," Beth said.

Deirdre moved to the edge of her seat on the golden brocade couch. "Tattoo?"

"A heart encircling the name Gemma," Beth said. "That bit of information has already been made public. His wife confirmed that Shelby had that exact tattoo."

"Somebody wanted him out of the picture," Jacopo muttered as if trying to digest this new bit of information. "But not Lorenzo. I swear on my sainted mamma's grave; he's not violent. The way this, this Jonathan Shelby's throat was slashed," he said with a shake of his head. "No. He must've messed with the wrong person."

"The poor man," Beth said. "I can't shake away the image of that *Bauta* mask. It was so creepy."

"I'd hate for all this morbid talk to spoil our appetites," Deirdre said standing. She moved toward Beth, seated on the adjacent couch, and plopped down next to her.

"No chance of that happening to Shane." Beth patted Deirdre's arm. "Until recently, he used to thrive on homicide investigations."

Jacopo understood the look Shane shot at Beth. He'd used the same look innumerable times when Deirdre had tried his last nerve by nagging, complaining, or just babbling way too much.

"But now my darlin' husband is about to start a new career in construction. He was just shy of attaining his architecture certification when he made an about-face and joined the sheriff's office."

Jacopo tightened his lips when the mother of the cleaning team, who Deirdre had upgraded to a housekeeper, entered the salon dressed in a crisp maid's uniform holding a platter of hors d'oeuvres. He swallowed his disdain, even though he didn't trust the woman, believing that she spent most of her time snooping instead of cleaning, and shook his head when she offered the tray in his direction. He watched as she sashayed from one person to the other and then deposited the silver tray on a table next to a crystal vase stocked with an array of pink and orange gerberas, yellow lilies, and white roses. Jacopo's favorite flowers. He had them delivered fresh every day.

Shane popped the Caprese crostini into his mouth. "Ummm," he murmured. "The flavor of Italy all in one bite."

Deirdre beamed. "For dinner, I made all of Jacopo's favorites."

Shane stood and headed toward the appetizers. He stopped and slowly turned around. "This is amazing. Looks like a set for a historical movie. Except, it's the real deal." He motioned to the two massive Murano chandeliers as he stepped closer to the grand piano. "This carpet must be thirty-feet long. The plasterwork, pilasters, and paintings..."

Jacopo couldn't stop the smile from forming even if he tried. "As an architecture aficionado, I'm pleased you recognize the magnificence of this room. The murals were painted by some of the most renowned Venetian artists from the sixteenth century. That one," he said pointing to a tondo encircled by plaster *putti*, chubby winged cherubs, "is my ancestor who was a Doge, Sebastiano da Parma. All the gold," he said gesturing toward the ceiling, "is 24-karat. The furnishings are also authentic though not as old as the *palazzo*. I see myself as the steward of this treasure, that is until my son inherits all of this." He waved an arm as if attempting to encompass the grand room.

Jacopo enjoyed their guests' moment of confusion. Deirdre chewed her lip as Beth and Shane exchanged puzzled glances.

"A family tradition," Deirdre said. "Jacopo doesn't want his sister's son to inherit the house. But with me not able to..." She shook her head.

Shane broke the moment of icy silence. "So, your home dates from the 1500s?"

"1479. This section of Dorsoduro is the oldest in all of Venice. People have lived here for a millennium." Jacopo's voice assumed a tone of authority. "To your eyes, the area may look a bit um ... *cadente* ... how you say—"

"Rundown?" Beth asked.

"Eh. Close enough." Jacopo gestured with a shrug and his palms upward and fingers splayed. He moved toward an arrangement of liquor bottles nestled on a marble-topped table. "Our streets are packed with history and character." He dropped a couple of ice cubes into four glasses, opened a bottle of Aperol Aperitivo liqueur, and filled them. "Then there are the treasures. Breathtaking churches, the Gallerie dell' Accademia, the Guggenheim Collection, ah, there's too much to count." He dropped an orange slice into each glass.

Shane moved next to him and took two glasses. "I think this area of Venice is the most authentic—the true flavor of everything the city stands for—pride mingled with a sense of real grit. Sorta like a painting by Guardi. But your gem of a house is the exception. Looks a bit outta place here."

"Guardi?" Jacopo asked under his breath. He realized Shane had paid him a backhanded compliment but what good was it, he thought, at the expense of insulting his beloved neighborhood.

Deirdre moved next to Jacopo and claimed a glass. He raised the remaining flute.

"A toast," Beth said taking a glass from Shane. "To Venice."

"To the Dorsoduro," Jacopo said.

The fine crystal glasses clinked just as a bell jingled. The housekeeper stood in the doorway holding a little brass bell. "*La cena è servita*," she said then turned away.

"Dinner can wait until after we finish our drink," Jacopo said still worrying over Shane's Guardi comment. But then he shrugged. *How could an American understand the beauty of the aging patina of time? Where he's from, a building fifty years old is considered ancient.* He raised his glass and took a sip. "Would you like a tour of the *palazzo* after dinner?"

Shane's faced brightened. "Sounds like a plan."

Jacopo emptied his glass. *Detective Shane Dalton hasn't seen anything yet.*

Chapter Fifteen

LIDIA GLANCED AWAY FROM the computer monitor as Rosa neared the door. She pulled off her glasses attached to a chain around her neck, released them, and they bounced against her chest. "*Buonasera,*" she said.

"You've had a busy day so don't stay too much longer." Rosa sounded like a concerned mother.

"I want to finish this itinerary for that couple who stopped by earlier today."

"The Swedish couple? So, they enjoyed the glass blowing demo and now they want to hike the trails in the Dolomites?"

Lidia nodded. "They requested a guided tour. Seems a bit last minute. They leave Italy in a couple of days for some Greek island."

"Regardless, I know you won't disappoint them. *Ciao.*" Rosa offered a tiny wave and exited the La Serenissima Travel Bureau, leaving Lidia alone.

She replaced her glasses and stared at the screen. The excuse of planning a hiking trip had been a ruse since she needed to research her next move with no prying eyes around. Lidia scrolled down the screen and stopped at a listing for Radstadt, a hamlet in Austria. Skimming the information, she shook her head. *Too small. I wouldn't be able to stay anonymous there.* A seed of panic mingled with frustration, heightening the fact that she had no time to lose. In a few days, Oriana would be in America, and then she'd have to be ready to flee the border. She brushed her fingertips through her hair, deciding that a larger town in Austria would be her safest choice. She'd grown up near the Italian border and spoke fluent German. No one would mistake her for an Italian kidnapper, let alone, a murder suspect.

She glanced at the bottom of the screen and caught the name Klagenfurt. *I've been there before—as a kid—on a skiing holiday.* She opened the site and skimmed the information offered about the town. "They have a small airport," she murmured hoping she'd be able to fly there directly from Venice.

She fished the cellphone from her purse and tapped in the number she'd long ago memorized. At the seventh ring, Lidia was about to click off when she heard his voice. Even though she was alone in the deserted office, she kept her voice low. "It's Lia. I need your help." She quickly explained to her "cobbler" that she needed an Austrian passport and prayed it wouldn't take long. She breathed relief when he explained that he had one available, but it would be pricey. Over the years, Lidia made sure that she'd squirreled away enough euros in case of an emergency. And this was a major one. "How long?" she asked under her breath.

She tapped the screen, ending the call, and leaned back in the chair. The passport would be ready within the week, but first, she had to wire him half the cost. The same as last time. Usually, the weight of her deceit left her overburdened with guilt. But now, she refused to yield to feelings, good or bad. If she didn't act fast, only God knew what would happen if the police uncovered her identity. The possibility of being arrested for Jonathan's murder not only petrified her but spurred her on. She reached for a pen and scribbled down the name the master forger had given her. She'd have to get used to it fast. Aleda Linser. Her new identity.

Lidia grabbed the slip of paper, folded it in half, and stuck it into her purse. She glanced at her watch and realized it was later than she'd imagined. *The rest will have to wait until tomorrow.* After all, she knew what it was like to destroy a family. She'd left her own in ruins.

Chapter Sixteen

WHEN LIDIA ARRIVED AT WORK the next day, Jacopo whisked her into his office. He rallied on about his proposed blueprint for their life together, but his grand words translated as worthless rubbish, since in a week's time, every trace of Lidia Feloni would be eradicated. He didn't seem to notice the disinterest covering her face.

He paused, and she found her voice. "Did you tell Deirdre you want a divorce?"

"I had every intention but..." He shrugged. "She'll know tonight; I promise. You see, she had planned a dinner party..."

Lidia blocked out his words. She longed to reveal the devastating event that had shattered all her plans and left her sorrowful, consumed by grief and weighed down by despair. In her fragile state, she'd only dare to share the depth of her heartbreak to someone who'd offer support. Understanding. Hope. Jacopo's faith in Lorenzo Caravello's innocence blinded him. She couldn't take the risk of divulging her secret pain with him. Ever.

She cleared her throat. "When the school term ends, Oriana will be visiting her father in California. And I'm—"

"Don't tell me. No. You're going with her?"

Lidia took a deep breath. "I've decided to leave Venice. I've accepted a job in Rome."

He sprung out of his chair. "What? You've done what? No. No, Lidia, you can't just pull up stakes and leave." He paced around the desk and hovered over her.

"You expect me to refuse a job offer in my field of study?" She didn't wait for a response. "I've taken an engineering job at Leonardo S. p. A."

90

Though a bald-faced lie, Lidia wished she could be starting such a dream job instead of assuming another false identity in a foreign country.

"For that, you would abandon Venice... and me?" His hand landed on her shoulder.

"Opportunities like this are rare. I'd be a fool to turn the job down."

He bent close to her ear. "No offer could outrank that of being my wife." His hot breath brushed her cheeks.

She looked down at the marble pattern of his office floor. "I can't stay here. All this talk of us being a couple and you willing to destroy your family, for what?" She lifted her face and looked into his eyes. "I don't love you."

The color rose to his cheeks as he swept a hand through his hair. "So, I'm driving you away." Jacopo crossed the room and paused at a small console. He lifted a framed photograph of his daughters. "If you're afraid that I won't care about Oriana, you're mistaken. I'll love her as if she were my own daughter." He replaced the picture and faced Lidia. "I can make you happy. Happier than you could ever imagine. Give me the chance to prove myself."

"I've written my letter of resignation."

"I won't accept it."

"You have no choice."

He moved next to her and took her hands. "Don't do this."

It would be so much easier to give in to him, Lidia thought. *Let him use some of his ample money as a bribe to protect me.* She pursed her lips. It took only a moment to brush that idea away. She'd rather be alone, assume the persona of Aleda Linser of Klagenfurt, Austria, and start her life over from scratch then be coerced into marrying Jacopo da Parma.

She stood and freed her hands from his grasp. Before she could take a step, he pulled her into an embrace. For the first time in days, she felt safe. She rested her head on his shoulder, closed her eyes, and for a moment, imagined she was nestled within Jonathan's strong arms.

"Please," he whispered in her ear. "Don't break my heart."

The spell shattered.

"There's no reason to upset Deirdre. Go home and enjoy your family. Forget about me." She pulled free.

"I can't live a lie," he said. "Once my marriage is dissolved, I'll prove that I'm the perfect man for you." He kissed her cheek. "So, go to Rome. But I swear, one day you'll accept my proposal."

His words rattled her, but she forced herself to respond. "Take the clouds from your eyes. I don't love you and never will."

Lidia raced out of his office and retreated to her desk wondering if he'd sack her on the spot. Not bothered if he did, she sat on the edge of her chair and fired up her computer. Her fingers flew across the keyboard and then paused as she waited for the information to fill the screen. She scribbled down the address. Without a word to Rosa, seated with a sugary S-shaped *bussolià* in hand and eyes glued to a spreadsheet, she left the office.

The trip to the *Istituto di Internazionale* where Deirdre taught consisted of a short jaunt on a waterbus, a five-minute walk down a narrow lane, and through a shady park with a stone fountain spraying a jet of water. She stood outside the main entrance of the stucco building while bolstering the courage to enter. First, she'd have to find the right words.

She glanced at her watch. Eleven. Normally school wouldn't let out until one, but with the end of year assessments, the dismissal was earlier. Students started to stream out through the doors. They flew down the age-old stone steps and spilled onto the sidewalk with lively voices. Most of them headed in the direction of the waterbus stop.

She walked back to the park and sat on a bench, knowing she'd have to act soon. As the throng of students dispersed, Lidia stood and smoothed the wrinkles from her lime-green sheath dress and took a few steps closer to the school. She glanced at the building and caught a glimpse of Deirdre. A small group of students nearly surrounded her, their faces animated as they vied for her attention. Lidia rushed toward them then stopped a couple meters away. Her mouth suddenly turned dry as a shot of adrenalin coursed through her, making her heart pound.

The chattering students continued with their banter even though Deirdre had stopped walking. "Now off with you," she instructed the half-dozen teenagers. They drifted away, their voices still charged with adolescent enthusiasm.

"Lidia? What are you doing in this part of town? Don't tell me Jacopo sent you?"

"I need to speak with you." Trying to settle her nerves, she couldn't keep the pitch of her voice level. She coughed a couple of times, attempting to clear her throat.

"You need something to drink. There's a *café* down the street."

Lidia swallowed hard. "No. I'm fine."

Deirdre linked arms with her and steered Lidia toward the bench she'd vacated minutes before. The sunlight had changed, and now blocks of shadow crossed the wooden seat.

"What's wrong?" Deirdre asked softly.

They sat side by side, though Lidia kept her sight focused on her clasped hands resting in her lap. "I'm sorry, Deirdre."

"Sorry?"

"I value our friendship and ... well, I don't want you to be hurt. I have no idea what Jacopo is going to say, so I want to set the record straight and tell you the truth."

Almost instantly, Lidia noticed that Deirdre's open and friendly expression had vanished, and a sense of wariness had taken its place.

"It's crazy, but Jacopo thinks he's in love with me," Lidia said the words so fast that she wondered if Deirdre had understood. Not about to repeat herself, she continued but tried to speak slower. "I've been stressed out over finances. Jacopo stepped up. Helped me out. But I'm afraid he mistook my appreciation for affection."

Deirdre's lips parted as if she were about to speak, but instead, she only looked into Lidia's face.

"I want you to know that I have no romantic feelings toward your husband. I've told him as much."

Deirdre slowly nodded as if finally understanding Lidia's words. "You don't need to be concerned. I know from experience that Jacopo's head is easily turned by a lady in distress. Especially a beautiful one." She patted Lidia's arm.

Lidia wanted to shout, but her words came out not much louder than a whisper. "It's more serious than you think. He's planning to divorce you."

"That's ridiculous."

"He's going to tell you tonight."

Deirdre shook her head. "Jacopo has a big personality, and everyone loves him. But, he has his flaws. One is that he sees himself as a smooth-talking charmer. A venerable Casanova. In reality, he's a family man."

"That may be true, but he wants a different family now. He blames you for not giving him a son. I know that's ridiculous. Jacopo talks as if *you* have the power to determine the sex of your children."

"Unlike your brilliant daughter, Jacopo was far from being a scholar. He must've missed that lesson in biology class." A touch of sarcasm touched her words. "But, I can't complain. He provides a good home for us. I've gotten used to pretty girls turning his head."

"Pretty girls? Why would he be interested in other women when he has you for a wife? You're beautiful. Young. Vibrant." Lidia noticed the color rise to Deirdre's cheeks. "He's a fool if he doesn't recognize that your beauty is more than skin deep. It radiates through you and shines on your face."

Deirdre looked downward as if embarrassed.

"If only you could see yourself the way I see you... you'd take your girls and leave Jacopo for good. There's a man out there who will respect and love you the way you deserve."

Deirdre nodded. "Perhaps, you're right." She raised her head, and Lidia noticed that Deirdre's eyes were wet.

"I wish you only the best whatever you decide to do. I'm leaving Venice for a job in Rome."

"Don't tell me you're moving away because of Jacopo."

"It's for the best. Jacopo thinks he loves me. Maybe he does," Lidia said with a shrug, "but I'm not a homewrecker." The words slipped out innocently enough, though deep down, she knew that was exactly who she was—she'd wrecked her own home, her family, and her only chance for happiness. "Anyway, I can't stay here. I've lost someone very precious and ... well, it'd be impossible for me to remain living in Venice." Lidia took a deep breath. "I want to ask for your forgiveness."

"Forgiveness? What is there to forgive?" Deirdre grasped Lidia's hand and squeezed it.

"I couldn't bear for you to think that I'd betray you after all the kindness you've shown to me and Oriana. I'll treasure your friendship forever, and I wish you only happiness." Lidia kissed Deirdre's cheek. She stood and took a step away from the bench. "*Addio*," she said. Though it lasted only a second, she detected a look of bewilderment on Deirdre's face. With a tiny wave, Lidia turned away and headed for the waterbus stop.

Part of her wanted to rush back to Deirdre—to urge her to unleash the anguish crushing her spirit—the result of her husband's callousness. And then both of them would curse Jacopo to hell. But she sensed Deirdre was the type to save face, a strong upper lip due to being ... British? Deep down, she feared her admission had pierced Deirdre's heart. *Both of us have that in common now.*

Chapter Seventeen

"ANOTHER GLASS OF WINE sounds good," Elena Borozzi said. She lifted her eyes from the empty glass and focused on Daniele Marinello, seated across from her on the patio of the *Gran Caffé Quadri*. A throng of tourists milled about the Piazza San Marco, and the mingling of their garbled tongues created a constant hum, but Elena hardly realized she was not alone with him. She'd known Daniele for years, yet never thought of him as anything more than her husband's second cousin and his closest friend. He'd been the best man at their wedding and chosen as Chiara's godfather. He was just one more member of her husband's large, extended family. *When exactly did that change?* she wondered.

As he placed the wine order with the waiter, she pressed her fork into a fruit tart and broke it into two mouth-sized pieces. A few stray crumbs fell onto the white tablecloth. Elena couldn't bring herself to eat the pastry, so she placed her fork back on the porcelain plate.

"Silly of you to think dessert will spoil your figure," Marinello said. "You need to gain a few *chili*."

He was right; she had lost weight. The last couple of years had been difficult since her husband, Marco, had been killed by a roadside bomb when he was on his way to a triage center outside of Kabul. He'd been assigned to work with a small delegation of international military physicians and was the only one who died—complications from a brain trauma. His buddy, Andrew, a Royal Australian Air Force doctor suffered barely a scratch and had paid her a visit last year with a letter from Marco. Just holding the envelope had brought a sudden rush of anguish. She'd refused to break the seal and read his final words. Elena couldn't face the finality—their life together would come to an end—forever. She wasn't ready to cut the last remaining thread that linked her to Marco.

For Chiara's sake, she'd done her best to hide her heart-shattering grief, though every day remained a struggle. Since that fateful event, she'd not only lost her appetite but the very reason for her own existence. The first few weeks, she went through the motions, if only to offer a pretense of normalcy. But with Daniele's presence and constant assurance, she found strength she didn't realize she possessed, which allowed her to carry on with her daughter, her job, and her own life, with a flicker of hope.

She looked away from the plate and studied his face. The late afternoon light was bright enough to detect the gold flecks in his hazel eyes. Marinello cleared his throat and replaced the cup of espresso on its saucer.

"Jacopo has stopped by the station three mornings in a row."

"Three times?" Elena shook her head. "You know, he and Marco were friends, and I'm fond of him, too. But," she paused a second, "he's never been one to keep his thoughts to himself, especially when he has a complaint. So, what is it now? Too many Venetians moving to the mainland, not enough stalls at the fish market, or what are you doing about the pigeon problem?"

He shot her a smile. "None of those this time. He's agitated over the recent arrest of Lorenzo Caravello. Every morning, it's the same thing. Release Lorenzo immediately."

"Which of course, you did." A touch of sarcasm touched Elena's voice.

"Today, I did."

"What?" She inched to the edge of the red wicker chair. "You released a murderer back onto the streets of Venice?"

"He withdrew his confession. Anyway, that was immaterial since we had no evidence to hold him." He looked beyond Elena as if studying the golden domes of the basilica. "Caravello is a nuisance. A lousy pickpocket and a braggart. It took only a couple of days behind bars for him to bare his soul. Explained his murder confession was a ploy to get noticed. He wanted to impress a girl."

"You're kidding?" Elena reached for the full wineglass, she'd just noticed, sitting next to her dessert plate. She took a sip. "You believed him?"

He cocked his head but didn't answer.

"Well, I wouldn't be too sure that he didn't kill that tourist. The way he struts around with that over-developed chest, and why did God have to give him such a beautiful face? No wonder he thinks he can get away with murder." Her heightened emotions made her realize that she was, indeed, hungry. She took a quick taste of the pastry then took another, larger bite. "I should be getting home. Chiara—"

"The girl Lorenzo wanted to impress was Chiara."

She dropped her fork. It made a clatter against the dish.

"Lorenzo said he'd been milling around the *piazza* looking for an easy mark, to pickpocket, when he noticed the commotion. He'd caught a glimpse of Chiara with Antonio, which made him mad. So, like an ass, Lorenzo thought if he confessed to the murder, she'd be overcome with respect for him, awe actually, and he'd have the prettiest girl in Venice for a girlfriend."

Elena squeezed her eyes shut as a flaring pain shot through her temple. "How dare he blame Chiara as the reason for his brutality?" She flashed her eyes open, took a sip of wine, and cleared her throat. "Has he been diagnosed?"

"Diagnosed?"

"Delusional disorder? Erotomania?" She read the confusion on his face. "The object of obsession is typically a person who is unattainable, due to various reasons such as high social or financial status or even disinterest."

"You may be overthinking this, Elena." He grasped her hand and stroked it. "I doubt Lorenzo is suffering from any kind of mental disorder."

"Onset is sudden. And Lorenzo has already exhibited anti-social behavior."

"True. He's a petty criminal looking for attention. But I've already read him the riot act. If he's within a *chilometro* of my goddaughter, he'll be arrested."

"How would I manage without you, Daniele?"

"Just fine, I suppose." He shot her a broad smile that lasted only a second. "I doubt Chiara even knows Lorenzo exists." He tented his fingers and pursed his lips. For a moment, he seemed lost in thought. "But, if she has been associating with that scoundrel then we'll have to take immediate

98

action. After all, she's naïve and could easily be misled by a sweet-talking jerk like Lorenzo."

"Chiara is an intelligent girl, but she is a bit boy crazy." Elena shrugged. "If she is socializing with scum like Lorenzo, I'll get to the bottom of it. For her own protection." She tapped her foot against the stone pavement. "Actually, I was thinking of sending her away to spend the summer break with my mother. She lives in Padua and has eyes like an eagle. I'm certain that she won't let Chiara out of her sight, let alone, allow her to mingle with the opposite sex."

"Ah, a perfect chaperone. Sounds like a reasonable plan."

"A temporary fix. If only the Sisters of Santa Angela de Merici would intervene and keep her locked up in the convent for the next three years." She shook her head.

"I'm sure the sisters would be up for the challenge," he said with a grin. The amused expression on his face froze for a second before fading away. "The couple who found the body is headed this way."

"That must've been a shock," Elena said looking into the crowded square. "I imagine they're still a bit disturbed by the incident."

"You'd think, especially since they're on their honeymoon. But, the man is a former police detective, and the woman seems a bit too interested in the investigation. The funny thing is that when I met Beth Getty, I swear, she looked familiar. I must know her. I rarely forget a face, but for some reason, I'm having difficulty placing her. It'll come to me, eventually. I'm sure of it."

Elena shifted in her seat to see the approaching couple. She immediately recognized the man—the one she'd wondered about at the crime scene. Apparently, she'd been correct. He had discovered the body in the canal.

Marinello rose and faced Shane and Beth. They approached with their arms wrapped around each other like so many other lovers exploring the streets of Venice.

"Chief Superintendent," Shane said slipping his arm free from around Beth's waist.

"Ah, Signore." Marinello offered his hand, and Shane grasped it. After releasing his grip, Marinello gestured to Elena. "This is Doctor Elena Barozzi."

"So lovely to meet you. I'm Beth, and this is my husband, Shane."

Elena nodded. *So, this is the woman Daniele thinks he knows. Hmmm ...*

even without all the trappings of celebrity, she's actually ... quite stunning.

"Congratulation you on your collar, um, arrest of the Canal Murderer," Shane said.

"Thanks, but..." Marinello paused. "Oh, what the hell." He waved his hand in front of his face. "Caravello was released this morning. Couldn't hold him any longer. No evidence. But, he's still a person of interest."

"How disappointing," Beth said. "We were relieved that the culprit had been arrested. I'm terribly heartsick for the victim's family. Maybe we could help. You see, according to the poor murdered man's..."

Elena recognized the look Shane shot at his wife—a mixture of caution and irritation.

Beth pressed her lips together.

"There's bound to be setbacks," Shane said. "You'll get the perp. I'm sure of that," He took Beth's hand. "Have a pleasant evening. Chief Superintendent. Doctor." He offered them a curt nod.

Elena kept her eyes fixed on the couple as they headed to a table a couple rows away. Marinello lifted his cup, looked inside, and then placed it back on its saucer.

"Are you familiar with Noelle Cosmetics?" Elena asked, dragging her finger around the rim of her wineglass.

Marinello frowned. "Cosmetics?"

"I know why *she* seemed familiar to you. She's Sibéal. The Irish model. Had Milan in an uproar a few years ago."

"A model?"

"And spokesperson for Noelle Cosmetics. Back then, her face was plastered everywhere—magazines, flyers, billboards—and in television advertisements."

Marinello rested his chin on his tented fingers. "Well, that's the last thing I need—some celebrity type wanting to stick her nose into my investigation."

Chapter Eighteen

BETH TOOK A QUICK SIP of tea, trying to keep her eyes off Marinello and his attractive tablemate. "Do you think he's in love with her?"

"What?" Shane lifted the glass and took a long swallow of Peroni beer.

"Marinello and his doctor friend."

"How'd you come up with that? I swear, you do have a way of letting your imagination run wild, Betty Getty. She's probably nothing more than a colleague. A medical examiner."

"This has nothing to do with my imagination. In fact, the moment I saw those two, my *fey* informed me they were much more than friends. Actually, a sixth sense wasn't necessary to pick up on the electricity crackling between them."

With a resigned shake of his head, Shane took another swallow of beer and placed the glass firmly on the table. "Why don't we focus on an actual love affair?" A half-smile played at the corners of his mouth. "Later, we can catch the sunset over the canal from our terrace."

She reached for his hand but then drew it away. "Look," she said pointing toward the crowded square, "there's Deirdre. Give me a quick minute to run over and say hello."

She jumped away from her seat and skirted around the tightly-arranged tables leading into the *piazza*. Beth called her friend's name as she popped around a gaggle of tourists and came into Deirdre's direct view. A look of happy recognition covered Deirdre's face the moment before Beth reached her and threw her arms around her friend.

"Have a drink with us at *Gran Caffè Quadri*," Beth said.

"Ah, no, I'm grand, thanks."

"Surely you can spare a few minutes, so."

"We're celebrating the end of the school year with the girls tonight. I'll be stopping at the market and then whipping up a special dinner."

"Lovely. At least walk back to the café with me."

"After all these years," Deirdre said with a sigh, "I still haven't figured out how to say no to you. Come on, then." She linked her arm through Beth's and made their way to the café.

As they approached, Shane stood and pulled out two red wicker chairs. Deirdre plopped down next to him and glanced at a nearby waiter. "I certainly could do with a good *cuppa*."

"I've already ordered a fresh pot," Shane said as Beth reclaimed her seat.

"What a darlin' man," Deirdre said. "If only my Jacopo was half as thoughtful." She cleared her throat. "So, what have you two lovebirds been doing today?"

"Visited San Giorgio Maggiore," Shane said.

"Ah, 'tis a marvel. Such a lovely church." Deirdre nodded at the waiter who deposited a black metal kettle and a white porcelain teacup in front of her.

"Look, why don't you two enjoy your tea and girl talk. I'm going to walk over there," Shane said motioning beyond the square, "and pick up an American newspaper." He kissed Beth's cheek and dropped a few bills onto the table. "Then I'll head back to the apartment."

As Beth watched him amble into the crowded square, she noticed that Marinello and his friend had left the café. The table now sported two white-haired men seated behind cocktails with cigars nestled between stout fingers.

She turned her attention back to Deirdre who was filling their cups. A chilling thread of coldness gripped Beth. *Something's wrong.* She rubbed her sore shoulder and discovered her muscles stiff—bunched up with strain. *Maybe Deirdre's in danger.* She shook her head remembering Shane's comment about her wild imagination. "There's something you're not telling me?"

"One of your premonitions?" Deirdre tapped her fingers against the linen-covered table. "It's Jacopo." She lifted the teacup but returned it to its saucer. "He's once again involved with another woman."

Beth's eyes grew wide. "He's cheated on you?"

"Truly, Beth, he can't help himself. He loves women. All types and varieties. And in most cases, unfortunately, they're equally attracted to him."

"But he's been unfaithful?"

Deirdre jutted out her chin.

She realized Deirdre was trying to be strong, but her quivering lip gave her away. She silently counted to ten to defuse the anger welling in violent swells deep in the pit of her stomach. "I don't care about how easily women may swoon over him. He's married to you. That's where his affection and commitment belongs." She gripped her hands together so tightly her knuckles turned white.

"This latest episode turns out to be an infatuation only on my husband's part."

She wanted to ask for details but decided to let Deirdre continue without her playing twenty questions.

"His assistant broke it off before the affair had a chance to start." Deirdre took a sip of tea. "All this time, I thought his brooding was over Lorenzo's arrest. But no, it was Lidia. His unwanted attention has upset the poor colleen so, she's leaving Venice and moving to Rome."

"Lidia Feloni?"

Deirdre nodded. "Lidia is really quite a decent sort. Like you, she's beautiful, but if you ask me, she plays down her good looks. No wonder, Jacopo was attracted to her. I can't compete when it comes to that kind of thing."

"What are you talking about? My Shane was saying just the other day that he thinks you're cute."

"Cute?"

"You remind him of a teacher he had a crush on when he was a lad."

"Cute can't compare with beautiful."

"Jacopo's a fool if can't see that you possess true beauty of character and spirit."

Deirdre reached for Beth's hand and squeezed it.

"I never would've dreamed he could be so cruel," Beth said. "Heartless the way he's hurt you. I'd like to give him a piece of my mind, so." She pressed her lips into a tight line.

"It's the same old thing. Guilt gets hold of him, he confesses, asks for forgiveness, but then turns around and repeats the pattern." Deirdre shrugged. "I don't think I have the strength to forgive him one more time. But ... what choice do I have? You know how seriously I take our wedding vows." She raised her cup and looked over its brim at Beth. "Truth is, he scares me sometimes."

"Scares you?"

"His emotions are so volatile. Laughing one minute then *effin'* and *blindin'* to high heavens the next."

"Erratic, so," Beth said. "But he always seems to come across warm and friendly. Outgoing."

"That's his public persona. At home he's ... well, no one's perfect," Deirdre said. "For being such a grand success in business, it's ironic that he doesn't show the same discipline in everyday situations. He tends to let his emotions take charge. Living with Jacopo is like being stuck on a never-ending ride on the Cú Chulainn Coaster."

"What are you going to do?"

Deirdre glanced at her watch. "I have to go." She drained her teacup and stood.

"I'll walk with you."

They crossed the piazza in silence as tour groups marched by, following guides with upraised umbrellas. Lovers walked hand in hand, and happy families laughed and licked streams of melting gelato from crispy cones while gesturing at the abundant pigeons. With each step, Beth sensed Deirdre's will strengthen.

They stopped at the portico leading into *Calle Dei Fabbri*, not far from the footbridge where Beth had discovered the body of Jonathan Shelby.

"I haven't a clue how to stop his maddening cycle of infidelity," Deirdre said under her breath. "I do know that I've got to away from Venice. I'm going to take the girls to Ireland for the summer. Stay with my folks. They'll love spoiling the twins, and it'll give me time to think."

They walked under the arch and through the portico then climbed the bridge's two sets of steps. Deirdre leaned against the bridge's iron balustrade and stared into the canal. Beth moved next to her, but instead

104

of looking into the water, she focused on the Hotel Leone. She wanted to forget the memory of the body in the canal.

"Do you miss it, Sibéal?"

Beth turned toward Deirdre. "Ireland?" She paused a few seconds. "Sometimes my heart aches for it. I miss the cool, fresh mornings—"

"And the soft rain... shady country lanes... and the corner pub, Guinness and gossip." Deirdre shot her a quick smile. "Ah, it's a different world—green, fresh, peaceful—home. There, I'm sure to find the answers I'll be looking for." Deirdre faced her. Instead of self-pity or despair, Beth saw strength and purpose, a capable woman who would determine her own fate. "You need to get back to Shane," Deirdre said. "Don't give me another thought. I'm going to be fine."

"Of course you'll be fine *me ould flower*." Beth offered her an encouraging smile, but the niggling of her *fey* made her doubtful that all was going to bode well for Deirdre and her marriage.

Chapter Nineteen

JACOPO STOPPED PACING WHEN the door opened leading into the *piano nobile,* the "noble" floor of his *palazzo.* He stood hidden in the small reception room adjacent to the grand hall. A sensation, akin to dread, mixed with a rush of adrenalin and surged through his veins.

"Jacopo! I bought some veal cutlets for dinner." Deirdre's cheery voice sounded from outside the room.

He took a couple of deep breaths, trying to abate the swarm of emotions clamoring inside him. His life with Deirdre had been solid but had fallen into a predictable, if not boring, routine. The spark of attraction that had made them dizzily craving each other had long fizzled out. An image of his twin daughters flashed through his mind. The last thing he wanted to do was to hurt them. He clenched his teeth, finding himself caught between duty and desire.

Jacopo paced again. There'd be no turning back once he severed their marriage. The notion of being free from Deirdre sent a shiver of delight down his spine. "Lidia," he whispered. The sound of her name caused a pulsating ache that bolstered the undeniable fact—he had to have her. *I'm committed. Lidia has to—no—she will wipe away her false pride and accept the fact that we belong together.*

He left the reception room and headed to the kitchen, knowing Deirdre would be there. It was her favorite room in the entire house, and this irritated him. Though it was impressive with its shining white cabinets, granite and marble countertops, and stainless-steel appliances, it was still a workspace—a place for servants—not his wife. He stood with arms crossed in the doorway. She hadn't changed out of her work clothes but had draped her suit coat over the back of a barstool. He watched Deirdre chop peppers, summer squash, and onions into neat slices. She dumped the vegetables into the sizzling cast-iron skillet and added a drizzle of olive oil over them.

"Deirdre." He said her name louder than he'd meant. She jerked around and knocked a metal spatula to the floor. "I didn't mean to startle you."

"You nearly scared the life out of me." She sighed with a shake of her head.

"We need to talk." His eyes flittered around the kitchen. "Are we alone?"

"I gave Santina the night off."

"Santina?" He squinted trying to place the name.

"Our housekeeper."

"Oh, her. That busybody," he said under his breath. He cleared his throat. "Good."

She stooped, retrieved the spatula, and placed it in the sink. "Whatever it is can wait until after dinner."

"Dinner can wait," Jacopo said.

"No, it can't. The girls have been looking forward to this celebration. I even picked up their favorite strawberry cake from the bakery."

"There'll be no celebration tonight."

"What are you talking about?" Deirdre's eyebrows shot up.

"I sent them to their cousins for the night."

She rested her hands on her hips. "They've had their hearts set on this dinner. Why did you send them to your sister's house?"

"Because we need some time together. Just the two of us."

"It would've been nice if you had run the change of plans by me first." She pressed her lips into a taut line.

"Whatever." He paused a second. "Look, I'll pour us some wine. We can sit on a balcony. There's a cool breeze, and the sun will be setting soon."

"We used to do that all the time when... well, seems like a long time ago." She shook her head. "I better fix dinner, and then I'm going to bed. I'm exhausted. If you have something on your mind, I can cook and listen at the same time."

"I'm not sure how to tell you." He stuck his hands into his pockets.

"I ran into Sibéal today. We had a good heart-to-heart. That's why—"

"I've had it up to here," he said touching his forehead, "with talk about Sibéal or Beth or whatever the hell her name is now. Can't you just shut-up for a damn minute and listen to what I have to say?"

She looked up from the pan and glared at him. "If all this fuss is about your feelings for Lidia Feloni, save your breath."

He frowned.

"Lidia stopped by the school. She wanted to prepare me for a shocking bit of news," Deirdre said.

"She did what?"

"Turned out not to be very shocking after all." She moved to the counter and reached for a package wrapped in butcher's paper.

"What did Lidia say?" Jacopo took a few steps deeper into the kitchen.

"That you want a divorce so you can marry her." She broke the string that secured the wrapping and freed the blood-soaked paper.

"Lidia never should've told you that," he snapped.

Deirdre wiped her hands on a dishtowel then dropped it on top of the counter. "After all this time, only God knows why I still love you. Because of that, I've overlooked a lot. But, I've had enough. I'm tired of your lies— and your infidelities. It hurts that you think so little of our marriage vows." She rubbed her hand against her chest as if trying to comfort her heart. "I'm going to spend the summer in Ireland. Try to sort out my feelings and decide what I want. The girls will be coming with me."

"Alright then." Jacopo nodded. "You go to Ireland. But the girls stay here." He paused a second as a smile tugged at the corners of his mouth. "With me and Lidia."

"Your imaginary lover."

"Lidia and I *are* lovers."

"Not according to her. Anyway, she won't be in Venice much longer." She grabbed an apron from a drawer and tied it around her thick waist. "You wouldn't have a clue as to how to take care of the girls." She waved her hand as if dismissing him, pulled a fresh spatula out of a drawer, and stirred the vegetables.

"You can run home to your parents, but the girls are staying here. That's final."

"And have your sister babysit them all summer? No." She twisted the knob on the stove. The tiny jets of bluish flames disappeared.

He grabbed her arm and yanked her around so close that his face almost touched hers.

"Let go. You're hurting me," Deirdre said.

He tightened his hold, squeezing his fingers into her fatty arms. "Lidia may be leaving Venice. But one day she'll come back to me."

"Don't be a fool, Jacopo. She's going to Rome to get away from you."

He released her but not before shoving her forward. Deirdre lost her footing and clutched the edge of the waterfall island for support. He stomped toward the door but then he spun around. She was rubbing her arm. Tomorrow, bruises would be a reminder of his rough treatment, but he didn't care.

"I'd never dream of purposely keeping the girls away from you," Deirdre said. "But they need to spend time with their grandparents. How about if we compromise? I'll bring them home at the beginning of August."

He liked the pleading tone lacing her voice.

She opened the refrigerator, pulled out a liter bottle of mineral water, and lifted it in his direction.

Now she's trying to placate me, as usual, to get her way. Ha, he thought with a nod, *not this time*.

"That temper of yours is out of control." Deirdre poured the bubbly liquid into a glass. "Your ranting and ravings frighten the girls." She handed the water to him.

"But do I frighten you?" He emptied the cut crystal tumbler in one long gulp.

"Don't be silly."

He hurled the glass across the kitchen. It smashed against a cabinet.

Deirdre pushed past him.

"Where are you going?" Jacopo demanded.

"Out. Until you calm down."

"This isn't an affair like the others." He softened his voice.

She stopped and faced him.

"They were only pleasant distractions that meant nothing. I still loved you. God only knows why with your constant nagging and fading looks.

How do you think I feel having to face people with a wife that looks like a cow? All I ever wanted from you was a son. We had the girls the first year we were married. Fine. Then you never conceived again?" He shook his head. "I've given you everything," he said waving his arm to encompass the kitchen. "But are you grateful?" He stepped closer to her. "I don't think so because ... because you've tried not to get pregnant on purpose."

"That's a lie."

"You always disappoint me," he said.

Tears welled in her eyes.

He touched her belly. "Is there a baby in there now? A boy? Hell, no."

She stepped backward, recoiling from his touch." You know what the doctors said." Her voice cracked. "Marginal fertility. We were lucky. Blessed to have had the twins." She glared at him. "If only you knew how many times I've pleaded with God to give me another child. A boy. To make you happy."

"If that's true, why do you keep refusing me in bed?"

Her face fell.

Jacopo felt no remorse knowing he had attacked where it hurt the most. Her inability to bear his children. "No wonder I look elsewhere."

"I've heard enough." She headed toward the door.

"Deirdre. Did I give you permission to leave?"

She ignored him and continued to walk away.

How dare she disrespect me? A blaze of searing, white heat shot through him like a bolt of lightning. "You're not going anywhere." Jacopo caught up to her. He snatched a handful of her hair, pulling it loose from her neat chignon. With a viselike grip, he yanked her head back, causing the fleshy folds of her neck to stretch taut. "I assure you; the new Signora da Parma will be a more worthy spouse than you ever were."

"You're delusional," she managed to say before he pulled her head back further.

She twisted, trying to break away from his grasp. With his free hand, he gripped her shoulder to stop her thrashing. She stopped struggling. He loosened his hold and released her.

She stumbled across the floor.

"So, this is what Lidia has to look forward to," she said.

"Unlike you, Lidia will obey me." He looked at his hand and noticed strands of hair tangled around his fingers. "Finish making dinner."

She swayed and grasped her head.

"Cut the theatrics. I'm hungry."

"I'm dizzy," she whispered.

"Dizzy?" A full smile crossed his face. "If you really want to know how it feels to be dizzy..." He took her in his arms and spun her around as if they were dancing an accelerated tango twirl.

"Stop," she said breathlessly.

He released her. She teetered then fell sideways, smashing her temple against the sharp corner of the island. A cracking sound filled Jacopo's ears as Deirdre collapsed onto the wide beamed floor.

An unfamiliar rush of panic rose from his gut and choked the breath from him. He gasped several times, inhaling deeply. Finally, he found his voice. "Deirdre, get up." He waited a second, but she didn't move. He crouched next to her and grasped her hand. "*Per favore, cara mia,*" he cooed. But still, she didn't move. "This is no time to play." His words stopped when he noticed a trickle of blood inching out on the floor from beneath her head.

A guttural sound erupted from her lips. The unexpected noise jolted him. She fluttered her eyes open for a split-second.

"Are you okay?" He stroked her hand a couple of times, waiting for an answer.

Instead of speaking, her body contorted and twitched as if she'd been shot with a charge of electricity. He released her hand and backed away. Mesmerized by the jerking movements, he stood transfixed, not knowing if seconds or minutes had passed. Then as suddenly as the fit started, it ended.

Deirdre opened her eyes. "My head," she whispered.

"I'm such an idiot. I don't know why I torment you. Please, *cara*, please forgive me. I swear; I'll be the perfect husband from now on. Just say you forgive me."

She pulled herself into a sitting position. He winced seeing the gash splayed across her temple. A line of blood flowed down her cheek and onto her blouse. Without a word, he untied her apron, folded it, and pressed the cloth against the wound.

"You're going to have to change. That temper—"

"Yes, yes. Anything you say."

The metallic smell of blood soured his stomach. The snowy-white apron now saturated and stained crimson hadn't seemed to stop the blood flow. "You're going to be alright," he said unsure if his words were to reassure Deirdre or himself.

She raised her hand to her forehead. It was then he noticed the blood dripping from her nose. She ran the back of her hand across her nostrils. "Help me."

He took her hand, raised it to the apron, and positioned it on the wet, sticky cloth. "Press. Add pressure. To stop the bleeding. I'll call for an ambulance."

"Hurry." Her eyelids sagged closed, and then she crumpled into a heap.

He raced to the phone and lifted the receiver. His finger shook as he tapped one-one-eight, the emergency number, but before hearing a ring tone, he cut the connection. He glanced at Deirdre, and dread filled him. If she was dead, how could he explain what happened? He needed time.

He let go of the phone's receiver. It swung on its curled wire attached to the cradle on the wall. Taking quick steps, he crossed the room and stopped at the window. He caught a glimpse of a rickety boat, its occupant stabbing the water with a weathered oar. Jacopo dropped his hand, and it fell to the edge of the wide porcelain sink onto something soft. He lifted the dish-towel Deirdre had abandoned and wiped his face blotting away beads of sweat.

I can't contact the police. The carabinieri would never believe this was the result of an accident. He shook his head, noting the marks on Deirdre's arms, now flamed angry welts.

He paced to the far side of the island and stopped at the refrigerator. Flinging open the door, he pulled out a bottle of Peroni, twisted off the cap, and swallowed a mouthful of beer. He shifted from one foot to the other then took another long swig before placing the half-empty bottle in the sink. He walked toward Deirdre. Not able to look directly at her, he whispered her name.

"I didn't mean to hurt you. Open your eyes." He dropped to his knees. "Deirdre," he said louder and shook her shoulder.

His stomach constricted as he touched her neck in search of a pulse. He cursed as his fingers probed not able to locate a single pulsation. He touched her lips and felt a wisp of breath. *Unconscious? Coma?* He wasn't sure but suspected she didn't have much time left unless he took some action.

He rose and pulled out one of the white barstools. Slumping into the seat, he covered his eyes with the palm of his hand. "What the hell am I going to do?"

A myriad of wild thoughts flittered through his mind. He forced himself to think. *Marinello will understand that I didn't mean to hurt her. An accident. Deirdre tripped. Hit her head. But how to explain the damn welts on her arms.*

Jacopo opened his eyes, but instead of focusing on his injured wife, he studied his hands. Blood stained his fingertips. The diamonds adorning his wedding ring waxed a dull luster in the muted evening light.

Not even Marinello could sweep something like this under the carpet, he decided. *No matter how high the bribe I'd pay. Anyway, how much money would it take to make this go away?*

"I've got two options," he said aloud. "Make it look like a robbery gone wrong or get the hell out of here. I could go to the South. Naples. Or better yet, Sicily." He shook his head. "What the hell am I thinking? I could never leave Venice."

He jumped off the stool, hurried from the kitchen, and headed toward the main staircase. In his rush, he banged into an antique lacquered table and sent the newspaper atop it flying. The headline, *Suspect Released*, stopped him dead in his tracks. He lifted the paper, and his eyes flitted across the newsprint. Jacopo reread the final line twice. 'Lorenzo Caravello says he's learned his lesson—never try to impress a lady by admitting to a crime you didn't commit.' He gathered the loose sections of paper, folded them, and hurried to the staircase taking the steps two at a time.

"So Marinello released Lorenzo. Leaving him with no suspect," he muttered. "Maybe, just maybe..."

He entered Deirdre's bedroom, rushed past the bed, and threw open the wardrobe. Clothes hung, arranged by color and type, neat and orderly. Familiar with her obsession with tidiness, he wasn't surprised. *It's here somewhere*, he thought looking above the rack of clothing to an upper shelf. He stretched his arm but couldn't reach the ledge.

With quick strides, he hurried to a small room used for storing cleaning and household items and grabbed a step stool. A moment later, he returned to the bedroom, opened the stool, and climbed up. Now eye-level with the wide shelf, he rummaged around until he touched a plastic storage bag. "This has to be it." A note of triumph filled his hushed voice.

He leaped off the stool and dropped the bag on the bed. He chewed his lip as he freed the box from its shelter of thick, clear plastic. Deirdre had already started planning for next year's *Carnevale,* and they'd come up with a new idea. Scrape the dramatic, colorful costumes they were accustomed to wearing and switch to a more traditional fare. He'd decided to wear the ancient *Bauta*. Deirdre hadn't gotten too far along in her selection of a mask and costume depicting *Colombina*, but she had purchased a half-mask. Elegant and handcrafted, it was decorated in twenty-four-karat gold leaf and accentuated with a lacy braiding, dotted with amber and clear crystal beads. He'd cringed when he first saw it, believing the mask's headdress too modern with its plume of yellow, black, and wine-colored ostrich feathers. But Deirdre had her heart set on it and promised to wear it only at the many balls they'd be invited to and not in the *piazza* during the bulk of the festivities. Then she'd wear the traditional golden baroque mask.

Jacopo pulled off the top of the cardboard box and freed the masks from a cushiony bed of tissue. He lifted the *Bauta* and studied its clean, crisp angles. With the mask in hand, he retraced his steps to the storage room, located a pair of latex gloves, and a dusting cloth. He rubbed the cloth along every cranny of the angular mask. Uncertain if fingerprints washed away in water, he wasn't planning to take the risk.

After returning everything to its proper place, he carried the mask and a box of heavy-duty trash bags to the kitchen. Deirdre hadn't moved. He fell to his knees and pressed his ear against her chest straining to hear the familiar thumping of her beating heart. But the pulsations had ceased. Even if he had wanted to save her, it was too late now.

He refused to dwell on emotions but only saw a problem that needed to be fixed. He dropped the mask and trash liners on top of the work island and tossed the dusting cloth from one hand to the other. Deirdre's death had to look exactly like the one in the canal. That way, he wouldn't be considered a suspect.

He presumed that Marinello would blame himself, believing he'd made a mistake in releasing Lorenzo. The thought caused Jacopo to smile, but almost instantly, a flicker of guilt caused it to fade.

Lorenzo. He exhaled loudly. *It'll be up to me to save his sorry ass once again. But that will have to wait. For now, I must be perceived as the poor, mourning husband deprived of my vibrant, young wife; then everything will work out fine.*

Jacopo moved to the large window above the sink, lowered the silk shade, and flipped on the pendant lights hanging above the island. He glanced at Deirdre. The warmth of her usual creamy complexion had vanished in exchange for a sickly gray pallor. He fell to his knees and smoothed the sticky strands of bloodied hair off her forehead.

Though he didn't have faith, he knew Deirdre would appreciate the gesture as he made the sign of the cross. He tried to recall the prayer for the dead. "Eternal rest grant, Deirdre," he stumbled over the words looking at her battered face, "and let perpetual light shine upon her through the mercy of God. Amen."

He stood, turned away from her, and eyed the block of knives on the onyx countertop. He shook his head realizing that he'd never be able to use the expensive set of knives again if he used one to slice Deirdre's neck. He patted the pocketknife he always carried. *Anyway*, he decided, *it'll be better to take care of that later. Outside.*

He pulled back the shade. The overcast sky stood black without a moon or any visible stars. A blessing. He released the shade and realized that one problem remained. Deirdre's weight. Even when they'd married, she wasn't skinny but light enough for him to carry her over the threshold. For an instant, he recalled the silkiness of her wedding dress, the feel of her arms draped around his neck, and her laugh tinkling in his ears. He closed his eyes, blotting away the memory and replacing it with a strategy of how to transport her body to the canal. The biggest hurdle, he decided, would be getting Deirdre out of the house. Once outside, he imagined he'd be able to carry her the twenty-five meters to the footbridge.

"It'll be my penance for not controlling my temper," he muttered.

The hours moved painfully slow throughout the night. He watched a *calcio* match on his cellphone. But even the win by the Italian national football league couldn't lift his spirits with the knowledge of his wife's body sprawled on the kitchen floor. Around eleven, he retreated to his study and fell asleep on the smoke-colored leather couch. When he woke, not even an hour later, he felt more agitated as he dreaded the ordeal to come. He stretched, slicked his hair back in place, and rose.

Jacopo stashed the items he'd need inside a sturdy plastic bag: the carnival mask, waterproof glue, and Deirdre's wallet. He remembered to empty her leather billfold before tying the bag's handles through a loop of his jeans.

After a series of stretches aimed to loosen his shoulders and biceps, he grasped Deirdre's wrists with gloved hands and dragged her across the kitchen floor. He stopped and took several deep breaths as fingers of cold fear crept up his spine. He'd barely moved her, and already, he was winded.

"What if I can't make it to the canal?"

He chewed the inside of his cheek and looked over his shoulder at Deirdre. Her eyes stared accusations at him. He dropped next to her, grasped her hand, and kissed it. Though splattered with blood, her simple gold wedding band seemed to glisten.

"You do understand, I didn't mean for this to happen. But the way you were mocking me. I just lost it. Anyway, I know deep down," he said placing his free hand on her lifeless heart, "you'd never want me to go to prison because of an accident."

He released her hand, and it banged against the cool, stone floor. He stood, filled with determination, but as he reached for her, Jacopo realized something wasn't right.

"*Dannazione,*" he cursed. The porous tile was streaked with blood. If he didn't act quickly, not only would the floor be ruined, but it would offer a tell-tale sign of what had happened in the kitchen. That was the last thing he wanted. Though it would push his timetable back, he couldn't leave a trail of blood behind.

Ten minutes later, with a bucket consisting of a mixture of water, powdered detergent, and bleach, he knelt on the floor with a scrub brush and the dusting cloth. He scrubbed and wiped until the floor gleamed. He glanced at Deirdre and pressed his lips together. Her seeping body was making a mess while offering a plethora of biological evidence. It took a couple of seconds before he remembered the plastic bags. He grabbed the box of biodegradable bags from the counter, pulled out one of the extra-large clear bags, and waved it open.

He decided to start at her feet and work upward. Droplets of sweat trickled down his face as he struggled to slide the bag over her body and lift the heavy weight at the same time. Rigor mortis hadn't set in yet, so by the time he'd finished stuffing her into the bag, Deirdre's knees had bent, causing her legs to fall sideways, even though her torso and head remained upright. He took the bag's corners and tied them together into a tight knot. Glancing down at his handiwork, he grimaced seeing her lifeless stare. The bag hadn't diminished the reproachful look filling her eyes.

He crouched and heaved the bundle over on its side, grabbed the pail, and cleaned the fluid-splotched floor where Deirdre's body had been lying. Satisfied, he pulled the knife from his pocket, grabbed another bag, and sliced it open. He laid the sheet of heavy-duty plastic on the floor, smoothed it out, and then rolled the corpse on top of it. The body moved easier when he grabbed the sheet and pulled. Jacopo breathed out a sigh of relief.

With measured steps, he guided the parcel down the long *portego* and across the entry *loggia*. When he finally reached the door, he whipped it open and glared at the elaborate Istrian stone staircase leading to the ground floor.

Though he couldn't bear to drag her body down the long flight, imagining the sickening sound of her head hitting against the risers, he didn't have much of a choice. He lifted the edges of the sheet and laid them over the plastic shroud. It was then he remembered the soiled dusting cloth. He made his way back to the kitchen, lifted the soppy cloth, and wrung it out over the pail. After dumping the water, he folded the damp cloth and slipped it into the bag tied to his belt loop. He spied the slices of veal on the counter and grabbed them—just in case—and stuffed the cutlets into his pocket.

Hell-bent on working quickly, he reached the enshrouded corpse and grabbed Deirdre's feet. He didn't dare turn on the light that would brighten the ground floor but depended on the illumination streaming down the steps from the *portego*. He tugged, and her head thumped against the top riser.

"Christo," Jacopo called out then grit his teeth.

Knowing there was no other way, he continued to walk down the staircase backward, surprised at how easily the body slid down the ancient steps. He left the bundle resting against the stairway as he waited for his night vision to kick in.

Jacopo clenched his jaw as a new emotion emerged. Anger. At Deirdre. She's the reason he was embroiled in this predicament. All because of her bullheaded attitude toward the divorce. The last straw had been her taunting that Lidia wanted nothing to do with him. Now because of her, he had to deal with the aftermath.

He stormed to the wood and glass door, yanked it open, and stepped outside. The thick air laid a wet blanket of humidity over the silent neighborhood. An eerie sensation of desolation enveloped him as he turned away from the courtyard and stepped back inside the house.

It took only a moment to shake free from the stifling bleakness that sought to debilitate him as an image of the portraits that lined the *portego* reminded Jacopo of his noble ancestry. With renewed purpose, he headed to the storage space in search of a metal wheeled cart. *It'll be a snap to dump her into the cart and roll her to the canal.* He couldn't help but smirk, remembering the brouhaha that had tourists scrambling a couple years ago with the news that wheeled luggage was going to be banned from Venice. *It's these carts the council wanted to get rid of—they're so squeaky—noise pollution.* He paused as the thought sunk into his brain.

"The cart will be too noisy." He panicked in a wild attempt to come up with another solution. He made a split-second decision. One he didn't like. He'd have to fulfill his penance and carry her.

He returned to the stairs. A fireman's carry would be the best way to transport the body, but with it encased in plastic, he wasn't quite sure how to proceed. He struggled but finally managed to get her torso across his back. Then he wrapped his left arm around her legs that brushed against his shoulder. The position of the body felt awkward.

After a few tentative steps, he strained under the heft of the load. Motivated to rid himself of the cumbersome burden, he managed to trudge through the door, cross the courtyard, and head to the edge of the narrow canal. Certain his lungs would explode after slogging fifteen meters, he doubted he'd make it to the little footbridge that seemed kilometers away. The bag of accruements banged into his thigh with every labored step. He paused, gulped a mouthful of air, and continued plodding along the narrow walkway.

With his senses heightened and his heart pounding, he moved through elongated shadows and hoped to God that he wouldn't be spotted. His leaden steps stopped as he sensed movement. He backed closer to a building, praying to meld into the darkness when he heard a snarl.

"Christo," he gasped seeing the lean, black canine, its sharp teeth exposed behind strained lips.

He cursed the smell of death that had attracted the dog. He moved closer to the building and pressed Deirdre's body against its crumbling stucco wall. With the dog only a few steps away, Jacopo reached into his pocket. He pulled out the slab of uncooked meat and tossed it in the opposite direction as far as he could manage. He exhaled relief as the emaciated creature raced away.

The few moments of rest renewed him. He continued plodding along the canal until reaching the footbridge. Spasms clenched his back, and his shoulder ached. He wanted nothing more than to toss Deidre's over-sized body into the water. Instead, he laid her down on the bridge's sturdy balustrade.

After catching his breath, he freed the knife from his pocket. With a long sweeping motion, he cut through the layers of plastic, peeled them open, and glanced at his wife's body. A flash of remorse filled him. The neck he was about to slice had been a favorite place to nuzzle. He remembered the taste of her skin and its smoothness nestled between his teeth.

He glanced up at the dark sky, took another deep breath, and jerked the blade across the lifeless flesh, leaving a clean, deep slash. As he wiped the stiletto's edge on Deirdre's already soiled blouse, he was surprised that a torrent of blood hadn't erupted from the laceration. He fumbled with the bag at his side but was soon rewarded when he grasped the glue bottle and the *Bauta*. He squeezed a bead of glue onto the top of the mask and then one on the bottom. Just enough to keep it secure since he didn't want his wife's face to become any more disfigured by the glue. He reached behind her head and tied the black ribbons.

With his gloved hand, Jacopo swiped the sweat from his face. He took a backward step and folded his arms realizing he'd have to dispose of the plastic bags, cloth, gloves, and glue.

That won't be a problem, he assured himself, aware that he could drop off the refuse at the garbage boat at daybreak. *It'll be immediately compacted with other bags of general waste.* He allowed the smile, which ached to form, to cross his face.

Still smiling he refocused on his wife's body. He jumped back a few steps as her arm rose in a quivering motion. "Can't be," he said as ragged breath burned his throat. He blinked a few times and rubbed his eyes. When he looked again, Deirdre's arm was as it had been, tucked across her abdomen.

"God. Now I'm seeing things." Lightheaded and shaky, his hand trembled as he retrieved the knife and plunged it into her belly—the barren belly—that had refused to give him a son. His vision became unexpectedly blurred with emotion. He didn't try to stop the tears that slid across his cheeks. Jacopo kissed the ravaged neck before shoving his wife's body off the railing.

She landed so softly, it took him by surprise. It was then he remembered that the canal was amid another repair and held less than ten centimeters of water. Deirdre's body had sunk into a pit of soggy, filthy, muck. He could make out the mask and the fullness of her heavy bosom in the shadowy night air as he fingered her billfold. The girls had given Deirdre the wallet as a birthday present. He pushed all thoughts of his daughters from his mind as he tossed the wallet into the narrow ribbon of water.

Chapter Twenty

BETH BOLTED UP IN THE BED. She shivered, and her heart banged wildly as if attempting to escape its cavity. *This means only one thing*, she realized gulping a mouthful of air then slowly exhaling through her nose. Her *fey* had issued a terrible warning.

Earlier in the afternoon, she'd spent nearly an hour talking on the phone with her friend, Skye Andrews, who was working on her latest film. On the set, things had turned from bad to worse. Skye's costar had been replaced, she'd been butting heads with the director, and an actress who had the producers wrapped around her little finger was trying to usurp her role. She had pleaded with Beth to use her *fey* instincts to find out if something more terrible was going to happen. Once again, Beth explained that her sixth sense didn't work that way and did her best to calm Skye's frazzled nerves.

But now, she wondered, *did this warning concern Skye?* Beth slipped out of bed, snatched her mobile phone from the night table, and padded into the kitchen. After flipping on the light, she grabbed a kettle, filled it with water, and plunked it on top of a burner. Though Italian tea couldn't compete with a good Irish *cuppa,* she didn't mind the mellow flavor of the *Bancha Florita* green tea.

She plucked a teabag from the canister and tossed it into a mug. As the water heated, she paced back and forth, only stopping once to check her phone messages. The time glowing from her mobile, a couple minutes passed three, assured her that if she telephoned Skye, she wouldn't wake her up—now that the movie was being filmed in Baltimore—instead of LA.

The shrill whistle screaming from the kettle made her jump. She twisted off the gas jet, poured the hot water into the cup, and waited for the tea to brew. After a couple minutes of indecision about making the call, she sighed and swallowed a couple sips of tea. The comforting effect of the pale liquid cleared her mind. She grabbed her mobile from the counter and began to tap in Skye's number, but then her phone beeped twice. An incoming call. She checked the screen. *Jacopo?*

"What's wrong?" she asked.

"Is Deirdre with you?" Panic laced his voice.

"Why would she be?"

"She's been gone for hours. Tell me she's with you."

"What are you talking about?" Beth felt like she was speaking with a mouthful of cotton. She raised the teacup, swallowed, and placed the cup on the counter.

"It's all my fault. We had a stupid fight, and she walked out. I regret not running after her with an apology, but my damn pride stopped me," Jacopo said.

"Must've been some fight to make her leave the girls."

"Our daughters," he whispered. "That's what started the whole mess. You see, Deirdre had planned a celebration for the girls, and I, like a stupid ass, sent them to spend the night with their cousins. I ruined everything. Deirdre stormed out saying she needed some air. I thought a walk would help her work through her anger. That was like seven hours ago." He paused a second. "You of all people know the force of her awful Irish temper."

His statement jolted her. *Deirdre's the most even-keeled, level-headed person I know.* Though she wanted to refute him, she let the comment pass. "I can understand Deirdre wanting to cool down and take a short walk, but to be away for so long ... that doesn't sound right." She remembered the warning issued by her *fey* and chewed her lip. "Have you called the police?" She noticed Shane, his eyes squinting from the light, as he stood in the doorway, running a hand through his tousled hair.

"Of course not. It's a private matter. After all, we both hold responsible positions. Making our spat public will tarnish our credibility within the community."

Though she wanted to shout him into action, she rolled her eyes, not believing he'd be more concerned about appearances than the welfare of his wife. "Listen to me. You must alert the authorities ... Marinello. He'll know what to do."

"No."

"For pity's sake, Jacopo. Call him."

"I've spent hours walking from one side of Venice to the other. Checking out bars and hotel lobbies. What else can Marinello do?"

"He's the police, for God's sake."

"I don't know—"

"Damnation, Jacopo. Look, if you won't do it, I will."

He sighed loudly. "*Va bene*. Okay. It's against my better judgment, but what choice do I have?"

"Right, then. Keep me informed. Let me know the minute you hear something." She swiped her mobile off.

"What the hell is going on?" Shane stepped deeper into the kitchen.

"Deirdre's missing."

"Missing?"

"They had a fight, and she walked out. But that doesn't sound like her at all."

He turned on the burner and dumped the remains of Beth's cup in the sink. "What do you think really happened?"

She shrugged not willing to tell him about the strong warning her *fey* had issued. "It certainly couldn't be over the fact that Jacopo sent their daughters to their cousins for the night." She paused a moment. "At the café, when you left to get a newspaper, Deirdre told me Jacopo wants a divorce."

His eyebrows shot up. Not saying a word, he placed a fresh teabag into her cup and refilled it with hot water.

"Turns out he's been cheating on her," Beth said. "Wants to marry his assistant."

"That blonde looker?"

"Lidia Feloni. I imagine the fight was over that. Anyway, Deirdre decided to leave him. Well, for the summer at least. She's going home to Ireland. Maybe that's what she did—except Deirdre would never leave the children behind." Beth couldn't push aside the building fear, causing her heart to pound once again. She lifted the cup and took a quick sip. "My intuition is telling me something terrible has happened."

Shane fingered the dimple in his chin. "My gut's been telling me that something's off with that guy."

She narrowed her eyes, taking in his words.

"All that back-slapping and glad-handing," Shane said. "Seems like a phony to me. I'm actually not surprised he's a damn cheat."

"Why didn't you tell me you didn't trust Jacopo?"

He shrugged. "Look, you said Deirdre's gonna leave him. She could've checked into a hotel." He lifted a peach from the fruit bowl and inspected its fuzzy skin before biting into it. A dribble of juice rolled down his chin. "She's probably sound asleep in some ritzy hotel and billed it all to Jacopo." He wiped away the liquid with the back of his hand.

She paced to the far wall of the efficient kitchen. "Then why didn't she call me? Deirdre's not the type to just take off. And what about her daughters? She'd never up and leave them even for a night."

"But the daughters aren't home, are they?"

Beth nodded.

"And Deirdre wants us to have a perfect honeymoon, right?"

She nodded again.

"So why would she bother you with news of a fight with Jacopo?"

Beth pursed her lip following his logic.

"Maybe that's why she didn't telephone, but instead checked into a hotel?"

"Could be," Beth said tentatively.

"Could be? Hey, I didn't become a decorated homicide detective for nothing." He tapped his temple. "I understand human nature. The motives that drive people to do what they do."

She wrapped her arms around him and kissed his lips. She tasted peach.

"Trust me, everything will resolve itself in the light of day." With one quick movement, he scooped Beth up and carried her back to bed.

Chapter Twenty-One

AFTER A RESTLESS HOUR OF trying not to disturb Shane's slumbering, Beth slid off the mattress, inched across the room, and out onto the balcony. Drowning in anxiety, she tried several deep breaths and a half-hearted attempt to clear her mind. Both actions proved useless. A sudden urge to do something physical took hold, so she paced. Four quick steps each way. Her slippered feet moved without a sound, but the unanswered question in her mind roared.

Where is Deirdre?

She stopped and leaned against the stone balustrade, gazed across the deserted *campo*, and sighed. The darkness surrounding her offered a strange sense of confinement and only intensified her unease.

She dropped into the chair pressed into a tight corner. A breeze rustled her auburn locks, and they danced around her face. She grabbed the irritating tresses and secured them with a hair clip she fished out of her dressing gown's pocket. She glanced at the adjacent side table with the white votive candle centered on its polished surface. To dispel the engulfing darkness, she reached for the lighter, kept on the table's lower tier, and struck the steel roller. As she brought the wavering flame close to the short wick, a gust of air blew it out. After another failed try, Beth gave up as she craned her neck attempting to locate any pinpoints of light in the sky, but only observed the scuttling of gray wispy clouds against an ebony background.

Stifling a yawn, she stood and turned back into the flat through the opened French doors. Relief washed over her with the sound of Shane's even breathing, relieved that she hadn't woken him. The last thing she wanted was to disrupt his night's rest again. She groped around in the dark until she located the clothes she'd taken off hours earlier. She snatched them from the back of a chair, crept into the bathroom, and clicked on the light. The brightness caused her to squint as she slipped into the wrinkled t-shirt and skirt so fast her eyes didn't have time to adjust.

No matter how hard she tried to believe Shane, the warning she'd sensed from her *fey* trumped his logic. Her stomach churned. She grabbed her tightening abdomen and realized her emotional state wouldn't improve until Deirdre explained the reason for her impetuous and erratic behavior.

She tiptoed out of the bathroom and across the room but stopped at the doorway long enough to glimpse Shane's form covered with a satiny sheet. After grabbing a couple items, it took Beth no time to steal out of the flat and into the deserted park. To her surprise, the breeze had vanished but the familiar heaviness of moisture-laden air heightened her anxiety.

She'd known Deirdre her entire life, and this wasn't like her. A soft smile crossed Beth's face as she remembered her ten-year-old self attempting to escape the penetrating eyes of her great aunt, Ealga, who minded her after her mother's death. She'd run to Deirdre's house so often, she now understood why Mrs. McKenna treated her like one of her own. A warm glow radiated through Beth as she turned her thoughts to Carmel McKenna, mother of five—nurturing and intuitive—she'd been the one to urge Beth to follow her dream of modeling in Italy and allowed Deirdre to be her companion.

Beth turned around amazed at how drastically Venice transformed at night. Gone with the lightness of day were the overflowing lanes of bustling tourists, music, and laughter. She hesitated a moment, wondering if she should return to the flat, as she took in the eerie quality their tiny *campo* had donned. But the need to physically work off the paralyzing fear that held her prisoner topped the thought of twisting and turning in bed.

She swallowed hard, closed her eyes, and waited for her *fey* to offer something—insight, direction, counsel—but nothing happened.

Not very clever to just stand here wondering what to do, she chided herself. She glanced at the shadowy gothic structure that housed their flat, standing like a phantom in the darkness. With a sigh, she crossed the square and headed in the direction of the Rialto Bridge, hoping that her usual route to the marketplace would lessen the sense of dread for Deirdre's safety.

The click, click, click of her heels striking against the paving stones filled her ears as she walked along the endless mazes of backstreets and deserted squares. Wishing she hadn't slipped into a pair of heeled mules, she dropped onto a bench. The *vaporetto* stop beyond her stood abandoned, but in a couple of hours would be humming with activity. She closed her eyes and listened to the rushing water flowing along the Grand Canal.

Words popped into her mind. Keep walking.

KeepwalkingKeepwalkingKeepwalking.

It was then she understood what this outing in the dark hours of morning was all about. She was on a mission to locate her missing friend.

Chapter Twenty-Two

DISTANT POUNDING WOKE MARINELLO from a sound sleep. He turned over and squinted at the clock's face glowing on the night table. Six forty-five.

"*Accidenti*," he muttered as his plans for sleeping in on his day off vanished. He ripped away the cotton sheet covering him, jumped out of bed, slipped into a robe, and tied its belt tight around his waist. The silk material flapped against his knees as he hurried down the steps. He'd been a Chief Superintendent long enough to presume an unexpected visitor at the break of dawn could only mean bad news. He steeled himself and flung the door open.

Jacopo faced him.

The panicked look on his face told Marinello something was wrong. He ushered the distraught man inside. Jacopo stood in the small foyer with his hands jammed into his pockets. His hair stood on end, and his eyes blazed as if lit by an inner fire. Marinello didn't smell any traces of alcohol, but Jacopo did reek of something more penetrating—fear.

"I need your help." Jacopo's normal, booming voice had been reduced to a croaking whisper. Marinello leaned closer to him. "I didn't know where else to turn and figured you'd know what to do."

It took Marinello only a split second to determine that whatever was bothering Jacopo had rendered him a shadow of himself. He pressed his lips together prepared to allow Jacopo as much time as he needed to explain.

"Something terrible has happened to Deirdre."

Marinello nodded urging him to elaborate.

"It's like she's vanished into thin air. I've searched everywhere. Walked up and down every lane and back alley in the Dorsoduro."

Marinello extended his hand toward a short flight of stairs. Jacopo's sigh filled the silence as he trudged up the staircase and into the small den. Marinello flicked on a light. "Sit down."

Jacopo sunk into a cushy wing chair.

"Now start at the beginning," Marinello said.

"We had a fight, and Deirdre took off. Around eight. Last night." Jacopo ran his fingers through his hair smoothing it into place. "It was all my fault. I'm scared, Daniele. I can't shake away this feeling of dread that something terrible has happened to her." His bloodshot eyes watered.

Marinello moved to an assortment of decanters arranged on a walnut credenza. He grabbed one, twisted off its crystal stopper, and poured an ounce into the tumbler. He handed the brandy to his troubled visitor.

Jacopo downed the drink in one gulp, stood, then walked to the decanter and refilled the glass.

Marinello pursed his lips. Something didn't add up. Jacopo wasn't the type to lose his head over a quarrel with his wife. Certainly, there'd been many of those. He was aware of Jacopo's reputation as a ladies' man, though he didn't place much stock in gossip. When he'd hear snide remarks, he'd always given Jacopo the benefit of the doubt. Even so, Jacopo's animated and outgoing personality lent itself to interacting with women. He remembered numerous occasions when he'd seen Jacopo at an intimate table in a café or a bar with a pretty girl seated across from him. Every time it made him think of Deirdre, a schoolteacher, mother of young twin girls, devoted wife, with a shake of his head.

"Maybe Deirdre's fed up with your flirtations," Marinello said.

"Huh?" Jacopo pulled the glass away from his lips. "What are you implying? That I've been unfaithful to my wife?"

Marinello shrugged.

"Maybe I haven't been the most steadfast husband." Jacopo wiped the back of his hand across his eyes as if to wipe tears away. Tears Marinello hadn't seen.

"If you've committed adultery—"

"Such an ugly word," Jacopo said with a shake of his head. "Dalliances is more like it. And Deirdre knew about all of them. She forgave me for my, um ... indiscretions." He swallowed the remainder of his drink. "Anyway, the argument was over a simple misunderstanding. She was angry that I'd sent the girls for a sleepover at their cousins."

"Hmmm." Marinello stared at the Berber carpet as if inspecting the woven design. Years of experience told him Jacopo was lying. "Interesting story but... I'm not buying it."

"I swear it's the gospel truth."

"Let's keep the good book out of this." Marinello paused long enough to look directly into Jacopo's dark eyes. "A saint would find it difficult to forgive one, um, *dalliance,* let alone ... how many did you say there were?"

"Alright. She found out about my latest lover. Got her dander up. But, she had never up and left without a word before."

"Maybe she had enough. Could've contacted a lawyer. Seems like she'd have a sound case in a court of law."

"She wouldn't do that." Jacopo looked at the empty glass in his hand. "So, I've made mistakes. Deirdre isn't perfect either." He slammed the tumbler down on top of an end table. "You think I've driven her away?"

Marinello winced, sensing the familiar pressure of an oncoming headache. He rubbed his forehead. "Relax, Jacopo. Most missing person cases turn out to be nothing. After a night or two at a friend's house or in a hotel, they usually find their way home." He noticed a flicker of hope cross Jacopo's face, but it disappeared just as quickly.

"I've already contacted her closest friend. Sibéal. And she hasn't heard a word from Deirdre."

"Sibéal?" Marinello's eyes widened. "You mean Beth Getty? The woman who discovered the body in the canal?" *Oh God, please no. Not that nosy model.*

Jacopo nodded.

Marinello sank onto the edge of the leather couch and tented his fingers in front of his chest. A moment later, he cleared his throat. "When did you start searching for her?"

"When I woke up this morning, around three o'clock, I couldn't believe that she hadn't returned. So, I waited and waited. When she hadn't shown up by five, I set out scouring the neighborhood."

"Let me get this straight. Deidre left home around eight pm and then you realized she was still missing seven hours later. So, she's been unaccounted for nearly eleven hours." Marinello flicked his thumb across his stubbly chin. "Maybe she wanted to teach you a lesson by staying out all night. I wouldn't be surprised if Deirdre is home now safe and sound."

Jacopo fished a cellphone from his pocket. He held it up. "This is Deirdre's. She left it behind. I'm going to telephone my home line." He swiped the screen and tapped. "The phone is on speaker." Ten rings sounded. Then Jacopo cut the connection. "Deirdre always answers the phone. On the first ring. She's not there."

Marinello pursed his lips. "Did you notice if she'd packed a bag or if any personal items are missing? Money?"

Jacopo shook his head. "Her billfold wasn't on the dresser, but she usually keeps that in the pocket of whatever she's wearing. She doesn't carry a purse. Pickpockets." He shrugged.

Marinello's temple started to throb. "So, there'd be money and credit cards in the wallet?"

Jacopo's eyebrows jumped. "Credit cards? Oh, no. I handle all the finances—the household expenditures, the girls' tuition, taxes. She only carries her identification and a few euros for incidentals."

"Does she have access to any bank accounts?"

A mystified look crossed Jacopo's face. "Why would she? Like I said, I take care of everything. That pittance she makes teaching wouldn't even pay the housekeeper's salary for a month."

Though he believed Jacopo was exaggerating, the fact was clear; if Deirdre had taken off, she didn't have enough money to get very far away from Venice. "What exactly do you want me to do?"

"I want your men to conduct a search for my missing wife."

Marinello sucked in a mouthful of air as a stabbing pain shot behind his eyes. "Be realistic. Deirdre needs some time to cool down. Leave it at that." Though his words sounded confident to his ears, Marinello was beginning to wonder if something had happened to the affable wife of Jacopo da Parma.

"She's had plenty of time to compose herself. I demand action. Now." Jacopo thrust out his chin as he crossed his arms.

Marinello sighed. "There are procedures that must be followed. I'll have to add the information into the database of the Central Directorate for the Criminal Police. Then the proper agency will begin the investigation. They will determine if the media will be alerted."

"*Va bene*. Do it then," Jacopo said.

"I'll start the ball rolling. The best thing for you to do is to go home. It's obvious, you're exhausted." Marinello rose, stepped next to the defeated man, and placed a reassuring hand on Jacopo's shoulder. "I'll walk with you since it's on the way to the *Questura*."

After a couple of seconds, Jacopo tightened his lips and then nodded in agreement.

After slipping into a t-shirt and pair of jeans, Marinello hurried down the steps and into the den. Jacopo sat in the chair asleep, his chin resting against his chest. For a moment, Marinello wondered if he should leave him alone. Thinking better of it, he shook Jacopo's shoulder, believing it'd be more beneficial for Jacopo to slumber in his own bed, especially if Deirdre was there.

After stepping outside, the two men walked in silence through the narrow streets and eventually wound themselves through the neighborhood of Dorsoduro. The sun, gaining strength and brightness, had broken through the early morning haze as they neared Jacopo's noble house, the Palazzo da Parma.

Marinello had been invited several times to Jacopo's impressive home. Its relatively simple façade composed of arched doors and matching windows that led to heavy marble balconies marked the edifice as one of the earliest mansions of its kind. But with its Tiepolo mural, period furniture, and Murano chandeliers, the house boasted not only of the elegance of a bygone era but wealth. Enormous wealth. He grimaced, recalling how after several drinks Jacopo eventually started complaining how the palazzo was going to be ripped out of the da Parma lineage when he died and his sister's son would take ownership. He hadn't been shy about blaming Deirdre for the suspected loss. *Maybe now that she's missing, he'll realize that Deirdre is worth more than his many possessions. Anyway, what does it all matter? Once he's dead, he won't be in a position to care about a house—ancestral or not.*

As the two men climbed the handful of steps leading to a footbridge, Marinello refocused his thoughts on the missing woman. Adjectives describing Deirdre jumped into his mind: friendly, kind, opened-hearted. He hoped to God she hadn't suffered any harm.

"There's been problems with this canal as long as I can remember," Jacopo said breaking the silence between them. "The city is draining it again for repairs." He stopped walking, pulled a cigarette from a pack, and stuck it into his mouth. He offered Marinello one, who reached for it, but then shook his head.

"There are always repairs in a city as old as ours. Can't be helped."

Jacopo exhaled a stream of smoke. "Thank God for tourists to help cover the cost."

Marinello detected a touch of sarcasm. "Without them, how would you keep up the old family homestead?" He shot him a quick smile.

Jacopo glared at him but didn't respond. Instead, he moved next to the bridge's sturdy stone balustrade. He stood there a few seconds then backed away. "Daniele." He dropped the cigarette. "That can't be. Another body?" He pointed at the channel.

Marinello glanced over the top rail and into the murky stream of water that barely covered the canal bed. "*Santo Dio.*" He sucked in a mouthful of air, feeling weak in the knees. With his eyes riveted on the muddied body, he pulled out his cellphone.

"I can't believe it." Jacopo's voice rose in pitch as he leaned over the railing looking into the mucky channel. "The body's mostly covered in mud but, I think it's a woman. What the hell is going on?"

Marinello didn't answer as he turned his back to Jacopo. He wanted to curse—yell obscenities into the still air—but instead, in a rapid-fire fashion, he relayed orders to the officer on duty. The white mask mottled with specks of mud seemed to mock him as he spoke. He disconnected and remembered Jacopo. "Go home," he ordered.

Though Jacopo nodded, he didn't budge an inch.

Chapter Twenty-Three

BETH STOOD, TURNED AWAY FROM the canal, and looked to the right and then the left. Not certain where she was supposed to walk, she took a few tentative steps in the direction of the Rialto. *Certainly, this is pure folly,* her rational mind screamed. "No." She shook her head. "I believe in my *fey,*" she whispered, "my God-given gift." Her gait quickened as a surge of determination wiped away all doubt. She raced along the gray pavers, almost running, as the mantra *keep walking* rang in her ears.

Her heart stopped pounding as she caught sight of the *Ponte di Rialto.* In the early light of dawn, the structure stood as a beacon, orienting Beth and drawing her near to what many in Venice considered the heart of the city. The bridge, one of four spanning the Grand Canal, stood in the faint light like a sentinel guarding Venice's main waterway with its wide stone arches and stately central portico. She wanted to climb the pedestrian ramp and enjoy the solitude, one that all too soon, would be replaced with milling crowds, mobbing its roofed inclined walkway and contained shops, but a burning need to keep moving stopped her.

As the sky's pale translucent blue glowed in the soft light of sunrise, she spied silver ripples sparkling on the water's surface. She inhaled as the magic of Venice washed through her, imparting a sensation of being enmeshed between the present and the past. The brief interlude shattered with the rising and clamoring voices streaming from the fish-market stalls. She turned away as bold-colored awnings unfurled over collections of tables and chairs on the canal's shore. *Waiters will be serving cappuccinos and flakey pastries within an hour*, she thought as her stomach rumbled.

Remembering her mission, she raced down winding alleyways and crossed picturesque footbridges, driven by an inner guide. Still unaware of

134

where she was heading, an elegantly-carved fount, planted in the center of a small square, beckoned her. She slowed her gait. Puffs of air escaped her parted lips as her heart rate lessened. Beth snapped her head from side to side and realized she was completely lost. She bent over the fountain and captured a mouthful of the enticing water, swished it, and spit it out onto the ground. She cupped her hands and splashed the cool, fresh water on her face. Then she took several deep swallows. Revived, she once again moved in the direction her sixth sense was leading.

It dawned on her that Shane would be worried if he woke up to find her not beside him in bed. She stopped walking, leaned against a crumbling façade, and patted the sheer fabric of her crinkly peasant skirt. She remembered tossing the flat's key into her pocket along with, God knows why, a pair of sunglasses.

"Damnation," she muttered. "How could I have forgotten my mobile?"

The phone's pedestrian mode had been a lifesaver as Beth navigated the city's twisty byways and narrow alleys. Yesterday, it had led her back to San Marco's Square and *Casa Codognato*, the famed jewelry store, where she'd purchased an exquisite silver-gilt frame with panels of agate and a band of carnelian for Deirdre and Jacopo. But after finding out the truth about Jacopo's brutish nature, she'd decided to frame a photo of the twins and give it to Deirdre for her birthday at the end of the month.

Disappointed about the mobile, but not defeated, she dashed along the narrow street amid a bewildering maze of bridges and waterways. She paused near an unassuming church composed of brick walls and a terracotta roof. It was obvious by the bands of slightly different colored bricks, which reminded her of the earth's strata, that the church had undergone many reconstructions. She slowed her gait and stopped at the church's small Renaissance porch facing a canal.

"Why do I know this church?" she whispered craning her neck to take in the enormous bell tower.

She turned away from the age-old building, headed toward the canal, and investigated its channel. Instead of water, wooden planks filled its bed. Following the path of the canal, she found a smaller waterway that branched off the main artery. She took a few steps along the narrower canal

135

and discovered that it too had been drained. Only about a half of a foot of muddy water filled the conduit.

She jerked her head up detecting a strange vibe in the air. As she glanced around, Beth breathed a bit easier, convinced that her *fey* had directed her steps to that very spot. Then she saw it—some kind of commotion straight ahead on a footbridge. Curious, but also cautious, she stepped closer and squinted to make sense of the scene. The red stripe along the length of a few of the men's trousers revealed their identity— *carabinieri,* military police officers. Her tired eyes struggled to make out what they were doing, but she was still too far away. She decided to inch closer.

As she approached the group, loud voices full of emotion, upset the early morning calm. She caught a glimpse of Marinello and her heart sank. A footbridge, police officers, and Marinello.

"Oh no," she whispered. "Please God, not another murder." Beth hesitated. She glanced back at the church, wondering if she should enter inside and offer up some prayers, but then she shook her head. *My fey led me here for a reason.*

She ran a hand over her rumpled shirt and smoothed back a lock of hair that had fallen onto her forehead. It didn't take a warning from her *fey* to know that Marinello wasn't going to be pleased seeing her.

Discretion caused Beth to stop a few feet away. She couldn't help but hear Marinello spit instructions as he motioned an agitated hand toward the shallow water below. She followed his movement and spied a body. The mud-spattered Bauta mask caused the breath to die in her throat. She backed away.

Now eager to know her location, Beth's eyes flitted in search of a yellow direction sign. The nearby corner building didn't have one. She headed back toward the church, hoping to find the rectory and the use of a phone. *Shane will be furious I left without my mobile,* she thought, rubbing away the ache in her recuperating shoulder. After a few rapid steps, she started to jog but cursed under her breath when she nearly twisted her ankle. She kicked off the mules, grabbed them, and continued running barefooted. She crossed the deserted *campo* and reached the church. Not waiting for the thudding of her heart to lessen, she halted in front of the

136

startling white entrance façade and pulled on the glass door, but it wouldn't budge.

She turned around in a slow-moving circle searching for someone who'd know the name of the church. She stopped mid-step after catching sight of two men. Laborers, she detected by their attire: overalls, boots, and hard hats. Beth ran toward them but stopped with a wince after stubbing her toe on an uneven paver. She dropped her shoes and stepped into them.

Beth felt the stares of the two men. *Is that amusement coloring their weathered faces?* She took a deep breath, tried to smile. "*Mi scusi, prego, il nome della Chiesa?*"

The taller of the two men offered her a wide, friendly smile. His teeth scattered among prominent gaps were stained a golden brown. He reached for her hand. Fearlessly, she grasped his gnarly fingers.

"*La Chiesa?*" He squeezed her hand.

The other man, younger and sporting a wisp of a mustache, spoke. In English. "The church is called St. Nicholas of the Beggars. Very old. Built over a pagan temple."

The man holding her hand pressed it tighter. She took a deep breath, knowing this might be her only chance to contact Shane. "*Cellulare?* Do you have a mobile I could use?" She looked from one man to the other.

The younger workman pulled one free from a back pocket and handed it to her. She turned her attention to the man grasping her hand, but before saying anything, he released it.

She tapped in Shane's number.

"Dalton," he whispered instinctively from his years as a detective.

"Did I wake you?"

"Beth?" He paused a second. "Where are you?"

"I had a devil of a time falling asleep. So, I decided to take a wee bit of a walk—"

"You're lost."

"That's beside the point but..." She inhaled deeply. "My *fey* led me to the scene of another canal murder. I caught a glimpse of the body and the mask. Marinello and a couple of officers are stationed on a footbridge."

"Another murder? What's your location?"

"I'm at a church. St. Nicholas of the Beggars."

"Look, I'll take a taxi to the church. You make sure to stay put."

Beth tapped off the phone and handed it back with a word of thanks. As the workmen ambled toward the footbridge, she dropped onto the red park bench that faced the church's portico. She tried to remember the purpose of the enclosed porch with its iron grille and sloping roof. After a few unsatisfying seconds of straining her brain, she gave up and decided to focus on the situation happening at the footbridge. But once again, she was too far away to see anything. She tapped her foot, impatient for Shane to arrive. A wave of exhaustion swept over her. She yawned. Her eyelids drooped with heaviness. Fearing she'd fall asleep on the wooden bench she stood, glanced at the church, and then in the direction of the bridge.

"Why not?"

With small, confident steps, she headed toward the narrow canal and the footbridge. Still yards away, she realized that a new facet of escalation had erupted with the arrival of the workmen. Marinello and the two laborers shouted at each other. The staccato cadences of their disputing words flew at lightning speed and left her grasping to understand. Marinello barked about the canal being a crime scene and the laborers about lost wages. Half believing they'd come to blows, Beth strained to hear Marinello's words when his voice suddenly dropped to a near whisper. She watched Marinello shake their hands, press his mobile to his ear, then offer a half-wave as the workmen walked off the footbridge and sauntered away from the crime scene.

Not able to contain her curiosity any longer, she moved even closer. Marinello, absorbed with his phone conversation, didn't seem to notice her, but she recognized a familiar figure on the bridge. Though she couldn't see his face as he talked with a uniformed officer, Beth had no doubt about his identity. Jacopo.

She frowned, wondering if Jacopo had discovered the murder victim while searching for Deirdre. *Or ...* The breath caught in the base of her throat. *No. This is not about Deirdre.* She closed her eyes and willed her *fey* to enlighten her. Nothing. At least that's what she wanted to believe. She flatly refused the notion that she'd been drawn to this place because it held the horrific murder site of her best friend.

Any caution that Beth had been clinging to, she shrugged off and raced to the footbridge. She called Jacopo's name. A flash of confusion crossed his face, but then his eyes lighted in recognition, and he opened his arms. A second of indecision filled her. She was angry with him. How could she even consider embracing him? But then his arms encircled and squeezed her. She took a sharp intake of air, immobile in his iron-like hold, and a wee bit shocked by his display of affection.

"There's been another canal murder," he whispered in her ear. "This time it's a woman." He released her and rubbed his eyes with the heels of his hands. "I'm really scared. The body ... I don't want to believe that it could be ... God, I can even say it—"

"No. NoNoNo. That body in the canal cannot be Deirdre."

"I don't want to believe it. God knows I don't, but look for yourself." He steered her closer to the railing.

Her heart pounded. Even though the body was mostly obscured in mud and fetid water, there rang something familiar about it. Was it the body's shape or the cut of the clothing? She took a few backward steps and bumped into Marinello.

"Why am I not surprised to see you?" Marinello's voice rang in her ears.

She turned and faced the *Commissario Capo*. She couldn't discern if annoyance or melancholy touched his face. "Do you know who...?" She moved her arm in the direction of the canal.

"Not yet. Forensics has been called." Marinello glanced at the phone in his hand. "This is an official crime scene. Both of you are going to have to move along." He flicked his hand back and forth as if shooing away an irritating fly.

Before she could protest, three men stepped onto the footbridge shod in knee-high rubber boots. Marinello turned his attention to the men, who Beth guessed were the anticipated forensic specialists. Marinello addressed the newcomers in hushed tones.

Jacopo grabbed her arm leading her to the opposite end of the bridge, down the steps, and along the walkway. He stopped. Though they stood several yards away, because of the bend of the canal, they were able to see the activity at the bridge.

"You look tired," Jacopo said.

"I've been up most of the night. I guess you have been too."

"Who would've thought that a little disagreement would turn into a living nightmare? Believe me. I've tried, but I can't shake the thought that Deirdre is ... is ... the Canal Murderer's latest victim."

"Don't give up hope." She wanted to believe her own advice but feared the words rang hollow.

"I've got a sick feeling in the pit of my stomach. I knew it the minute I looked into the canal. I recognized the skirt. Deirdre was wearing one like that when she stormed out last night. My God, does this makes me responsible for her... for her murder?"

"You need to stop assuming that it's ... the authorities don't know who the victim is ... Anyway, Shane is on his way. He's an amazing detective. If anyone can figure out where Deirdre is, my Shane can." She looked into Jacopo's drawn face. "I'm meeting him at the church." She waved her hand in the general direction of the ancient structure.

"I've been begging for the saint to intercede. You remember, Deirdre and I were married there." Jacopo blinked his eyes but not fast enough to stop a tear from escaping.

She grabbed his arm and patted it. She now understood why the church looked so familiar. "When Deirdre's home safe and sound, we should have a Mass of Thanksgiving. Certainly, your cousin, the pastor, will agree to be the celebrant."

He shook his head, though a trace of a smile crossed his face. "Uncle. Old Uncle Guido. The blessed Monsignor da Parma has since gone to his heavenly reward. It's been three years now. I can't help but fear Deirdre has joined him."

"Don't think that way. After all, Deirdre isn't the only sturdy, conservatively-dressed woman in Venice."

"That's true."

"Whoever the poor woman is, she didn't deserve to end up dead in a wretched canal." She released his arm and focused on the forensic team who'd lowered themselves off the bridge. Their boots emitted a sucking sound as they moved along the muddy surface. She focused on the officer hunched over the body. He tugged the mask.

"*Incollato*," the forensic tech called to Marinello who was leaning over the bridge's stone railing.

"Glued on just like the other murder." Beth took a few steps closer to the bridge.

"*Un portafoglio.*" The officer waved the compact wallet like a flag.

An intensifying mixture of tension and fear escalated inside of Beth. Disregarding Marinello's orders, she flew back to the bridge and ran up the steps. She heard Marinello's instructions. "Look for identification."

Her heart pounded in her ears. The unexpected pressure of a hand on her shoulder made her jump. Jacopo had joined her.

She focused on the officer's gunk-splattered gloves as he flipped the wallet open. It took a few seconds for him to check the various pockets. He shook his head then placed it into an evidence bag. Marinello hurried off the bridge and moved to the edge of the canal. He reached toward the forensic specialist, took the bag, and stared at the muddy wallet.

"Come on," Jacopo said, ushering Beth in Marinello's direction. They stopped a couple of steps away from the Chief Superintendent.

Marinello faced them. "Why are you still here?"

"I pray to God I'm wrong," Jacopo said, "but, she's wearing a wedding band." He motioned toward the body. If the ring belongs to Deirdre, there'll be an inscription. JdP to DBM. My Eternal Love."

"Check the ring for an inscription," Marinello called to the men in the canal.

Beth tapped her foot for the longest minute of her life as she watched the investigator remove the ring, look at the inside of the band, and nod. He slipped the ring into a plastic bag and handed it to Marinello.

He inspected the ring, stepped closer, and grasped both of Jacopo's shoulders. "I'm sorry."

For a second, Beth couldn't breathe. Then, from a place deep within, a tortured, gasping sound escaped her lips. An arm surrounded her waist. She turned and buried her head against Shane's shoulder.

Chapter Twenty-Four

BARELY AWARE THAT SHANE hovered over her as they sat in a taxi that skimmed along the Grand Canal, Beth's tears had stopped, but crushing grief covered her with an icy numbness. Shane wrapped his arm around her shoulders. For several silent minutes, she closed her eyes and rested her head against his chest.

The queasiness that rocked her stomach lessened as the fog enshrouding her mind began to dissipate. She found her voice. "Deirdre murdered? How can that be possible?" She pulled away from Shane and faced him.

"What happened to Deirdre was vicious. Makes no sense." He paused a second. "Murder never does."

She caught a flash of anger cross his face. The same fury that gripped her also had a stranglehold on Shane. She reached for his hand, and he encased it between his two strong ones.

"Nothing is going to undo the sickening fact that Deirdre is gone," he said.

She freed her hand and swiped her hair away from her face. "I bloody well understand that some hateful, repulsive monster has stolen my best friend's life. But I won't rest until I find the creature responsible for her death."

Shane rubbed his temples then cleared his throat. "You're still in shock. Exhausted. You need sleep. The five minutes we were in the apartment you were like a caged animal. This boat ride is supposed to help calm—"

"You really think I can relax with Deirdre lying dead in a filthy canal?" She sucked in a mouthful of air.

"I get it." He shook his head. "All too well."

In an instant, it became clear why Shane had resigned from the sheriff's department—innocent people being murdered sucked the life out of your soul—she'd never again attempt to steer him back to his old profession.

"You and Deirdre were close as sisters," Shane said. "You loved her. But babe, this isn't your battle to fight. It's Marinello's and the state police."

"Right. And I'm going to make sure he's doing his damnedest to find her killer."

She jumped up from the cab's upholstered bench and moved to the open window separating her from the driver. "Signore, take us to police headquarters ... *per favore portaci alla Questura.*" She swayed as the boat turned.

Shane shot up. He grasped her waist and steadied her. "I agree. We need to meet with Marinello, but not now. It's gonna take some time to come to grips with this awful tragedy. Maybe in a couple of days." He led her back to the bench.

"I know you have my best interest in mind, but darlin', I won't find a moment's rest until I speak with him. Find out what Marinello has uncovered about Deirdre's murder." She blinked a few times trying to disperse the tears gathering under her eyelids.

"Alright then." He blew out a stream of air. "But only if you eat some breakfast. I guarantee you, it's gonna be a long wait. He's trying to sort out this whole ugly business. Now that there are two bodies, Marinello could be looking at a serial killer."

She paused a moment, waiting for a sudden rush of dizziness to pass. "I don't care if we sit there all day. I need to find out something—anything—as to why Deirdre was targeted by this ... this crazed killer."

"Okay. I've been meaning to touch base with him anyway. We still haven't filled out the paperwork concerning the first murder."

"The first murder. There must be some connection. But what is it?" She tried to still her mind long enough to recall everything she knew about Jonathan Shelby.

He was in Venice searching for his abducted daughter. Maybe....

She grasped Shane's hand and squeezed it.

AFTER WHAT SHANE HAD told her, she was surprised that Marinello met them so quickly. They'd just finished writing a formal statement regarding their role in discovering Jonathan's Shelby's body when Marinello appeared and ushered them into a spacious office. He looked tired and hadn't changed out of the clothes he'd worn at the canal. They both had that in common. Marinello waited for them to be seated before he settled behind his desk.

"First," Marinello said, "I want to offer my condolences. It's been a shock for all of us. Jacopo had to be transported to *Ospedale Civile,* Venice's main hospital. He suffered some kind of breakdown."

"Breakdown?" Shane's brow furrowed.

"Flung himself into the canal. Pulled out a pocketknife and slashed his wrist."

Beth pursed her lips, a bit mystified. That didn't seem like the Jacopo she knew, but perhaps seeing his wife's lifeless body made him regret the shabby way he'd treated her. Her heart softened with the thought that maybe Jacopo realized what a jewel he'd lost and lamented his transgressions.

"Jacopo tends to be hyper-emotional." Marinello's comment drew Beth away from her musings. "He can turn on the charm just as easily as being a major pain in the..." Marinello's words trailed off as he glanced at Beth. "Anyway, I'm sure a day or two in the psych ward will help calm his nerves."

"What about the girls?" Beth moved to the edge of her chair. To her dismay, this was the first time she'd considered the fate of Deirdre's beloved daughters. "They must be confused. Terrified."

"No worries. They're safe under the care of Jacopo's sister. She's going to break the news to them."

She shook her head. "This tragedy will affect so many lives." The thought of the grieving little girls reminded her of the pain and loneliness she experienced in losing her own mother. "The girls will be devastated."

Tears stung the back of Beth's eyes. She promised herself that she'd keep her emotions in check, knowing this wasn't the time to wallow in her heart-wrenching despair. Her mission was to cajole Marinello into spilling all leads about Deirdre's murder.

"But, please," Marinello said glancing from Beth to Shane, "know that resolving this case is our top priority." He stood. "Thank you for stopping by."

Beth leaned further back in the chair. She glanced at Shane and sensed he wasn't about to budge an inch from the Chief Superintendent's office.

"Have you spoken with Nicole Shelby?" Shane asked. "The first victim's widow?"

Marinello's brow knotted.

"I've been in contact with my former LASD partner, Detective Gavin Collins," Shane said.

Marinello pressed his fingertips together forming a pyramid.

"You're aware of the details regarding an ex-wife—a noncustodial parent, who kidnapped her child." Shane didn't wait for a response. "And I'm sure it's crossed your mind that Shelby's death wasn't random. That he could've been targeted." He paused a second. "I'd bet my last dollar; Deirdre's murder wasn't arbitrary either. So, what the hell is the connection?"

Marinello stroked his stubbly jaw as his eyes narrowed.

"I've been thinking," Beth said not much louder than a whisper. "Deirdre could've been the innocent victim of a crazy lady's scheme to keep her daughter to herself. It's very possible, the abducted girl could have been one of Deidre's students. Maybe she confided in Deirdre and told her the whole story. The girl could've slipped up and told her mother she'd shared the information with her teacher... well, that could explain Deirdre's murder."

Marinello glanced down at his desk and lifted the elegant Bortoletti ballpoint pen lying next to a green folder. He rolled the shaft fashioned from Murano glass between his fingers. After what seemed a full minute, he lifted his eyes and focused on Beth. "A very interesting theory, Signora. But, as you know, this is an official police matter. I couldn't possibly allow civilians, let alone foreigners, to interfere with my investigation."

"I already know you're working with the LASD and my former partner. He told me as much," Shane said. "I'm also aware that Nicole Shelby is scheduled to arrive today in order to identify the body we found in the canal."

Beth shot him a quizzical look, wondering why Shane hadn't shared that bombshell with her.

"What you don't know is that Collins set up a meeting with Mrs. Shelby and me. Via...." Shane slipped out his cellphone and flashed it at Marinello.

Beth attempted to interject but instead forced her rising temper down to a simmer, waiting to hear what other revelations Shane was about to share.

"She was pretty much tight-lipped. But she did talk about her love for her husband and the shock she suffered from the news of his murder. Mrs. Shelby seems to think her husband's ex-wife is somehow involved. That point aside, she insisted that I'd accompany her to any meetings she may have with you. Apparently, she's somewhat uncomfortable talking to the Italian authorities. Seems to think there may be a breakdown in communications."

Beth wanted to yell, *Why didn't you tell me all this?* But she didn't want Marinello to know that Shane hadn't confided in her, so she pressed her lips into a tight line.

"We both know the name of Shelby's ex-wife," Shane said.

Marinello pursed his lips.

"Early this morning, when Beth contacted me about another canal murder, I checked my texts. Collins had sent me a photo of Lia Renner."

Beth could barely contain her mounting frustration. She took a deep breath and squeezed her folded hands so hard that her knuckles turned white.

"I would like to see the image of this mystery woman," Marinello said under his breath.

Shane placed the phone, screen-side down, on the edge of the wooden desk. "I don't mind sharing information as long as you keep us in the loop. I get it. This is your investigation. But things have changed big time. Now, it's personal."

Marinello offered Shane just the tiniest thrust of his chin.

Shane lifted his phone, tapped the screen, and handed it across the desk to Marinello. "It's an old photo, taken about twelve years ago. Mrs. Shelby told Collins she found it a couple days ago while going through her husband's belongings."

Marinello stared at the image. "There's something about her that seems familiar but...." He shrugged then handed the phone back.

Beth leaned closer to Shane. Instead of handing her his phone, he slid it back into his pocket.

Marinello flipped open the lid of a fragrant Spanish Cedar box. He reached inside and withdrew a cigar, clipped the tip, and handed it to Shane. He rose, walked around the desk, and offered Shane a light. A smile dispelled the seriousness from his dark eyes. "I do not see why we should not share our thoughts. Perhaps, we can solve this heinous crime before another unfortunate winds up dead behind a carnival mask."

Chapter Twenty-Five

OUTSIDE THE *QUESTURA*, Beth stood with her arms folded. She couldn't trust herself to say a word, fearing she'd later regret it. She stared straight ahead and wondered how such a horrific, tragic act—a crime of pure malice—could happen on so perfect a day. The cloudless sky, like a sea of lapis lazuli, reflected on the canal, making it sparkle a deep azure. She gulped a mouthful of air and released it slowly, trying to soothe her tortured heart.

"Beth," Shane said, "I know you're pissed at me—"

Her mobile phone sounded. She pulled it free from the depths of her tote bag and glanced at the screen. "Jacopo. How are you holding up? Marinello told us your grief sent you to hospital." She purposely spoke in Italian to exclude Shane.

He moved closer, but Beth turned her back to him. Though she tried to concentrate on Jacopo's hurried words, she couldn't help but hear the tapping of Shane's foot against the pavement.

"Okay, then. Talk to you soon." She tossed the phone back into her tote and refolded her arms.

"I get it, Beth. I should've told you about Collins—"

She pressed her lips into a tight line.

"You know Collins is strictly by the book. Seems like Nicole Shelby was able to crack through his professional shell."

She jerked her head in his direction.

"Collins slipped up. Told Shelby we were in Venice on our honeymoon." He paused a couple of seconds. "That's all she needed. Next thing, she was begging to talk to me. Usually, he's unflappable, but, I guess her obvious sorrow over losing her husband reminded him of the loss of—"

"His brother in Afghanistan."

Shane nodded. "Collins texted. Wanted to know if Shelby's killer had been apprehended. Then he sent the photo. I swear, I was gonna tell you but then ... Deirdre."

"Darlin'." She rubbed her eyes with her fingertips. "I'm sure I've overreacted. I'm so emotional."

"I'd be worried if you weren't." He pulled her into his embrace. "I'm gonna take you home and tuck you into bed, make you a pot of tea and ... and some of those tasty little sandwiches with all the crusts cut off."

The corners of Beth's mouth tugged into a smile. "Truly, the only thing I want is a couple of aspirin and an ice pack."

"Headache?"

She nodded.

He kissed her forehead as if the touch of his lips would make the pain disappear and then released her. "What did Jacopo have to say?"

"As Marinello said, he was taken to hospital. The doctor agreed with Jacopo that the shock of finding Deirdre's body made him mad as a box of frogs. The cut wrist turned out to be nothing more than a scratch. Didn't even need stitches. He was released about an hour ago."

"Hmmm." Shane fingered the cleft in his chin.

"Jacopo does have a flair for the dramatic," she said.

"So, you think he was just putting on a show?"

"Good Lord, I want to believe that Deirdre's death has devastated him."

"But you're not sure."

"He's been unfaithful numerous times and was about to ask for a divorce. Still, it wouldn't be impossible that somewhere deep in his heart, he regrets his mistreatment of Deirdre. That he seeks redemption."

"I guess it's possible." Shane shrugged.

"When is Mrs. Shelby supposed to arrive?" Beth asked rubbing both temples in a circular direction.

"Around noon. She's taking an early train out of Rome."

"Good. I want to get her take on my theory. That Lia Renner killed her ex-husband, who had a legal right to the child, and then Deirdre because she knew too much."

"Forget it. You need sleep."

"But, but—"

"But nothing. Look, our taxi." Shane pointed to the boat approaching them. He wrapped his arm around her waist and walked her down the narrow pier.

Chapter Twenty-Six

NICOLE SHELBY SAT AT THE TABLE closest to the arcade. The café, tucked into the corner of the piazza, was not even half full despite the crowds thronging the square. As the minutes dragged by, she inspected the people seated near her, so obviously tourists, and evaluated everything about them from their clothing to their hair color. She wasn't impressed, except for the exquisite handbag belonging to a grossly overweight woman.

She reached for the wineglass and noticed her hand tremble. "Damn," she said under her breath. *Why the hell am I nervous? He's nobody to me. Not anymore.* She glanced at her cellphone. It had remained silent for the past twenty minutes, ever since she'd placed it on the linen-covered table. *Five more minutes then I'm out of here.*

Though grateful for the afternoon shade cast from an imposing building, she lifted the napkin from her lap and pressed it against her damp forehead. Pinpricks of anxiety gathered in her chest as her heart pounded. She blinked a couple of times behind oversized sunglasses and swallowed a few deep breaths.

I was the one who insisted on this meeting for God's sake. To let him know exactly what I think of him. Oh please, don't let me cave. If he wasn't so ... so ... She closed her eyes and envisioned an image of him, which made her heart beat even faster. But then she remembered their last meeting and a new sense of resolve buoyed her confidence. Checking the pink-gold Cartier watch encircling her narrow wrist, she noticed that four minutes had ticked away.

"Nicole."

She tilted her head and eyed the man facing her. Bernardino Moro. She took in his appearance and forced herself to appear calm—relaxed— in charge.

"Sorry to have kept you waiting. But," he said with a shrug, "it couldn't be helped." He pulled out a chair opposite her and sat.

Nicole removed the sunglasses that shielded her turquoise eyes. "I didn't expect you to look so ... so continental. Must be living in Italy that has changed you." She flashed him a perfect smile. She waited for a compliment, but instead, he pulled a package of Marlboro's from his dress shirt pocket and offered her a cigarette. "Thank you, no."

A flash of anger shot through her and warmed her cheeks. It wasn't that she craved flattery, but it had been over four years since they'd seen each other. Though the parting hadn't been amicable, she'd been troubled, wondering if they'd pick up where they had left it. Probably not. No. A wave of relief flowed through her now that she'd decided against hooking up with Dino. She lifted the glass and drained it.

He lit a cigarette, removed it from his mouth, and held it between his thumb and index finger. A hint of a smile played at the corners of his mouth. "You know you're a beautiful woman. You don't need me to say so."

"Well, Dino, it wouldn't hurt you—"

"For your sake, I'm sorry about your husband."

"Are you?"

"Not really, no."

"I thought as much." She glanced at her empty wineglass then refocused on him. "I'm meeting with an American detective in about an hour. I have to identify the body."

He frowned.

"Though you don't believe it, Jon was a good man. He had his faults, but doesn't everyone?"

He sucked deeply on the cigarette then slowly exhaled.

"We had a wonderful life, actually."

He raised his eyebrows but said nothing.

"If only he could've forgotten about Lia Renner and her daughter," she spat out the words as if she'd tasted something foul.

"Ori—I mean, Louise was his daughter too." He rested the cigarette in a little tin ashtray.

Nicole waved her hand impatiently as a narrow shaft of sunlight glinted off the three-carat diamond on her finger. "I still don't understand why he cared so much about a child he hadn't seen for over ten years. What about our sons? Why weren't they enough for him?" She paused a second to brush a strand of blond hair off her cheek. "But my God, when I heard that he was going back to her—a psychotic, baby-snatching, money-grubbing bimbo—I hate to admit it; I was crushed."

"Lia was my friend. She was just as blinded by him as you were."

"I forgot that you, Jon, and *she* were like the three musketeers back in the day." Her words dripped in sarcasm.

"For all of a minute. Anyway, I couldn't understand what Lia saw in him. Or for that matter, what you saw in that jerk."

She pursed her lips for a second, trying to come up with an answer that would placate him, but she knew that wouldn't be possible. "He was handsome. And charming ... when he wanted to be. Together, we were the shining, successful, beautiful couple that people envied. Then for no good reason, he decided to throw it all away for *her*." She glanced away from the dark eyes that seemed to be drinking in her face.

"Maybe he wasn't going to do that."

"What?" The breath caught in the back of her throat.

"You were led to believe that Jonathan was returning to Lia so that the three of them could be a family again. True?"

She nodded.

"I disagree. I think it was all a clever scheme to reclaim his daughter. Once he had Louise safely in LA, well, then Lia could go to hell. I wouldn't have been surprised if he'd had her arrested for kidnapping. So, I think your marriage was never really in jeopardy. He would've found his way into your arms. That is, if you would've taken him back."

Could this be true? No. Jon was planning a life with her. Nicole rubbed the center of her forehead with her fingertips. "I would've welcomed him home in a heartbeat. But, if what you're saying is true, why did Jon's lawyer advise me of his plans for a divorce?"

"He had his lawyer tell you?" Dino shook his head. "You know, Nicole, I've had a long time to try to figure out why the hell you decided to stay with him. I guess, it all boiled down to the fact that I couldn't offer you prestige—status—all the shiny things you craved. I guess you needed that more than love."

"Love? That's what I thought we had until I overheard you boasting, telling Jon about our affair," Nicole's voice rose accusingly. "Seems that I was only a means for your revenge."

He turned his head as if suddenly fascinated by the parade of people walking by.

"I need a glass of wine," Nicole said.

"*Cameriere,*" he said sharply to a nearby waiter. "*Un bicchiere di Prosecco.*"

Silence stood between them like a wall. Her cellphone pinged. She grabbed it and scrolled down the screen. "A text from the detective. We're going to meet in the lobby of the Gritti Palace in forty-five minutes."

"Your hotel?"

She nodded.

"Ah, of course. You would be staying in the most expensive hotel in Venice." He lifted his cigarette only to crush it into the ashtray. "I imagine it was Jacopo da Parma who arranged your travel plans."

Nicole didn't want to tell him she was grateful that he had connected her to Jacopo. They clicked instantly on the phone, and after talking daily for over a week, he'd paid her a visit in person, for eight glorious days. They hardly left the bedroom. "Since Jon had mentioned a while ago that you'd moved to Venice, I really didn't know who else to contact in this... this unusual city. Thanks for referring me to Jacopo. He was a tremendous help with the travel arrangements and reservations."

"I figured you'd only want to deal with the best."

She offered him a curt nod. "Anyway, the detective is going to accompany me to the morgue." She reached for the glass of sparkling wine the waiter had deposited in front of her. "I'll be relieved when all this gruesome business is finished." She took a quick sip then set the glass down.

"Look, you don't need that detective. I'll go with you to the morgue."

"So you can gloat?"

"To support you."

"That's rich coming from you. The man who used me to get back at my husband. And all because you were crazy about that *woman*. I'm still angry about that."

"Ah, come on, Nikki," he softened his voice.

She glanced away. Dino only used her nickname when they were making love. A flash of heat shot through her and a wave of dizziness made her head feel funny.

"I told Jonathan because, I don't know," he said with a shrug. "I guess, I wanted to one-up him. Lord it over him that we were lovers." He tapped his finger against the table for a couple of seconds. "And I'm not lovesick over Lia. You're the one I was head over heels crazy about. I still am." His hand shot across the circular table.

Sidestepping his touch, she reached for the stem of the glass. "Just because we had a fling doesn't mean that I didn't love my husband."

He nodded.

"Jon was a great father and knew how to make me happy. I almost blew it by becoming involved with you. But even though he overlooked my indiscretion since Jon mostly blamed you for the whole affair, sometimes he'd get a distracted look on his face like he was miles away. That's how I knew he was thinking about *her* or that long-lost kid of his. Then he'd become sulky and disengage himself from me and the boys." She pulled her eyes away from Bernardino and focused on the diamond ring encircling her finger. "But with you, oh I don't know, you were always so interested in what I had to say. You gave me back the confidence that Jon had stolen away from me. That's why I had the inner strength to trust you. To be your lover. But then you betrayed me." She looked directly into his eyes. "I don't know if I'll ever be able to forgive you."

"I was an idiot. I probably don't deserve your forgiveness."

"I don't see how it matters now. It's water under the bridge."

"It doesn't have to be."

She bit her lower lip. The whole time he'd sat across from her, she'd been careful not to scrutinize his face. Afraid that she'd lose her nerve and never be able to tell him off. But now she took in his warm, expressive brown eyes, his broad forehead beneath a mass of wavy black hair, and his square and strong chin. A dimple creased his left cheek, adding a boyish charm to his handsome face.

He reached for her hand again. This time she let him encircle it with his fingers. "Maybe we can meet later. Tonight?"

"I better get going. I don't want to keep the detective waiting."

He released her hand.

She stood and placed the sunglasses on her face. "I'll call you."

In one fluid movement, Bernardino stepped next to her and kissed her cheeks. "Until tonight."

Chapter Twenty-Seven

NICOLE LOOKED AT HER WATCH for the umpteenth time. *The detective is beyond late*, she fumed. She stood and tossed the magazine onto a lustrous mahogany table. Though she couldn't read the Italian words, the jewelry advertisements had captured her imagination. But now, she was just pissed.

Her stilettos clicked against the hotel lobby's polished marble floor. She stopped at the front desk's ornate counter and gripped her purse as the concierge fumbled with a set of keys. She jumped, not expecting the light touch on her shoulder.

"Mrs. Shelby?"

She spun around and faced two men. "Yes? I'm Mrs. Shelby."

"Sorry for being late. I'm Shane Dalton, and this is Chief Superintendent Marinello."

"I regret that we must meet under such dire circumstances," Marinello said. He ushered Nicole beyond the couch she'd been camped on for the previous fifteen minutes and led her into a more private room off the lobby as Shane followed behind.

She faced the men with her hands clutching her tiny waist.

"The Chief Superintendent has a few questions for you before we head over to the morgue," Shane said.

Nicole dropped onto the plush red velvet couch while Shane and Marinello sat in the cushy, matching armchairs flanking a coffee table. She lifted one of the golden pillows and hugged it to her chest. "It's difficult enough, Superintendent, that my husband is dead. But to be interrogated? It's too much for me to handle." She glared at him.

Shane pressed his lips into a tight line while Marinello seemed to be studying his fingers. After a few moments, Marinello broke the silence.

157

"Your husband's death is a shock and a tragedy to all of us in Venice. It's my duty to uncover who committed this horrific crime. Please, Signora, help us find the culprit responsible for your husband's murder."

"What do you want to know?"

"There's a bit of confusion as to why your husband was visiting Venice?"

Nicole flipped her long blond hair over her shoulder and focused on the pillow she'd dropped onto her lap. For an instant, she tried to come up with a plausible story, but then almost as quickly, she decided on the truth. "A private family matter."

Marinello waited as if expecting her to elaborate.

"He was visiting family members then?" Shane asked.

"Well, not exactly. His ex-wife. Lia Renner." She looked directly at Marinello. "It's a long story. But I think it has everything to do with his death." She tossed the pillow aside.

"Please, go on," Shane said.

"I'd rather not talk about *her*." She glanced at Shane. "It's been nearly two weeks since my husband's murder. I would've thought by now you'd have some kind of lead. Maybe even arrested someone."

"Investigations sometimes take years," Shane said.

"Years? Oh, no. I need closure. Jon was my soulmate. Our world revolved around each other's happiness. I need to know who did this awful thing and why." She closed her eyes but not quick enough, as a tear slid down her cheek.

Shane rose and sat next to her. "Detective Collins told me that your husband was close to locating his daughter who'd been abducted years ago."

She opened her moist eyes and focused on Shane knowing her irises would be sparkling like the waters of the Caribbean Sea. "Jon never stopped searching for his little girl. Even hired a couple of private investigators but that ex-wife of his outsmarted all of them." She noticed how he rubbed the cleft in his chin as if thinking.

"His daughter's name is—"

"Louise." Nicole cut Marinello off. "Louise Anne Shelby. But Jon had a nickname for her. Gemma. Means flower bud, or gem, something like that. He even had the name tattooed on his right arm. That's how crazy he was about her." She shook her head. "But you already know about that 'identifying mark'," she said making air quotes.

"The tattoo is not definitive," Marinello said.

"I understand. That's why I'm here. To identify the body." She gulped a mouthful of air. "Anyway," she said reaching for her purse. She pulled out a photograph. "Here." She waved the picture in Marinello's direction. "It's the last photo Jon took of his ex and Louise before the divorce. Louise is about four years old, but now she must be at least fifteen."

Marinello took the photo and studied it. "Do you know the alias his former wife is using?"

"According to Jon, she must've had a long list of false names. But," she said with a shrug, "I don't think he had a clue as to her current one."

Marinello squinted at the photo. "There's something about Renner's eyes and nose that seem familiar, but I can't place her."

"Lia has probably changed her appearance so many times, you shouldn't be surprised if she now weighs three hundred pounds, has flaming red hair, and wears a thick pair of bifocals. After all, she'd want to look radically different than that." Nicole gestured toward the photo then grasped the pillow again. She ran her manicured fingers through the golden fringe edging the cushion.

"May I keep this photograph?" Marinello asked.

"I have no interest in ever seeing it again. So, yes. Keep it." She exhaled. "The truth is, my husband was played big time and lost his life to a conniving bitch. Can we go to the morgue now?"

"You think Lia Renner killed him?" Shane asked.

"Or hired someone. Who else would want my husband dead? After all, she had motive and means."

Marinello narrowed his eyes but didn't respond.

"Lia wanted to hold on to her precious Gemma. At any cost." Nicole looked at her hands folded on top of the pillow. She frowned, noticing that the polish on one of her nails had chipped. "Now our children have lost their father and me my husband, but Lia has what she's always wanted ... her daughter. But Louise was Jon's daughter too, It isn't right, Detective." She lifted her head and looked directly into Shane's eyes.

159

Shane brushed his fingers through his sandy hair, replacing a lock that had fallen onto his forehead. "Did your husband have any enemies?"

"Really?" Nicole jumped up from the couch. "The only enemy he had was the woman who stole his child. She has to be responsible for Jon's death," she said between clenched teeth.

Marinello stood. "We should head for the morgue. It's a bit of a walk." He glanced at her four-inch heels. "Perhaps you'd like to change into more comfortable shoes."

"I'll be fine." Nicole grabbed her purse, exited the room, and headed across the hotel's grand foyer. She pulled open the glass door and disappeared.

It took only a few seconds for the men to catch up. Sensing them at her side, she continued to stare at the Grand Canal with her arms folded. "Was he found in there?" A solemn note touched her voice.

Shane moved closer. "Ah, no. Actually, my wife and I discovered your husband's body. In a little canal near St. Mark's Square."

She turned away from the canal and offered Shane a sad smile.

"It's about a fifteen-minute walk to *Ospedale Civile*, the hospital and morgue. We need to go this way." Marinello took a few steps toward the little square, *Campiello Traghetto*.

As they walked in silence, she chewed her lip, trying to prepare for the sight of Jon's body. She hoped he wouldn't look grotesque. She'd hate that to be her final memory of him. For an instant, she visualized her sons' faces, splotchy and tear-streaked. *They loved their dad so much. I'll never let them know how obsessed he was over their half-sister.*

She sighed, fluffed her hair away from her face, and then remembered Dino. Though his invitation was tempting, she wasn't about to jump into bed with him. *That will require a lot more than an earnest apology. Anyway, Jacopo promised we'd hook up.* A smile tugged at the corner of her lips.

"Signora, this way," Marinello called.

A bit startled, she stopped and realized that she'd walked past the left turn the men had made onto *Campo Santi Giovanni e Paolo.*

When she caught up to them, Marinello flung out his arm, gesturing beyond an enormous church toward a gleaming white façade of a Renaissance building standing adjacent to a canal.

Nicole's heart sped up. "I don't think..."

Shane stepped a bit closer.

"I can't bear the thought of looking at him," Nicole said under her breath. "I want to remember Jon as he was."

"That's understandable," Shane said. "You won't be alone. I promise; I'll be at your side the whole time."

"That means so much." She grabbed his arm. "I may have to rely on your strength to get through this ordeal." She glanced at him. Though she kept her face filled with solemnity, she wondered what it would be like to snuggle within his strong arms and kiss his mouth.

Chapter Twenty-Eight

SHANE STOOD IN THE MAIN HALL of the *Scuola Grande di San Marco* and absorbed its harmonious splendor. Earlier when they'd hurried inside the building leading to the *Ospedale Civile*, he hadn't time to inspect the Renaissance hall. Instead, he had concentrated on the muted sounds as they walked along the red runner protecting the marble floor's geometric design to steel himself, once again, upon entering a morgue. But now, as Marinello spoke to Nicole in a hushed tone, he seized the opportunity to look around. He glanced at one of the identical ten Corinthian columns seated on a tiled pedestal that towered upwards toward the beamed ceiling. The remnants of the morgue's grim atmosphere that lingered inside him were thankfully being replaced with a measure of pure architectural beauty.

Standing in the morgue had allowed memories to crash down around him, causing his stomach to constrict and his throat to dry. He'd had his fill of investigating homicides, and his final case, the murders of four teenage girls, had sealed the deal with his resignation from the Los Angeles County Sheriff's Department. Though he wanted nothing more than to shut down his investigative mind and blot out his detective instincts, they emerged in full force as he observed Nicole view her husband's corpse. He'd prodded himself, knowing from experience how differently people mourn but ... a *smile*? He forced the distracting thought from his mind and focused on the conversation.

"Detective Marinello," Nicole said. "I'm planning on leaving Venice as soon as possible. Maybe tonight."

Marinello frowned. "You have the death certificate." He gestured to her leather purse. "But you still must make arrangements for the shipment of the body."

"Well ... I want him cremated."

Marinello nodded. "Then you brought with you the proper paperwork."

Nicole raised her neatly arched eyebrows.

"Evidence that Signore Shelby wanted to be cremated."

"He's dead. What does it matter now?"

"If you have his written permission, it can be done easily enough. But it will take several weeks for the ashes to be delivered from the crematorium."

"Weeks?" A stricken look crossed her face.

"The funeral director will make all the arrangements. If you decide to ship the body, then the preparations will take four to seven days."

"Funeral director?"

"The Venetian funeral home, *Impresa Rallo*, is in Mestre, on the mainland. I can take you there first thing in the morning."

Nicole focused on Shane. "Would you mind going with me? I'm sure the superintendent is busy—"

"I'm not familiar with the procedure. Anyway, I don't think it's appropriate for me—"

"Okay. But can you, at least, walk me back to my hotel? I'll never find it on my own." She didn't give Shane a chance to answer. Instead, she addressed Marinello. "What time do you want to head over to the funeral home?"

"I can meet you at the Hotel Gritti Palace tomorrow morning at nine."

"Fine." Nicole put on the sunglasses she'd pulled free from her purse, took a few steps, and then glanced over her shoulder at Shane. "Detective?" She walked away from the two men.

A wave of irritation rolled through Shane. "If you'd like me to go to the funeral home, I could probably swing it." *Beth will, no doubt, want to tag along*, he thought waiting for Marinello to answer.

"That won't be necessary."

He picked up on the flicker of amusement that crossed the Chief Superintendent's face.

"I think the signora is waiting for you." Marinello extended a hand.

Shane shook it. "We'll be in touch."

He turned and spied Nicole on the other side of the vast *campo*, gazing into a shop window. He didn't hurry, but instead took measured steps trying to figure out Nicole's motivation for chumming up to him for support. For all intents and purposes, she didn't come across much like a grieving widow. A flash of Beth's grief-stricken face wet with tears over Deirdre's death provided quite a contrast to Mrs. Shelby. He stopped a couple of feet away from her and stuck his hands into his pants pockets.

"Oh, there you are." Nicole grabbed his arm. "I have no sense of direction. I'd be lost in no time." She offered him a half-smile.

"You're handling all this like a trooper. It must've been a terrible shock discovering that your husband was murdered."

"You can't imagine." She paused a second eyeing a pair of shoes in the store window then looked directly at him. "I'm thankful that Detective Collins told me you were in Venice. I'd be lost having to deal with all of this by myself. It's not that I have anything against Italians, *but* I don't think they're the most efficient people. Look at how long it took them to realize that it was my husband's body in that stinking canal." She thrust out her chin. "And really, if you want to accompany me to the funeral home tomorrow, I'd appreciate it." She lifted her sunglasses for a second and looked at him with pleading eyes.

"I'd like to help you out but...." Shane said steering her down a narrow arcade quickening his step. She had no problem keeping up with his stride. "My wife—"

"Oh, yeah. Detective Collins ... Gavin told me you're honeymooning."

Gavin? Shane frowned. *They're on first name basis?* "Um, yeah, that's right. The whole month of June. Did Gavin also tell you I've resigned from the force?"

"It takes more than a couple of weeks to forget how to be a detective."

Though he wouldn't admit that she was right, he wished the most pressing problem facing him was setting the correct degree on a miter saw at a construction site.

They exited the alleyway and headed across a small square. He wondered if he should spill the beans regarding Deirdre's death. He wavered but then decided, even though the details hadn't been officially released, that it would be better if she heard the news from him, instead of through unreliable hotel gossip. "What Detective Collins doesn't know is that there's been another murder."

"Another murder?"

"A replica of your husband's."

"What?" She pulled off her sunglasses and stopped walking. "What do you mean ... a replica?"

"The autopsy hasn't been performed yet, but on the surface, everything matches up. The victim was discovered in a canal, suffered a slit throat, and a *Bauta* mask was attached to the face."

"So, he was killed like Jon." She slipped her glasses on top of her head.

"She." Shane hesitated to tell her any more details.

"A woman?" She squeezed his arm tighter. "Another tourist?"

"Not at all," he said taking a few steps. "That's why I need to be with my wife tomorrow. The victim was her best friend. They grew up together in Ireland."

"I'm sorry."

He glanced at her. No trace of sympathy crossed her face.

"So, she was Irish, but not a tourist?"

"She moved to Venice about ten years ago."

"I can't imagine anyone choosing to live in this stinky, sinking, pile of rocks. It's musty, old, and crumbling—anywhere you look there's scaffolding—trying to cement it all back together. Plus, it gives me the creeps."

Shane wanted to shake her, point out the architectural wonders of the lagoon city. Instead, he allowed a sigh to escape between his teeth. Then he remembered her husband was murdered here.

"What was she? Some kind of tour guide?" Nicole asked. "They seem to be everywhere holding those damn umbrellas."

"Huh?" Her question jolted him from his musing. "Oh, no. A teacher. An English teacher."

"I'm trying to understand why a murderer decided to kill an American lawyer and an Irish teacher?" She gripped his arm tighter as Shane directed her to turn left.

"That's for Marinello to figure out."

"Your wife must be broken up about it."

"We all are."

"We?"

"Her husband, kids, family."

"She was married then. Her husband's Italian?"

"Yeah. A businessman. Works the Travel Bureau over in St. Mark's Square. He was so shaken up, he was taken to the hospital."

She stopped walking and looked at him, frowning. "I'm sorry," she murmured, "it's just a shock to know that another person was murdered so ... so savagely. Was she an older woman?"

"Twenty-seven."

"Damn." She shook her head. "Well, you know what they say, 'The good die young.' You said she had kids."

"Twin girls."

"Twin girls," she repeated under her breath. "And I have two sons. You said the husband is a travel agent."

"He owns the business."

She let out a little gasp and began walking so unexpectedly that Shane had to hustle to catch up. "You okay?"

"What do you think, Shane?" Her voice had lost its softness and taken on a demanding tone. "Are the murders connected or just random acts of violence?"

"Connection? No. It's unlikely Deirdre da Parma knew your husband."

"Deirdre da Parma?" She turned away and focused on the pieces of hand-blown glass in a shop window. "Jon never mentioned her."

He studied Nicole as she stared at a Murano glass *millefiori* bird perched on a golden branch. It wasn't until then that he realized she wasn't a classic beauty, but most people probably didn't realize that. *After all, she carries herself like a damn movie star.* Attractive, very, he decided taking in her willowy frame, turquoise eyes, and blonde tresses. *Appealing, absolutely, the way her lips pout and her boobs well, they're most likely fake.* He felt certain, Nicole Shelby was used to turning heads.

She stepped away from the window and faced him.

Had she realized I was assessing her? His cheeks burned.

"I think I know." Her voice sounded strained.

"What?"

"The connection."

"I don't think there is a connection."

"My God, are you blind? It's obvious."

He stepped closer. "You've been through a trying ordeal. Let's get you back to the hotel where you can relax. You'll feel better after a bath or a massage, or even a stiff drink. I'm sure the hotel can accommodate—"

"Don't patronize me." She placed her hands on her hips and threw him daggers.

"Look, Mrs. Shelby. Nicole."

Her face relaxed. "It's Nikki. And please, hear me out."

He folded his arms and nodded.

"The killer is targeting non-Italians."

"Yeah." He didn't want to admit that fact hadn't occurred to him.

"Oh my God." Her face seemed to crumble.

"You okay?"

"How can I be? First Jon. And now this Irish woman. I could be next." She took off jogging across the square.

Shane's only thought was that she was going to break her neck running on the stone pavement in heels. "Nikki," he called as he ran to catch up with her. She wasn't moving very fast, so it didn't take long. He grabbed her arm. She stopped and faced him.

"There are thousands of non-Italians in Venice. Why do you think you'd be a target?"

"He killed my husband. Maybe, killing Jon was just a ploy to get me here. So, he could...."

Shane realized that the strain of the day had caught up with her. "It's natural to think crazy things when you're stressed. Look, you had a long flight on top of an uncomfortable train ride to perform a grisly chore. I'm telling you; you'll feel a helluva lot better after a solid eight hours of sleep. Come on," he said placing his hand on her back, "we're almost there."

"I've got a strange feeling. Call it a sixth sense. I'm very intuitive."

God, no. Without responding, he directed her down *Calle delle Ostreghe*. They walked amid an awkward silence. When they entered the Hotel Gritti Palace's elegant lobby, he offered her a curt nod. "Take my advice and get some sleep."

"Sleep? Are you kidding me?"

He shrugged and turned away.

"Shane, please."

He glanced at her over his shoulder.

"I'm scared. I might be able to relax if I had police protection. Could you come up to my room?"

"I can't help you there. Remember, I'm a former detective." The widening of her eyes and pleading expression hadn't been lost on him. "I'm sorry for your loss." He caught a glimpse of her pout then continued walking toward the exit.

Chapter Twenty-Nine

NICOLE PACED THE LENGTH OF THE wide room, not impressed by the stunning suite adorned with luxuriant furnishings, a Murano glass chandelier, and plush, oriental carpets. Her strides slowed to a stop in front of the balcony door. She opened it and stepped outside. The view offered an unparalleled sight of the Grand Canal and the famed church, Santa Maria della Salute. Instead of looking at the water or the church, she stared at the graying sky.

After identifying Jon's body, she'd had an inkling of hope that her visit to the lagoon city would be brief. Though that hadn't panned out, the walk back to the hotel had been informative. Shocking, actually. It explained why Jacopo hadn't contacted her. *How surreal.* Both of our spouses were killed *and* in the same gruesome manner. A cold chill ran along her spine.

She turned her back to the view and considered the scene earlier at the morgue. Marinello had instructed her to wait in the corridor while he obtained Jon's death certificate. She'd dutifully sat in an uncomfortable wooden chair and pulled out her cellphone. She was scrolling down a list of texts when a mortuary assistant muttered something in Italian. She looked up. Not interested, she was about to resume checking her phone when he lifted the sheet covering the corpse, said something that sounded like a curse and turned away from the gurney.

"Hmmm. No problem leaving him—it's not like that dead guy will be going anywhere," she had said under her breath. Nicole stood and rolled her shoulders. She glanced at the abandoned autopsy table then moved a few steps closer to it. In his haste, the mortuary worker hadn't pulled the sheet entirely over the body. She could clearly see the russet hair and the pallid skin of the half-covered face. She hurried next to the gurney and peeked under the scratchy sheet.

The stocky figure had been washed, cleansing any blood residue, but the vicious cut across the woman's neck went from ear to ear. Nicole dropped the sheet, hurried back to her seat, and resumed looking at her cellphone screen.

The assistant had returned about two seconds later carrying a clear plastic bag which contained a white form caked with dried mud. He tugged on the sheet, straightening it, then wheeled the table to the autopsy room.

Nicole shook her head as if trying to shake the memory loose from her brain. She leaned against the balcony's railing, closed her eyes, and released a deep sigh. "I'd bet my last dollar that corpse had been Jacopo's wife. The poor woman," she said opening her eyes. But now she wondered how an Irish teacher married to Jacopo fit into the killer's plan. "Why was she murdered ... and in the exact way as Jon?"

She decided there was only one way to find out. She reached beneath her cotton voile tunic and freed her cellphone from the pocket of her crepe trousers. She tapped the numbers she'd memorized weeks ago. "Jacopo will know what the hell is behind these murders. My husband ... his wife?" She let out another sigh.

Chapter Thirty

SHANE BALANCED THE TIN FOILED covered plates of gnocchi and tortellini in one hand as he used the other to softly click the apartment door shut. Determined not to disturb Beth, he slipped out of his tasseled leather loafers and walked in his stocking feet through the living area into the kitchen. With high hopes that she'd sleep straight through until tomorrow morning, he pulled open the refrigerator and deposited the tortellini, anticipating that when she woke, Beth would be hungry.

"Shane!"

He tapped his forehead in frustration and turned away from the refrigerator. She stood in the doorway. He wanted to throw his arms around her and whisper in her ear that everything was going to be okay. Except it wasn't. After Nicole had identified her husband's body, Marinello had ushered him toward another body waiting for an autopsy. The carnival mask had been removed and though the face belonged to Deirdre, the lively, intrepid, fun-loving girl was gone, and what remained was only a shell of that vibrant life.

"How are you holding up?" He tried to gauge Beth's emotional state from her appearance but came up empty.

"Better." She attempted a smile but failed.

"I brought you some tortellini from that carry-out place you love." He turned to retrieve the plate from the refrigerator.

"Thanks, but, I'm not hungry."

"You only had a slice of pizza for lunch and left most of it on your plate." He took a step closer. "I'm worried about you. You have to eat."

"I will, love. But...." She shook her head.

"Then I'll make you a cup of tea."

"Sounds lovely." She took a few steps closer to him. "I rang Mrs. McKenna—Carmel—Deidre's ma."

"You broke the news to her?"

She shook her head. "Jacopo had already contacted her. We talked, and cried, and even laughed a time or two remembering... Anyway, she'll be arriving in Venice in a couple of days. The rest of the family will be following behind her throughout the week. I'm going to help Carmel plan Deidre's funeral."

"Shouldn't Jacopo be doing that?"

"Apparently he's too distraught and asked Carmel if she could handle all the details. He wants to spend the next few days honoring Deidre's life by writing her eulogy."

"You think he's sincere? I mean after what you told me about his cheating, I wouldn't be surprised if he's now finding solace in his current lover's bed."

She moistened her bottom lip with the tip of her tongue. "I am a bit torn. I really think Deirdre's death shook Jacopo. Maybe he's regretting the way he treated her, but either way, I'll be givin' him the benefit of the doubt, so."

"Doesn't surprise me. Your heart is so kind."

"I'm not sure that's the reason. But I am certain he once loved Deirdre. And there are the children to consider. Anyway, I want my best friend's funeral to reflect her warm personality and unfailing love—for her kids, her family, friends, for me."

He noticed that she blinked rapidly a few times, probably trying to prevent new tears from springing to her bloodshot and swollen eyes.

"I give Jacopo credit for preserving his family's magnificent Renaissance palazzo," he said. "But I've got an uneasy feeling about the guy. On the surface, Jacopo seems like a good old boy—friendly, back-slapping, hand-shaking, wide smile kinda guy. Except, I can't trust anybody who treats his wife like crap. I think he's a two-timing, sympathy seeking phony."

"Your detective's instinct is telling you that?"

"Right here." Shane tapped his abs. "Feeling in my gut I can't ignore. Jacopo is a jerk."

She walked across the kitchen and leaned against the marble countertop. "It feels as if my *fey* has dried up. I'm numb. My heart is broken."

He moved closer to her and slipped his hands into his pockets.

"I don't think I ever told you that after *me ma* died, Carmel McKenna became like a mother to me. Unlike my Aunt Ealga who was hell-bent on fashioning me into her spitting image, Carmel showed me possibilities I never dreamed of—gave me books to read, and listened to my thoughts and ideas; then she urged me to spread my wings—to become the person that was in here." Beth pressed her hand to her chest. "Carmel and Granny. If it wasn't for those two," she said with a shrug. "Both of them urged me to trust my *fey* and follow my dreams. It's just that Deirdre was always a part of that dream. I thought of her more like a sister than a friend. Now there's an aching, gaping hole, and I don't know how to deal with it."

"You're not alone. I'm here for you." He drew Beth into his arms. "Tá mo chroi istigh ionat," he whispered the Irish Gaelic words into her ear.

"My heart is in your heart. I love you too, my darlin' boy."

He took a step back, releasing her and wiping the dampness from her cheeks. "Now, my *darlin'* Betty Getty," he said with his best Irish accent, "I want you to get comfortable in the living room while I make you a good *cuppa*." He winked. A wave of relief washed over him when he spied a glint of light shining in her eyes.

A few minutes later, Shane entered the living room holding two mugs of tea. With a flicker of relief, he noticed that Beth was looking at her camera. Since "retiring" from modeling, she seemed to always be on the lookout for new pursuits. Photography and volunteering at a cat rescue had become her two current interests. He prayed to God that solving murders hadn't made her list.

"Just the way you like it. A dollop of milk and a teaspoon of sugar," he said.

She placed the top-of-the-line camera on a nearby end table, grabbed the hot mug, and blew across the cup's lip. "How did the poor lass hold up at the morgue? I managed to say a couple of Aves for her. Poor Mrs. Shelby. My heart surely breaks for her."

Shane took a quick sip and silently cursed as the liquid burned the back of his throat. He looked into the mug, trying to find the right words to describe Nicole Shelby. "If I didn't know better, I would've believed that Mrs. Shelby and Skye share the same DNA." He recognized a spark of puzzlement cross Beth's face. "More specifically—the old Skye—when she believed the world revolved around her. The loss of a loved one kinda changed Skye's perspective, making her a little less self-absorbed. I wish it would've affected the widow Shelby that way."

Beth set her mug on the table next to her camera. Though she didn't respond, Shane knew he'd gotten her full attention.

"If she's grief-stricken, she has an odd way of showing it. On top of that, I believe she was flirting with me," he said.

"What?" Beth moved to the edge of the soft leather chair.

"I walked Nicole Shelby back to her hotel. Not only did Nicole, I mean, Nikki," he said rolling his eyes, "grab hold of my arm, she did that hair flipping thing, and... and then she invited me to her room."

"To her room. She thought you and she—?"

"Would fool around. Yeah, I'm sure that's what she was going for. But that wasn't the worst of it."

"What could be worse than propositioning you? And on your honeymoon no less."

Her cheeks flushed, and he read the anger brewing in her eyes. *Dammit*, he thought. *Stupid. StupidStupidStupid. I never should've told Beth. The last thing I want is to upset her.* "I agree. Beyond tacky. Especially with her recently murdered husband on a cold slab in a morgue. But get this. When Marinello led her to the autopsy table and lifted the sheet, she stared at the corpse for like twenty seconds. I watched her face—resembled granite—but when he dropped the covering, I detected the faintest smile cross her face. I'm sure Marinello noticed it too."

"Hmmm."

Beth's furrowed brow told him she was considering his words.

"I told her about Deirdre. I thought it only fair that she should be informed there'd been another murder with the same M.O. That's when the twenty questions started."

"What kind of questions?"

"Everything except what was Deirdre's favorite flavor of gelato." He took a quick sip of tea. "Nicole did come up with a good observation that both victims weren't Italian. But for some weird reason, she believes she may be the killer's next target. Thinks her husband's death was a means to get her to Venice. According to her, she's the reason for the murders."

"That doesn't make sense. I've thought a lot about it and have concluded that Deirdre's death was the work of a copycat. After all, there's no link between Jonathan Shelby and Deirdre. They didn't even know each other."

"Could be. But Nicole thinks there's a connection. Swears she has this feeling—"

"Feeling?"

"Mrs. Shelby says she has a sixth sense. You know..." he bit his tongue not wanting to upset Beth even more by once again reiterating his lack of belief in that hocus-pocus stuff.

She lifted her cup but then cradled it in her hands as if warming them. "I'd like to meet Mrs. Shelby—and not only to offer condolences. If she does have the gift and her intuition is correct, maybe she'll offer to be the bait so we can snare a vicious killer."

Chapter Thirty-One

LIDIA HAD JUST FINISHED BLOW-drying her newly-dyed, golden copper hair when a pounding on the apartment door rang loud and insistent. Thinking Oriana might have forgotten her key, she unplugged the hairdryer, hurried out of the tiny bathroom, and rushed down the narrow corridor that led to the living area.

The unrelenting banging increased in intensity. She stood like a statue, realizing that it couldn't be Oriana. *She'd never hammer on the door, demanding me to drop everything and race to her need. She's a considerate, thoughtful girl.* A shiver ran through her as the whacking thuds filled her ears. Her fingers played on the handle, and then with a deep breath, she cracked to door open.

Taken aback by Jacopo's disarray—his rumpled clothes, hair bristly and wild, and swollen eyes—she allowed no emotion to touch her face as an idea flew through her mind. *This could be a ruse to keep me in Venice.* "Come in," she said softly.

Jacopo stepped inside and slammed the door shut by leaning against its scarred wooden surface. He covered his face with his well-manicured hands.

She stared at him with her lips pressed together. After what seemed an eternity, he emitted a rattling sound, a cross between a sigh and a cough. He removed his hands.

Confused by his extreme behavior she wondered what was going on.

"Have you heard?" Jacopo's voice cracked.

"Heard what?" She frowned.

"Deirdre. She's dead. Murdered."

She grabbed his arm and pulled him into the small living room. "What are you talking about? Deirdre murdered?"

He sunk onto the lumpy settee and raked his fingers through his unruly locks. She waited for an explanation with arms crossed. With each passing second, her disbelief intensified.

Will he say anything to keep me here? This has gone too far. "I don't understand this game you're playing—"

"Game?"

He jerked his head up, and she caught his eyes. They looked wet.

"This isn't a game. For God's sake, my wife was murdered just like the other one—"

"The canal murder?"

"Deirdre stormed out last night after I asked for a divorce. I searched for hours, contacted her friends, even called the hospital. Finally, Marinello joined me, and it was then…." He wiped the back of his hands across his eyes. "I spotted her body, except, at first, I didn't know for sure that it was Deirdre. A *Bauta* disguised her face. It was ... horrifying."

She dropped next to him.

"I came here directly from the morgue since I had to identify her body. They're about to perform an autopsy. Deirdre has suffered enough already, but now they insist on mutilating her corpse." His sobs seemed to shake the room.

Confusion like a surreal blanket covered her. Dumbfounded and struggling to make sense of his disturbing words, she found her voice. "Why would someone murder Deirdre?"

He glanced at her.

Lidia's breath caught in the back of her throat realizing he resembled a lost, frightened little boy. She wanted to wrap her arms around him and offer soothing words of comfort, but at a time like this, touch is cold and words are useless. He'd have to find his own way.

"I knew the first victim." The moment the words slipped from her lips, she believed some kind of mad impulse had overshadowed her. She wanted to take them back.

"You knew...?"

"Jonathan Shelby." She nodded gathering she'd have to shift to damage control. "I met him at the Travel Bureau. He'd stopped by asking about must-see sites. We kind of hit it off. He took me to lunch a couple of times. Jonathan was a nice person. But, poor Deirdre. She was one of the kindest, most genuine—"

"You've talked to Marinello about your friendship with the canal victim?"

"Um...." She chewed her lip a couple of times, trying to digest the shift in his demeanor. An accusing guise had replaced the anguish. "Of course," she lied. "I couldn't offer much, since I knew next to nothing about Jonathan. We talked mostly about our children. He had two sons."

"So, this Shelby person was interested in you."

The shift in his tone had progressed so swiftly that her head spun.

"You made love with him." Jacopo stood and moved in front of her.

"Of course not."

He gripped her arms and pulled her upright. "You're lying."

"Let go. You're hurting me."

Jacopo released her. "Forgive me. I'm out of my mind with grief. I'm not thinking straight." He moved toward the door then turned and faced her. "I don't know what to say to my girls. They loved their mamma so much. How can I face them?"

"It's going to be difficult. You'll have to swallow your emotions and be strong. In the end, all you can do is love them."

"How can I do that without you?" He stepped closer to Lidia and brushed a stray lock off her forehead. A strange look crossed his face. "What did you do to your hair?"

She couldn't believe that at a time like this he'd be interested in her dye job. But then she considered his grief and guessed that any change, even a small one, like her hair color could upset his tenuous emotions. "I needed a change. After all, I'll be starting a new life in Rome." She didn't dare tell him the actual reason—the first step in changing her appearance to assume a new persona, that of Aleda Linser.

He took her arm. Tugged her toward him. "There's no need for you to leave Venice. Though I'd never wish for this, Deirdre is out of the picture. We can start our life together." He pulled her into a tight embrace.

She stiffened in his arms. If she acquiesced to Jacopo's wish, it would make her the obvious suspect ... if the authorities discovered that Oriana was Jonathan's missing daughter, the distinct motive would surface that she killed him to keep Oriana for herself and Deirdre to steal her husband. A child would be able to determine the reason—a struggling, single mother winds up living a pampered life in a mansion with servants, and a doting millionaire. She wasn't about to let that happen.

As she pushed the damning thought aside, she realized that Jacopo was spreading kisses along her cheek, and his fingers were busy unbuttoning her blouse.

"What are you doing?" She pulled back, but he only tightened his hold.

"I'm sick with grief. I can't face my daughters. I need you to get me through this. Don't deny me." He ripped open her shirt. He yanked her brassiere, popping open its front clasp. Never had she felt so degraded as his tongue swept along the curve of her bosom. "Stop it." She clawed at his face, his neck, his eyes.

"What the hell are you doing?" he bellowed, flapping her hands away.

Lidia ran to her bedroom, slammed the door, and locked it. She covered her ears, trying to block out the sound of his voice. It had taken on a timbre of contrition as he pleaded for her to open the door. Waves of anger crashed through her. "I'll be relieved when I get away from here—and you."

"Don't say that, Lidia. Look, I'm sorry."

She fixed her bra, slipped out of her blouse, and pulled a sweatshirt over her head. Then she opened the door. Jacopo faced her with arms crossed.

"Try to understand. I can't comfort you, hold your hand, or make love with you. Now or ever." She noticed the tightening of his jaw.

"What can I say to change your mind?"

She looked into his beseeching eyes. His fierce determination and unwanted sexual advances made her wonder what Deirdre might've put up with being married to him. She wanted no part of Jacopo da Parma, Now or ever.

"Nothing."

"Listen to reason," he raised his voice. "I've been planning a life with you for months. The girls need a mother, and I need you to be my wife. I can give you the world—"

"Stop it, Jacopo. I'm sick about what happened to Deirdre, but I'm not about to take her place."

He reached out to touch her arm.

She took a backward step into her bedroom. "I think you better leave. Now."

The pleading expression vanished as his eyes narrowed and his nostrils flared. His opened mouth exposed his teeth. Fearing he was about to hit her, Lidia retreated further away and grasped the door, ready to slam it in his face.

She expected him to yell, but instead, he whispered, "You've made a big mistake. I promise; you'll regret rejecting me for the rest of your life." He thrust out his jaw, spun around, and walked out of the apartment.

FILLED WITH RAGE, Jacopo stood in the deserted hallway outside of Lidia's apartment. He balled his hand and swung at the wall, but stopped before his fist touched the plaster surface. It'd be stupid, he realized, to bust up his hand because of her stubborn refusal to accept the magnificent plan he'd devised for the two of them. He sunk onto the first step of the dilapidated staircase not thinking about his freshly pressed hand-tailored trousers.

He struggled to quell his rising fury. If he didn't get a grip, he'd lose all perspective and do something rash that would ruin his carefully laid groundwork to win not only the joys of Lidia's body but her steadfast devotion. The thudding of his racing heart filled his ears, and he feared his blood pressure had spiked to a level that'd be off the chart. He gulped mouthfuls of air and imagined flickers of sunlight dancing on the gentle swells of the Grand Canal. The image of Venice's mighty waterway had a cathartic effect, and soon, the pounding of his heart lessened—and so did the confusion clouding his brain.

"Could I have been mistaken?" His whispered words gave him pause. *For months, Lidia's been sending out signals—those doe eyes meeting mine with the look of desire, the soft touch of her hand on my arm, and that kiss. That damn kiss. Could her flirtations have only been a devious ploy to squeeze money out of me to pay her kid's tuition?* He chewed the inside of his cheek. *In fact, she hasn't even tried to pay me back one damn euro.* A new bout of outrage begged to spiral out of control. He tapped his foot in a failed attempt to squelch the rising anger. "She only pretended to care for me," he muttered. "The truth is, she only cares about her precious Oriana." He balled his fists. *That bitch blindsided me. Played me for a damn fool.*

He stood, hurried down the dingy staircase, and crossed the lobby. He reached for the door, but let his arm drop as the breath died in his throat. For an instant, he thought he was having a heart attack. A wave of dizziness made his vision blur. "I have to get out of here," he huffed pulling the door open. Every fiber of his being rebelled against his analysis of Lidia's motive, but gut-wrenching anguish told him it had to be the truth.

Deirdre was right.

Lidia doesn't love me. Never did. She only loved that I was able to help her darling brat. She must have a long roll of pawns that cater to her biddings. I bet Dino Moro tops the list ... after me. Dammit. Now that she's finished playing me, she's ready to move on ... send the kid to relatives to hijinks them out of money ... hightail it to Rome and hook up with another starry-eyed schmuck—and scrounge up more money.

His thoughts rambled so quickly that he stopped walking to sort them out. He leaned against a footbridge's wooden railing and stared at the stagnant water filling the narrow canal.

What it boils down to, he thought squeezing his eyes shut for a moment, *is that ... Deirdre died for nothing.*

Though he wanted more than anything to expunge the troubling thought from his mind, he couldn't. A whisper of guilt fluttered through him. He trembled with the realization that he could've tried to save Deirdre's life instead of devising a morbid masquerade of a cover-up. Full-fledged remorse settled in his stomach like a lead weight.

But, I'm not to blame. It's Lidia's fault. The way she exploited my love for her. She'll have to pay—and her damn daughter too.

A slow smile curved his lip. He inhaled deeply as a thread of relief moved through him. Though he had no idea how to enact his revenge, he was certain that Oriana would have to be first.

And when Lidia feels as if her heart has been torn out of her chest then I'll execute my measure of justice toward her.

A thread of relief moved through him as he pulled his sight away from the putrid canal. He freed his cellphone from the inside pocket of his suitcoat and checked the screen. Four texts. All from Nikki. A hint of a smile crossed his face as he remembered his little deceit. While everyone believed he was on a business trip at the Riviera, he'd jetted to California to meet his new long-distance friend. Mrs. Nicole Shelby. Their relationship had started innocently enough when she'd contacted him about making travel arrangements to Venice. But the more she talked, the more he became intrigued. Her sexy, "bedroom" voice captivated his imagination and caused him to wonder what she looked like. On a lark, he'd asked her to email a photo of herself. He hadn't expected much knowing that voices hardly ever matched up with the faces but, hell, he was shocked after opening her email. Nikki Shelby was gorgeous.

Moving away from the footbridge, he scanned her texts, but the words didn't register as an idea began to blossom. *With Deirdre gone and Lidia's betrayal, their usefulness is finished. But Nikki is already the mother of two sons. She could easily bring another one into the world.* His son—if he played his cards right.

Chapter Thirty-Two

NICOLE OPENED THE DOOR of her hotel suite, expecting a maid with extra towels. Instead, Jacopo stood there. A flutter of emotion caused her eyes to tear. It took her only a second to realize that the events of the day had finally caught up to her.

"Welcome to Venice." A smile crossed his face, lightening his eyes with warmth. "For you!" He lifted a colorful bouquet of wildflowers enveloped in a cloud of green tissue paper.

It was then she noticed a bottle of champagne cradled in the crook of his arm. "Come in."

Once inside the elegant living room, he handed her the bouquet.

"They're lovely," she said.

"Though sun-kissed, aromatic, and delicate, these flowers pale in the presence of your radiant beauty."

She couldn't help but smile, thinking that Jacopo had mastered the art of offering admiration mixed with a healthy dose of flirting—a trait she'd decided Italian men had taken to another level in the game of seduction. But she wasn't going to let his flattery go to her head.

"While I tend to these," she said bringing the bouquet to her nose, "why don't you pour the champagne." She pointed to a platter on a buffet holding several wine glasses.

She hadn't cared for the long-stemmed pink flowers she'd found in the hotel suite earlier that day, so she grabbed the arrangement out of the ivory porcelain vase and tossed them into a waste bin. Artfully, she arranged the new bunch then turned and looked at him.

He handed her a glass. Instead of taking a sip, she focused on the effervescent bubbles.

"What's wrong, Nikki? You're not happy to see me. When I read your text messages—"

"It's not that..."

He took the glass from her and placed it on an end table. Then he wound his strong fingers around her slender hand, bowed low, and raised it toward his face. She barely felt his lips brush her cool skin. He squeezed her hand as he stood upright and touched her cheek, ran his fingertips to her chin, then lifted her face. She looked into his dark eyes for a second before he kissed her lips, lightly at first, then deeply. The scent of his musk cologne filled her nostrils as his tongue probed the warmth of her mouth. A tingle of desire ran down her spine—an emotion she wanted to repress.

"I've missed you so much," he whispered.

She pulled away without responding.

"Nikki?"

"Either you're a damn good actor or a cold-hearted bastard," she said. "It was your wife's body I saw at the morgue?"

He blew out a stream of air.

She crossed the room and sat on the silky, golden couch. He followed but chose an imitation Rocco armchair that faced her. "Deirdre was killed exactly like your husband," he said.

"What the hell is going on?"

"It's not so bad that your husband is..." He shrugged.

She narrowed her eyes. "Financially, no. But emotionally—I'm a wreck. You know I loved Jon. He was my world." She wanted to believe the words, but they rang hollow to her ears.

"Stop lying, Nikki. You happily welcomed me into your bed because you hated him for dumping you—for his ex-wife. You're glad he's dead."

"Well, maybe I'm not all broken up over Jon's death. But what about your wife?"

He crossed his arms. "We fought. She walked out on me and into the path of a deranged killer."

"I don't see you shedding any tears for her." She gestured to the glass in his hand. "If you ask me, this whole meeting looks like a celebration."

A slow smile crept across his face. "Why shouldn't we celebrate? Your no-good husband is dead, and my wife, who just about everyone thought was a living saint, has gained her heavenly reward. It looks to me like a win-win situation."

"You're one cold S.O.B."

"Cold, no, never. My blood blazes with irrepressible passion. You of all people know I speak the truth." He stood, raised his glass from the cocktail table, and emptied it. After replacing the flute, he walked around the table that separated them and offered her his hand. "Be honest, Nikki. You're glad he's dead. It's what you wanted after all, isn't it?"

She didn't want to answer his question lingering in the air. Her breath caught in the base of her throat as he scared and excited her all in the same moment. The only thing she wanted was to give in to the desire burning within her. She extended her hand and was surprised that it trembled.

On the verge of giving herself to him, something stronger than passion made her pull her hand away. Curiosity. Nicole wanted to know the truth. She took a deep breath and waited a moment as she read the understandable look of confusion that claimed his face.

"I want some answers," she said. "In California, we both agreed that Lia Renner needed to be punished for wrecking my home. But now, my husband is dead, your wife winds up murdered, and Renner, I imagine, is unscathed. She still has full possession of Jon's daughter. Something isn't adding up here. How can such a devious woman live so charmed a life?"

"I know we came up with some amazing ways to punish her. My favorite one was to tell her daughter what a rat she has for a mother, but I think you rather liked the idea of staking her to the ground, covering her in bird food, and letting the pigeons peck her to death. But Nikki, what do you want me to do? I don't even know the woman."

"Liar." She had no idea if he was telling the truth, but she decided to let her instincts take over. "How do I know that you didn't kill Jon? To get me over here. To continue the affair with the woman whose voice you fell in love with over the phone." Her words rose accusingly.

"Don't be ridiculous. You're getting yourself worked up over nothing."

"Am I?"

"I didn't kill your husband. As for my wife, someone was trying to be clever, to confuse the police by copying your husband's mode of death. Why he chose Deirdre, I haven't a clue."

"Lia Renner has to fit into the equation somehow."

She noticed him pull his eyes away from her and settle on the richly carpeted floor. He stood that way for nearly a full minute. She gathered he was trying to come to some kind of decision.

"You're right. I did lie." He looked her squarely in her face.

She parted her lips wanting to speak but then pressed them together.

"Lidia Feloni."

She frowned.

"Renner's alias. And you're right about her. She is a conniving bitch."

"Well, finally, a name." She crossed her arms. "How do you know that this Lidia person is actually Renner?"

He shrugged.

"Alright. Keep your little secret to yourself. But you are going to alert the police."

"In good time."

"What? You know who killed my husband and—"

"Shhh." Jacopo placed a finger over his lips. "Trust me. Lia Renner's going to get exactly what she deserves." He stepped closer.

Waves of anger rushed through her. *He's playing a game, and I don't like it.*

"Deep down, if you're honest with yourself, I think you're relieved your bastard of a husband is dead." He lifted a lock of her golden hair and wound it around his finger. "If it wasn't for Renner and her scheme to get your husband over here, we never would've met."

"Dino should get some credit. After all, he suggested I contact you in the first place."

"Damn Dino, too." He released the tress of blonde hair.

"Ah." She widened her eyes in understanding. "You two aren't friends. So, you did have something in common with Jon beside me. Jon hated Dino too. Probably because he and I had an affair." She was surprised that his face remained impassive. "Jon about drove me into Dino's arms with his endless brooding over his lost daughter and that *woman*. So, you're right. I'm not really sorry Jon's dead. Anyway, I chalk it up to karma dealing out payback."

"I thought as much." He took her into his arms, kissed her, and released her.

Nicole read the look of desire in his dark eyes. She decided not to keep him in suspense and moved toward the corridor that led to the bedroom. It took only a couple of seconds to realize that he wasn't following behind. She turned and glanced at him. The change in him was startling.

He stood with his head bowed and shoulders stooped. He trembled as he ran his fingers through his hair.

She folded her arms as a question jumped to her lips. Instead of asking it, she believed she already knew the answer.

He's broken up over his wife's death. And now he's feeling guilty because he'd betrayed her. With me. A sad smile touched her face. *With a little luck, I'll be able to sooth away his guilt and lessen his grief. And in the process, I'll forget about that little home-wrecking bitch, Lia Renner, ever existed. For a little while, at least.*

She cleared her throat. "Aren't you coming?"

The dazed look on his face didn't surprise her. "Of course, Nikki," he said.

"Bring the champagne with you. You are right. We do have a lot to celebrate."

Chapter Thirty-Three

THE SOFT RAPPING ON THE DOOR was loud enough to rouse Nicole from sleep. She fluttered her eyes open, patted the space next to her, and realized that Jacopo had left. She glanced at the gilt bronze mantel clock—the face read five minutes after ten—slid out of bed, and slipped into a robe. *Perhaps, Jacopo has returned*, she thought with a smile.

Nicole clicked on a light and smoothed her hair into place as she padded through the living room. She swiped her tongue across her lower lip then pulled the door open. Bernardino faced her. "Dino?" Disappointed, her voice sounded flat to her own ears. It was then she remembered how they'd left their meeting earlier in the afternoon with a hint of getting together later. "Kind of late for a visit."

"I texted several times. When you didn't answer, I got worried."

She stifled a yawn. "I turned my phone off. I was wiped out and needed to crash."

He stepped past her and walked into the suite.

"Sorry Dino, but I'm not up for company. Damn jet lag." She shrugged and offered him an apologetic smile.

He stepped close, caught her in his arms, and kissed her.

She twisted to free herself, but he held her firmly.

"Seeing you today reminded me how much I've missed you." He moved closer for another kiss, but she turned her face. He dropped his hands and slipped them into his jean pockets. "I must've jumped to the wrong conclusion. I thought you'd be happy to pick up where we left off especially since Jonathan is..."

"Dead." She shook her head.

Earlier, she'd wavered about resuming her relationship with Dino, but now she knew she'd made the right decision. Though she and Jacopo weren't exactly mourning the passing of their spouses, it was still a loss, and they had each other for support. *Not to mention, the sex isn't bad either*, she thought repressing a smile.

"I'm crazy about you."

She liked the level of fervor building in his voice.

"Crazy enough to have killed Jon so you could get back with me?" She folded her arms against the robe's silky material.

"Kill Jonathan?"

"Maybe I'll tell that detective, Marinello, to take a look at you."

"Have you lost your mind?"

She pressed her lips into a tight line and glared at him.

"Don't tell me. You're actually mourning Jonathan's death?" Bernardino took a step closer to her.

"Of course. I'm devastated. He was my husband. We shared an unbreakable bond, rooted in our love for each other."

"Love? Damn, Nicole. You need a reality check."

"How would you know?" She puffed out a stream of air. "After you moved here, Jon and I patched things up. Our marriage hadn't ever been stronger."

"The only thing you were to Jonathan was the perfect trophy wife who took the place of the one who unceremoniously dumped him. Love had nothing to do with it. After all, I heard it from the horse's mouth."

She dropped on the edge of a chair and stared at the floor. She didn't want him to see the seething in her eyes or the rage filling her face. *Jon loved me. JonlovedmeJonlovedmeJohnloved me.* She silently repeated the mantra and then took a deep breath. *If it wasn't for that damn Lia Renner ruining our marriage....* She exhaled slowly. "I don't know why you insist on degrading Jon. After all, it was *you* who betrayed him."

"It takes two to tango." A smile tugged at the corners of his mouth.

She felt the weight of his eyes as if he were appraising every inch of her.

"A couple of weeks ago," he said, "Jonathan and I had a heart to heart, in his suite in this very hotel. A couple of times we almost came to blows. Though we both agreed we'd never be friends—or even like each other, we established a truce. He admitted that he screwed up with his first marriage and though he'd talked himself into loving you, he realized that marrying you was a mistake—that is except for the birth of his sons. It was all about soothing his bruised ego. He wasn't even upset about the affair, except for the fact that you cheated with me."

He crossed the room and stopped in front of the carved marble fireplace. Cloaked mostly in shadow, he mumbled something. She strained to hear his words.

With a slow turn in her direction, he said, "Once Jonathan had his daughter safely back in the States, he was going to make a go of your marriage. Though he wasn't in love with you, he wanted the kids to have a stable home life and believed you could accomplish that."

"But what about the divorce and Lia Renner?"

Bernardino shrugged. "I guess Jonathan wanted Lia to believe he was being legit. I wouldn't be surprised if he made the call to his lawyer about starting divorce proceedings while she was listening. Because once he had Louise safely on that plane to California, he was going to drop the very idea of divorce."

"Jonathan told you that?"

"Not in so many words but ... I gathered that was his intent."

She stood and walked toward the balcony doors and looked outside. The light cast from ornate lampposts reflected off the Grand Canal. "Then I've been right all along."

"Right?" Bernardino stepped next to her.

"Lia Renner must've found out Jonathan was stringing her along. She killed my husband."

"That's absurd."

"Is it?" She spun around and faced him.

"According to Jonathan, Lia wanted to do the right thing and relinquish Louise into his care. She wanted forgiveness. Redemption."

"Forgiveness," Nicole said. "Are you kidding me? We both know she had a motive for killing Jon. What could be stronger than maternal love?"

"Like you're an expert on that. As soon as your own kids were old enough to walk, you packed them off to boarding school."

She narrowed her eyes. "I want my boys to get a good education."

"Right." He shook his head. "If anyone had a reason for wanting Jonathan dead, it's you. The way he treated you like a possession. Showing you off in public, but in private barely acknowledging you as a person, let alone his wife." He paused a second. "And I wouldn't blame you one bit."

"Me? You think I was involved in Jon's death? Well, you have a lot of nerve." A flash of anger made her head pound. "I wouldn't be a damn bit surprised if you and Lia plotted to kill my husband. The way he was murdered, she couldn't have done it on her own."

His lips slipped into a curved line that hinted at a silent threat. He stepped closer, grabbed her arms, and kissed her hard, forcing her lips open. He released her and laughed.

The sound of it chilled her.

"Since when have you become *un investigatore privato*—a private eye?" Sarcasm colored his words.

"You'd be surprised by what I know." She'd heard enough and was ready to put him in his place. She sashayed to the couch, landed on its supple fabric, and lifted a pillow. She traced her finger along its satiny pattern. Believing she'd kept him in suspense long enough, she lifted her eyes and noticed the brooding expression filling his face. "For instance, I know your precious Lia is using the alias, Lidia Feloni."

"What?"

She noticed his expression changed from swaggering confidence to anger, and then settled on bewilderment. Even though the room was dimly lit, she saw the color rise to his cheeks. "After I have a word with Marinello, it won't take him long to slap a pair of cuffs on her. Then she'll get what she deserves. Do they have the death penalty in Italy?" A slow smile crept across her face. "Now that would be sweet."

"How did you—"

"I have my sources."

Before she even acknowledged his movement, he grasped her arms and pulled her up from the couch. His face was so close to hers that all she could make out was a blur of fury. "Tell me."

Too shocked to speak, Nicole said nothing, but then he shook her. "Who told you that name?" His voice sounded like a bullhorn.

"Quit it." She found her voice.

He released her and took a few steps away. She saw that the color had intensified, flushing his cheeks though his expression now displayed a combination of contrition and stubbornness. His eyes sad, but his jaw fixed and strong.

"What kind of hold does this Lia Renner have—Jon loved her, Jacopo hates her, and you ... some kind of loyal lapdog?" Though he ignored her slur, she sensed her words had caught his interest.

He cleared his throat. "Why would Jacopo hate her?"

Bernardino's words rang in her ears sharp as barbs. She shrugged.

He paced across the room and lingered at the French doors. He turned with crossed arms and glared at her. "Jacopo told you."

"What if he did?"

"How the hell would he know that Lidia is...? He paused with a frown. "Why is Jacopo talking to you about Lidia anyway?"

"So, I'm right." She clutched her slim waist.

"She must've confided in him. God, this is a mess."

Nicole realized he was talking more to himself than to her. "What are you muttering about?"

Without another word, he strode to the door, yanked it open, and left her question hanging in the air.

Chapter Thirty-Four

LIDIA KNELT ON THE WOODEN kneeler in the chapel of the Church of San Silvestro. The main church had been closed due to major ceiling renovations since bits of plaster had been falling for years. The morning Mass had ended, but she stayed behind and now found herself alone in the cool, tiny chapel. The tall, golden curtains were drawn, and a soft glow filled the simple room. She tilted her head to the left and focused, beyond the altar, on the small, bronze crucifix. With her hands clasped, she didn't search her mind for a prayer or word, but, instead, gazed at the image of the crucified Christ.

Unaware of how much time had passed, she rose from the kneeler, sat in the pew, and freed a missal from her tote bag. *Father Busato will return to the chapel soon,* she told herself, *if only to extinguish the two candles illuminating the modest altar. And to lock the building.* She understood the church closed every day at eleven-thirty and didn't reopen until four in the afternoon.

The sound of footsteps startled Lidia. For an instant, a spark of irritation fired through her. She wanted to be alone, surrounded by the solace found in the sacred space. She pulled her sight away from the crucifix and recognized the stooped, white-haired man, scurrying toward the sanctuary. Undetected, she observed his humility as he bowed with hands folded and then climbed the three steps leading to the altar.

She edged closer toward the narrow aisle. "Padre," she whispered. A flare of anxiety caused her stomach to flip. Though she dreaded this meeting, she didn't have a choice.

He snuffed out the candles and smoothed his hand across the crisp, white altar cloth.

She raised her voice and addressed him again.

"Lidia?"

"Please, hear my confession."

He ambled from the altar, turned and bowed, and then approached her. "Come," he said gesturing to a pew near the rear of the chapel.

Once seated, Lidia crossed herself, methodically as if exaggerating the movement, to buy a couple more seconds. She had done her best to examine her conscience while alone in the church, but too many thoughts had crowded her mind—Jacopo's threat, Jonathan's death, and Oriana—who, within a few days, she would probably never see again. "Forgive me Father for I have sinned."

He sat with his eyes closed and his fingers loosely interwoven as if patiently waiting for her to recite a litany of offenses. A couple minutes ticked by, and she still hadn't said a word.

"Lidia?"

She lifted her head and looked into his face, etched with lines and filled with compassion. She sucked in a mouthful of air. "I killed Jonathan Shelby." She fell to her knees and bowed her head. She felt his hand rest lightly on her shoulder and guessed he was praying for her soul.

"You killed Jonathan Shelby?"

She looked into his confused face. "I didn't actually plunge the knife that took his life, but...." She tried to thwart the tears that had sprung to her eyes. "While he was here, Jonathan had set into motion the steps needed to begin divorce proceedings. Once that came through, he'd be seeking an annulment. His wife jumped to the conclusion that we'd reconciled." She inhaled deeply then slowly blew out the air. "My prayers were answered when he forgave me for stealing Oriana away. That's more than I could ever have hoped for. He'd even hinted that we might someday become a family again. But it wasn't definite—only a seed planted that hadn't yet sprung."

The priest nodded as if encouraging her to continue.

"I swear Father, though we had rediscovered the love we have for each other, Jonathan wasn't leaving his wife because of me. Even if she did accuse him of it. I wouldn't be surprised if she had something to do with his murder. I've racked my brain, and that's the only reason I could come up with as to why he was killed. Nicole thought I had broken up his marriage when, in reality, she had done that all by herself." She took a deep breath. "But I'm truly the guilty party. If he hadn't been in Venice.... Anyway, I took away his daughter, and now I'm responsible for his death."

"Have you discussed this with the Chief Superintendent?"

She shook her head. "I can only imagine what he'd think—that I killed Jonathan to keep Oriana to myself. The irony of it all is that in a couple of days, Oriana will be on her way to Jonathan's family in California."

"And then what? You refuse to face the authorities and continue this charade? Taking on aliases and running away like a fugitive?"

"I have no choice."

"The time has come for you to take full responsibility for your actions."

"I promise, Father, when I get to Austria, I plan to spend the rest of my days in a convent, atoning for my sins."

He offered her a thoughtful nod. "You know that I am bound by the seal of the confession and cannot disclose a word of what that you have told me. I advise you, no, I beseech you to go to the authorities. Tell them everything you know about the murder."

The walls seemed to be closing in as her heart started to pound. "I seek absolution, Father," she whispered, "but what you ask of me is impossible."

"Your anguish in relinquishing Oriana, though very real, cannot make up for years of deceit and betrayal. You denied a father his own child."

"I've done everything you've asked of me. I contacted Jonathan. Begged his forgiveness. Offered him Oriana. But, if I must spend the rest of my life in a cell, please let it be the cell of a cloister not that of a jail."

"God knows the depth of your heart and forgives your sins. He loves you, Lidia—enough to sacrifice himself for you. Now, it's your turn to sacrifice the remainder of your life for him."

She clasped her hands together. "Oh, my God, I am truly sorry for having offended you..." Each tumbling words of her act of contrition grew stronger until she said the final amen.

"Go then, my child, in peace," he said blessing her with the sign of the cross. "Your sins have been forgiven. I absolve you in the name of the Father and of the Son and of the Holy Spirit."

Chapter Thirty-Five

BETH CHOSE HER FAVORITE RESTAURANT on the island of Murano, hoping that a change of scenery would brighten her mood—as well as that of Nicole Shelby, who'd spent the morning planning for the shipment of her husband's body. She hoped the fresh, inviting atmosphere of the eatery would revive the young widow's spirits. Earlier, Shane had texted Nicole with an invitation to lunch at noon. He'd also touched base with Marinello, who offered to put Nicole in a taxi that would let her off at the restaurant's door.

Though not hungry, Beth perused the menu and considered a Caesar salad then changed her mind. She dropped the menu on top of the blocky wooden table, took a sip of wine, and gazed out through the wall of Palladian-style windows, which offered a brilliant view of the Venetian lagoon.

"I've never seen so many different types of pizza," Shane said looking over the top of his menu at her. "Like forty-eight different varieties. The one that grabbed my attention sounded simple enough—tomato sauce, mozzarella, but then—bam—French fries. There're lots of unusual toppings: asparagus, lard, walnuts, tuna... amazing."

"You're ordering pizza?"

He shook his head. "Spaghetti with clams. What about you?"

"I can't handle anything too heavy. I think the Di Bosco salad."

He glanced at his watch. "I wonder what's taking Nicole. I'm glad you suggested I make reservations. The place is filling up."

"I think she just walked in. You failed to mention that she's quite beautiful."

"Not from my point of view." Shane rose and crossed the room. "Nicole."

She noticed the easy smile that sprung to Nicole's face and the way she grabbed Shane's arm. He escorted her to their table. "Beth, this is Nicole Shelby."

"Please, call me Nikki." A quizzical look crossed her face. "Oh. My. God. Aren't you Sibéal?" Nicole didn't wait for an answer. "I only use Noelle cosmetics. They're fantastic." She glanced at Shane. "Why didn't you tell me who your wife is?"

He shrugged then pulled out a chair for her.

Nicole swiped the knife and fork off the folded square napkin in front of her and dropped the cloth onto her lap. "I could so do with one of those," she said nodding toward Beth's wineglass. "Anyway, I'm so relieved that chore is finished. Jon's body is being prepared and should arrive in California within the next two weeks. I really wanted him cremated, but that would take like forever for his ashes to arrive home. I'm certain the media will try to make Jon's funeral into a three-ring circus, but I will be planning a semi-private and tasteful memorial service. I swear to God; I'll be glad when this whole thing is behind me." She offered a half-smile in Shane's direction.

Beth pursed her lips, remembering how Shane had told her that Nicole didn't seem upset at the morgue and had even smiled after identifying her husband's corpse.

Nicole shifted her sight from Shane and looked at Beth. "Oh, Sibéal, I'm so sorry about your friend's passing."

"Thank you. And, please, call me Beth."

"Beth? Okay. Don't you think it's just plain creepy the way both were murdered exactly alike? What the hell is that mask supposed to mean?"

"That *is* a mystery," Beth said under her breath, trying not to dislike Nicole Shelby. "Shane told me that you have a sixth sense. What is your intuition telling you?"

"About the mask—nothing. But it's funny that you ask. On the ride over here, I got the strongest feeling that the murders aren't connected at all. I think Shane," she said with a quick glance in his direction, "is right. Your friend's death had nothing to do with my husband's murder. That was the singular work of a hateful woman who stole a child away from her father."

"Lia Renner," Beth said.

"Exactly."

A young server approached their table dressed in black with a long, blue apron tied around his waist. He handed Nicole a menu. "No thanks, I'm ready to order. I'd like to start with a Cinico." She looked at Beth. "Have you tried one? The drink takes Prosecco to the next level with added lime, mint, and cinnamon liqueur—it's to die for." Not waiting for Beth to respond, she finished her order, "And cuttlefish in ink sauce."

Beth couldn't believe that Nicole was waxing on about a cocktail when she should be heartbroken with grief. Her *fey* was telling her loud and clear that Nicole's smile at the morgue had unveiled her true feelings about her husband's death.

The waiter looked at Beth then Shane with questioning eyes. Shane ordered for both of them, and the server headed toward the kitchen with the order written on his pad.

"Lia Renner," Nicole said picking up where she'd left off. "That bitch. If it wasn't for her stealing Jon's daughter, he'd be happily living with me and his three children in LA." She shrugged.

A shiver ran through Beth as her *fey* issued a warning. *Nicole is lying.*

"Are you alright? You're white as a ghost." Nicole said with her eyes glued on Beth.

"Babe?" Shane reached for her hand.

Beth heard the concern in Shane's voice. She raised her glass and took a sip of the Pinot Grigio and allowed the zesty liquid to remain in her mouth for a few seconds before swallowing.

"I'm fine, darlin.' No need to fret. But Nikki, I was wondering, it was your sixth sense that suggested Lia Renner—"

"It didn't take ESP to figure that out. It's obvious. Who else had anything to gain from Jon's death? Nobody."

Beth pursed her lips, welcoming the thought that raced through her mind. *Nicole will benefit not only materially—but gain what she desires the most—freedom.*

"I trust that your husband hasn't left you in financial straits." Beth glanced at Shane who seemed attentive as he fingered the cleft in his chin.

"My husband was a stickler for planning, especially for the future. Not only did he set up trust funds for our two sons, he also had one for his daughter, Louise. Too bad she'll never benefit from it. Well, unless the poor girl is located somewhere in this tourist-trap of a city." Nicole glanced away as the waiter placed the glass of Prosecco next to her plate. She raised the glass and took a quick sip. "He had a gigantic life insurance policy, and of course, there're savings, the houses ... my family will be able to continue living the lifestyle we're accustomed to. Jon made sure of that." She paused a second. "I'm starving. What's taking so long with the food?"

Shane ignored her question and posed one of his own. "How is it that you're so sure Lia Renner was not sincere about relinquishing her daughter? Isn't that the reason your husband traveled to Venice in the first place?"

Nicole ran a long, tapered finger around the rim of her cut glass tumbler. "Tell me, former Detective Dalton; would you trust a woman who kidnapped a child and hid out for over ten years? Renner dangled a carrot in front of his eyes and lured him over here with the sole purpose of having him murdered."

Shane frowned. "You think Renner hired someone to do the job."

"A woman would use a simpler, but just as deadly, method to commit murder. Poison, perhaps. Don't you agree, Beth?"

In a flash, Beth recalled how, only a few short weeks ago, a masquerading murderer had concocted a deadly cocktail of poison that had almost stolen her own life. "Poison, well, yes, a possibility. But my *fey*, my sixth sense, is telling me that two individuals worked together to kill your husband."

Nicole drew her eyebrows together. "Two people strangled and knifed him? Do you have any idea who the killers are?"

She wanted to point her finger at Nicole and announce that she'd been the mastermind behind her husband's death. But, in reality, she hadn't an inkling as to who had killed Jonathan Shelby or Deidre. She looked at Nicole and noticed that the woman had chewed off her lipstick. "Really, I have no idea."

An audible sigh escaped Nicole's lips.

"Too bad the original suspect was crossed off the list." Shane drained the last mouthful of his beer. "Lorenzo Caravello."

"Suspect?" Nicole frowned. "Why didn't Marinello tell me there was a suspect?"

"Probably didn't see the need to get your hopes up, only to have to disappoint you. I'm sure he'll notify you when there's been an arrest that sticks."

"He better," Nicole said. "I've decided to stay in Venice for a few more days. Though I'm not fond of the city, you can't deny there's some wonderful shopping to be done here. Plus, the food is good. Speaking of which, our lunch," she said nudging out her chin in the direction of the waiter, "it's finally here."

BETH LEANED AGAINST SHANE on the *vaporetto* Water Bus Line 4.2 as they departed Murano and headed back to Venice. She'd remained silent, absorbed with her thoughts regarding Nicole Shelby. It hadn't taken her long to conclude that Shane had been right about her. Nicole definitely wasn't mourning her husband's death. The conversation during the meal had focused on Nicole's dislike of Venice, her summer plans for her children once they return home from boarding school, and a gala she was organizing to support the endangered sea green turtle. All talk swirled around Nicole and her activities. It was as if Jonathan Shelby never existed.

"How are you doing?" Shane asked.

She sat up straight and looked at him. "I think Nicole is responsible for her husband's death." She couldn't read any expression on his face but sensed he didn't agree.

"How'd you come up with that?"

Beth sucked in her lower lip and silently counted to ten. He'd scoff if she told him it was because she didn't like Nicole or the way she looked at him. *Good Lord, could it be that I'm jealous? Of Nicole Shelby?* She shook her head. *My Shane wouldn't give her the time of day. Would he?* She chewed her lip.

"Beth?"

"Sorry, darlin.' I'm finding myself a wee bit distracted. But, getting back to Nicole, something about her doesn't sit right with me," she said. "She seems angry about her husband's death, but not really broken up about it. I think she's kind of pleased that he's dead."

"Even if that's true, it doesn't make her a murderer."

She was about to refute him but caught sight of the island of the dead through the window. "San Michele."

Shane twisted, looked through the window over her shoulder, and sighed. "That's one place I never thought I'd be visiting during our honeymoon." He grabbed Beth's hand and squeezed it.

"Tomorrow I'll start working on Deirdre's funeral arrangements. But first, I think I'll drop by that mask store around the corner from us."

"Why?"

"Maybe learn a little more about *Bauta* masks."

"Look, I know you want to understand why this horrible thing happened to Deirdre. But stop torturing yourself trying to make sense out of the senseless. Marinello has his work cut out for him, but it's his job, not yours or mine."

"You're probably right. Carmel will be arriving tomorrow evening, so I guess I should concentrate on consoling the brokenhearted, except that's a bit hard when your own heart is broken too." She nestled next to him and closed her eyes.

Chapter Thirty-Six

LIDIA BREATHED RELIEF WHEN she opened the door. The insistent knocking that woke her from a fitful sleep had sent her into a tizzy, believing Jacopo had returned. Instead, Bernardino stood there, but it took only a second to sense something was wrong.

"It's urgent, Lia; let me in."

Though he'd spoken only a hair louder than a whisper, she cringed when he said her real name. She took his arm and led him into the living room.

"Is Oriana around?"

"She's spending the night with Chiara. A sleepover to celebrate the end of the school term."

"Good," Bernardino said with a curt nod. He placed his hands on her shoulders and looked directly into her eyes. "You need to leave Venice immediately. There's no time to lose."

His words told her the worst had happened. Her stomach twisted, and her throat went dry.

"You don't have to worry about money. I'll give you as much as you need to hightail it out of here." A tone of urgency filled his voice.

A sharp jab of pain shot through her temple, causing her to lose her breath. With it rose a terrifying fear that forced Lidia to realize that she'd waited too long to act. Her plan of escape had been irretrievably foiled. She hadn't even received her new passport—her main vehicle of introduction to her new life.

"Let's get you packed." Bernardino's words startled her. He headed toward the narrow hallway leading to her bedroom.

She grabbed his arm. "What about Oriana? I can't leave her."

"You don't have a choice. Understand?"

"What's happened?" Her eyes pleaded for him to explain.

"That bastard, Jacopo. He told Nicole Shelby your true identity. Nicole is adamant. She's going to reveal your secret to Marinello."

Her heart sunk, realizing that Jacopo had made good on his promise. *I've been so careful. How did he figure out I'm Lia Renner?* She frowned. "How in God's name did Jacopo find out?"

He shrugged.

"I've never breathed a word to him." She shot an accusing glance at Bernardino.

"Don't look at me."

"Well, then how?"

"*Accidenti*," Bernardino cursed under his breath. "Can't be...."

"Tell me."

"Dammit." He raked his fingers through his wavy hair. "I don't know how you feel about Nicole Shelby, but over the years, the two of us became close. She sensed Jonathan had become tired of her, and then he blindsided Nicole with news he was divorcing her."

Lidia kept her lips clamped into a tight line.

"Nicole suspected that he wanted to resume his relationship with you. She became desperate to talk him out of it. When she was planning to come here, I hooked her up with Jacopo to make all the travel plans. Turns out, the two of them became chummy over the phone. Maybe she asked Jacopo if he knew Lia Renner. Hell, for all I know, she could've texted him a photo of you. And if she did that—"

"Then Jacopo has known my true identity for weeks."

"It's a possibility."

"A strong possibility." Lidia took a few steps then sunk onto the edge of the ragged couch. She buried her face in her hands.

"There's no need to panic," Bernardino said. "You've pulled this disappearing act for years." He paused a moment. "Look, I'll take care of Oriana. I'll tell her you had an emergency—that you'll be back in a couple of days. Then, in a week or two, I'll tell Oriana the truth and take her to you."

"She'll have to come with me. Now." Lidia freed her face.

"That would only reinforce the fact that you killed Shelby because of Oriana. Leaving her behind will help quash that lie."

She paced across the dingy room trying to calm her trembling dread. "I loved Jonathan. The guilt I suffered because I stole Oriana away from him nearly caused me to lose my mind. I fell into deep depression. Thought about killing myself. But Oriana came first. She always comes first."

He pulled out his cellphone. "I'm going to make the plane reservation. Where to?"

"Klagenfurt. Austria." She watched as he scrolled down on his phone's screen. When he began tapping, she placed her hand on top of his. "No, Dino." The decision had come in a split second. She was tired of running away. "I'll go to the *Questura*. Explain everything to the *Commissario Capo*."

"You can't do that. No."

"I don't have a choice."

"Marinello won't listen to reason. All of Venice is clamoring for an arrest. He'll have no alternative but to take you into custody. Then what will happen to Oriana?"

"You said you'd watch over her." Lidia moved closer to him but stopped at an end table. She lifted her purse, unzipped a pocket, and removed an envelope. "Oriana's plane ticket to California." She handed him the ticket. "Make sure she gets on the plane."

He crossed his arms.

"Please, Dino. Please. Protect my little girl. I don't care what happens to me, but my daughter is innocent." The thought of losing Oriana forever pierced her heart.

Bernardino took the envelope and withdrew the plane ticket. He folded it in half and stuck the ticket into the back pocket of his jeans.

"Thank you," she whispered.

"Even though you may not care what happens to you, I do. I'm going with you to see Marinello. I'm ready to confess my role in this whole deception."

Chapter Thirty-Seven

LIDIA PACED THE LENGTH of the living room, her feet skimming across the thin carpet. She'd been awake most of the night, ever since Dino dropped the bombshell that Nicole Shelby knew her true identity. But as the sun rose, she decided to come clean—and tell Oriana the whole story. An unexpected sense of peace settled her nerves with the resolution of finally revealing the entire, unvarnished, self-serving tale.

More times than she could remember, Oriana had begged her to explain. Why were they always on the move, changing their identities, keeping secrets? Lidia sighed. *But, would I tell her? No.* She glanced at the cellphone in her hand. Not wanting to make her daughter suspicious, Lidia had texted Oriana with the pretext of a breakfast date at a nearby eatery. She paused by her purse, dropped the phone inside, and continued pacing in anticipation of Oriana's arrival.

She spun around when the apartment door opened.

Oriana's exuberant voice filled the room. Lidia didn't listen to the words but only to the sweet tone, which warmed her heart. "Sit with me. I want to talk to you." She dropped onto the settee and patted the spot next to her.

"What about breakfast? I'm starved."

Lidia wanted to pull her daughter into her arms and tell her how much she loved her. That everything, no matter how despicable, had been done out of love for her. Instead, she patted the cushion again.

Oriana bounded to the couch and plopped down next to her mother. "Chiara is so mad. Dottoressa Barozzi is sending Chiara to her grandmother's in Padua for the summer. No more Antonio. Or any other boy. Her *nonna* has eyes like an eagle. Because of that, she won't be able to go with me to California." She sighed. "We would've had the best time, but I guess the most important thing is that I'll be with Papà. Finally."

"That's what I want to discuss with you."

Oriana's face clouded. "The trip's been canceled?"

"No, nothing like that. But, before you leave tomorrow, there's something I need to tell you. It's high time you know the truth." Lidia read the puzzled look that crossed her daughter's face. "About Papà and me." She smiled, trying to lighten the mood as she brushed a few stray hairs off Oriana's forehead. "As you already know, Papà and I met when I was earning my engineering degree in California."

Oriana nodded.

"He was in law school then. As soon as he passed the bar, we were married, and then you were born. He was so happy. You were the joy of his life, and that's why he gave you a pet name." Lidia paused a second. "Gemma."

"Gemma?" Oriana's eyes grew big.

She sensed that Oriana was about to make the connection but rushed ahead with her unscripted discourse. "We were a happy little family. I'd gotten a job at a top design firm, and your papà—back then you called him daddy—doted on you. But he was busy starting his own career, and I fell into a deep depression. Nothing Papà tried could snap me out of it. Then I made the biggest mistake of my life. I told him I didn't want to be married anymore. I left him." She touched Oriana's hand. It felt cold. "I left him—and you." A rush of dread clutched her. She feared she wouldn't be able to continue.

"Mamma?"

"I bought a ticket, determined to fly home to Italy, but then I started to feel more like myself. I tried to patch things up with your papà, but I'd hurt him too deeply." Tears welled behind her eyes. She blinked a couple of times, forcing herself to be strong—to accept the consequence of her long-ago folly. "He filed for a divorce. At the time, I thought he was being cruel. Spiteful. Keeping you away from me. I feared I'd lose you forever. But one day, Papà allowed me to take you for the afternoon, for a picnic in the park, but instead, we went to the airport. I've been running ever since."

"You kidnapped me," Oriana whispered.

"I did. Yes."

"I don't understand."

"I can offer all kinds of excuses. I've been telling them to myself for years. The bottom line is—I was wrong. Terribly wrong. Your papà never stopped searching for you."

Oriana opened her mouth as if to speak, but then she snapped it closed. Lidia reached for Oriana's hand, but this time, she snatched it away.

"I finally came to my senses." Lidia's words tumbled on top of each other. "I contacted Papà. We talked and texted for months. I begged his forgiveness, and I offered to give you back to him."

"Is this what the trip is about? You giving me back to him? Like I'm some kind of possession to be traded back and forth."

"Of course not," Lidia said. "We love you."

"Love?" Oriana muttered the word.

"Your papà came here last month. Though you didn't realize it, he'd spend time following you, cherishing every glimpse he got of you. Smart and beautiful. That's what he kept saying. He was so proud—"

"He spied on me?"

"I thought it'd be too big of a shock—I wanted to ease you into the idea of meeting your Papà—after you knew the truth."

"How could you've lied for so long?"

Lidia let Oriana's question hang in the air. "It was the truth when I told you that Papà and I worked things out. There was plenty of tears and apologies. In the end, we realized that after all the misunderstandings and lost years, we still loved each other. It was like a miracle." A sad smile crossed Lidia's face. "We came up with a plan. You'd spend the summer with him, and then I would join you. Hopefully, if everything turned out well, we'd work on becoming a family again." She looked at Oriana. Her face was set like flint.

"Why didn't you tell me the truth sooner?"

"At first, I thought you were too young to understand, and then as the years passed, I guess I couldn't bear for you to know how cruel I'd been to your father ... and to you."

"You had me believing that Papà didn't care a whit about me? What kind of mother does that?"

Lidia bit her lip, knowing she had no answer for Oriana. She couldn't even explain it to herself.

"And now all of that is forgotten in one big, happy family reunion?"Oriana flung out her hands as if in exasperation.

"No. No happy ending. No family reunion."

Oriana narrowed her eyes.

"We named you Louise. Louise Anne Shelby."

"Shelby?"

"Jonathan Shelby—"

"No. NoNoNo. Don't tell me the dead man in the canal was my father."

Lidia's heart broke. She ached to comfort Oriana, cradle her baby in her arms, and whisper soft words of consolation in her ear. Instead, she said, "It's my fault your papà is dead."

A strangled yelp died in Oriana's throat as she rocked with her arms clasped across her chest.

"Even though we named you Louise," Lidia said wanting her to understand, "I decided to call you Oriana because you were like the sunrise, offering me a new day. A fresh beginning."

"How did that work for you? With us running like fugitives from one end of the country to the other. How could you be so selfish?"

Oriana's voice rung accusingly in Lidia's ears. She hung her head. Never had she seen such a look of betrayal on her daughter's face. "I pray to God that one day you will be able to forgive me."

"I have to get out of here." Oriana jumped up from the sofa and hurried across the room. Lidia flinched, as if she'd been slapped, as the apartment door slammed shut.

Chapter Thirty-Eight

JACOPO PULLED HIS CHAIR CLOSER to the Chief Superintendent's desk. Earlier that morning, he'd walked aimlessly with his mind in a fog. When he finally stopped, he realized he'd traversed the city and stood adjacent to the police headquarters. He took it as a sign. But now, facing Marinello, he wasn't sure.

"Why are you here? Lorenzo Caravello has been released. He recanted his confession."

"I know," Jacopo said with a nod. "Do you believe him?"

"He's still a suspect. We just don't have enough to hold him—yet."

"Lorenzo is a thief—but not the murderer of the American tourist. I know who committed that crime."

Marinello leaned forward.

Determined to pin the murder on the woman he'd foolishly believed deserved to be his wife, a twinge of regret caused him to reconsider ... for only a couple of seconds. He blew out a stream of air. "My assistant."

"What? Rosa—a killer. Are you mad? She's a cousin of mine and won't even kill a damn mosquito."

"Not Rosa. My personal assistant, Lidia Feloni."

Marinello pursed his lips, rested back in his chair, and crossed his arms. "That's a wild accusation. How'd you come up with it?"

Jacopo wasn't surprised by his reaction. Anyone who'd met Lidia would consider her an angel instead of the devil dwelling deep beneath a beautiful façade. "She was once Shelby's wife—the one who kidnapped their kid."

Marinello stared at him. Seconds ticked by and still no reaction. Jacopo started to wonder if he'd known all along and had scratched Lidia

209

off his suspect list. If that were true, he'd have to do a whole lot of talking to persuade Marinello to again aim his target on her. He couldn't risk not convincing Marinello because that would thwart his all-consuming desire to see Lidia suffer. *If I'm successful,* he gloated, *she'll not only lose her damn daughter that started this whole charade; she'll lose her freedom, as well.* A smile tugged at the corners of his lips.

"How do you know about the kidnapping?"

He offered Marinello his opened palms. "I found out through Deirdre's friend, Sibéal... Beth Getty. Her husband has connections with the Los Angeles police and the murdered man's wife."

"*Accidenti,*" Marinello cursed under his breath. "So, if what you say is true, why do you suspect she'd want to kill him?"

"She slipped up. Told me that she'd been spending time with Shelby during his stay in Venice. That they were friends." He tried to gauge Marinello's reaction, but his face revealed nothing. "I think Shelby probably let his guard down and then she ... killed him ... or hired someone to do the job," Jacopo said with a shrug.

"If she was the ex-wife who kidnapped his child, why in heaven's name would he trust her?"

"She has a way of bewitching men." Jacopo tried not to scowl but failed. "Look at the facts. Lidia has no family except her daughter, who happens to be the same age as the kidnapped girl. She's worked for me, close to three years, and still, I know next to nothing about her. Lidia has no friends well, except for that overbearing Bernardino Moro, who no doubt, forced himself into her affections ... she probably didn't have the good sense to tell him to get lost. Anyway, she keeps to herself and spends most evenings at a convent. If that doesn't make her seem guilty as sin, I don't know what will. Not to mention her mental illness."

"Mental illness?" Marinello raised his eyebrows.

"Suffers from bouts of depression. Has headaches. So bad, she's missed more days from work than I like to remember. I'd describe her as unstable."

"Then why didn't you fire her?"

"Can I help it if I have compassion? How could I throw her out on the street when she has a daughter to care for?"

Marinello glanced at the ceiling then looked directly at Jacopo. "It's not unusual to be a single parent. Hordes of people suffer depression and headaches, and they don't come up with elaborate murder schemes. Anyway, I've only heard good things about her kindness toward the Sisters of Santa Angela de Merici. You still haven't answered my question. Why would Lidia Feloni want to murder her former husband?"

"It's obvious," Jacopo said. "She wishes to keep Oriana for herself."

"What's really going on here? As far as I see it, Lidia Feloni is above reproach."

"Trust me, Daniele. She killed that man." He swept his tongue across his bottom lip. "I wouldn't be a damn bit surprised if Dino had a hand in it too. Look, why don't you come over to the Travel Bureau. Check out her computer. You might find some interesting items there." He sensed that the commissioner was weighing the value of his words. "Oh, and about Lorenzo. You know that he's like a son to me, and I'd fight tooth and nail to save his butt." Jacopo jumped up and began pacing. He crossed the office twice then stopped at the far end of the room. "This about breaks my heart to say … but I wouldn't be surprised if he *did* kill Deidre. My wife, may God rest her soul," he said crossing himself, "despised Lorenzo. She was jealous of the time I spent with him and told Lorenzo as much. The canal murder may have sparked his imagination—not just to turn a young lady's head—but as the perfect opportunity to remove Deirdre from our lives. So that our relationship could return to the way it was before I married. You may be looking for two different Carnival Mask Killers. Shame that it is," he said with another but louder sigh, "I wouldn't overlook Lidia or Lorenzo." He rose and stepped closer to Marinello's desk. "I've wrestled with the necessity of sharing this information with you, but deep down, I just couldn't neglect my civic duty."

"No one would ever accuse you of not being a conscientious citizen."

"*Grazie*, Daniele, *grazie*." Ready to exit the office, Jacopo reached for Marinello's hand and shook it. He took a few steps toward the door.

"Hold up, Jacopo."

He turned and faced Marinello.

"I have a few questions concerning your wife."

"Oh?" Jacopo narrowed his eyes. "I've already told you everything."

"You two had a disagreement. Then Deirdre left the house around eight pm. Correct?"

"Yes, but I've already—"

"I have the autopsy report. Your wife died from an epidural hematoma. Brain injury."

Jacopo hung his head, trying to work up a sense of grief. A few tears would do the trick, but his eyes refused to water.

"Deirdre smacked her temple against a sharp object. The curious thing is that there're bruises on her arms as if she'd been violently grabbed and perhaps slammed into the article that caused her injury. In addition, there are contusions on the back of her head and lower extremities."

"What does that have to do with me?" Though his words held a sharp edge he sensed the strength of his natural bravado weakening. He raised his head and looked Marinello straight in the eyes. It seemed as if Marinello could see into his very soul.

"That fight between you and Deirdre ... was it physical?"

"What are you implying? That I battered my wife? I swear to God, I never ever laid a hand against her."

"I only bring it up because the first victim's cause of death was strangulation, but unlike him, Deirdre was beaten to death."

Jacopo felt his knees give out as he sunk into the visitor's chair. He hid his face in trembling hands. Now he didn't have to fake emotions as Marinello's words rang in his ears. *Beaten to death. No. NoNoNoNoNo. That's wrong. It was an accident. I didn't mean to...*

"I know this is difficult to hear," Marinello said. "But, at this point, we can't rule out anybody. Including you."

He dropped his hands. "What the hell? How can you even imagine that I'd have something to do with Deirdre's death? I adored her. She's the mother of my children. We were building a life together that only death ended." He shot up and pointed a finger at Marinello. "I want you to find her killer. Stop judging the innocent and laying blame where it doesn't belong. I told you who to look at—two people I trusted above all others— who betrayed me." Tears now easily welled in his eyes and trickled down his face.

"Then you'd have no objection to a polygraph."

"Polygraph?"

"A lie detector test. It'll clear you of all suspicion."

Beads of sweat broke out on Jacopo's forehead. He chewed his lip, trying to think, but his brain failed to work. He muttered a protest under his breath, needing to end the deafening silence between them.

"What? Speak up," Marinello said.

He swallowed hard, trying to lubricate his throat that had gone dry. "Of course, Daniele. That will be fine. The lie detector will prove that I have nothing to hide." He glanced at his watch. "I've got to get to the Travel Bureau. Let me know about the ... the—"

"Polygraph?"

"Yes." Jacopo turned and hurried out of the office.

Marinello withdrew a cigar from the box and gently squeezed up and down its smooth body, inspecting its construction. "What the hell is Jacopo up to?" He reached into a drawer and grabbed his cigar cutter. *Trying to blame the murder on Lidia... and his about-face regarding Caravello doesn't make much sense. But what does make a hell of a lot of sense is that within twenty-four hours of releasing Caravello another canal murder took place. Which in my book is beyond suspicious.*

He cut off the end of the cigar, stuck the Havana between his lips, and struck a match. He took a puff and rolled the cigar ash against the edge of the marble ashtray, but instead of raising it to his lips, he rested it in the repository. He stared at the thread of blue smoke rising in the air.

I'll send an officer to bring him in for questioning. A few more days behind bars might give us enough time to collect evidence proving that Caravello is the culprit responsible for the murders. He crossed his arms. *A really dumb move killing another victim right after being released from jail. But then, Lorenzo Caravello has never been known for his intelligence.*

He stood and paced to the far side of his office. *Couldn't hurt questioning Lidia Feloni too. Except, it'd probably be a huge waste of time.* "Dammit," he said raking his fingers through his hair. *Jacopo's polygraph should be interesting. It's obvious he didn't want to cooperate but if he's innocent what's the big deal? But what if he is right about Lidia—could she be Lia Renner?*

He walked back to his desk, pulled out the center drawer, and withdrew the photograph Nicole Shelby had given him of the mystery woman. He started at the dark-haired beauty. "I guess it could be Lidia," he muttered. He dropped the photo onto his desk and resumed pacing. "Elena." He snapped his fingers.

She knows Lidia. Chiara and Oriana are friends. I'll get her take on Jacopo's accusation. Plus, it'll give me an excuse to take her out to lunch. He grabbed his jacket from the hook on the back of the door and dashed out of the office.

Chapter Thirty-Nine

BETH HURRIED DOWN THE NARROW lane toward the tiny store that captivated her imagination. *Casa della Maschera*. House of the Mask. Several times during her jaunts around the city, she'd paused in front of its window, which boasted a variety of handmade Carnival masks. Their exquisite details fashioned from paint, gold leaf, lace, and feathers assured her that these masks were a cut above others she'd seen displayed around Venice.

She pushed opened the door, and a bell tinkled above her as she stepped inside and turned around, overwhelmed by the number of masks that lined the red velvet walls. Every inch was covered except for a doorway that gaped like a black hole. It stood among a riot of shapes—humanoid, animalistic, and fantastical heavenly bodies that combined sun, moon, and stars, all adorned with vibrant, electrifying colors.

A young woman stepped through the aperture. "Welcome to my shop. May I help you?" Her voice, rich and warm, was tinted with a heavy accent. She gestured to the nearest display with a latex-gloved hand. "We have a wide selection."

Besides the gloved hands, it was obvious that she'd been working in the back room, since a paint-spattered apron was tied around her waist.

Beth decided it might be easier to communicate if she addressed the woman in Italian. "*Buongiorno. Le tue maschere sono fantastiche.* Are you the artist?"

"You speak Italian." A relieved look crossed the woman's face. "Yes. All of these are my creations."

Beth detected the hint of a proud smile playing at the corners of the mask-maker's mouth. She guessed that the woman was about her age. Perhaps a bit younger. Twenty-five, probably.

"I was wondering about the Bauta."

"Ah. The mask that protects those who wear it from other people's eyes. Its heyday was during the 17th and 18th centuries when the mask and costume could be worn outside of the weeks reserved for Carnival. It was used most effectively by both men and women to conceal their identities."

Beth nodded urging her to continue.

"A woman wearing a Bauta could enter a casino and play cards. While a man could have a love affair while hiding his true self. Like Casanova was rumored to do. Actually, the Bauta is also called the Casanova mask."

The woman gestured to a collection of Bauta style masks, elaborately decorated with shiny acrylic paints, raised stucco relief covered with gold leaf, and snippets of musical notes decoupage. Though striking, Beth was interested in the traditional mask, like the ones glued onto the faces of Deirdre and Jonathan Shelby.

"Do you sell the plain white ones?"

"Of course. I sell quite a few of those. Especially, though sadly, since the murders."

"Oh?" Beth's hope of discovering the killer's identity plummeted.

"I was about to begin one when you entered the shop. Would you like to see?"

Beth perked up. Maybe the killer didn't purchase the masks after all, but made them. "I'd love to," she said following the artisan into her workshop.

The space was almost as large at the store. A wall of shelves held molds and unadorned masks waiting to be decorated. Beth stepped next to a long table protected by an oilcloth that hung so low, it almost touched the scuffed wooden floor. A container filled with a white, watery paste stood next to a paintbrush and a plaster block.

"This is the Bauta mold." The mask-maker flipped the block over. "See, it's a negative form. The first step is *cartapesta*."

Beth frowned not recognizing the word.

"Papiér mâché?"

"Sì," Beth said with a nod.

She watched the experienced hands brush the paste onto a sheet of thick, gray paper, tear off a generous piece, and press it inside the mold. The process was repeated until the entire form was covered.

"After several layers are applied and dried, I'll wiggle it free, tear off the excess paper, and paint the mask white. Then I'll add the finishing touch; fasten black ties through tiny holes on the sides of the mask. All in all, a fairly simple process. The other masks require much more expertise."

Beth nodded as she glanced at one of the shelves stocked with the finished products. She moved away from the worktable after catching a glimpse of a half-mask. A cat half-mask. She reached out to touch it but paused. "Do you mind?" she asked the young woman.

"Ah! You like cats."

Beth nodded.

The woman moved next to her, freed the mask from the shelf, and handed it to Beth. "Cat masks are very important in Venice. Because of our long history."

"Why is that?"

"Centuries ago, the city suffered from plagues brought by rats that scurried off the vast convoys of merchant ships that docked in the lagoon. Because of that, every household made sure to have at least one cat to kill the disease-bearing rodents. To this day, we believe that cats protect the safety of our homes."

"I have to buy one," Beth said. "I know a little girl whose mother just surprised her with a family of kittens. She'll love one of your beautiful cat masks."

Beth smiled, recalling the surprised look on Emma's face when she'd brought one of the kittens to Baltimore. Emma, the young daughter of her friend, Skye, had suffered a terrible trauma, and Beth thought a furry companion would help soothe the child's troubled spirit. Emma immediately bonded with the fluffy white kitten and, no doubt, was waiting in anticipation to be united with the litter on her return home—when Skye finished the film—but with the recent problems on the set, she wondered if there would be a delay. *But no matter, the kittens will be waiting for Emma at the Cute Cat Rescue whenever they return to Los Angeles.* "The mask will be a wonderful welcome home gift for Emma," she said under her breath.

After going back and forth between at least a dozen masks, she finally made her selection. A gold one with a harlequin design painted black, red, green, and orange. *The wee slip of a lass is going to love this*, Beth thought. She placed the mask, which the artisan had gingerly enveloped in bubble wrap and neatly covered with a sheet of shiny silver wrapping paper, into her oversized tote bag.

It took only an instant for her pleased feeling to dissolve. *Unless the killer is a mask- maker, he couldn't have fashioned the quality masks that had glinted in the water of the murky canals. And now with the newfound notoriety of the Bauta, it'll be next to impossible to determine who might've purchased those two masks.*

She checked her watch. Her appointment with the pastor of *San Nicolò dei Mendicoli* was less than a half-hour away. They were slated to discuss possible options for the funeral—details that she would later share with Carmel upon her arrival in Venice. She imagined the meeting would be short, leaving her plenty of time to stop by Jacopo's house to select an outfit to give to the funeral director. Beth had wondered if the casket would be closed but had been assured that the undertaker's talent in presenting a lifeless corpse, even one with a broken body, was exceptional.

She dreaded the morbid task. The idea of rummaging through Deirdre's clothing watered her eyes, but Beth knew this wasn't the time for giving in to her emotions. Particularly since Jacopo refused to assist with any of the funeral arrangements. He had told her several times that he had no choice but to swallow his grief and focus all his energy on writing Deirdre's eulogy ... and running the Travel Bureau.

She pulled out her mobile and pressed the speed dial number for the taxi service she'd saved into her phone. It took only a moment to reserve a taxi. By the time she'd drop the cat mask off at the flat, the private-hired boat would be waiting at the steps leading from their little *campo* to the canal.

The staccato beat of her heels striking the stone pavement filled the narrow lane as she raced against the clock. She sighed audible relief as the *campo,* which abutted the building that housed their flat, came into sight. She picked up speed, aiming for the building's entrance when, from out of nowhere, a chill prickled her skin. She almost tripped over her feet to stop. With measured steps, she moved into a shadow cast from a building that showed more brick than stucco and took a deep breath. The briny air filled her nostrils as she attempted to banish all thoughts—to make her mind a blank slate—on which her *fey* could write its message. Though she tried to relax and listen to her inner voice, all she heard was the sound of her own heartbeat.

Unsure of how many minutes she'd stood transfixed in hope of receiving insight from her sixth sense, Beth reluctantly pulled her mind back to her list of chores. She clutched the tote bag to her chest and continued the mad dash across the square. The word rang out so loudly, she thought someone had yelled at her. She slowed her gait and glanced over her shoulder. No one was there. It was then she realized her *fey* had spoken.

Beware.

Chapter Forty

MARINELLO WAITED IN THE HOLE-IN-THE-WALL tavern near the Rialto market. The place had been in business since the mid-fifteenth century when it offered hospitality to both aristocrats and gondoliers with the opportunity to chat, drink a glass of wine, and engage in a game of cards. He liked the spare simplicity of the place—the plaster walls, wood floors, and heavy beamed ceiling—but especially the sense of continuity that intertwined the distant past with the here and now. But, like all things in Venice, tourists had discovered the *osteria*, not so much for its staid ambiance but rather for its delectable dishes. He took a sip of wine and wondered what was holding up Elena.

He replaced the glass on the age-worn table, looked around the small room, and noticed it was already filling up. A few faces he recognized and offered a friendly nod, but the bulk of people flooding into the room didn't belong—they lacked a bond, a lineage to the place. They were interlopers, gawkers ... tourists. Usually, they didn't bother him. Like every other Venetian, he realized that tourists were the city's lifeblood. No matter how much he despised that fact, there'd be no Venice without them, with their polyglot of languages, cellphones snapping photos, and money—especially their money—euros, pounds, yuan, dollars, yens, rubles, riyals. He lifted his glass and drained it.

Though tourists are always welcomed, murder isn't. He couldn't recall a recent murder except for the case of the young Iranian fashion designer whose body was found stuffed in a suitcase floating in the lagoon. *But she was killed in Milan, and her body was dumped here. And that incident happened more than five years ago.*

He glanced at his watch then tapped the scuffed wooden tabletop with his fingertips. After a minute, he opened the menu and perused the selections, even though he already knew what he was going to order.

An image of Nicole Shelby burst into his mind. Instinctively, he made a face as if he'd tasted something foul. His gut had told him she was feigning grief when he and Dalton had questioned her in the lobby of the Hotel Gritti Palace. And then that wisp of a smile after she identified her husband's body.

He resumed tapping his fingers as he tried to quiet the thoughts tumbling through his overburdened brain. Though he tried, he couldn't blot out the fiasco at the funeral home. That performance shined a blinding spotlight on the authentic character of the young widow. Sharp words and anger exploded as she argued then tried to bully the funeral director to cremate her husband's remains.

Luckily, I was able to soften her words through the translation, but the elderly undertaker, a true gentleman, I fear, saw through my efforts. He recalled that her first attempt was to use her femininity, and when that failed, she spat demands. Still getting nowhere, she whined like a spoiled child. *She carries more than a chip on those shapely shoulders ... a giant boulder camps out there. Thank God she finally, with an angry smirk, agreed to ship the body back to California.*

Determined to forget about the demanding American woman—at least for the time being—he shifted his thoughts to Elena. Even if he'd wanted to, Marinello couldn't prevent the corners of his lips from turning upward. Then he remembered the reason for their lunch, and the hint of a smile faded. Lidia Feloni. He didn't know Lidia personally, but word of her charity toward the Sisters of Santa Angela de Merici wasn't a secret. Though most of the sisters suffered the ravages of age, the fervor of their prayers hadn't waned, and their generous hearts to the people of Venice, no doubt, had inspired Lidia Feloni to come to their aid. He frowned wondering why Jacopo had insisted that she was the Canal Murderer.

"What's wrong?"

Marinello snapped out of his reverie. He jumped up, kissed Elena's cheeks, and pulled out a chair for her. He recognized the concern clouding her eyes even if she tried to hide it with a wan smile. "Nothing's wrong. It's just work," he said.

"I hope you haven't been waiting long," Elena said. "I had to run a few errands and then bumped into one of my patients. The mother of a toddler who is keeping her on her toes." Though Elena lifted a menu, he noticed that she kept her sight focused on him. "I'm getting a feeling this lunch is more than just sharing a meal."

"There is something I need to discuss with you."

The waitress approached their table. "Are you ready to order?"

He handed his menu to the waitress but waited for Elena to order. She asked for the sea bass. Marinello added two glasses of Prosecco and an entree of potato gnocchi with meat sauce. Once the server turned her back to them, he cleared his throat. "Elena—"

"It's about the murders, isn't it?"

He folded his hands on the table. "How well do you know Lidia Feloni?"

"Lidia? Why do you ask?"

"Just wondering."

"Well," she said with a shake of her head, "unlike our daughters, we're not especially close. It's obvious she's beautiful, but that beauty isn't just skin deep. She's assisted the Ursuline Sisters for years. Lidia helps bathe them, prepares meals, prays with them." She paused as the server placed the wineglasses on the table. "I know she gets terrible headaches and that Oriana worries a great deal about her. Oh, and she works for Jacopo da Parma."

He stroked his jaw. Elena hadn't told him anything he didn't already know.

"You don't think Lidia has something to do with the murders?"

"Well, there's a possibility—"

"That's the most ridiculous thing I've ever heard." She lifted her glass and took a sip.

"I agree with you. It just that," he said extending his opened palm toward her, "Jacopo stopped by the office this morning with quite a tale. He swears that Lidia is the canal victim's ex-wife. Not only that, apparently, she kidnapped Oriana years ago and fled to Italy. When Shelby arrived in Venice, to reclaim his daughter, Lidia killed him."

Elena's mouth fell open. After a silent moment, she said, "Why is Jacopo blabbering about Lidia Feloni when his own wife's body lays stone-cold dead in the morgue? Shouldn't he be comforting his children and planning Deirdre's funeral instead of playing detective?"

"Jacopo thinks he's helping. His accusation might be the result of stress—or it could be that he really does know something." He pursed his lips a moment. "His polygraph may tell us something."

"Polygraph? Jacopo's a suspect?"

"It's mostly routine. To eliminate him as a suspect." He reached for her hand resting on the table. "I'd really like to know what you think. Is Lidia Feloni capable of murder?"

"This is crazy, Daniele. I believe Lorenzo is the killer? Even if you did release him. Not Jacopo or Lidia."

"You might be right about that. Before leaving the office, I sent a couple of offices to bring Caravello in for additional questioning. Even though he'd recanted his confession and we didn't find any hard proof—fingerprints, hair, fibers, DNA—for the initial murder a new angle has surfaced. Though it's circumstantial, we'll hold him until we're certain he's not the Canal Murderer."

The waitress reappeared and deposited the steaming food in front of them. Without speaking, Elena cut a piece of her fish and placed it in Marinello's bowl. He scooped a couple spoonfuls of gnocchi onto hers. Sharing their meals had become a habit they started months ago.

Absently, he moved the dumplings around in the shallow bowl. "I'm going to have to interview Lidia. No matter how preposterous that may seem."

Elena stabbed a mouthful size of sea bass. She jerked her head up, and Marinello felt her eyes boring into him. "If what Jacopo said is true, then Jonathan Shelby was Oriana's father." She tilted her head with her lips pursed. He suspected that Elena was piecing together the bits of information he'd shared with her. "How can that be?" She questioned him. "In a day or two Oriana is going to California—to spend the summer with her father."

"Is Lidia going with her?"

"I don't know."

"*Dio mio!*" He stood, grabbed the linen napkin from his lap, and dropped it on the table. "I better contact Lidia Feloni immediately. The last thing I'd need is for a possible murder suspect to flee the country."

Chapter Forty-One

ORIANA'S HEAD FELT LIKE IT WOULD explode as her mother's words replayed over and over. She wanted to rip them from her mind. Blot them from her memory. She ached to pack her suitcase, fly to Los Angeles, and spend the summer with her father ... Papà ... Daddy. Now that'd be impossible.

She shifted on the park bench and lifted her eyes from the ground. She followed the movement of the boys kicking a football in the square. *How carefree they are*, she thought, *like I was until*... She clenched her fingers into a fist and pounded her thigh. She sighed, stood, and made a decision. She had to tell someone—someone who would understand—Chiara.

The quickest way to reach Chiara's house would be to hop onto a *vaporetto,* but she chose to walk. She focused on the worn pavement and hurried along the meandering back-streets to avoid the crowds. Still a way off, she broke into a jog, which turned into a full-fledged run. The rhythmic slapping of her sandals against the stone *calli* lulled her tormented mind into a quieting trance. As she approached the grand stucco building with pointed arched windows and lacy ornamentation, she bent over to catch her breath. Still a bit winded, Oriana slipped through the wrought-iron gate, crossed the ancient courtyard, and entered the lower floor through the exquisite entrance. She hurried to the staircase that led to the *piano nobile* apartment. Usually, the stateliness of Chiara's home triggered a flicker of awe, but not this time. Her mother's devastating news had numbed her senses. She hustled up the gleaming Istrian stone staircase and rapped on the apartment's stained-glass entry door.

A few seconds passed before Chiara appeared with her cellphone in hand. She opened the door. "I just texted you. I'm surprised you're back so soon. Weren't you and your mother going out for breakfast?"

Oriana mumbled a half-hearted, "We were supposed to" as she followed Chiara down the *portego*. Through the space felt airy with sunlight spilling in through the floor to ceiling windows located at the end of the hall, it hadn't raised her spirits.

"Are you hungry then?" Chiara asked.

"Not really. No."

Chiara turned into the rustic den with its heavy wooden beamed ceiling and honey-toned stone walls. She plopped into a sleek leather chair and gestured for Oriana to sit on the matching couch. Instead, Oriana stood facing her.

"My whole life has been a lie," Oriana said.

Chiara frowned.

"Everything I believed was real turns out to be an illusion. My papà hadn't deserted me. What I'm about to tell you might seem crazy, but it's the God honest truth."

Oriana wasn't sure if it was a flicker of confusion that raced across Chiara's face or worry. She swallowed hard. "I just found out that my mother kidnapped me when I was four-years-old. She fled to Italy, and we've been on the run ever since."

Chiara moved her lips as if trying to form words but then pressed them together.

"What kind of mother does that?" Oriana hoped against hope that her friend would have an answer. Her mother's reason that it had been out of love seemed insipid, trite ... selfish.

Instead of responding, Chiara inched closer to the edge of the chair.

"My real name is Louise Shelby."

Chiara jumped up. "Shelby? Isn't that the name of the man—?"

"My father was the canal victim."

Chiara pulled Oriana into her arms and held her close. For the first time since hearing the awful truth, Oriana gave into her emotions. She wept softly as Chiara patted her back.

After a minute, Oriana pulled free and wiped the back of her hand across her damp face. "Tell me what to do."

Chiara grabbed Oriana's arm and led her to the kitchen. She pulled two cans of Fanta Chinotto from the refrigerator, flipped open the tabs, and poured the dark-colored soda made from the juice of myrtle leaf oranges into two crystal goblets. Oriana sunk onto a barstool next to the work island, reached for the glass Chiara offered her, and took a deep swallow of the bittersweet beverage.

"My mamma can help you." Chiara sat next to Oriana. "Except, right now she's at lunch with Godfather Daniele. Then she's scheduled to meet with patients until seven. I could call her." She removed her cellphone from her back pocket.

Oriana didn't want to interrupt Doctor Barozzi's busy day. "I think it'd be better to wait until she comes home from work. Can I stay here?"

"As long as you like. But what do you want me to tell your mother when she telephones?" Chiara shook her cellphone in Oriana's direction.

"Tell her you don't know where I am."

"You want me to lie?"

"I can't face her."

"*Va bene*," Chiara said. "Alright. But you do realize that you're going to have to go home eventually."

"I'll worry about that later." Oriana raised the glass and took a sip. "I'm ashamed to say that for an instant, I thought she had killed my papà just to keep me all to herself. But then, I saw the devastation filling Mamma's face. Her eyes were so sad. She told me that the two of them had worked out their problems. We were going to be a family again. In California."

"So horrible," Chiara whispered. "Your life's story could be a plot ripped right out of a novel or a movie."

"Except it's not." Oriana raised the glass but returned it to the granite countertop. "You'd think adults wouldn't make crazy, insane decisions like my mother did. Papà was devastated that I had become lost to him. But he never forgot me. He searched for years. He even got remarried, trying to forget about Mamma and me. I have two half-brothers."

"Your little brothers lost their papà too."

Oriana looked into her friend's face and noticed her eyes were wet.

"If you do go to California, please make it a short trip."

"After all that's happened, I doubt I'll be going. Though it would be the perfect way to get away from my mother. I can't believe how she deceived me and devastated Papà."

"In the end, she tried to make things right," Chiara said.

"*Troppo poco troppo tardi*," Oriana said. "It's only after my papà was murdered that she tells me the truth. How can I ever forgive her? Like I said, too little too late."

"But, she's you're mamma. She's the only parent you have now."

"Can I spend the summer with you and your grandmother?" Oriana noticed the sparkle return to her friend's deep brown eyes.

"What a great idea." Chiara raised her glass, holding it mid-air. "But don't you have a grandmother in California that's expecting you?"

Oriana shrugged. "I'd much rather be with you. Anyway, I bet my mother is already in search of a new town for us to live in. I don't want any part of it. I want to stay in Venice."

"Well ... there really isn't any reason for your mother to be on the run anymore."

It took Oriana a moment for the words to sink in. "You're right. There's no reason for us to hide anymore now that my papà is...."

"She can stay in Venice and be Lidia Feloni, like, forever," Chiara said with a smile.

"Maybe. Oh, I don't know. I don't know about anything anymore." Oriana tried to blink back tears, but a couple escaped and trickled across her flushed cheeks.

The girls sat in glum silence for a couple of minutes, both seemingly lost in their own thoughts until Chiara broke the stillness binding them. "I've come up with a plan. Why don't you forget about going to California and live here with me? We'll be like sisters. Better than sisters because we're best friends. Nothing will separate us. After all, we fatherless girls have to stick together."

"Would your mamma agree?"

"I know how to handle her. Leave it up to me. It'll be a snap."

"Maybe things will work out after all." Oriana tried to believe her words but feared a happy ending wasn't in store for her.

Chapter Forty-Two

BETH TOOK A DEEP BREATH, steeling herself for the chore at hand, as she stepped into the Palazzo da Parma through the rear entrance. She glanced around the cavernous first floor. Centuries ago, this space would've contained a storehouse of exotic fare—silk, spices, sugar—within its service rooms belonging to Jacopo's merchant ancestors. Though grand with its marble floor, coffered ceiling, and impressive staircase, she noticed that it had suffered water damage by the discoloration on the wood-paneled walls. *Venice is sinking*, she thought with a low sigh.

She hurried up the stairs and paused in front of the lustrous hand-carved door decorated with a lion head, which led into the noble floor, housing the mansion's grandest rooms. Without hesitation, she pressed the bell and waited. She tapped her foot, a full thirty seconds, before reaching again toward the bell when the door flew open.

Expecting Jacopo, she was instead greeted by the housekeeper—minus the crisp uniform. "*Cosa vuoi?*" The woman spat the words, but then a look of recognition claimed her face. "*Mi dispiace.*" Her voice softened with the apology. She opened the door widener and ushered Beth inside. "I'm beside myself with anguish. The poor signora. I can't believe she is gone. Please, forgive my bad manners."

Beth patted her arm. "There's nothing to forgive," she replied in Italian trying to recall the housekeeper's name. By the time she'd removed her hand from the stout, steel-grey-haired woman, she'd remembered. "All of our hearts are broken, Santina."

The housekeeper nodded. "Every few minutes there's a messenger or delivery at the door," Santina said. Flowers. Cards. Food."

"I'm not here to drop something off, but to pick up something. Deirdre's clothing for the funeral."

Santina puffed out a mouthful of air. "I should be dressing the signora. But no," she said raising her voice, "the viewing isn't going to be in the house. Only at the church."

Beth recalled the night before her mother's wake in their family's parlor. She'd crept into the room and sat with her mother until she'd fallen asleep. She hadn't wanted her mother to be alone.

"Let me take you." Santina's words startled Beth from her memory. The housekeeper pointed upward. "*Il secondo piano nobile.*"

Beth had never been on the second floor, knowing that the exquisite bedroom Deirdre shared with Jacopo was on the main floor. Assuming that the housekeeper had misunderstood, she waved her off. "Thank you, but no. You're busy. I'll find what I need on my own."

"*Grazie. Grazie.* My daughters and I are busy preparing food for the funeral reception. There's sure to be all of the Dorsoduro, if not all of Venice, attending." Santina flicked away a tear that escaped from her watery eyes.

A flood of emotion rushed through Beth. Though she tried to stop the flow of sorrow, she found herself shaking and softly weeping within the housekeeper's sturdy arms. After a few moments of shared grief, Beth gently pulled away. "Is Jacopo in—"

"That man. He didn't deserve the signora. She was a true saint and he ... well, no, he's out."

About to agree with the woman, Beth was startled by the sound of thunderous banging on the door.

Santina threw up her arms. "See. So many people loved her. She opened the door, and a delivery man handed her a large bouquet of white flowers— lilies, mums, and carnations—enveloped in gold wrapping paper tied with a white ribbon. Behind him stood a woman holding a casserole dish.

Though her cheeks were still wet, Beth smiled realizing how much her *ould flower* was truly cherished, perhaps not by her husband, but by the community of people surrounding her.

Beth left the housekeeper and headed down the *portego* in search of Deirdre's wardrobe. She remembered how Deirdre had loathed their bedroom, telling her it was like sleeping in a gymnasium. *Actually*, Beth thought, *Deirdre really didn't care too much for Jacopo's ancestral home and referred to it as the museum.* But she did love the kitchen. Jacopo had it renovated to her specifications, which, along with all the upgrades, included a drop ceiling to make it feel a bit more intimate and welcoming.

She stopped at the threshold of the antechamber that led into the bedroom. Deirdre had enjoyed making over the smaller room into a cheerful den and had decorated it with mementos from Ireland: her Belleek porcelain vases and Waterford crystal figurines, comfortable overstuffed armchairs, and an elaborate stained-glass Celtic fireplace screen. Deirdre made sure the vases were fully stocked with an array of wildflowers, and strands of sweet Irish tenors would often flow from the state-of-the-art sound system. With a sad smile, she remembered the excitement that had lit up Deirdre's face when she'd seen the wedding gift Beth had surprised her with—an antique Williams and Gibton tea table—and it became her most cherished possession. After a hectic day at work, Deirdre would relax with a good *cuppa* and enjoy a bit of old Ireland within the massive Italian palace.

Eager to be surrounded by the objects Deirdre loved, Beth stepped inside the room. She blinked a couple of times not believing what faced her. Deirdre's sitting room was gone. An office had taken its place. A desk that would've looked new during the Renaissance held a PC and printer. The castered, creamy leather desk chair had been rolled across the glass mat and stood next to a fax machine. The plush carpet held a modern, geometric design while the LED desk lamps looked out of place in the golden room with a wooden coffered ceiling.

She dropped into the swivel chair and slowly turned around in an attempt to make sense of the room. She stopped when she faced the far wall. Arranged like those in the *Casa della Maschera* hung a group of masks. But unlike those in the mask store, these lacked the ornate decorations and plumes of feathers. She rose, moved closer to the wall, and recognized a few of the classical Venetian masks—the black velvet Muretta that caused women to be mute, the bird-like beaked Plague Doctor, the Bauta, and the black Harlequin half-mask with its tiny eyeholes and wrinkled forehead that would be worn with a diamond checkered costume.

"These are rare antiques," she murmured taking in the array of over a dozen different types of masks—most of which she'd never seen before.

She reached out to touch the Bauta, but thinking better of it, withdrew her hand. "This doesn't make sense. What in heaven's name happened to Deirdre's sitting room?"

She took small steps, inspecting everything from the leather couch to the bookcase that housed a wide variety of novels. It was then she remembered what Santina had told her—that Deirdre's bedroom was upstairs. She sunk into the couch's soft leather and pressed a tasseled pillow against her chest.

Their marriage must've really been on the rocks. She frowned wondering why Deirdre hadn't breathed a word of the difficulties plaguing her marriage until only a few days ago. *And to think it's been only a handful of years since they married and were so madly in love.* She shook her head. *How it was possible that their passion for each other had so rapidly shriveled and withered into a stony estrangement.*

She traced the jagged scar that crossed her cheek. After being the victim in a drunk driving collision, Beth had shunned just about everyone—except Deirdre—who offered her words of hope and comfort. Her efforts had soothed away some of the hatred and resentment Beth had harbored for the inebriated motorist. The endless hours she spent at the Cute Cate Rescue had also helped as she gingerly cared for abandoned and unwanted kittens. And then, by some miracle, she met Shane, and the world went from dull gray to full color. Though they'd been married a hair less than a year, deep in her heart, she knew their love would last whatever the future had in store for them.

Though she'd been giving Jacopo the benefit of the doubt, Beth couldn't help but sense the flowering of a newfound hatred toward him. She tried to suppress the emerging negativity, but it took so much effort that a wave of exhaustion washed over her. She closed her eyes, wanting nothing more than to curl up on Jacopo's sofa, fall into a sound sleep, and forget the tragedy that had befallen her dearest friend.

Beth woke with a jerk. She blinked a couple of times then looked at her watch. Twenty minutes had passed. Chastising herself, she stood, rolled her shoulders, and took one more look around the room. It hit her like a flash. Jacopo had been so vindictive that, in his growing disenchantment with Deirdre, he'd callously torn away her oasis—her sanctuary—the link to her beloved homeland—and had transformed it into his own private workspace. Not only to hurt Deirdre but to crush her spirit. With her jaw set, she stomped into the *portego,* but an instant later, she remembered her tote bag that she'd dropped on top of Jacopo's desk.

She rushed back inside the room and grabbed the bag. As it slid across the desk's polished surface, it took a piece of paper with it. The cream-colored sheet floated to the floor. She rolled her eyes, bent down, and retrieved it. The paper's thick texture surprised her, but then she guessed that Jacopo would have only the best *even* when it came to a piece of stationery. She glanced at it and noticed the letterhead of the famed auberge, Hotel Gritti Palace, embossed in gold at the top of the leaf. She pursed her lips. *Probably a condolence note,* she thought spying a matching envelope on the desk. She replaced the letter and hurried out of the room.

She'd gotten half-way down the *portego* when a chill ran through her. She took a couple of deep breaths, attempting to still her hammering heart and understand the warning from her *fey*. Not knowing what to do, she decided to complete her chore by gathering a couple of Deirdre's outfits to take with her. She'd let Carmel make the final decision. The sound of her Cuban heels striking the marble floor filled Beth's ears until she reached the elaborate staircase. She grabbed the banister and hurried up a couple of steps. But then her *fey* struck again, and she nearly lost her balance. She leaned against the heavy handrail and clutched it tighter.

"Enough," she said under her breath.

She marched back into Jacopo's office, stopped at the desk, and lifted the slip of paper that turned out to be a handwritten note in English. Her eyes flew across the words but they didn't make sense. She read them again this time out loud:

"J—,

You were amazing last night. Since I've arrived in Venice, the sweetest thing I've tasted is your bare skin on my lips. Can I taste you again ... tonight?

N—"

Disgust washed over her. She released the note and it fluttered onto the desk. Beth folded her arms and paced the length of the room. When she looked up, she was eye to eye with the Bauta mask. *Deirdre isn't even in the ground yet and he's having ... having what? Sex? An affair? Good Lord, what kind of man is he?* She rummaged for a moment inside her tote bag until she found a hair clip. It took only a second to grab her tresses, twist her hair into a knot, and secure it with the clip. Then she paced again.

Seeing red, she tried to shake her anger so she'd be able to think. It took a good five minutes of pacing for her fury to subside enough for her to look at the note again—to study it—and hope to God that her *fey* would give her the insight needed to understand why this slip of paper was so important. She noted the feminine handwriting abundant with loops and curly-cues. But it told her nothing. "Hotel Gritty Palace. N," she said the words over and over. It finally became clear in a blaze of illumination.

"Nicole Shelby is staying at the Gritti Palace." She chewed her lip. "Could she be the mysterious N?" She grabbed her tote bag and headed down the golden corridor, pulled open the lion door, and descended the stairs leading to the first floor. "Jacopo and Nicole," she whispered. "Nicole and Jonathan. What is the connection?" She hurried outside and squinted as the brightness of the day assaulted her eyes. She ran across the courtyard then stopped. "Jacopo, Nicole, and Jonathan—could they form some kind of unholy triangle?"

Though she had no idea, Beth was hell-bent on doing whatever it took to find out.

Chapter Forty-Three

LIDIA COULDN'T CONCENTRATE ON Bernardino's words as he steered her down the *Questura's* long corridor. Her singular concern targeted on locating Oriana. She'd called and texted Oriana so many times she'd lost count. Contacting Chiara hadn't helped either since the girl had insisted she hadn't any idea of Oriana's whereabouts. And that was a red flag. Those two, close as sister, share everything. She couldn't help but wonder if Chiara was keeping something from her? Don't worry, was the only advice Chiara had offered. But how could Lidia not worry as a sickening dread clutched her heart? *I don't care what happens to me. Marinello can arrest me as long as Oriana is safe.* She focused on the movements of her steps and the wild beating of her heart began to slow. A group of uniformed officers breezed past them and filled the air with excited cadences of hurried words. She stopped.

"What's wrong?" Bernardino faced her.

"The *poliziotti*." She pointed to the officers turning a corner. "They're talking about another murder. A woman." The blood rushed from her head, and the walls began to spin.

His strong hands clasped her shoulders. She collapsed against his chest.

"Lidia. Relax. They're talking about Jacopo's wife. You already know she was murdered," he whispered into her ear.

"Yes," she breathed the word out. "But where is Oriana?"

"After we speak with Marinello, I'll scour every lane and back alleyway in Venice for her. Trust me. In a few hours, you'll be wondering why you were so worked up."

"How can you be sure?" She pulled away. "I've deceived her. Oriana hates me."

234

"She needs time. She'll come around and realize everything you did was for her benefit."

"What if she doesn't?" She looked out a window at the Grand Canal. A new thought seized her. "What if the killer has Oriana?"

"The killer?"

"He could've lured Oriana into some kind of trap... what if she's floating in a canal ... her face covered with a *Bauta*—"

"Get a grip. You're letting your imagination run wild."

"I spoke with Deirdre only two days ago, and now she's dead. Oh, God," she whispered. "He's stalking and killing people I care about. Jonathan. Deirdre. Oriana?"

His fingers encircled her biceps. "Marinello can help. We'll ask him to send out a search party."

"I've got to go. I need to find her." She pulled away, her heart in her in throat, as she sped away from him.

Chapter Forty-Four

BETH FOLLOWED THE DIRECTIONS on her mobile's screen, aware that she'd never locate the Hotel Gritti Palace on her own. As she walked, she offered up a quick prayer in hopes that she'd find the right words when facing Nicole. Never really good at multi-tasking, she tried to focus on the directions shining on the phone's screen while seeking to uncover a thread that would link Jacopo, Nicole, and Jonathan. *Well*, she told herself, *Jonathan and Nicole were spouses but Jacopo ...* She lifted her eyes from the screen a moment too late and plowed into the back of an unsuspecting tourist. That's what she thought until the man turned and faced her. Marinello.

Uh-oh.

"*Mi scusi, Commissario Capo.*" She flashed the mobile at him.

"Signora Getty." He folded his arms across his chest. "Sightseeing?" The flicker of amusement that crossed his face vanished. "Ah, of course not. No."

She moistened her bottom lip with the tip of her tongue, wondering if she should tell him about the puzzling note she'd discovered in Jacopo's study. After a moment of indecision, she chose not to share the information. She didn't know if she'd decided to keep the info to herself because of Shane's comments regarding her bouts of "flights of fancy" or because she didn't want Marinello to think she was ingratiating herself into the investigation.

"Actually, I'm on my way to the La Salute to pray for Deirdre's soul."

He pulled his lips tight and offered her a curt nod. "A good place to pray. When I was a boy, my mother explained that the basilica was built to resemble an inverted chalice—one that shelters the city's piety." He shook his head. "The plague is far behind us, but now Venice needs to be sheltered from the machinations of a murdering phantom."

"I pray to God you find this madman. Soon."

"Or woman."

She widened her eyes. "You don't think that Lia Renner is behind the murders?" He opened his mouth as if about to answer, but she didn't give him the chance. "Maybe you should consider a different woman."

Marinello frowned.

Beth bit her lip. *Damnation. Now I've done it.*

"Another woman?"

She shrugged. "Just an idea playing..." She tapped her temple. "And a strong feeling. I have a sixth sense about these kinds of things?"

He offered her a lopsided smile. "We base our findings on evidence."

"True. But don't be ruling out the *fey* of an Irish lass. It was a true asset in solving my Shane's last case."

"Be that as it may," he said with a shrug. "I'm searching for the person who might be behind these vicious killings before she leaves the country."

She stepped closer. "Fleeing Italy could be a sign of guilt." Though she said the words, her *fey* was signaling that the Chief Superintendent was wrong about Lidia Feloni—that she had abducted her daughter for a good reason. She concentrated, hoping that her *fey* would reveal exactly what Lidia's good reason was, but after a couple seconds of nothing, she gave up.

"When you reach the Accademia Bridge, cross it, and make a left. You can't miss the church," Marinello said.

"Thanks." She swiped the mobile's screen and slipped the phone into her tote bag.

"And please, say a prayer for me. The way things look now, only divine intervention is going to lead us to the perpetrator."

"Of course," she said with a little wave and continued walking. Beth hated that she'd lied to Marinello, especially since he'd asked for her prayers. As she hurried down the narrow lane and weaved around slow-moving tourists, she offered a decade for the repose of Deirdre's soul, for Marinello, and for the repentance of the blackened soul of a murderer.

Chapter Forty-Five

NICOLE STOOD ON THE BALCONY and gazed across the Grand Canal. She'd never seen a circular church before and wondered what the inside looked like. The thought vanished when her cellphone pinged. She glanced at the text and smiled. She'd wondered how long Jacopo would manage to stay away. *Not very long—not even a whole day.*

She stepped inside, closed the ceiling to floor French door, and looked at her reflection in the gilded wall mirror hanging above the couch. Deciding she looked perfect, she practiced her come-hither expression. Satisfied with the smile, a mixture of pouty and pleased, she checked her watch. A knock sounded on the door. Perfect timing.

Taking slow, measured steps, she reached the door and opened it. This time there were no flowers or wine. Only Jacopo. And he didn't look happy. The smile slipped from her face.

He stormed into the suite and dropped into a chair. "That damned Marinello wants me to take a lie detector test." He pulled the tie loose from his collar.

Nicole wrinkled her nose but imagined she understood. "He suspects *you*? Of what? Killing your wife?"

He lowered his head and slumped forward. This wasn't the Jacopo who shared her bed last night. She didn't like this version.

But then as if being energized by an electric current he jumped up. "Well, damn Marinello to hell." Jacopo paced across the elegant room, stopped, and faced her. "The nerve of him even suggesting that I had anything to do with Deirdre's death."

She frowned. "What's the big deal? You didn't kill your wife. So, take the damn polygraph and be done with it."

He raked his fingers through his unruly locks.

"You didn't kill your wife ... did you?" She sat on the satiny couch and crossed her long shapely legs.

"Of course not." He stepped in front of her and sunk into an adjacent armchair. "But to be honest, I'm not sorry she's dead. I'm actually quite grateful to whoever did her in. We have that in common," he said gesturing from himself to her. "You're happy, or should I say relieved, that your husband is dead too."

She widened her eyes. "I never said I wanted Jon to die."

His eyebrows jumped.

"I just wanted revenge on that damn Lia Renner. I told you that. If Jon happened to come to an unfortunate end..." She shrugged. "Then Renner wouldn't be able to get her claws into him, and I'd get to keep everything. No 50/50 split after a messy divorce. But I never told you or anyone that I wanted my husband murdered."

"True." A slow smile crept across his face.

"Don't tell me you killed—"

He shook his head. "Let's just say that the responsible person will soon be behind bars."

"What? Why the hell didn't Marinello tell me?" She jumped up and marched to the telephone seated on a marble-topped console table.

"No need to contact the Chief Superintendent. Because, well, because you're going to get exactly what you wished for. Your husband is dead, and I told Marinello that my assistant is Lia Renner."

"Your assistant? You never told me she was your assistant!" Nicole clutched her narrow hips. She caught a glimpse of color crossing his cheeks.

"*Va bene*. Alright. I'll tell you. I discovered the truth quite by accident. I was scrolling through Twitter and came across an article. An interview. All about the pain and frustration of living through the horror of having a child kidnapped."

"Jon?"

He nodded. "It wasn't the interview that caught my attention. It was the photograph. A young woman holding a child. There was something familiar about her."

She wanted him to spit it out, but Jacopo seemed to be enjoying every word that he carefully pronounced.

"I'm an expert when it comes to photography."

She pressed her lips together and silently started counting to ten.

"I photoshopped the picture."

She stopped counting and ran a fingertip across her lips.

"I straightened out the little bump in the nose, changed the hairstyle and color, added a bit more cleavage, and what do you know? My assistant, Lidia Feloni." He paused long enough to look her straight in the eyes. "Everything fell into place. Questions answered. I knew Lidia's secret and decided it was an ace up my sleeve. I'd use it if I had to."

It wasn't until he stopped talking that Nicole realized she'd been chewing one of her perfectly manicured fingernails. "If you'd informed Marinello sooner things might have turned out differently." She glanced at the nail. It was unharmed. "But," she said with a shrug, "I'm just relieved that woman is where she belongs. In jail. Now I can think about returning home." She caught a glimpse of her reflection in the mirror. "It's not that I want to leave you. I've enjoyed your company, but—"

"Renner hasn't been arrested. Yet."

"But you said—"

"Lorenzo Caravello was taken into custody."

"Who the hell is he?"

"That doesn't matter. The important thing is that I put a bug in Marinello's ear. I'm sure he's on his way to arrest her now."

Nicole sunk onto the couch. "I can't believe this. She's got to be apprehended, found guilty, and sent to prison. For the rest of her life."

"Not to worry. I'll see to that."

She wanted to believe him, but a lingering thread of doubt made her wonder.

"What you need is a good Venetian meal. Let's go downstairs to the outside terrace for lunch. The food here, as you probably already know, is the best in Venice."

"I've lost my appetite."

"Then maybe…." He moved toward the couch, sat next to her, and turned her face toward his.

She looked into his dark eyes and hoped that she could trust him. She was about to ask again for confirmation that Lia Renner would be arrested when his lips touched hers. Lightly. Teasingly.

"Perhaps we could move into the bedroom?" he asked.

"Well, I do need something to take my mind off this terrible turn of events." She took his hand and led him down the hallway toward her bed.

Chapter Forty-Six

JACOPO HUMMED UNDER HIS BREATH as he smoothed back his hair. His eyes caught the glimmer of his diamond wedding band. He smiled. The answer to all his problems had been staring him right in the face—or to be more specific, next to him in the bed. He moved to the chair where he'd carefully draped his Cucinelli suit coat and took a quick glance at Nicole. She looked like an angel with her halo of golden hair spilled against the cream-colored satin pillow, her cheeks rosy, and her fringe of ebony lashes, long and silky. She stirred and a moment later flashed open her eyes.

"You were looking at me?"

"Admiring you."

"Oh?" Nicole paused with a hint of a smile. "That I don't mind." She inched up in the bed.

He lifted his navy-colored coat, brushed away an imaginary speck of lint, and slipped into it.

"You're leaving so soon?"

"I have a business to run." He wanted to blurt out his ingenious idea but knew it might take a bit of finesse to persuade her. He'd have to think it through. Use just the right words and point out the logic and brilliance of his plan.

"I thought you wanted to get lunch?" She slipped off the bed and padded toward him.

The breath caught in the back of his throat as he took in her flawless figure. He reached for his silk tie but stopped short of pulling it loose. "Lunch." He nodded.

It took Nicole nearly an hour to make herself presentable, the word she'd used, as he impatiently waited. At first. The minutes allowed him the perfect opportunity to hone his plan from a disjointed idea into a master blueprint guaranteeing happiness for both of them. He couldn't wait to share his strategy with her over antipasto ... *Baccala mastecato* and *polenta crostini*. His mouth watered.

She glided into the living room clad in a turquoise dress that matched the color of her eyes. Sleeveless and wide skirted, its thick wraparound fabric belt accentuated her tiny waist.

"*Bellissimo*," he said.

"You like it?" She did a little twirl. "I picked it up in a dress shop yesterday. It's completely handmade out of some kind of silk, I think."

He gestured toward the opened door leading to the balcony.

"What about lunch?"

"We'll have it sent up here."

"I'd much rather go out. The view from the restaurant—"

"Is the same view from the balcony."

She pouted.

The last thing he wanted was to upset her. "I have a proposition."

She raised her perfectly arched eyebrows. "About lunch?"

He shook his head. "About us."

"Us?"

He draped his arm across her shoulder and led her to the couch. She took a seat, and he sat next to her. "We lost our spouses in the same horrific manner." He noticed she'd narrowed her eyes as if trying to decipher where he was headed, but then she offered him a nod. "It couldn't be a coincidence. It has to mean something."

"It means that crazy assistant of yours went on a killing spree." She started to stand, but Jacopo placed a hand on her arm and pressed gently. Nicole scooted to the cushion's edge and folded her hands in her lap. "So, what do you think it means?"

"Ah." He inhaled deeply anticipating that she'd buy into his plan. "Regardless of who committed the crime, your Jonathan and my Deirdre, God have mercy on their souls, are gone. Forever. Now you're a wealthy widow and me..." He shrugged. "I come from an ancient, proud line of Venetians—one who accompanied Marco Polo and another who was a Doge—merchants, bankers, architects, explorers."

Her eyes glazed with boredom.

"What I'm trying to say is that my ancestors accumulated great riches, and through my business and savvy investments, I have increased that fortune many times over."

She leaned closer.

"I live in a palazzo—a palace."

"Oh God, not one of those run-down decaying ruins."

"No. No." He shook his head. "It's magnificent."

"Well, good for you. Now, I'm starved." She stood.

"Nikki," he said patting her vacated spot on the couch.

Though she rolled her eyes toward the ceiling, she reclaimed her seat. He grabbed her hand and massaged the top of it with his thumb.

"I think we should combine our assets."

"What?" Confusion covered her face.

"If we were to marry—"

She jumped up and rushed to the opposite end of the room. "What the hell?"

Jacopo swallowed hard. "We like each other." He tried to send her an encouraging smile, but she only turned away from him. He rose from the couch and stood behind her. "I'm not talking about a traditional marriage," he whispered into her ear.

"Then what?"

"A merging of two families. We marry and live in my palazzo. I'd even adopt your sons. The eldest would inherit my fortune unless…." He reached around her and patted her belly.

She turned, and he was surprised that no expression claimed her face. "I hate Venice."

"But you love money?"

She half-shrugged.

"You'd be free to spend as much time in your California home as you like. And when we become tired of each other, we'd be free to look elsewhere for companionship. But there'd be no divorce. Ever."

She pursed her lips and lowered her eyes as if considering his proposal.

"Fate brought us together. The threads of our destiny have become woven together through misfortune, but if we unite, that very tragedy will become our triumph," he said.

With eyes big and questioning, she seemed to be appraising him. "How rich are you?"

He crossed his arms and smiled.

"So, you're suggesting an open marriage."

"If that's what you want."

She dropped into a chair and started chewing a fingernail. "Oh, I don't know, Jacopo. This is so sudden—out of the blue."

"Perhaps. But you can't deny that we're two of a kind. Cut from the same cloth. We'll do just about anything to get what we need. And ... we need each other."

She dropped her hand. "I'm not naïve. You don't love me. What is it that you really want?"

Though he'd hinted at it, Jacopo didn't want to tell Nicole the driving need for a son had triggered his stratagem. After all, he was attracted to her, and maybe one day he'd eventually develop feelings for her. An image of Lidia flashed through his mind. He shook his head, attempting to dislodge the memory. She'd spurned his affection. Rebuffed him. Humiliated him. *Lidia deserves to be punished. A jail cell may not be enough.* Though he didn't know how he couldn't wait to get his hands on Oriana to make Lidia suffer more. He gritted his teeth together.

"It's not like we're strangers or anything," she said.

He looked into her face, and the tension caused by the thought of Lidia slipped away.

"My BFF, Cindi, met her husband, and a week later, they eloped. They're still married. We've been involved with each other for way over a month. But I want to be sure."

"I just want to make you happy, Nicoletta."

"Nicoletta," she whispered the name. "I like the sound of that." She crossed her arms. "But, why me? Why do you want to marry an American woman you've only known for weeks? I'm sure there are plenty of local women who'd jump at your proposition."

"*Va bene.* Okay. The truth is that from the first minute I heard your sexy voice on the other end of the phone, I believed it was kismet that caused our paths to cross. When I first saw you, my darling Nicoletta, your beauty overwhelmed me. You took my breath away. Since becoming lovers, I could never be happy if you weren't in my life." He feared his words had been too flowery but then her face beamed with pleasure.

"I had no idea you felt that way. But I don't love you—"

"In Venice, like all of Italy, in centuries past, marriage wasn't about love. It was about forging political alliances... and sealing fortunes. I don't expect you to love me, but perhaps, over time...." He shot her a tentative smile.

"There's no reason to rush into a marriage. The engagement would have to be at least a year out of respect for our spouses."

"Are you accepting my proposal?"

She half-shrugged.

"Nicoletta, please say yes."

She bit her lip.

"I can give you everything your heart desires—jewels, furs, houses, vacations—anything. The only thing I ask of you is for a child. A boy. To guarantee our dynasty."

"Our dynasty?"

"Once we're married, you will become a da Parma and a rightful recipient of the benefits of my magnificent line. You'll become a part of history."

"I ... I don't know what to say."

"Say yes."

"Yes."

Before he realized it, he'd taken her in his arms, lifted her, and spun around. Their laughter bounced off the walls and wafted through the opened French door. He placed her on the floor and she managed to say between spurts of giggles, "Ridiculous. Completely insane. But what the hell."

He kissed her with such passion that Jacopo believed he did love her.

Nicole pulled away. "If you want a son that badly, I think we should start working on that right away." She placed a finger over pouty lips and fluttered her upturned silken lashes.

Coy. Charming. Adorable. His heart thumped wildly with his tour de force and craving for her delicious body. *She's bound to give me my heart's desire.*

He grabbed her hand and led her to the corridor leading to the bedroom. A loud pounding on the door stopped them in their tracks.

Chapter Forty-Seven

BETH KNOCKED ON NICOLE SHELBY'S hotel door. She tapped her foot as she waited, realizing that once again, she'd allowed her emotions to take control and hadn't thought things through. Now she wondered how she'd broach the subject of the note she'd found in Jacopo's study. A twinge of pain shot through her shoulder, but she ignored the dull throb. About ready to give up, she decided to try again and rapped on the white paneled door. To her surprise, it opened—but no wider than then a narrow crack.

"Sibéal?" Nicole said. "Oh, I mean Beth. I wasn't expecting—"

"I couldn't bear the thought of you all alone after facing such a devastating tragedy. I was feeling a bit low and thought maybe spending a wee bit of time together would help to bolster our spirits."

Nicole opened the door a bit wider. Beth noticed Nicole's dress, hair, makeup. Seemed as if she was expecting company ... Jacopo?

"That's really kind of you." Nicole dropped her eyes.

"It'd be lovely to enjoy such a beautiful day together. We could start off with lunch at the hotel's Terrace Restaurant. It overlooks the Grand Canal." Beth sensed the woman's nervousness by the way she absently chewed on her fingernail and was betting she'd decline the offer. But to her surprise, Nicole agreed as she stepped into the hallway and closed the door.

After a short elevator ride that led to the outdoor restaurant, they were seated at a table, facing a perfect view of the canal. Beth sent up a quick prayer for guidance as she watched a gondola lazily float by.

"It's funny, but I haven't eaten here yet," Nicole said.

"It's pricy, but the food is wonderful." Beth tore her eyes away from the canal, focused on Nicole, and noticed that her demeanor had changed. The anxiety seemed to have disappeared. She couldn't read a trace of sadness in Nicole's blue-green eyes as a smile played around her lips, giving off a hint of merriment.

"I'm glad you stopped by," Nicole said. "A day like today, so perfect and fresh, makes me appreciate life." She gestured toward the canal with an opened palm. "All the worries and fears banging around in here," she said tapping her temple, "have vanished. For the first time since Jon's death, I feel almost normal again."

A waiter in formal attire approached their table and handed them menus.

"Two champagne cocktails," Nicole told the waiter. As he hurried away, she turned to Beth. "I hope you don't mind me ordering for you. But, I feel like celebrating. Heart crushing as it is that Jon is gone," she said fingering the embossed leather menu, "I've been able to work through the grief because a trace of him will always live inside my two sons. So, I've decided not to dwell so much on his death, but rather embrace life. I think it's what he'd want me to do."

An image of Deirdre's girls sprang to her mind with a pang of sorrow. She hoped to God that Jacopo was enveloping them with the comfort and love that only a father could provide. She suspected Nicole hadn't noticed her moment of reflection since she was busy perusing the menu.

"My mother died when I was just shy of ten," Beth said.

Nicole raised her eyes away from the menu.

"*Me da*—my dad—took grand care of me. He wiped away my tears and told me that *me ma* would live forever in my heart. I'm guessing only that kind of solace can come from a parent. I'm sure you'll be anxious to get back home to your children."

"Of course." Nicole smiled at the waiter as he delivered their drinks. "They're in boarding school until the end of the term, but when I get home, I plan to spend a lot of time with them."

Wanting to know if Nicole had even told her sons that their father had died, but thinking better of it, Beth bit her tongue. She inhaled deeply and tried to come up with something—anything—that would confirm her suspicions about Nicole and Jacopo.

"To life." Nicole raised her glass in a toast.

Beth followed and touched Nicole's glass with hers. "*Sláinte.*"

Nicole took a sip of the cocktail. She placed the glass on the table and leaned closer to Beth. "I have a secret."

"Oh?"

"I'm going to explode if I don't share it. Promise you won't tell a living soul." She rose from her seat opposite Beth, walked around the table, and sat next to her. She tilted close to Beth's ear.

"You can trust me," Beth said, trying to keep the excitement out of her voice.

"I'm not one to do anything on the spur of the moment but...."

She saw Nicole's eyes shift away from her. Beth jerked her head over her shoulder and spied Jacopo moving in their direction.

"Beth. What a surprise running into you here." He took her hand, raised it to his lips, and kissed it.

His eyes seemed to sparkle, filled with mirth, not masked with grief. She wanted to accuse him of being a heartless fraud, but instead, she asked how he was holding up.

He shrugged. "It's only natural that the girls are devastated. Thankfully, my sister is caring for them. I haven't even begun to deal with my own grief." Jacopo looked down at the wooden floor. "I'm lost."

Yesterday Beth would have believed him, but now she had grave doubts. "Do you know Mrs. Shelby?" Beth said.

"Shelby? That's the name of the other canal victim. Are you...?"

Nicole dabbed the linen napkin to her eyes. Beth could plainly see they glistened not with tears but amusement.

"I'm so sorry. My wife...." He covered his face with his hands.

"Nicole, this is Jacopo da Parma. It's his wife who was murdered a couple days ago."

"I'm so sorry." Nicole's voice broke with emotion.

He removed his hands. There were no signs of tears; in fact, his eyes still sparkled. Beth pulled her lips into a tight line. She didn't need help from her *fey* to know this charade was for her benefit.

"You must be heartbroken. Would you like to join us?" Nicole motioned to the chair next to her.

"I was on my way back to work when I decided to stop here for lunch."

"Please, join us," Nicole said.

Jacopo nodded before taking a seat.

"I'm surprised the two of you haven't met." Beth looked from one face to the other. Jacopo appeared nervous as he silently tapped his fingers against the linen-covered table, though Nicole seemed to be holding back a smile. "I thought the *Commissario Capo* might've introduced you since both of your spouses suffered the same horrific fate."

"Marinello," Jacopo said shaking his head, "I'm beginning to believe he hasn't the slightest clue on how to conduct a murder investigation. He had the nerve to ask me to take a polygraph test."

Marinello suspects Jacopo? Beth pursed her lips but said nothing.

"From what I understand, the police always want to rule out the spouse first," Nicole said.

"Yes. Yes. Even so, it's still insulting." He glanced at his Rolex. "I didn't realize it was so late. I have to get back to the office." Jacopo looked at Nicole. He offered her a shake of his head and then brushed his lips with his index finger.

Beth wondered if he was giving Nicole some kind of signal.

"But you have to eat?" Nicole said widening her eyes.

"Don't worry about me," he said standing. "I'm swamped at work and still have to finish composing Deirdre's eulogy." He glanced at Beth. "Thank you for the help with the funeral."

"I'll have to stop by the house to pick up clothes for the viewing," Beth said. "Tomorrow, okay?"

"Yes, yes. Take whatever you need." He turned to Nicole. "I grieve not only for my sorrow but yours as well." Jacopo offered her a half-bow and left them.

Beth waited a beat before asking Nicole about her secret.

Instead of answering, Nicole lifted her glass and took a swallow. "I wonder what happened to our waiter. I'm starved."

Beth lifted the menu but didn't look at the list of offerings. *Whatever that little scene was between the two of them, Nicole got the message loud and clear. Keep your mouth shut.* She lifted her drink and took a sip. *Whatever their secret is, no matter what it takes, I'm going to find out,* she vowed.

Chapter Forty-Eight

SHANE HUMMED UNDER HIS BREATH as he wound his way along Le Mercerie, several connecting streets that formed Venice's high-end shopping district. Though he'd hated deceiving Beth with a story about visiting the basilica in Murano, he wanted the gift to be a total surprise. The locket was beyond extravagant—concentric hearts—the larger one glittered with one hundred and fifty-nine diamonds and the smaller center one shone brilliantly with eighty-three Burmese rubies—totaling three carats. He wanted more than anything for Beth to know how much he treasured her and what better way than by presenting her with a treasure. Their anniversary wasn't for six more days, but with the ongoing tragedies of their ill-fated honeymoon, he decided an early celebration might bring the sparkle back into Beth's eyes before facing the gloom of her best's friend's funeral.

That morning, he'd held his breath as he riffled through Beth's giant tote bag in search of her wallet. Inside her billfold was a plastic covered pocket meant to display a driver's license, but Beth had instead inserted a photograph of her mother. The picture had been taken shortly after Beth's birth, and from the image, it was easy to see where she had acquired her beauty. With the photo in hand, he felt like a little kid who'd stolen the proverbial cookie from the cookie jar. His first stop had been at the photograph shop to have a reduced copy made of the picture. With the copy in hand, it had only taken the jeweler at Salvadori's a few moments to fit the beloved image inside the jewel-encrusted locket.

Though he was pleased that he'd checked off two items from his to-do list, he grimaced, running into gridlock on the narrow lane boasting upscale shops from Gucci to Hermes and everything in between. He took a deep breath and searched for an opening between leisurely moving crowds to dart through, but quickly realized that plan was hopeless. He'd just have to slog along and work on patience, a virtue he lacked. But exasperation won out, and he ducked down a side street, figuring an alternative route, one that wouldn't be as direct, but would still lead to Campo San Luca.

Walking down the meandering alleyway he vowed to stick to his guns since gondoliers were famous for driving a hard bargain when it came to fees. *But what the hell*, he thought with a shake of his head, *after spending a small fortune on the pendant what's a couple more hundred euros*? He wanted the whole enchilada—at least an hour ride, champagne, and song—romantic Italian songs at sunset.

Beth's gonna be blown away. Especially since he'd hinted that the marbled paper she's so crazy about would be a perfect anniversary gift. After all, he mused, paper is the traditional gift for first wedding anniversaries. He would give her the box of stationery he'd purchased days ago along with the Bortoletti ballpoint she'd admired on June 26th—their anniversary date. *But this little trinket*, he thought patting the gift-wrapped present nestled in his shirt pocket, *I'll give her tonight at dinner after being ferried along the Grand Canal.*

Setting up the private gondola ride went smoother than he'd expected. Though a bit disappointed that an hour ride was out of the question, he'd been able to expand the usual thirty-minute tour by ten minutes. He'd been assured that the singer had a voice like Caruso and would be accompanied by an accordionist. Satisfied, Shane made the reservation and was surprised that the fee was less than he was expecting to pay for a floating serenade on the picturesque canals of Venice.

He glanced at his watch and realized there was plenty of time to catch a boat to Murano and visit the church. Beth was planning to spend the afternoon with Deirdre's mom so he wouldn't be missed. He hadn't been aware of the close bond between the two women until Beth had shared how Carmel McKenna had been like a mother to her growing up. He figured she'd appreciate alone time with the grieving older woman who'd played such an important role in Beth's young life. With quick steps, he headed to the Zaccaria waterbus, a bit pleased by how easy it'd been for him to learn how to navigate the labyrinth of Venice's back streets.

He'd never lied to Beth, and even though setting up a romantic anniversary celebration was a good enough excuse, he didn't ever want to deceive her. *Too bad Beth didn't feel the same way.* A smile tugged at the corners of his lips as he realized that Beth would never admit to lying, but only the stretching of the truth a wee bit.

Chapter Forty-Nine

"WHERE CAN SHE BE, DINO?" Lidia stopped walking. She eyed the short flight of curved steps leading to the heavy wooden doors of San Silvestro church. A teenage girl was sitting on a step, but it wasn't Oriana. "We've been searching for hours and nothing."

"It's time to go home. After all, Oriana is probably there by now. Then all this worrying would've been for nothing."

"I have a sick feeling here," she placed a hand on her abdomen. "No, something terrible is going to happen. Call it a mother's intuition if you like, but I can't shake the horrible thought that Oriana is in danger. We have to find her."

"You have faith," he said pointing to the church. "Much more than me. Maybe you should act on that."

"You're right." She turned and climbed the five steps leading into the church.

"I'll wait for you here while you pray."

"No. Go on," Lidia said looking over her shoulder. "I want to talk with Father Bustato." She pulled open the door and entered the narthex. With hurried steps, she entered the nave, dipped her fingers in the holy water font, and made the sign of the cross. She scanned the sanctuary with its massive Corinthian columns and golden altar flanked by marble angels kneeling in prayer. Only one small scaffolding remained along the wall of the northern ambulatory. She clasped her hands and walked along the outside aisle. The sound of her heels hitting the marble floor echoed in the deserted church. She hurried past the sacristy and stopped at the closed door leading into Father Busato's small office. She took a deep breath and knocked.

"*Entra.*" The priest's voice rang.

With a bit of trepidation, Lidia opened the door. She believed he'd blame her for Oriana's disappearance, and she didn't need his admonishment because she already blamed herself.

He removed his glasses as she stood in the doorway. "Come in, Lidia."

"Oriana is missing. I've looked everywhere."

He stood and moved to her side. "You told her the truth."

She nodded. "It was too much for her. I shouldn't have divulged all of it at one time."

"Perhaps, not." He fixed his sight on her. Instead of condemnation, she read compassion in his tired eyes. "At the convent, I will offer up the Mass for Oriana's safe return. The sisters are expecting me in twenty minutes."

"I'll come with you."

"It's obvious you're overwhelmed with worry. You should go home. Wait for Oriana there."

"How can I just wait for her? I'll feel like a caged animal."

He reached into the pocket of his cassock and withdrew a rosary. "Keep company with our Lady. After my rounds of home visits, I'll stop by your apartment. Ah, I almost forgot. First, I must pay a visit to Jacopo da Parma. The murder of his wife has been a terrible shock. She was a good Christian woman; God have mercy on her soul. I'm sure he's in need of comfort." Father Bustato handed her the ebony string of beads. "Pray for Jacopo also. His heart must be broken."

ELENA WANTED TO CRADLE ORIANA and soothe her distress as the girl shared her story. Instead, she remained silent as the emotionally-charged words tumbled from Oriana's lips. Flashes of anger flew through Elena as she listened, unable to fathom the level of deceit that had unwittingly permeated the girl's life. It was one thing hearing the story from Daniele, but it broke her heart as she detected the raw pain in Oriana's quivering voice. Though Elena prided herself on being nonjudgmental, she couldn't stop from forming the opinion that Lidia Feloni had been reckless, selfish, and notoriously devious by whisking Oriana away from her unsuspecting husband. And now the child would never have the opportunity to know her father ... or he, her.

Daniele's question rang through her brain. *Could Lidia be capable of murder?* She wanted to believe the worse about Lidia but found it hard to imagine that she'd commit murder for any reason, even out of love for her daughter. *Lidia works hard, scrimps to pay for Oriana's education, and gives selflessly to the Sisters of Santa Angela de Merici.* She shook her head. *Maybe there was a good reason, at least in Lidia's mind, for why she abducted her daughter.*

"Mamma. Are you even listening?"

Chiara's question jerked Elena away from her thoughts. She stood and faced the two girls seated on the couch. "I'm so very sorry for you, Oriana. What your mother did was wrong, but I suspect her intentions were sincere."

"How can you say that?" Chiara's eyes blazed with anger. "What her mamma did was cruel and illegal. Even though Papà is now gone, at least, I spent most of my life with him, but Oriana never had the chance to know her own father."

Elena searched Oriana's face. She read the depth of despair in her ashen-colored eyes, though her expression remained like granite.

"Oriana doesn't want to live with her mamma anymore. Please, let her stay here. With us." Urgency filled Chiara's voice.

Elena squatted in front of Oriana and took her hand. It felt cold. "I'm not saying what your mamma did was right. Because it wasn't. But I suspect she did it out of a misbegotten desire to give you a better life. Because she loves you. More than her own life, I suspect."

Oriana opened her mouth as if to speak but then pressed her lips together.

"You need to go home. Talk this through with her." Elena released her grip and stood.

"Talk? What good will that do?" The tone in Chiara's voice rose. "Oriana's papà is dead. She wants to live with us. Mamma. Why can't you understand?"

"It's fine with me if Oriana wants to spend the summer in Padua with you but, her mother must give permission." Elena crossed her arms as defeat spread over Chiara's face.

"Thank you, Dottoressa Barozzi. I understand," Oriana said.

"Understand?" Chiara shot up, facing Elena with her arms outstretched. "Her mother kidnapped her and you want her to go home like nothing ever happened?"

Oriana rose and slipped her arm around Chiara's waist. "Your mamma is right. I have to face my mother. Let her know what I think about all of this."

"I'll telephone Lidia. I'll explain that you're having dinner with us. She must be wondering where you are," Elena said.

Oriana shook her head and faced Chiara. "I'll call you later." She moved close to her ear and whispered, "If only we could've been sisters for real."

Chapter Fifty

GRIEF CHOKED THEIR WORDS as Beth faced Carmel McKenna after she disembarked from the airport *vaporetto*. Beth blinked back tears but managed a smile as she opened her arms to embrace Carmel. All of the pent-up anger and frustration melted as Deirdre's mother wrapped her strong arms around Beth and held her close. She didn't want Carmel to release her, fearing that the hatred festering toward Deirdre's killer would resurface with added intensity. Carmel's hold weakened, and Beth dropped her arms.

Though the clamor of Venice swirled around them, the walk to Beth's flat had been silent as she wheeled Carmel's suitcase with one hand and linked the woman's arm with her other one. She stopped at the entrance of the once Gothic palace turned apartment building, reached for the access control panel, and tapped in the code. The lock clicked, and Beth pulled the door open. She guided Carmel across the grand foyer to the lift.

"My darlin' girl." Carmel broke the silence between them. "It's a blessing that you're here to help us through this tragedy." She touched Beth's shoulder.

The elevator opened, and the two women stepped inside. Beth pressed a button and faced Carmel as the door closed. "We're only in Venice because Deirdre insisted we go ahead with our long-awaited honeymoon. She'd pointed out the obvious to me ... that there's nowhere on Earth more romantic than Venice at sunset with the light shimmering on the Grand Canal. And, of course, I agreed." The door opened. Beth stepped out, still gripping the suitcase handle, and motioned down the short corridor. "Deirdre wanted everything to be perfect and found us this lovely flat." She fished the apartment key from the bottom of her tote and opened the door.

Then she took Carmel's hand and led her into the living room. "As you can see, it's romantic and cozy, perfect for my darlin' Shane and me." She released the suitcase and moved her hand in a sweeping motion. "Through the window, you can see a quaint little park that overlooks a canal. And the French doors in the bedroom lead to a charming balcony."

A pensive smile moved across Carmel's face. "That would be my Deirdre. She'd move heaven and Earth for you, Sibéal. She loved you so much."

"And I, her. Deirdre was the sister I never had." Beth took Carmel's arm and walked her to the sofa. "Make yourself comfortable while I put on the kettle."

"Where's your *acushla*, your Shane? Deirdre couldn't say enough glowing things about him."

"If it wasn't for my Shane, I don't know how I would've gotten over the accident. His love helped me heal ... here." Beth placed her hand over her heart. "But he's off to Murano for the afternoon. He wanted to visit the Basilica di Santa Maria e San Donato. Shane's an expert when it comes to architecture. Since the church originates from the 7th Century, he was curious about the design. Not to mention the bones belonging to the dragon that the saint is believed to have slain. He wanted you to know he'd be lighting a candle for Deirdre and offering up a prayer."

"That'll be ever so thoughtful of him." Carmel lifted her hand and with a featherlike touch ran her fingertip along the jagged scar crossing Beth's cheek. "My heart breaks that you had to suffer so all because a *bosthoon* couldn't hold his drink."

"Don't fret on my account. I'm fine now." Beth patted the sofa. "Take a load off while I brew us some tea." She headed toward the kitchen but paused and glanced over her shoulder catching a glimpse of Carmel. She'd moved to the window.

When Beth entered the living room holding two mugs of *Bancha Florita* tea, Carmel sat on the couch's edge with her hands clasped and lips moving as if in silent prayer. She cleared her throat, and Carmel fluttered her eyes open.

"Surprisingly, this makes a good *cuppa* considering it's Italian tea," Beth said.

Carmel took the cup and then a sip. "Not Lyons, for sure. But, good enough."

"You must be exhausted. We can talk tomorrow. Let me call a taxi to take you to Jacopo's *palazzo*," Beth said.

"I won't be going there. Apparently, he's too upset and couldn't take the added strain of having our family stay there until the funeral."

"What? As big as his house is? Dear Lord, he wouldn't even know that you were there."

Carmel pulled her lips tight.

"Where are you planning to stay? Not a hotel?" Beth didn't wait for an answer as she patted the sofa. "This is a sleeper. You can stay with us."

"Thank you, darlin,' but Caterina opened her house to our whole family."

"Caterina?" Beth narrowed her eyes trying to remember.

"Jacopo's sister. Caterina has always been friendly. That's more than I can say for Jacopo. My granddaughters are staying there, and I'm anxious to see them. I can only imagine their heartbreak. They loved their mother, and the twins were Deirdre's whole world."

"I know how they feel—the poor colleens." Beth raised her mug and took a quick sip. "But you're emotionally spent. Depleted. Why don't you spend the night here? In the morning, it'll be easier to face the challenges of greeting family.

"Thanks for the kind offer but..." Carmel glanced at her watch. "I'll have to leave in about an hour. You see, Caterina has planned a special family meal as a sort of memorial dinner for Deirdre. I suspect it's going to be difficult for all of us."

"Jacopo will be there?"

Carmel took a sip of tea. "He will. Yes. And actually, it'll be his first time seeing the twins since Deirdre..." Her eyes watered and a tear slid down her cheek. "Forgive me; I fear I'm still in shock. I can't believe that my baby girl is gone."

A wave of sadness washed over Beth. Carmel had mothered five children—born only a year or two apart. Deirdre was her fourth and the only girl. Growing up, Beth had all but lived in the McKenna home. Along with Deirdre and her mischievously playful brothers, the household offered a lively and warm atmosphere that was welcoming to a little girl who'd lost her own mother. But by an evil twist of fate, she was the one now comforting Carmel.

"It's like a living nightmare," Beth said. "I keep thinking if only I can wake up, everything will be grand. But then I realize it's not a dream; I'm wide awake, and I'm never going to see Deirdre again." She blinked a few times, fighting back tears, knowing she had to be strong if only for Carmel's sake.

"Come here to me."

Beth scooted closer.

"It seems like only minutes ago when you were a wee coleen confiding in me about your hopes for a modeling career or being a nun, or even a railroad conductor." A flash of a smile crossed Carmel's face. "But the sad truth is, it's been donkey years." She sighed. "If only we could relive those precious days."

"If only." Beth shook her head. "What I most remember is how you encouraged us to spread our wings. And it was in this city of fantasy and illusion that Deirdre's dreams became reality. She loved everything about Venice—its pageantry, history, food ... she didn't even mind the tourists. But as you well know, her true joy was her family. And teaching her vocation." She gulped a mouthful of air. "If only my *fey* would've warned me that Deirdre's life would be so savagely destroyed."

"Now don't be blaming yourself." Carmel patted Beth's hand. "It's that husband of hers I hold responsible."

"Jacopo?"

"If he'd been treating her right, she never would've run out into the night and come face to face with death."

The last thing Beth wanted to do was to upset Carmel any further. She took a swallow of tea wondering if she should bring up Deirdre's marital troubles.

"I'm afraid that Deirdre's happiness had become a bit tarnished," Carmel said. "Jacopo was insisting she become pregnant. If that wasn't bad enough, considering her health issues, he was punishing her because she hadn't produced a baby boy."

"He took away her little Irish parlor."

"Among other things. She was at her wit's end. I kept telling her to come home for a visit. But—"

"Didn't you know? Deirdre was planning to spend the summer in Ireland with you and the family. She was going to bring the girls with her."

"That would've been lovely." Carmel wiped her eyes with the back of her fingertips. "My Deirdre sugarcoated everything. I suspect things between she and Jacopo were worse than she'd let on."

Beth took the moment to look into Carmel's face. Instead of crinkling with amusement, the skin around her eyes sported dark circles, lines she'd never noticed before etched her forehead, and her deep auburn hair now looked dull and faded. If only there was something she could do to ease her sorrow. "Can I get you another *cuppa*?"

"I'm fine, love." Carmel leaned her head back and closed her eyes.

Beth slowly eased off the sofa. *A wee nap would do Carmel a world of good.* She moved to a window and looked outside. A handful of boys were playing football; running across the *campo's* stone pavement behind a skidding ball.

"Do you remember how much Deirdre loved to write?"

A bit startled, Beth spun around in Carmel's direction.

"Deirdre had an active imagination," Beth said. "Used to entertain us with her stories when we were mere *cailíní*—carefree girls—eager to discover what the future would hold." She paused a second. "Surely, she had the gift. I thought one day she'd become a famous author. But now...." She shrugged.

"Truth be, she never stopped writing."

"Oh?"

"She kept a journal ever since she was so high." Carmel touched her shoulder. "The tales she wove were truly magical."

"I had no idea. Why didn't she tell me?"

"Poor girl lacked confidence. Jacopo didn't help any. He belittled her for even thinking that her stories could be published."

Beth seethed but tried to hide her anger.

"She was so proud of your achievements," Carmel said. "For some reason, Deirdre thought she didn't stack up being only a housewife and a language teacher. Not very glamourous she used to say. She planned to surprise you with the news of her first published work."

"Bejesus! Why did she think that? My career was totally frivolous. Deirdre made a huge difference in so many people's lives." Beth shook her head. "With her passing, one of Earth's brightest lights was forever extinguished."

Carmel focused on her folded hands resting in her lap. "Thank you, Sibéal." When she raised her head, a smile brightened her face. "I truly believed that one of her stories was going to be published soon. She'd been so excited when an Irish editor had shown interest. Ah, what could've been, perhaps?"

"So, tell me; where are these stories?" Beth asked with a bit of excitement in her voice.

"Tucked away in a box inside a *press*, I'd imagine."

"That *palazzo* is full of cupboards and wardrobes." Beth brushed back a stray lock off her forehead. "I'll be going over there tomorrow to pick up one of Deirdre's outfits for the viewing. While I'm there, I'll snoop around a little and try to find her stories."

Carmel pressed an index finger against her pursed lips. "She told me that she'd stop hand-writing when she began outlining a novella. It was a mystery, I think. That's when she started using a computer. Maybe she saved all her stories to her laptop."

"I'll look for her laptop too. Just to be sure."

Carmel shot up. "The time's just flown by, darlin.' I really must be going."

"I'll call for a taxi."

"Now, don't be bothering yourself. I'm fairly familiar with Venice and her winding byways. Anyway, Catarina doesn't live very far from here plus," she said freeing her mobile from her skirt pocket, "I've got GPS."

"Before you leave, I have something for you." Beth walked to the far end of the room and stepped into the dining area. She returned with a package. "I was going to give this to Deirdre for a birthday present."

Carmel took the parcel and carefully unfolded the heavy wrapping paper. She ran her fingers around the silver-gilt frame accented with agate and a band of carnelian.

"I thought you'd like this photo of the two of us. It was taken the first time we visited Venice. It's when Deirdre fell in love with the city and decided to stay."

"'Tis lovely." She raised her head and looked at Beth. Tears had gathered in her eyes. "I'll treasure it forever."

Chapter Fifty-One

AFTER SPENDING THE BETTER PART of an hour secretly celebrating his pending nuptials in the Aventi Bar, Jacopo decided to walk home before heading to Nicole's for the night. He'd had a good time, *maybe too good*, he thought as his right temple began to throb. But it was worth it, he decided remembering how he'd kept the drinks flowing and the lively conversation focused on last year's crushing failure of Italy's non-qualification in the World Cup. That topic surrounding the beloved *gli Azzurri* always caused emotions to flare.

The camaraderie at the bar turned out to be the tonic he'd needed to blot out the lingering scene at his sister's house. There, the heartbreak and sorrow were palpable, and it pained him to see his little girls' tears. Though he tried to suppress it, his temper flared at the travesty of Deirdre's death, knowing she died in vain all because of Lidia's deception. He'd been with his family only ten minutes when he begged off saying he was too distraught to stay for the memorial dinner. Then he made his way to the bar. The minute he entered the *bacaro,* the cloying aroma of grief that clung to him like cellophane fell away.

Now on his way home, he walked around the church of San Silvestro and gulped several mouthfuls of the night air, relieved that the hordes of tourists had vacated for the mainland. Now he could enjoy the magical beauty of his beloved city without pressing against a sea of foreigners with gawking eyes and garbled tongues.

"*Buonasera,* Signore da Parma."

Jacopo stopped. His eyes flickered from one side of the narrow street to the other. A girl sat on the church steps. *Could it be?* In the dim twilight, he wasn't sure. His heart pounded. He moved closer, and a trill of excitement rushed through him. "Oriana? What are you doing here?"

"I wanted to go inside and pray for Mamma, but the church is locked."

"She has another headache?"

Oriana shook her head. "A special intention for something that happened a long time ago." She lowered her eyes for a second.

Now that he had Oriana in his grasp, he sure as hell wasn't going to let her get away. He held back the smile that ached to form, not believing his luck. Jail wasn't nearly enough punishment for Lidia, but this chance meeting with her daughter provided the opportunity to destroy the one woman he'd been willing to kill for. A myriad of ideas flew through his brain of how to dole out a measure of sweet revenge. He took in the forlorn figure seated on the step. *Too bad for you, little girl,* he thought shaking his head, *that you're the unfortunate offspring of that thankless harpy.*

He trembled even though the balmy night air hung thick with humidity. It'd never struck him before how much the girl looked like Lidia, even now, with her face drawn lacking the usual bright assurance of youth. In fact, he couldn't read any sign of emotion besides a stony quietness. "Come and walk with me." He held out his hand.

"I need to go home. It's late, and my mother will be worried."

By the careless way she'd said the words, Jacopo sensed that she didn't really want to leave. "Allow me to escort you there. With the recent murders," he said with a sigh, "the streets aren't exactly the safest place after dark."

She rose and walked down the couple steps.

"You must be excited about your upcoming adventure in California," he said. "When do you leave?"

"Tomorrow," Oriana said. "But I doubt I'll be going with everything that's happened."

"Happened?"

"You don't know?" She frowned.

"I know your mother is moving to Rome because of a new job. You don't want to move?"

"Something like that." Oriana shrugged.

They neared the edge of the square when Jacopo's brain began to tick. First, he'd take her to the bar. After that, he'd figure out his next step. "Are you hungry?"

"A little."

"Then it's settled." He took her hand and led her around the church's imposing bell tower. He stopped in front of a collection of black and white tables that flanked a weathered brick building.

"Oh, Signore. Please forgive me."

He noticed a flash of alarm cross her face.

"I haven't offered you a word of condolence. I'm so sorry. Signora Deirdre was one of the kindest ladies I've ever known. Your heart must be broken."

Jacopo had forgotten that he should be mourning his wife's passing. He wiped every vestige of delight from his face and forced an unnatural solemnity. "I'm still in shock over what happened to my poor Deirdre. I must've walked straight across Venice trying to shake the incredible depth of loneliness that's taken hold of me. It's funny because when I saw you on the church steps, I realized that I too wanted to enter that sanctuary— to offer a prayer for the repose of my wife's soul."

She nodded.

"With Deirdre gone, I've become a shadow of myself. Rationally, I know that I must keep on living, if not for me, but for my precious daughters. But the emptiness here," he said tapping his chest, "will probably remain with me for the rest of my life."

An awkward silence stood between them.

"Do you have any idea who might've committed the murders?" Oriana asked.

He detected a trace of hope touching her words. "Not the slightest hint, but I pray to God the police catch the culprit soon."

Her face dropped.

"Look. This hasn't been made public yet but ... between you and me ... the Chief Superintendent is about to make an arrest." *Incarcerating your damn mother*, he thought with a smirk. "The good news is that an innocent man will not be accused of being the Canal Murderer."

He'd been amused that Marinello had taken heed of his suggestion that Lorenzo could've killed Deirdre and had rearrested him. Even so, he hadn't a trace of doubt that Lorenzo would be released since there wasn't any reasonable motive or actual proof that he killed Shelby or Deirdre.

"No need to worry," he said. "Justice will be had for Deirdre and that murdered tourist." He shot her an encouraging smile. "Take a seat while I run inside and get you a Fanta Chinotto and a bite to eat."

"It's so kind of you. *Grazie*."

He entered the bar through the wide doorway and stepped next to the long wooden bar. "Tomasso," Jacopo said addressing the barman.

"What ... back so soon?"

He offered his opened palms and a shrug. "Two *chinotti*. In one, add two shots of Cavalli vodka."

Tomasso's eyebrows jumped. "Ah, so you've found a companion."

A slow smile spread across Jacopo's face.

"You don't waste time when it comes to the ladies." A strain of admiration filled the barman's words.

"What can I say? They can't help themselves. I guess I'm just damn irresistible."

Jacopo chortled as Tomasso shook his bald head.

A few moments later, Tomasso placed two glasses in front of Jacopo and indicated the one with alcohol.

Jacopo turned away from the bar, motioned to a waitress, and placed an order. He took the drinks and stepped outside. Oriana didn't look at him; she'd wrapped her arms across her chest and rocked back and forth on the woven black wicker chair.

"Oriana?"

She looked up startled. "With you losing your wife and me losing ... anyway, I was thinking about how unfair life can be."

"That's a weighty subject for such a young lady." He handed her the alcohol-laden glass and watched her take a quick sip. "Like *chinotto*, life is a mixture of the bitter and the sweet. So, drink up Oriana, and like me, embrace life."

"It was wrong of me to impose." She rose and stepped away from the table.

"You've done nothing of the kind. Actually, being with you has eased some of my sorrow. Please, sit down, and remind a grown-up what it's like to be young and carefree."

She reclaimed her seat. "Sometimes unbearable burdens are placed on the young, crushing their spirits, too." Oriana lifted the glass and took a deep swallow.

"Enough of this morbid talk. Let's make a pact. Tonight, we'll cheer each other up."

"*Va bene*," she said with a nod. She lifted the glass and took a couple of sips. "How are your daughters?"

"Only happy talk allowed, remember?" He shook his head. "What's your favorite subject in school?"

"Math and science are my favorites."

"Ah, so you plan on being a researcher or ... *professoressa*?"

Oriana took a long draught from the glass. "I'm not sure. Maybe an engineer." She shrugged. "Or an archeologist."

A smile crossed his lips, seeing that she'd finished her drink. "Archeologist. Sounds fascinating."

She rubbed her forehead. "I'm feeling a little funny."

"Probably because you're hungry. Ah, here's our food." The waitress landed two plates filled with generous slices of chicken and spinach couscous pie and a side of grilled vegetables. "The food here is delicious," Jacopo said as the waitress retreated inside the bar. "You start eating, and I'll get the drinks refilled."

When Jacopo returned, he was pleased that she'd barely eaten a couple mouthfuls.

"You don't like it?" he asked.

"Oh, no. It's fine. But, I feel kind of ... I don't know, not right."

"Tired?"

She shrugged.

"Well, at least drink your soda. The caffeine will help energize you."

"Right." She guzzled down half the drink then landed the glass on the table with such force that it tottered on its narrow base almost tipping over.

"We better get going," he said pleased that the alcohol had affected her so quickly.

Oriana swayed when she stood. "I can't imagine why I feel so ... so dizzy."

He jumped up and grabbed her upper arms. "*Calma.* You got up too fast. Let me help." Without waiting for an answer, he wrapped his arm around her shoulders and supported her. With gentle prodding, he urged her to walk.

"I don't understand what's happened," Oriana said.

"Probably a reaction to stress. With the news of your father's death."

"Mamma told you?" She pulled out of his grasp and nearly fell. He grabbed her arm and steadied her. "How many people did she talk to about Papà being murdered before even thinking of telling me?"

"That probably was a mistake on her part."

"I don't want to hear excuses. My whole life has been a lie because of her."

"Look, Oriana." He jutted his chin in the direction of the *vaporetto* stop. "You're in no shape to walk home."

Each labored step added to the struggle of keeping her upright. Just when he believed he was getting the walking thing under control, Oriana stopped, looked into his face for a split-second, and then bent over retching. He weighed his options: leave her here in the shadows with her stinking pool of vomit or continue his mission. Though he wanted to be finished with the girl, getting Lidia's precious daughter drunk wasn't enough to bring that bitch to her knees.

She wiped her mouth with the back of her hand, and he urged her onward. She muttered slurred words. A few meters away from the dock, her voice became louder. "She must've had a good reason. She'd never want to hurt me. Mamma ... loves ... me."

Oriana's declaration made him seethe. *This damn girl is going to forgive Lidia. But by the time I'm through with her, Oriana won't be capable of excusing Lidia for her deceit.* His lip curled.

"I have big plans for you, my dear," he said in her ear.

"Plans?" she mumbled.

He tightened his hold around her shoulders, noticing the light emanating from the large windows of a *vaporetto* as it glided toward the stop. "We're just about there. You can do it. Keep walking."

She stumbled along as he strived to aim her forward. For an instant, he chided himself for plying her with too much booze but shook the idea from his mind. If his strategy was going to be successful, then she'd have to be a willing participant, and Oriana, sure as hell, wouldn't be an active part of his plan sober. Anyway, he brightened, if he couldn't have Lidia, then he'd take her precious daughter instead.

Half carrying her up the ramp and into the boat, he landed her on the first vacant bench. He dropped next to Oriana and patted her knee as her slack body slumped against his. She smelled of alcohol and vomit. Instead of allowing the stink to disgust him, a flash of triumph strengthened his resolve.

"How many times have I warned you about those friends of yours?" He raised his voice, hoping to satisfy the curious glances of those around him. "It's always up to Papà..." He turned his head toward the middle-aged couple seated across from them. Not knowing if they were bemused or sympathetic, he offered a shrug. "Kids. Please God, help me survive these teenage years." He rolled his eyes upwards. Smiles erupted on the couples' faces while the woman offered him a knowing nod of her graying head.

After a sweat-inducing effort to direct Oriana off the waterbus, he realized that the short ride hadn't done much to sober up the girl. Once out of the light cast from the ornate lanterns along the Grand Canal, he swept Oriana up and landed her across his shoulders like a sack of grain. The claps of his hurried steps filled the night air as he made his way home.

Winded and irritated, Jacopo clenched his teeth as he turned the key in the door and entered the first floor. Eager to be freed from his burden, he hurried across the darkened entry but paused a second in front of the daunting staircase. He sighed but forged onward as he carried Oriana up the steps and onto the *piano nobile*, the main level. He rushed a few steps down the *portego,* stepped into the small reception room, and clicked on the light. He eased her onto an elaborate-cut velvet couch. She fluttered her eyes open.

"Where am I?" She bolted upright and clutched her head. Her eyes flickered around the room. "Signore, this is your house."

Jacopo pulled a handkerchief free from his back pocket and blotted his face. He willed his thumping heart to slow and swallowed hard. "Don't tell me you don't remember?"

"Remember?"

"You took ill. Since you didn't want to upset your mother, I suggested you stay here until you feel better."

She frowned. "I'm fine. Really. Please, Signore, take me home. Now."

"No headache. Upset stomach?"

Oriana bit her lip.

"Remember our pact? Let me help you."

She nodded.

"Ah. That's better." He dropped next to her and kissed her cheek. Though the acidic odor of stale vomit lingered, he felt strangely excited. He turned her head and looked into her questioning eyes. "I'm so heartbroken. My little girls have lost their mamma, and I well, I've lost the love of my life." He inched closer so that their hips touched. "Poor Oriana. Never having the chance to know your father all because of your selfish, self-righteous mother."

She slid away from him.

Oriana had the look of a caged animal. He sensed her fear. That excited him even more. "I know how both of us can forget about our loss. Let me show you." He reached for her.

"No, Signore."

"We need each other."

She jumped up and took a few steps but then swayed and landed on the floor. She grabbed her head. "I have to go."

"I didn't mean to upset you. I'll take you home. But first, I'll get you some aspirin." He lifted her back up onto the couch. "Be right back."

He'd only taken a few steps out of the room when the sickening thought that the girl might flee made him stop. *Dammit. I bet she has a cellphone, too.* He turned back and stood in the door's threshold. Oriana had drifted off. He shook her. "Give me your phone."

Her eyes fluttered half-open. "I want to call your mamma. Tell her you're okay."

She fumbled with her back pocket and finally pulled out the cellphone. "I'll call her." She attempted to swipe the screen and frowned.

"Let me help." He took the phone. She slumped back against the couch, kicked off her flip-flops, and closed her eyes.

The moment he'd been waiting for had arrived. He moved close, pressed his lips against hers, and forced her mouth open. At first, she accepted his kiss as a soft murmur of delight filled his ears. A second later, she ripped her head away. Undaunted, he dropped to her neck and sucked on a mouthful of skin. He jerked, uttering a curse as she flayed her balled fists, hitting his arm.

The expression of outrage on her face made him laugh. "You're a desirable woman, Oriana. But I understand. You're not interested. Eh?"

"How dare you?" Her words trailed off into an unrecognizable utterance.

"I almost forgot the aspirin."

He jumped off the couch, exited the room, and ran down the *portego*. He raced through his office and into his bed-chamber. Not slowing down, he flew into the en suite and pulled open the medicine cabinet. He bypassed the aspirin and grasped the prescription bottle of sleeping pills. During his brief stay at the hospital, after Deirdre's death, he'd requested the prescription, fearing that the look on Deirdre's lifeless face would haunt his dreams. Luckily, that hadn't happened. But the ruin of Lidia's daughter would have the opposite effect, making his dreams come true. He found it difficult to reign in his elation but realized he didn't have to bother as a full smile crossed his face.

A couple of minutes later, he returned to the reception room holding a mug of sparkling water and a couple of sleeping pills. He stood in front of the slumbering girl, overcome by her drunkenness. She looked like an angel. Her skin, still a bit flushed, appeared luminous, her softly curled blonde hair brushed her cheeks, and her strong, dimpled chin gave way to her long, delicate, neck. He dragged his finger under her chin and moved it along the sensuous contour of her neck. He stopped at the patch of discolored skin where a bruise had already started to blossom.

When they find her, they'll know she was a damn whore just like her mother.

"Oriana."

She didn't open her eyes.

"I have aspirin."

He waited as she struggled to sit upright on the settee. Her eyes opened a mere sliver.

"Take this."

She shook her head.

"Dammit. It's for your own good." He took a pill and pressed it between her lips. "Swallow it."

He stood with arms crossed, fearing she'd spit it out. She didn't. He placed the cup against her lips, and it seemed like more water splashed on her chin then went down her throat. Stepping away, he paced across the floor, bidding his time. The last thing he wanted was for her to wake up. Knocked out, she'd be pliable like putty in his hands—no struggle and especially no complaints. He trembled with the sweet thought of payback so close that he could taste victory. After a quick glance at the sleeping girl, he decided he'd waited long enough.

Jacopo stuck his hand into his pocket and touched the knife. He wanted Oriana's death to mimic the other two, but he feared that wouldn't be possible. The only remaining *Bauta* he owned was the one hanging in his study, which dated from the eighteenth century. A prized possession. He resumed pacing but had only taken a few steps when the thought hit him.

The girls. They have a trunkful of costumes. Deirdre made sure that the twins had plenty of items to nourish their young imaginations. If only Fortuna will smile on me again, he thought crossing his fingers.

Ten minutes later, he returned to Oriana's side, elated that he'd located a mask inside a teak chest that stood between his daughter's wardrobes. He'd also discovered a silky scarf—one of those touristy types of bandanas found almost anywhere in Venice—that he'd be more than glad to dispose of after choking the life out of Lidia's daughter. He dropped the mask and scarf on a chair and pulled the knife free from his pocket. With a flick of his thumb, the blade flashed open.

Jacopo knelt next to the couch and placed the stiletto against her neck. He added a bit of pressure but then dropped the knife. The carpet's thick pile muted the blade's landing, making the knife seem harmless. The beating of his heart pounded in his ears as a rush of heat blazed through him.

The time of retribution had finally arrived.

Chapter Fifty-Two

BETH TOUCHED THE HEART-SHAPED locket resting against the hollow of her neck.

"You like it?" Shane slowed his pace as a mischievous grin claimed his face.

"Like it? It's gorgeous. My darlin' boy, everything about this evening has been magical. From the gondola ride to the dinner and especially this." She brushed the pendant again. "And so thoughtful of you to place a photo of *me ma* inside." She grabbed his hand and squeezed it. She'd never seen him this relaxed and carefree before and now, like Shane, she believed he'd made the right decision to leave the Sheriff's Department. "I love you, Shane Dalton."

"Really, it was nothing, Betty. Just planning and a tiny bit of deceit." He offered her a wink. "My aim was to get us back on track. Our honeymoon was meant to be a time for us to celebrate our marriage. But with all that's happened—"

"Seems like it was doomed from the start." She pointed at the bridge where she'd first spotted Jonathan Shelby's body.

He hurried Beth up the bridge's two sets of steps. Instead of crossing over the bridge, she stopped at the balustrade and looked into the canal that blended seamlessly with the darkness. His arm encircled her waist. "Come on," he whispered in her ear.

"This is where it all started." She shivered.

Instead of commenting, he kissed her cheek.

Her heart thumped against her ribcage. There was no question this time what her *fey* was telling her. "There's going to be another murder."

"What?"

"My *fey* warned me. We have to do something."

"You're letting your imagination run wild. It's being on this bridge that's upsetting you."

She pulled away from him. "I know you don't believe in anything besides cold, hard facts, but I was right about Deirdre." She looked into his face covered mostly by shadows. "I'm afraid something terrible is going to happen." She tried to conceal her frustration because the last thing she wanted was to spoil their amazing evening. *Why is it so hard for him to trust my sixth-sense?*

"Look. I'll call Marinello in the morning. I'll tell him I got it from a good source that there might be another murder."

"You will?" She faced him. "Dear Lord, I hope it won't be too late."

"What would you rather do? Spend the whole night walking up and down every canal in Venice. All one hundred and fifty of them?"

"My *fey* led me to Deirdre." Even if her *fey* did lead her to the scene of the crime, Beth wondered if she'd be capable of stopping the crazed killer. "You're probably right."

"Sorry, Betty, but twelve years as a homicide detective trumps your sixth-sense every time."

She opened her mouth to protest, but he pressed his lips against hers. "Why don't we skip that nightcap at Florian's and head back to the apartment?"

"I think you must have a touch of the *fey* yourself since you just read my mind," she said with forced enthusiasm, believing Venice was about to see its third murder in as many weeks.

Chapter Fifty-Three

JACOPO REACHED FOR ORIANA'S blouse. With nimble fingers, he undid the pearl-like buttons, pulled it open, and flicked free the bra's front clasp. He swiped away the brassiere's silky material and held his breath admiring her firm, round breasts. Dizzy with desire, he opened his mouth and enveloped a nipple. A swipe of his tongue probed gently, but as the excitement of tasting the virginal flesh intensified, he began suckling like a baby, greedy for his mother's milk. He moved to the other breast and started nibbling the downy skin as his hands encircled her tiny waist and then moved down to her hips. His breath, now ragged, came out in quick spurts as he tugged at her slacks.

Loud banging filled his ears.

"*Cazzo*," he cursed. "Who the hell?" Ignoring whoever was at the door, he focused on Oriana's pants and noticed a side zipper. He yanked on the tag, pulled down the zipper, and slid his hand inside her waistband. Another loud knock sounded. He froze. "Oh no, she didn't," he said under his breath, remembering how Caterina had insisted that the girls return to their home—of their need to be with him—and that she'd bring them to his palazzo after Deirdre's memorial dinner. He'd begged for a couple more days to deal with his own grief and believed that his sister had reluctantly agreed.

"What the hell am I going to do with her?" He lifted himself off Oriana and sat as if in a stupor. His brain refused to work. He tapped his forehead a couple of times with his balled fist before reaching for the girl. He did his best to close her shirt, grabbed the mask and bandana, and slid them under the couch. Patting the floor he found the knife, flicked it into its sheath, and slipped it back into his pocket. He stood and glanced at the antique mirror above the couch, smoothed back his hair, and closed the room's door behind him.

With quick steps, he rushed to the source of the banging. Jacopo paused for a second to assume a grief-filled countenance; he rubbed his eyes to make them red, drew his lips downward, and slouched. He'd have to show Caterina he was incapable of caring for two active children. He pulled open the door leading into his foyer expecting to see his girls, but instead, he faced an elderly priest. Father Bustato.

"Ah, Jacopo. I've awakened you?" He pointed to Jacopo's opened shirt.

"Um ... No. No, Father." Not remembering that he'd undone his linen shirt, Jacopo began buttoning it up.

"Your door was open." The priest motioned to the staircase behind him.

"Come in," Jacopo said pulling the door, adorned with the carved lion head, wider.

Father Bustato stepped inside. "May God strengthen you. Though we might not understand why such tragedies happen, our faith will sustain us."

Jacopo nodded furiously, thinking of a way to make the priest go away. "I'm still in shock ... Deirdre murdered ... it's impossible to believe she's gone."

The priest took a few steps down the *portego* and stopped at the reception room. "Why don't we sit a while and pray." He reached for the pocket door.

"No. I mean, I appreciate your concern, but I haven't been sleeping well and was about to retire. I'll stop by the church tomorrow."

"I understand. But, I'm in no hurry. Sometimes baring the depth of our grief helps."

"I'm not up to it. But tomorrow, I'll stop by the rectory."

"Then I will remember you in my prayers."

"Thank you, Father." Jacopo placed a hand on the priest's back and directed him down the hall. They'd only taken a few steps when a scream shattered the silence.

Father Bustato stopped and looked at Jacopo. Confusion covered his face.

"My girls. They've been having nightmares. Please pray for them too," Jacopo said, hiding his panic and wondering how the hell Oriana could've awakened. He'd been sure she'd swallowed the sleeping pill.

The door to the reception room slid open, and Oriana tottered out. Alarm riveted her blanched face. Jacopo chewed the inside of his cheek, taking in her mussed hair, water-spattered misbuttoned shirt, and bare feet.

"Oriana?" Father Bustato flew to her side. "What's happened? Your mamma is sick with worry."

She clasped her temples and started shaking.

"I can explain," Jacopo said. "I found her drunk, wandering the streets, and brought her here to sober up. Christian charity impelled me to help the poor girl."

"No," Oriana protested. She moved her collar and exposed a bruise on her neck.

"Look, I don't know what happened before I found her. Like I said she was drunk," Jacopo said.

Father Bustato opened his arms and cradled Oriana.

"I swear on all that is holy, I didn't do anything wrong," she said into the priest's chest.

Father Bustato glared at Jacopo. "If you have anything to confess—"

"For the love of God, I didn't do anything but try to help."

"I want you to telephone Lidia and tell her Oriana is here," Father Bustato said. "Once Lidia arrives, we'll get to the bottom of this."

LIDIA STROKED ORIANA'S hair as the girl rested her head on her mother's shoulder. When Jacopo had telephoned, she breathed relief, but then, almost immediately, a blast of anger began to bubble. His words hadn't made much sense. *Oriana drunk?* Now seated in Jacopo's salon, she stared at him, not knowing what to think.

"I'm telling you. I found Oriana sprawled on the steps of San Silvestro. Drunk." Jacopo flung out his hands in exasperation.

"Is this true?" Lidia whispered in her daughter's ear.

Oriana sat upright on the couch. "I don't understand, Signore. We met at the church and had dinner at the Avanti. I felt sorry because you were sad about your wife's death. I ate a little and drank chinotto. After that I don't remember too much ... being on a waterbus ... waking up here ... and...." She shook her head.

Father Bustato stood with his arms folded. "Don't be afraid." He moved next to Oriana and rested his deeply veined hand on her shoulder. "Would you like me to hear your confession?"

She nodded. "But first, I want to tell Mamma something."

"The alcohol must have addled her brain." Jacopo rose from his seat across from Lidia and stepped in front of her. "Remember you can't trust the words of a drunk."

"Go on." Lidia prodded Oriana while ignoring Jacopo.

"In private," Oriana said.

"Are you kidding me? Once she's alone with you, she'll make up some kind of story to diminish how much I helped her."

Lidia stood. "We can talk in the kitchen."

Oriana stood too quickly and swayed. Lidia wrapped her arm around Oriana's waist, led her out of the reception room, and down the *portego* toward the back of the house. They walked in silence, but once within the comforting space of Deirdre's favorite room, Oriana began to weep softly.

Lidia's heart ached for her daughter, and she silently cursed this hellish nightmare that had victimized her beloved Oriana. It was her fault that Oriana wound up in such a state.

Oriana wiped her eyes and looked directly into her mother's face. "I was so angry at you," she whispered. "I told Chiara to lie. To tell you that I wasn't with her. That I will confess to Father Bustato. But, what Signore da Parma said wasn't true." She shook her head. "The only thing I drank was chinotto. It was then that I started to feel strange. After that, almost everything is a blank. But..." she paused and inhaled deeply. "Signora da Parma—he kissed me."

Lidia's heart fell to her gut. "A kiss? What else did he do?"

Oriana shook her head. "My head was spinning; I was so dizzy. He gave me a pill. Said it was aspirin. I tucked it under my tongue, and when he left the room, I tossed it behind the couch."

She hugged her daughter close. "You did nothing wrong." Though she assured Oriana, Lidia wanted to convince herself that Jacopo had stopped with only a kiss. She guessed he didn't. *He hates me that much he'd assault my daughter?*

"I'm sorry, Mamma."

"Sorry? No, Oriana. I'm the one that's sorry." Lidia released her. "We're going home. You'll feel better once you're in your own bed." They walked down the grand hall hand in hand. "Wait for me on the first floor," Lidia said pointing toward the lion door at the end of the grand hallway. She didn't move until the heavy door closed behind Oriana.

She hurried back inside the salon. Jacopo jerked toward her. Lidia sensed he was nervous by the way he drummed his foot against the plush carpet. She crossed her arms and remained silent.

"As I was telling Father Bustato, girls Oriana's age have such fanciful imaginations. I wouldn't put much stock into whatever she told you. But please, don't be too hard on the girl—"

She cut off his words with a sharp slap across his face.

Chapter Fifty-Four

BETH SAT AT THE CAFÉ'S SMALL TABLE with a white porcelain cup cradled in her hand. A habit that'd developed over the past few mornings. A cappuccino and a flakey pastry. This morning, she was distracted more than usual. Shane had been good to his word and had telephoned Marinello only moments after arising and pouring himself a tall glass of *succo d'arancia*— the blood orange juice—now his favorite with its distinct sweet flavor and a hint of raspberry. She'd kept her eyes glued on Shane as he explained to the Chief Superintendent about her premonition of another murder. The telephone conversation had been brief, and after ending the call, he took a sip of the crimson juice and then pulled Beth into an embrace.

"No new murders," he whispered into her ear. Relived, she wiggled free, sensing he had more to tell her. He brushed a few stray locks off his forehead. "Marinello has a couple forensic IT investigators checking out Lidia Feloni's work computer. Seems like Nicole might've been right all along."

"Lidia's responsible for Shelby's murder?"

"Marinello is fairly confident that she might've played a part. They've discovered that she'd checked out towns in Austria as if searching for a place to plan a new life."

"Or a vacation?"

He shrugged. "Marinello seems to think it's more than that since he also found out that she'd wired deposit money for an apartment. Seems like she was planning a get-away before she became a suspect but wasn't quick enough."

This latest bit of information unnerved Beth as she sat at the café. She clutched her coffee cup tighter and frowned, unable to chase away the

281

thought of Lidia Feloni being a cold-blooded murderer. She glanced around St. Mark's Square unfolding beyond her and lingered on the basilica. The church shimmered in the morning light—five domes affixed with crosses, mosaic lunettes, arches, and golden spires—it seemed like a giant, golden ship offering a safe-haven to anyone who entered through the massive bronze doors. She took a quick sip of coffee as an overwhelming need to bolt into the church washed over her. Beth placed the cup on its saucer, rose, and stepped into the square, but then shook her head. Deirdre's funeral, slated for tomorrow morning, stopped her from heading to the church since there was still so much to do. She walked back to the table, drained her cup, and popped the final bite of pastry into her mouth. First stop, Jacopo's *palazzo.*

Beth walked in the direction of the basilica as she crossed the square but then turned away from it. She hurried along the *Procuratie Vecchie,* in the shade cast from the ancient building, one of three, that formed the perimeter of the Piazza San Marco. She picked up speed wanting to finish the disagreeable task of selecting an outfit for Deirdre's viewing as quickly as possible. After passing the clock tower, she became distracted, noticing a couple of teenaged girls trying on masks at a souvenir kiosk. Even though they were cheaply crafted, unlike the masks she admired at *Casa della Maschera,* their ornate decorations and colors captured Beth's attention. She joined the girls and spotted a white *Bauta.* She lifted it from the rack and placed it over her face. A shiver ran through her as the memory of the murdered bodies seemed to swirl in front of her eyes. She returned the mask and continued her mission, feeling like a raindrop in a torrent as she navigated among the throng of sightseers filling up the square.

She couldn't help but pause after spying a toddler laughing as pigeons gathered around her. The little girl released fistfuls of contraband seed as if sowing a cobblestone field. With a giggle, she dropped the paper bag of grain and ran toward her father. With opened arms, he lifted the child, spun her around, and her laughter filled the air like soothing music. A woman, standing a few feet away, snapped their picture on her mobile. Captivated by the charming scene, Beth watched until the man with his daughter, snug in his protective arms, met the woman and kissed. For an instant, she imaged Shane holding a child and kissing her, but with a shake of her head, she knew that little scene would never be possible thanks to a drunk driver who failed to take her life but stole away her capability of becoming a mother.

Beth lifted the discarded bag of birdseed that was still half full. She decided to use it later when Shane was with her since it amused her the way he complained about the pigeons. It would be worth the seven hundred euro fine just to see his expression as she scattered the seed and a throng of hungry birds descended around them. With a smile touching her face, she creased the top of the bag and slipped it into the back pocket of her Bermuda shorts.

Though she could've taken a water taxi, Beth felt like walking. It would take a half-hour, that is, if she didn't get lost. She fished her mobile free from her tote bag and tapped Jacopo's address into her navigation app. Once off the main tourist lanes, she slipped into a rhythm following the instructions sounding from her phone. Her mind wandered back to the conversation with Carmel and of Deirdre's aspirations to be an author which reminded her to search for Deirdre's stories and laptop. She'd do that before heading to the church to finalize the funeral arrangement with Carmel.

Since she'd decided against arriving by taxi, Beth wouldn't have the opportunity to admire the elegant façade of Jacopo's *palazzo*. She believed it was one of the grandest in all of Venice with its coral stucco walls ornamented with ogee arched loggias, balconies, a terracotta roof, and bell-shaped chimneys. The escutcheon, the de Parma coat of arms, had stood proudly for half a millennium above the impressive entryway that caused her to wonder how brilliant it must be to have a direct connection to ancestors spanning back centuries.

As she approached the edifice, Beth realized that the back view of Jacopo's *palazzo* wasn't too shabby either. The adjoining buildings hadn't been kept up as well and appeared to sag, neglected with crumbling stucco walls and overgrown courtyards.

With a renewed sense of purpose, she hurried through Jacopo's elaborate *piazzetta*. Her sandals slapped against the white pavers as she skirted around the carved Istria stone cistern sealed with a metal wellhead and large planters filled with blossoming flowers.

She paused in front of the door, fearing that rummaging through her friend's clothing would not only be difficult but bring with it a fresh bout of melancholy. *I don't have a choice*, she thought swinging open the heavy door. With quick steps, she crossed the wide entry and building up speed jogged up the broad staircase. After a light rap on the door with the carved lion's head, she waited in hopes that Jacopo would be home. Then she'd be able to question him about his relationship with Nicole Shelby. She was in the proper mood to ream into him if he even suggested involvement with Nicole only days after Deirdre's death.

Santina opened the door and a smile sprung to her tired face. She ushered Beth inside and offered a warm greeting. Beth kissed her cheeks and asked if Jacopo was somewhere within the stately home. Santina shook her head.

"Silly me, I left yesterday without picking up an outfit for the viewing," Beth said. "I'll have to hurry since I have an appointment at the church within the hour."

"The signore put in an order for his dinner, so I need to stop by the market," she said peeking at her watch. "Will you need my help?"

"Don't let me interrupt your schedule. I'll manage fine on my own."

"*Va bene.* But if you're unsure of what to choose, Signora da Parma had a special fondness for the cream-colored Gucci dress with the red and blue silk trim. It's hanging in her wardrobe."

Beth thanked her as Santina scooted out the door. With purpose in her steps, she walked up the curving stone staircase to the *secondo piano nobile*. In all the years she'd visited Deirdre, she'd never been to the second floor. She breathed relief realizing that it was laid out exactly like downstairs with rooms anchored to the main grand hall. Now the trick would be to figure out which of the seven bedrooms belonged to Deirdre. She glanced into opened doorways and spied the opulence of the décor—satin brocade couches, marble inlaid tables, thick carpets over shiny parquet floors—and the bedrooms boasted damask curtains, hand-painted murals, elaborate moldings, and gold—so much gold—accenting everything from fabrics to wall coverings.

She figured Deirdre's room would be near the one the girls' shared. Deirdre had been adamant that her daughters would not have their own rooms. She'd disagreed with parents who gave into their children's every whim and thought learning how to share a living space would offer an invaluable life lesson for her little girls. Somewhere among the grand lavishness, Beth knew a room existed that would reflect Deirdre's loving hand—a place where little girls would feel welcomed and not overshadowed by centuries of extravagance.

"Aha," she said looking into a room, unlike the others. Two matching beds stood side by side, covered with lilac duvets and lacy pillows piled high against cream-colored upholstered headboards. Positioned beyond the beds sat a sturdy wooden puppet stage flanked by an array of marionettes dressed in elaborate costumes hooked onto the wall. In an opposite alcove stood a child-sized playhouse. Between laced curtained windows stood built-in shelves stocked with books, boxes of board games, and art supplies.

She entered the room and slowly turned. An easel caught her eye and the colorful painting displayed there. As she moved closer, Beth realized it wasn't a painting at all, but a pastel drawing of a lady. The use of several layers of color and the strong hint of realism struck her as an example of exceptional artistic skill for a seven-year-old.

"I wonder which girl is the artist." It wasn't until she glanced at the top of the drawing that she noticed the neatly written words. "*Mia Mamma bella*—My beautiful Ma." Tears sprung out of nowhere and blurred her vision.

Her heart ached for the motherless children. Though it'd been nearly seventeen years since her own mother's passing from breast cancer, the hole in Beth's heart had never quite healed. After Deirdre's funeral, she decided to take the girls out for *gelati* and offer support; let them know it's okay to feel angry and lonely, even scared.

With one last look, she took in a carved teak chest separating two gleaming white wardrobes, which reminded Beth of her purpose. She headed toward the wide doorway on the far wall of the girls' room, certain it would lead to her destination. The room was small and probably somewhere along the line belonged to a nursemaid. Though the bed was covered with an elaborate spread made from rich blue and green velvet, there lacked any personal touches that would make the room welcoming or homey. She walked to the window, pulled back the drapery, and opened the shutter. Light streamed into room. She looked around and found in its unassuming simplicity the presence of her friend.

Beth remembered how she'd tried to persuade Deirdre to purchase a vacation home in California. They'd often talked about it, especially when Deirdre would share that the weight of the years, the shadowed ancestors, and the ghosts that roamed Jacopo's house had taken their toll. Or maybe it was the cruel way Jacopo had treated her. If only Deirdre had unburdened her heart sooner. But now glancing around the room, she wished her friend had fled the lagoon city and found security in a cottage facing the Pacific. She sighed knowing it was too late for wishes.

She focused on the imposing eight-foot-tall wardrobe, which she guessed had to be at least a couple hundred years old. She opened the doors, slid out the brass rack, and began sorting through the array of clothing arranged by color. She paused finding the Gucci dress. The fabric felt creamy in Beth's hand and was smartly cut and had a simplicity that reflected elegance. She pulled the dress free from the hanger, crushed it against her chest, and held it there until the tears stopped running down her face.

Wiping her cheeks dry with her fingertips, she remembered her next task. Deirdre's laptop. She glanced at the burl walnut davenport near the window and not seeing the computer checked the drawers inside the wardrobe. Nothing. "*Janey Mac*," she said, "it could be almost anywhere in this monster of a house. Where to look?"

Beth closed her eyes. She fought to chase away all thoughts hoping against hope that her *fey* would lead her. *Upstairs.* She flashed her eyes open. *UpstairsUpstairsUpstairsUpstairs*. The words rang in her ears. She laid the dress carefully on the bed and headed for the hall.

The purpose of the rooms under the eaves, if she remembered correctly, was to house servants. But now, she assumed, it would be used as an attic for storage. She located a wooden staircase and hurried up the well-worn treads. At first glance, Beth's assumption had been correct as she peeked into several rooms filled with old trunks and what she guessed to be furniture shrouded beneath dusty sheets. The third room she wandered into made her heart skip a beat.

286

Deirdre's possessions from Ireland filled it—the couch, cushy chairs, Belleek pottery, Waterford crystal—and on top of the Williams and Gibton tea-table stood a vase of withered roses. She touched one of the red petals, and it crumbled, reminding Beth of dried parchment stained with blood.

She dropped onto the oversized ottoman surprised that the room wasn't blazing hot but then noticed the shutters were open allowing air to circulate and fill the room with light. A rush of anger flooded through her.

"How dare Jacopo send all of Deirdre's precious belongings to the attic." She stood and began to pace. After a solid two minutes of trying to blow off steam, she dropped onto the chintz-covered couch and ran her fingertips over the floral upholstery armrest. She wanted nothing more than to curl up on the comfortable cushions, close her eyes, and forget the distressing facts regarding Deirdre's marriage. She turned her head and noticed that on the couch's end cushion sat Deirdre's reading glasses atop an opened book, left as if she expected to return moments later to continue reading.

She jumped up and resumed pacing. "It all boils down to Jacopo's damn pride. If he hadn't baited her into a fight, Deirdre never would've run out that night smack into the hands of a murderer." She paused at the window and looked out. The view opened onto the rear of the house. She stood there for a few moments hoping to see Santina arriving back from the market as threads of cold dread filled her. Was it a warning from her *fey* or only her common sense? Either way, she didn't want to be alone in the house. She pulled away from the window, gathering she'd been wasting time.

I've got to find Deirdre's laptop and get to the church. Carmel will be waiting. She looked around the room. "Ah." She walked to the simple pine writing table pushed against a wall. There sat the laptop. She ran her fingers along the surface of the Irish-made table with a longing for home that she hadn't felt in a long time. Blowing out a stream of air, she decided that this must've been where Deirdre worked on her writing. "Her stories have to here, so."

She grasped the center wooden knobs and pulled out the drawer. A short stack of folders filled the space. She opened the top file and smiled seeing a paper-clipped document. Scanning the top page confirmed that it was one of Deirdre's short stories. She grabbed the remaining folders and found more of her friend's writings. All in Italian. *Carmel won't be able to read them*, she thought with a frown. The very least thing she could do, Beth decided, was to translate the words, but it would take some time. Knowing Carmel, she'd wait without a whisper of protest, regardless of how long it took to convert her daughter's stories.

She glanced at the story's title in her hand—The Cat Who Ate the Clue—*oh my, is that right?* She searched inside the drawer for a pen to jot down her translation. Not finding one, she pulled open a side drawer and looked inside.

"What's this?" She lifted a little pack that looked like business cards secured by an elastic band. It took only a second to release the bundle. On top was Deirdre's plastic-coated Italian Identity Card. Upon marrying, she became eligible to obtain Italian citizenship, which Deirdre wholeheartedly agreed to as a sign of her commitment to Jacopo and her new homeland.

Underneath the ID card, Beth found Deirdre's International Teacher's Card, and then two credit cards. She placed the plastic cards side-by-side on the desk. Three pocket-size photos remained in her hand. She laid them out one by one next to the cards: a picture of the twins, one of Deirdre's parents, and the last one pictured Shane and she on their wedding day.

"These belong in Deirdre's wallet. The empty wallet that was fished out of the canal. Why would she leave the house with an empty wallet?" She knew Deirdre better than anyone. "She wouldn't have. That leaves only Jacopo."

But why?

The thought grabbed her and wouldn't let go. She snatched the laptop, folders, and the contents of Deirdre's wallet and slipped them into her oversized tote bag. Her heart raced as she flew down the two flights of stairs, realizing that her *fey* had guided her upstairs for more than gathering Deirdre's literary works.

When she reached the *portego,* a sharp pain seared through her shoulder. The added weight of the tote bag caused her recovering injury to flair. She tried to steady her fingers enough to adjust the bag's strap as she lengthened it and placed the leather strip over her head, resting it on her good shoulder, and crossing her chest. Then she continued racing down the hall with the sound of her slapping sandals against the wood floor filling her ears.

She had to confront Jacopo. *I pray to God he's here because he's got a boatload of explaining to do. But if he's not ... right after I meet with*

Carmel, I'll head over to the Travel Bureau. She slowed her steps. *How can I trust his explanation? He'll try to play it off by pouring on the charm. I wouldn't be surprised if he castigates me for snooping around his house.* Indecision filled her. Should she demand an explanation and face Jacopo's reaction or contact Marinello? Not knowing what to do, she grabbed her mobile from her tote and called Shane.

She tried to keep her voice from trembling, not wanting Shane to detect something was wrong. But it didn't work. By the time she shared her suspicions that Jacopo might've had something to do with Deirdre's death, his response was to the point. "Get the hell out of there. I'll meet you at the police station."

Though she'd agreed to meet him after touching base with Carmel, she paused at the doorway leading into Jacopo's office. She peeked inside. He wasn't there. "Oh my gosh," she whispered. "Deirdre's dress." She was about to return upstairs for the dress when a strong pull to enter the office overcame her.

She stepped inside the room and walked to the desk, half hoping to spot another note from Nicole Shelby. The work surface was clear except for a couple of invoices. She glanced at them.

All from the funeral home. She dropped the slips and headed for the door but paused to look at the ancient leather and wood masks on the wall. She had to leave—*the church, Carmel, Shane*—but something kept her from moving forward. Beth prayed for guidance as she sunk into the plush swivel chair. Without thinking, she reached for the desk's center drawer and pulled it open. Everything was arranged in neat little piles—stamps, notepads, folders—she opened a narrow wooden box and found a couple of sharpened pencils and an expensive-looking pen. She shook her head, ready to close the drawer when something caught her eye. She ran her fingertips across the soft leather cover and pursed her lips. The word "Passport" was stamped into the leather in English.

She lifted the folder and flipped it open. For a split second, she believed her eyes had deceived her. The photo staring at her didn't belong to Jacopo. Nor did the driver's license tucked into the cover's pocket. The image was of Jonathan Shelby.

Chapter Fifty-Five

EARLY AFTERNOON LIGHT BATHED Lidia and Oriana as they neared the automatic glass doors leading into the Marco Polo Airport. Bernardino followed close behind, lugging two large suitcases. Lidia's brow wrinkled as she moved into the terminal and faced the queue of people creeping within the line dividers. Months ago, she'd believed her days of running had ended, but now, she resigned herself to the obvious. Jacopo would stop at nothing to ruin her, even if it meant going through her daughter. They'd have to flee Venice if she wanted to keep Oriana safe. Yesterday Lidia had picked up her altered passport with the mail from the post office but Oriana would have to use her current Italian one. With Lidia assuming her Austrian persona of Aleda Linser, it would be impossible for them to travel as mother and daughter.

Though the morning had been busy with packing and tying up loose ends, two serious matters had been addressed. Hours before sunup, Lidia had tiptoed into Oriana's room and found her awake. With voices hardly louder than whispers, they'd candidly discussed the events of the previous day. Oriana poured out her heart, and Lidia apologized for her profusion of lies. At the end of the conversation, Oriana half-heartedly agreed that it would be better if she joined her mother and relocated to Klagenfurt, Austria.

The second issue had been just as pressing. Oriana needed to be examined by a doctor. It was four a.m. when they entered the *Ospedile Civile* emergency room. Because she'd suffered a possible assault, Oriana was seen right away. To both of their relief, Oriana hadn't been raped, though there were visible signs of sexual abuse. Lidia had wanted nothing more than to press charges against Jacopo for molesting her daughter. But her fear of being arrested for Jonathan's murder trumped justice for Oriana. And that sickened her.

Perhaps, I'm being a coward. But since there hadn't been time enough to contact the Chief Superintendent and explain her innocence regarding the canal murders, Lidia's good sense urged that they leave Venice immediately. She hoped for a silver lining—that with a change of scenery, her daughter would rebound from the assault and the loss of her father.

Oriana made a beeline for the snaking queue while Lidia kept pace with Bernardino. She asked him if this was the right move. His nod wasn't exactly encouraging. "I don't know Dino; maybe I should send Oriana to California. Being with relatives could help her heal quicker."

"It might, but I doubt it. Oriana needs to be with you. You're the only relative she knows and, most importantly, loves. You're doing the right thing."

"I pray to God I am," she said under her breath as she inched between the stanchions. "And now that monster, Jacopo, has won."

"He's won nothing," Bernardino said. "You were the prize, Lidia— the prize he wasn't able to possess. That mask of benevolence he wore for so long has been torn off, and now his true depraved self has been unveiled. I pity any woman who becomes involved with him."

"But because of me, my innocent Oriana...." She blinked back tears.

"Oriana is strong, just like her mother. You don't have to worry about her." Bernardino placed the suitcases down and touched Oriana's arm. She looked at him over her shoulder. "Are you ready for really snowy winters?"

Oriana shrugged.

"Don't rely on your mamma teaching you how to ski. She's terrible."

Oriana's eyes widened as she turned and faced them. "You know how to ski, Mamma?"

"Enough that I can teach you the basics."

"I'd like that," Oriana said. "Will you come and visit us, Signore Dino? At Christmas time we could have a skiing holiday." Her face brightened.

"You bet. I'll even teach you how to jump."

"I don't know about that. I'd be happy with just learning how not to ski into a tree," Oriana said with a touch of a smile. "If only Chiara...."

"You're sad about leaving her?" Bernardino said.

She nodded. "I never had a best friend before. We're more than friends—we're like sisters. The worst part is that I can't tell her where I'm going."

"I hate to see you so sad," Lidia said. "This is all my fault."

"No, Mamma." Oriana dropped her carry-on bag to the floor and touched her mother's arm. "This is for the best. I want to be with you."

They'd snaked up and down two aisles, and the check-in counter was in sight. "We're almost at registration. Get ready to act like we're strangers," Lidia said.

Oriana nodded.

For the next ten minutes, they remained quiet as if preoccupied with their own thoughts. Lidia held Bernardino's hand, now that he had a free one, after relinquishing one of the suitcases to Oriana.

With only a couple of people ahead of them in the line, Lidia turned to him. "I can't thank you enough." She kissed his cheek. "You've been my rock. I love you."

"You're stronger than you think. I—"

"Oh my God. Look." Lidia motioned to Marinello and a couple of uniformed officers flanking the Chief Superintendent. They marched toward them with determined steps. She clutched Bernardino's arm. "Please, no," she whispered.

Marinello stopped and looked into her face. "Lia Renner?"

Before she could answer, Bernardino said, "Is there a problem?"

"We were at your office yesterday." Lidia found her voice. "I wanted to set the record straight. But now my daughter and I ... we need to ... we're going on a vacation." Her heart thumped, drowning out the hum of the airport.

"Vacation is canceled. I'm arresting you for suspicion of murder," Marinello said.

"You can't do that," Bernardino protested. "Lidia hasn't—"

"What is he talking about?" Fear filled Oriana's voice.

The one thing Lidia hadn't told Oriana was the likelihood of her being the main suspect in Jonathan's murder. She broke out in a cold sweat as her temples pounded, and her feet felt like lead rooted to the ground. "It's nothing to worry about." She forced her voice not to shake. "Once I clear up a few details with the Chief Superintendent, we'll be able to carry on and enjoy our vacation." Lidia turned to Bernardino. "Please, take care of her."

An officer unhooked the stanchion's retractable belt as Marinello gripped her arm and directed Lidia to move into the open space. He escorted her around the maze of line dividers and out of the airport.

Chapter Fifty-Six

AS HE DASHED OUT OF THE APARTMENT, Shane held the cellphone to his ear. He'd been put on hold and impatiently cursed the wasted minutes waiting to be connected to Marinello. Quick steps led him toward the San Zaccaria waterbus stop. He'd catch the #1 line down the Grand Canal to *Ponte della Liberta*, the bridge near the *Questura*. He pulled the *vaporetto* pass out of his pocket and stepped onto the waterbus platform.

"Signore." A woman's voice met his ear.

Finally. The long stream of unrecognizable words made him interrupt. "Please. Do you speak English?"

"Chief Superintendent Marinello is unavailable. Would you like to leave a message?"

"Yes. I'm Shane Dalton." He spoke slowly and spelled out his last name. "I have urgent information regarding the canal murders. I will meet the *Commissario Capo* at his office in about a half-hour."

"Yes, sir. I will give him the message."

A loud click sounded in his ear as the vaporetto glided into the stop. A few minutes later, he settled back for the ride along the *Canalasso*— Grand Canal. Even though Beth's discovery filled him with a strange sense of uneasiness, he decided not to dwell on his initial suspicion that Jacopo was mixed up in his wife's murder, but instead, chose to soak up the amazing view of the architectural masterpieces lined along the reversed S-shaped channel. There'd be enough time for discussion once he and Beth faced Marinello.

He'd just gotten comfortable when his phone ringtone jangled. Expecting to hear Beth's voice, he didn't check the screen. "Hey."

Marinello's voice jolted him. "Urgent information?"

Shane explained about the items Beth had uncovered and that the two of them were on their way to the *Questura*.

"I'll meet with you as soon as possible. Right now, I'm fifty minutes outside of Venice."

"Got it." Shane ended the call. The uneasiness that'd bothered Shane earlier hit him stronger as his gut twisted into a knot. "Dammit," he said under his breath. *What was I thinking? I should've met Beth at Jacopo's house.*" He tapped her number and placed the cellphone to his ear. It rang until voicemail clicked on. "Hey, Betty Getty. I spoke with Marinello. He's not at the *Questura* but is on his way. You'll probably get there first since you're taking a taxi. Call me as soon as you get this message."

He stared through the vaporetto's large window. Majestic *palazzi* glimmered in the dazzling sunlight, but they didn't register. His sight was blinded by an alarming thought—*I told her to get out of that house—did she follow my instructions?*

He tapped the edge of the phone against the palm of his hand. "For once, I hope to God, Beth did what I asked." He reached into his shirt pocket and withdrew the miniature bottle of antacids—he hadn't quite shaken the habit of carrying them from his tenure as a detective. He flipped the cap open and downed a few of the chalky tablets.

Chapter Fifty-Seven

"WHAT THE HELL ARE YOU DOING?"

Jacopo's unexpected voice startled Beth and she almost dropped the leather passport case.

"Good Lord, Jacopo. You about scared me half to death." She attempted to hide the passport behind her but realized it was too late for that.

"So, you've been snooping." He crossed his arms. "Deirdre told me how you like to play detective. Tell me Sibéal; do you think you've put all the pieces together?"

"I don't know what you're talking about. I have to go. Shane is waiting for me." Her heart seemed to be beating right through her chest.

She didn't allow her fear to show as she threw back her shoulders and walked past him toward the wide doorway. She could only come up with one plan; after escaping the office, she'd run like hell out of the *palazzo*. *Dear Lord in heaven*, she prayed, until his fingers clenched around her arm.

"You haven't answered my question," he hissed into her ear.

"Let go of me."

"So that you can give Shelby's damn passport to your detective husband? Like hell." He pushed her down into the leather office chair.

Though she tried to simmer the anger swelling through her, an image of Deirdre flew through her mind, and she gave in to her "Irish." She jumped up. "You're nothing but pure evil. The way you treated Deirdre like she was a worthless piece of *merda*." She said the word in Italian so he'd fully under her meaning, "It's reprehensible. And then what...you killed her? The wife who forgave you countless times ... cherished you ... who was the mother of your children." She paused for a second and stared

296

into his sneering face. "I swear; nothing will stop me from revealing the truth of how you robbed the world of one of its most precious treasures."

"*Brava.*" He clapped his hands. "A speech straight from the heart. Too bad I'm the only one who's going to hear your impassioned point of view. Though I must say your opinion is a bit skewed."

"Opinion? No. Facts, Jacopo."

"You don't know what the hell you're talking about. I loved Deirdre. But she could be bullheaded. Knew how to push my buttons." He shrugged. "Her death was an accident ... and if I played any role in it at all, I can be forgiven. Sticking your nose where it doesn't belong into my personal effects is beyond reasonable. Not only illegal but unforgivable."

"Then call Marinello. Let's see what he has to say about this." She waved the passport in his face.

"Now you're being ridiculous." He ran a finger along her scarred cheek. "I used to fantasize about you—like most men who'd ever cast their eyes on you. But now, I see you're no more than a conniving, lying, malicious shrew just like Lia Renner. My Deirdre may not have been a beauty, but she possessed the rarest of qualities like honesty, loyalty, kindness ... respect. I'd take a thousand like her for one of you—or that bitch, Renner." He pursed his lips as he stared into her face. "It'll be a damn shame to mar such loveliness, but you leave me no choice."

"You don't scare me." Beth slipped the passport case into her tote bag and withdrew her mobile. She tapped Shane's number on speed dial. The phone rang once before it flew out of her hand and landed on the floor. Jacopo walked to the still active cellphone, picked it up, and threw it against the wall.

"You think I'm some kind of monster. Contrary to what you may believe, my heart isn't made of stone. Actually, it was chaste, untainted affection that drove me to do these things. But in the end, my love was rejected, debased... perverted by the woman who scorned me."

She wanted to hear his wild ramblings. They'd reveal the twistedness of Jacopo's psyche but she wanted to escape more. Pinpricks of fear made her stomach constrict. She strained to come up with a plan.

"The sad truth is that I was smitten with my assistant. Yes, she was easy on the eyes, but most importantly... Lidia would have presented me with sons. Turned out Deirdre only had one viable egg in that body of hers—one that split into two—two girls." He frowned. "What else could I do but divorce her?"

"Except you changed your mind. Was it because murder was quicker than a drawn-out divorce?"

"Murder? I didn't murder Deirdre. She hit her head and died. I only made it look like she was killed by the Canal Murderer. A clever move on my part."

"Drop the charade." She patted the bag lying against her hip. "You *are* the Canal Murderer."

"Lorenzo Caravello has that honor."

"Lorenzo?"

"That boy will do anything I ask out of deep-rooted gratitude. Even though Lorenzo committed the deed, it was my brilliant plan to dump the body in a canal and cover the face with a mask. Disposing of Jonathan Shelby's body brought me great satisfaction." He paused as a far-away look filled his dark eyes. "But not to worry. Lorenzo will be released from prison. Today most likely. Tomorrow at the latest. You see, I did a little creative writing on Lidia Feloni's work computer. When Marinello gets an eyeful and presents it to the jury that ungrateful whore will spend the rest of her life where she belongs. In a jail cell."

"You framed Lidia?"

A touch of amusement crossed his face. His smile, always so warm and open, that magnified his handsome countenance, now reminded her of an image painted by Michelangelo in the Sistine Chapel depicting the devil. She shivered.

Jacopo didn't respond. He pulled out the bottom drawer of his massive desk and grabbed a couple items. "I had a suspicion these would come in handy soon." He showed her the *Bauta* and the tourist scarf.

Her heart skipped a beat. She'd have to think fast, but her mind refused to work. She shut her eyes, trying to channel her *fey* for guidance.

"Don't tell me you're praying? A lot of good that'll do." He laid the items on the desk.

When he turned his back to her, she raced to the door. It took Beth only a second to realize she hadn't been fast enough when he grabbed her arm and pulled her into a tight embrace.

Positioned so close to him, it'd never registered how short Jacopo was since his big personality made up for his lack of stature. She had to be at least three inches taller, but she knew he was stronger.

Beth sent up a silent prayer, and an immediate sense of calmness chased away her panic. She was able to think again.

"You are so damn beautiful." Jacopo touched the hollow at the base of her neck then ran his fingertips along its contour, across her jaw, and stopped at her lips.

She didn't react but bided her time.

He placed his hand behind her neck and pulled her head forward, close to his face. She braced herself for the touch of his lips. When the featherlike pressure brushed against her, nausea ripped through her stomach. She forced herself to kiss him. His tongue pried its way into her mouth. She ached to recoil, but she waited a few seconds as he explored every cranny of her mouth. Then she jammed the chunky heel of her strappy sandal into his foot. He released her with a yelp, and she took off.

Chapter Fifty-Eight

SHANE DOWNED A COUPLE MORE antacids. A few minutes ago, Beth had called, and he'd exhaled relief as he swiped across the phone's screen. But, to his dismay, she didn't respond to the handful of times he'd repeated her name. To alleviate his intensifying unease, he figured the problem had to be a lost connection and that being on the canal might be the root cause.

But what if it wasn't. What if Beth ran into trouble?

The vaporetto stopped, its motor humming, as he followed behind the flow of disembarking passengers. A new sense of impatience or fear, he wasn't sure which, had taken hold, causing his temples to pound and his throat to parch. He stood on the platform, needing only a few moments to get his bearings. Then he headed toward the massive terracotta building. He hoped Beth was inside the *Questura* waiting for him.

He looked around the lobby. No Beth. His stomach tightened.

"Dalton."

Shane looked over his shoulder and spied Marinello heading toward him. He turned in time to see two uniformed officers escorting Lidia Feloni around a corner.

"You arrested her?" Shane jutted his chin in the direction of the disappearing officers.

"We can hold her for as long as necessary. But in a couple of days, we should have enough evidence to arrest Lidia Feloni, or should I say, Lia Renner for the murders," Marinello said. "Where's your wife? She has the items belonging to Deirdre da Parma?"

"She's not here. My gut's telling me something's not right." Shane freed his cellphone and tapped in Beth's number. He shook his head. "No connection." He slipped the phone back into his pocket. "Beth was alone in the house. But maybe da Parma returned ... and if he is guilty of murdering his wife, then Beth could be in trouble."

"I've known Jacopo for years. And though he's got an inflated ego and a reputation as a womanizer, I doubt he'd ever hurt his wife, let alone, kill her." Marinello squinted as he tapped his chin with a forefinger. "It is odd that the items your wife found were in Jacopo's attic and not in Deirdre's wallet. Hmm," he said squinting his eyes. "I scheduled Jacopo for a polygraph, which he confirmed, but he never showed up."

"Seems a bit hinky."

"I'd rather err on the side of caution, so I'll send an officer to Jacopo's house—to check on your wife. In the meantime, would you like to accompany me to the Travel Bureau? I have a few questions for Jacopo da Parma."

JACOPO FUMED AS HE rubbed the top of his woven leather slip-on. "Damn her." He grabbed his business crossover bag, stuffed the mask and scarf inside, and slipped it over his shoulder. He touched his trouser pocket and smiled, assured that the switchblade would make the task of ending Beth Getty's life effortless. Adrenalin rushed though him picturing his stiletto slicing her lovely neck.

He raced down the wide staircase and onto the first floor, ran to the door, and found it open. *She can't be too far away.* He jogged across the courtyard and almost ran headlong into Santina. "Damn you, woman," he muttered. "Have you seen Signora Getty?"

Santina narrowed her eyes. He read suspicion there as easy as words on a page.

"She forgot Deirdre's favorite scarf. To hide the cut on her neck during the viewing." He silently cursed the housekeeper as he patted the leather bag at his chest.

"She ran right by me without a word."

"Which way was she headed?" he asked.

"That way," she said pointing in the opposite direction of the church. Santina watched as he half-walked, half-jogged down the narrow walkway. As she turned back toward the *palazzo,* Santina sensed she'd done the right thing by lying to the signore. Beth's warning still rung in her ears. *"Stay away from Jacopo. Go home. Go anywhere. Just don't enter his house."*

Santina decided she'd heed the words of her late mistress' best friend.

Chapter Fifty-Nine

BETH ENTERED THE NARTHEX OF San Nicolò dei Mendicali, gasping for air. Her heart pounded, and the touch of Jacopo's hands, lips, and breath clung to her like a coating of grimy, mucky filth. After a minute of rest, her breathing returned to normal. She pulled a silk scarf from the outside pocket of her tote, wrapped it around her shoulders, and slipped inside the church. In the soft light of the cool nave, she spied Carmel praying with a rosary entwined around her fingers.

She genuflected, slid into the pew, and sent up a quick prayer of thanks. Carmel opened her eyes and faced Beth. An aura of serenity seemed to envelop the older woman as she kissed Beth's cheek.

"Where's Deirdre's clothes for the viewing?" Carmel whispered.

Beth shook her head but kept her lips sealed. This wasn't the time or place to discuss what'd happened at Jacopo's. Plus, there was no use upsetting the poor woman again. "I think we're close to discovering who killed Deirdre."

Carmel sucked in a sharp intake of air.

"It might be best to hold off an extra day for the funeral until the perpetrator is soundly locked up and unable to hurt any more innocent people."

Carmel seemed to be considering Beth's words. She nodded. "I'll let Father Bustato and Father Martini know. I'm sure they'll agree it'd be wise to hold off a bit longer. My darlin' Deirdre won't be able to rest in peace until the poor, misguided soul who took her life has been apprehended." She looked at the string of beads in her hand. "I've been praying for mercy on his soul."

She patted Carmel's arm. "He is, indeed, in need of mercy..." She swallowed the words that wanted to spill out—not only did Jacopo belong in hell, but he'd get along just fine with the demons that populated the place. "My Shane is waiting for me."

"This hasn't been any kind of a honeymoon for you," Carmel said with a shake of her head.

"Don't be worrying about us, so. Finding Deirdre's killer is more important than any vacation." She squeezed Carmel's hand, rose, and hurried out of the church.

Beth shielded her eyes from the assault of blinding sunshine as she stood near the church's Renaissance portico. Without a mobile, she couldn't call for a taxi or contact Shane. She'd have to walk. *But to where?* Jacopo might assume that she'd head to the *Questura* to turn in the items she'd found. *One thing for sure, I can't be standing here in the open like a feckin' target.*

She hurried to the canal and looked up and down the channel, wishing that a taxi would appear. It's common for taxis to line the major thoroughfares of metropolitan areas, but here, with streets made of water and the price of private taxis exorbitant, she conceded one wouldn't be passing by any time soon. With an abrupt turn, she headed away from the canal, determined to leave behind the ancient lanes of the Dorsoduro as quickly as possible.

Lost without her GPS, Beth prayed that she wasn't walking around in circles as she skirted narrow alleys and followed the windings of a residential street. She decided that St. Mark's Square would be her safest bet where she could become anonymous among the vast throng of visitors. To help disguise her appearance she'd stop by a shop and buy a big hat and large dark sunglasses. *Once there, some kind soul will surely lend me their mobile so I can contact Shane.* Satisfied with her plan, she felt the weight of worry slip off her shoulders.

She slowed her steps as the street led to a square anchored by a church. Her heart lifted as she spotted a directional sign posted on a stucco building pointing the way to Piazza San Marco. She raced through the small square and found another sign. Before too long, the "drawing room of Europe" would be opened up in front of her.

JACOPO CURSED UNDER HIS breath as he looked into the church and spied Carmel; her head together with two elderly priests. No sign of Beth Getty. He left the church and walked along the canal, trying to figure out where the hell she would've gone. *She's too clever to have set off for the Questura or that damn apartment until she contacts Marinello. But without a cellphone, that might take a bit of time.* Time. It was ticking against him. He exhaled loudly, knowing what he had to do.

Chapter Sixty

NICOLE SHELBY COULDN'T HELP but second guess her decision to marry Jacopo. Especially now. He'd promised to stop by the hotel last night and then came up with some half-baked excuse about a remembrance dinner for his wife. *And now he's more than an hour late for our lunch date. If he's not here in ten minutes*, she huffed, *then the whole marriage thing is off.* She glanced at her rose-gold watch and started counting. The minute hand had jumped twice when the rapping on her suite's door pulled her attention away from the sapphire crystal watch face.

She didn't rush to the door but paused by the wall mirror, finger-combed her hair, and practiced her dejected expression. Another bout of banging sounded. "Alright," she said under her breath as she opened the door. Though she wanted to give Jacopo a piece of her mind, she couldn't because his hangdog expression reminded her of a little boy caught in the act of being naughty. "Come in," she said opening the door a bit wider.

He stepped into the middle of the living room with his eyes focused on the floor. "Please, Nicoletta, please forgive me."

"If this is any indication of how our married life is going to be then—"

"I wanted nothing more than to be with you, *mia cara*, but work is crazy."

She knew what living with a man chained to his work was like. She wasn't' going to repeat the same mistake. "If you're going to let your business come between us—"

"That's what I've been trying to tell you." He looked into her face. "I've had enough. Every summer it's nothing but headaches. So, I've decided that my assistant and bookkeeper can hold down the fort for a few weeks. I've already made some plans for us."

She widened her eyes, wondering what he had in mind.

"I've booked a flight to Los Angeles, and from there, it's your choice. I think we both need a pre-wedding holiday. We leave tonight."

Nicole's first impulse was to throw her arms around him, but she didn't want to give in so fast. "Are there any limitations—I mean—if I want to go to the Arctic Circle that would be okay?"

"I said anywhere. You really want to go to the Arctic Circle?"

"Of course not. But there's this little bungalow in Fiji that overlooks a white sand beach and a turquoise lagoon. It would wonderful to unwind there from all of the stress of the past few weeks."

"Fiji, it is." He pecked her cheek. "I'll stop by the office and make the arrangements while you pack. I'll pick you up around eight. That'll give us plenty of time to get to the airport."

Something was niggling the back of her mind. Then she remembered. "Ah. Tomorrow. Isn't it your wife's funeral?"

He nodded.

"You're going to miss it?"

He threw his hands up in the air. "Deirdre was my wife. But her damn family and that nosy friend of hers want to run the whole show. They've planned every aspect of the service without consulting with me about anything—from the music to the grave marker. Anyway, Scripture says, 'Let the dead bury their dead' and I'm going to follow that advice."

"I don't think that's supposed to be taken literally."

"Whatever. The bottom line is that I don't want to deal anymore with death. I want to live to the fullest—with you." He reached into his pocket and withdrew a little, midnight-blue velvet box. "That is if you'll have me."

She snatched the box and flipped the lid open. "Oh. My. God." Nicole stared at the seven-carat round diamond surrounded by a ring of smaller round diamonds and an additional row of diamonds that encircled the band.

"Nicoletta, will you marry me?"

She lifted her sight from the ring and looked into his eyes. "Of course, Jacopo. Yes."

He released the engagement ring from the satin cushion and slipped it on her finger.

"It's too big," she said with a touch of disappointment as it slid around her slender digit.

"No problem. I'll have it fitted when we arrive in California."

"But ... but I want to wear it now. It's amazing." She turned the ring so that the center diamond sat in the middle of her finger. "Why don't we spend the night here and in the morning get it fitted. Then you'd be able to at least say farewell to your wife at the gravesite."

"No, my *gattina*—my sweet little kitten—we leave tonight."

She sighed. "Okay. But the first thing we do when we arrive in LA is to stop by a jewelry store."

NICOLE HAD WANTED him to stay, but Jacopo begged off with the excuse of planning their little holiday to Fiji. That could wait. He had more important things to take care of like settling things at the office. Rosa was capable enough when it came to the accounts, and Arturo, his new assistant, a cousin of a cousin, was itching to run the show. *Well, he'll have his chance to prove himself.* But he wasn't really concerned because of Arturo's impressive work history and impeccable references.

He patted his pocket and felt the ring box. No way was he going to let Nicole take possession of the ring until he was certain she could be trusted. *The ring. Deirdre's engagement ring.* He remembered it like yesterday, the way he'd worked one-on-one with the jeweler to design the perfect ring. Everyone who saw the masterpiece exclaimed that it was breathtaking. That is, except Deirdre. A rush of heat raced through him with the memory. "It's too ostentatious," she had complained, saying that wearing the ring would make her uncomfortable. She preferred simpler ... less showy ... fewer rocks on her finger. Deirdre never wore it. Only that plain gold band until the day she died. If she'd had a reaction like Nicole, maybe things wouldn't have become strained between them well, that is if she'd produced a son for him.

He entered La Serenissima Travel Bureau and breezed through the main lobby without acknowledging Rosa hunched over a pile of invoices with a cannoli in one hand and a pencil in the other. He glanced at Arturo who seemed engrossed by his computer screen.

Jacopo entered his private office and removed the faux panel that revealed a steel biometric safe. He stuck his index finger into the scanner and then twisted the knob. The door swung open. He withdrew three thick stacks of euros secured by elastic bands. *There's enough money here to live in Fiji for ten years. More than enough*, he decided, to *hold me over until this canal murder drama works itself out and I can return to Venice. Shouldn't take more than a couple of months. God, if only I'd been able to finish Beth off. Then I wouldn't have to flee like a damn dog with its tail between its legs.*

He placed the money into a thick manila envelope and secured the packet within an inside pocket of his leather business cross-body bag. He exited his office and stopped at Lidia's old desk, now occupied by Arturo. "How are the new itineraries shaping up?"

"See for yourself." Arturo motioned at the screen.

Jacopo sucked in his lips as he concentrated on the printed words. "Looks good." He crossed his arms. "There's something I want to go over with you."

Arturo lifted his head and pressed the bridge of his glasses, inching them further up his aquiline nose.

"I leave tonight for the Cinque Terra. Some difficulty with a couple of my guides."

"I hope it's not all work and no play. How long will you be gone?"

"At least a month."

Arturo frowned but didn't comment.

"I'm putting you in charge of the operations here. Do you think you can handle running the Travel Bureau for that long a time?"

"Absolutely. Don't worry about a thing. I'll have this place humming as sweet as a well-oiled machine."

The over-confident tone of his voice rubbed Jacopo the wrong way. Even so, he trusted the young man and figured he wouldn't have to worry with Arturo at the helm.

"Signore."

Jacopo shifted his attention to Rosa.

"Another business trip?"

"The Italian Riviera."

"Again? More trouble?" she asked with a frown crossing her wide forehead.

Jacopo sighed with a shrug.

"You're not leaving until after the funeral."

"Of course not. I'd never miss offering my final respects to the woman I adored," he said, wishing he could produce a tear or two.

"Well, yes," she said as she lifted another cannoli.

Jacopo offered them a quick wave as he exited his business. He touched his stomach, realizing he hadn't eaten anything since last night at the Avanti Bar. A quick lunch seemed in order, but a visit with his daughters topped his hunger since he hadn't the slightest idea when he'd see them again. If only he could bring the twins along. *But,* he thought shaking his head, *that'll never work.* He moved along the shadows cast by the imposing buildings as a pang of regret caused him to almost cancel his plans with Nicole.

Preoccupied with his thoughts, he accidentally bumped into a silver-haired lady walking a small dog with a glittery collar. "*Mi dispiace.*" He reached for her shoulder to keep her from tilting over. A bit shocked that the woman hadn't chastised him for being careless, she only offered him a nod and a tiny smile, as Jacopo presented her with another heartfelt apology.

He started to walk across the grand piazza, having changed his mind about lunch. He'd order a glass of wine and a club sandwich at Caffè Florian. The usual crowd mobbed the square, but today, that didn't bother him. This would be his last view of his beloved city's noblest square for who knew how long.

As he weaved his way around tour groups, a woman caught his eyes. He couldn't see her face hidden behind oversized sunglasses and a wide-brimmed hat. But he was certain of her identity. Sibéal Beth Getty.

Chapter Sixty-One

BETH'S ATTEMPT TO HIDE IN PLAIN sight led her to mingle with the shoppers in Le Mercerie along the upscale stores lining Salizada San Moisè. Surrounded by people, a sensation that she was ensconced in a bubble of safety, eased the pounding of her heart. As she browsed inside the classic Italian boutiques, she fought to suppress the terror set to paralyze her by focusing on the beautiful items on display. The fine leather goods offered by Prada to the eye-catching colors and bold prints of Etro's over-sized purses and dresses distracted her. But only momentarily. As she lingered on the street, she didn't let her guard down, since with every turn, she envisioned running headlong into Jacopo.

It wasn't until she glanced at her watch that Beth realized it was early afternoon. *No wonder my stomach is growling,* she thought with a toss of her head, bouncing the newly-purchased hat fashioned of woven hemp.

Forgetting about her empty stomach she hurried her steps. *Shane.* He'd be sick with worry since she hadn't shown up at the *Questura* according to plan. The last thing she wanted was to cause him any more grief. *If only Shane understood the workings of my fey, he wouldn't worry so much. But he refuses to trust my sixth-sense.* She exhaled a puff of air. *I'll have to gain access to a phone soon and let him know that I'm okay.* Though she didn't want to return to the flat, fearing Jacopo might be lurking about, she wondered if she had another choice.

She patted her heavy tote bag, and her heart quickened with the thought of handing over Jonathan Shelby's passport and driver's license to Marinello. Unequivocal evidence that Jacopo was the mastermind behind Shelby's death and, though he hadn't admitted to it, Deirdre's as well. *After all this, Shane won't be able to belittle the veracity of my fey. Ever again.*

Her nerves tingled. She didn't need the power of her sixth-sense to know that Jacopo wouldn't stop hunting for her. Even being swallowed up amid the daily influx of sixty thousand tourists, a creeping sense of unease inched up her spine. She needed a safe haven—a place where Jacopo wouldn't find her. She inhaled deeply, trying to shake off the curls of fear somersaulting in her stomach. It didn't help.

As she walked along the periphery of St. Mark's Square, she forced all thoughts from her mind and decided to rely on her instincts. Her route alongside the Procuratie Nuove led her to the Caffè Florian.

She stopped in front of the wide expanse of patio crowded with tables and chairs. *Why hadn't I thought of this earlier?* Tucked inside the gilded interior of the famed coffee shop with its large oval mirrors and diamond-patterned tile floor, she'd be able to regroup and most importantly contact Shane. *Mario, that darlin' maître d'hôtel, will gladly offer me his mobile so I can get Shane up to speed.*

She'd taken only a couple steps toward the café when she glanced into the bustling square. To her amazement, she caught a glimpse of Shane. Not believing her fortuity, she quickened her stride and called his name. Intent on reaching him, she nearly tripped before coming to a complete stop as a tour group ambled in front of her. "*Suminasen,*" she said one of the few Japanese words she knew. "Please, excuse me," she repeated the request, and an elderly man half-bowed and stepped out of the line, offering Beth a space to cut through.

Those few seconds of delay were long enough to lose sight of Shane. Even so, she wasn't about to quit as she sidestepped numerous tourists and scooted around clusters of milling people. To her relief, she spotted him again. Shane and Marinello. It didn't take long to guess where they were headed. The Travel Bureau.

She ached to be within the security of his strong arms. Only then would the driving fear sparked by a conniving killer drain away. With added determination, she hurried her pace. She'd taken only a few steps when a viselike grip seized her arm.

"Don't say a word."

Jacopo.

Beth yanked her arm, trying to free it, but he only intensified his hold.

Now that the dread she'd been fearing had become reality, she faced it head-on. "You won't get away with this."

"Watch me." He steered her away from the Travel Bureau so that they were walking toward the basilica. She felt pressure against her back and feared it was a knife's blade.

"Venice is crawling with people. All I have to do is scream."

A smirk crossed his face. "But you won't."

She chewed her lip, trying to cobble together an escape plan, but her mind refused to work.

"I'm no fool," he said. "I own a dilapidated building on Fondamenta Bonlini near the gondola workshops. A canal runs right behind the building."

"Stop this madness right now. Let me go." She felt the pressure increase and now didn't doubt that it was a blade pressing against her.

"And allow you to ruin my life? No way is that going to happen. You see, I've got everything planned out. Tomorrow this time, I'll be with my future wife, Nicole Shelby. In Los Angeles."

"What?" Beth stopped walking.

He laughed.

"You and Nicole?" It took a few seconds for the implication to sink in. "She was your accomplice?"

"Throughout our relationship, I sensed that Nicoletta wanted to be rid of Shelby for good. But I swear on my daughters' heads it was me, and only me, that ended Shelby's miserable life. The plan was that once Shelby was out of the picture for good, Lidia Feloni and I would marry. But instead of embracing my offer, she showed me what an ungrateful harpy she is. That was a big mistake—as big as the one you made by snooping around my *palazzo*." He paused long enough to shoot her a wicked grin. "Once Marinello fishes you out of the canal, minus those bits of incriminating evidence, there'll be nothing to keep me from returning to Venice. With Nicole. By that time, she'll certainly be pregnant with my son." He tugged her arm urging her to move.

"It's not too late to repent. Don't you fear God?"

"God? Don't be ridiculous. Now, shut-up." He cinched his arm around her waist and pulled her next to him. "Keep walking."

A pang of despair hit when they neared the spot where she'd been amused by the little girl feeding the pigeons.

The pigeons.

Offering a silent prayer, she slipped her free hand slowly enough as not to arouse Jacopo's suspicion into her back pocket. With quick tugs, she wiggled out the little paper bag of grain and flung it. Birdseed sprayed around them like a shower. It took a split-second for a mass of pigeons to descend. They flew so close that the air breezing from their flapping wings brushed her face.

Instinctively, Jacopo raised his arms and released Beth.

Running through the kit of pigeons, she moved straight ahead toward the basilica.

A KNOT, LIKE A FIFTY-POUND weight, in the pit of his stomach had Shane reaching for more antacids. Close to two hours had passed since he'd touched base with Beth, and his police instincts were clamoring that something was wrong. Very wrong.

He glanced at Marinello, chatting with his cousin, Rosa. The words seemed to fly from their mouths, Italian words, which he couldn't make heads or tails out of, but he picked up clues from their faces. Marinello's expression jumped around a lot, but a frown seemed to dominate and that told Shane the news wasn't good.

"*Grazie mille,*" Marinello said. He turned to Shane and shook his head. "We just missed Jacopo. Apparently, he's got business to attend to on the Riviera. Rosa wasn't sure when he was leaving, but if he did have something to do with Deirdre's death, he could be planning a quick escape."

"If he's got Beth, we'll have to work fast," Shane said.

"I agree. I'll dispatch officers to the airport and train station to be on the lookout for him. In the meantime, we need to head to Jacopo's residence."

Marinello withdrew his cellphone, and Shane moved toward the kiosk of glossy rack cards. He grabbed a leaflet and stared at the photo. It was hard to believe that only three weeks had passed since they'd stayed at Villa Saraceno. *We should've stayed there instead of returning to Venice.* He exhaled a long breath. *Beth ... where in God's name are you?* He fought to expunge the rollicking swell of emotions racing through him and to think like a detective, but he couldn't. All he could do was remember his last words to her as she raced out of the apartment early that morning—'I love you, Betty Getty.'

"You ready," Marinello said.

"Yeah." Shane returned the card to the rack and followed Marinello out of the Travel Bureau.

RUNNING WITH ALL HER MIGHT, swerving around pedestrians and dodging between tour groups led by guides clasping unfurled umbrellas, Beth concentrated on only one thing, reaching the basilica. She'd find sanctuary there. But that measure of safety depended on if she could outrun Jacopo. She sensed he was close, on her heels, so she pushed even harder until she feared her lungs would burst. Her hat flew off, and her sunglasses bounced against the bridge of her nose. She pulled off the glasses and dropped them.

The seemingly impenetrable mass of people waiting to enter the church stopped her. Jogging to the end of the group, she didn't even consider waiting her turn. She began to weave through the crowd, apologizing with a breathy, "An emergency. Let me through." Most of the people gave way to her appeal, though enough grumbled and spat sharp words of protest that she almost wanted to stop and explain the gravity of her situation. The uproar behind her confirmed that Jacopo must be following her lead. Nearing the basilica's entrance, a crushing doubt washed over her. Dress code. She didn't have time to open her tote and find the scarf that she'd covered her bare shoulders with earlier when she'd entered Jacopo's parish church to touch base with Carmel.

After what seemed like an hour, she reached the guards. One looked at her with suspicion. She figured he'd seen her pushing through the crowd. "Shoulders must be covered. Ticket."

The other guard pointed to an opened door. "All bags must be checked."

"I need your help. Call the police. Chief Superintendent Marinello," Beth said in Italian. She peeked over her shoulder and spied Jacopo so close she could almost reach out and touch him.

"Hold her. Don't let her enter," Jacopo's voice boomed in her ears.

She rushed past the guards.

"*Aspettate*! You wait," One of the guards shouted.

At first, she believed that it would be safer to mingle among the tourists within the golden sanctuary until she saw that stanchions directed their steps. "Won't do," she whispered. "I need a hiding place."

Barging into the basilica had been necessary, but she doubted she'd get away with running up the restricted staircase leading to the museum. At the ticket counter, Beth slapped down the blue colored banknote, which she'd stuck into her front pocket that morning before leaving the flat. She didn't bother to wait for the ticket or her change.

She ran to the wide staircase and took the knee-crunching steps two at a time. When she reached the landing, she didn't miss a beat and hurried toward the small museum. She stepped through the main entrance right as a group of tourists pushed past her and exited. The room stood empty of visitors. Instead of gazing at the ancient example of mosaics or even pausing at the authentic *Triumphal Quadriga*, the ancient four Greco-Roman gilded bronze horses and one of the most enduring symbols of Venice, she scanned the room for a shadowy alcove, a deep space below a display case, or even another exit to make a quick escape.

Not able to even find a cubby hole, Beth feared she'd made a big mistake. No hiding place. No other exit out of the building. Dizzy with fear, she gulped a mouthful of air and steeled herself for the worse. She pressed against the plaster wall behind the arch that framed the massive bronze horses and grasped the sculpture's monumental base trying to steady her nerves. Maybe, she reasoned, Jacopo had given up, but not a second later, her intuition told her otherwise.

A wisp of movement. She dropped down. The stone floor felt cool on her knees as she crouched behind the pedestal.

A shadow crossed her face. "You thought you could elude me?"

She backed closer to the wall.

"Like a rat in its hole." He stooped with his arm outstretched and reached for her wrist. She shot up. With a turn of her shoulder, she jammed it into his chest and slipped past him.

Jacopo spun around. He lunged at her, missed her arm, but with his claw-like fingers, he found the knot of hair twisted at the base of her neck.

He pulled hard, sending her hairclip to the floor, and wrenched her head backward.

She glimpsed at his bulging eyes and his face flushed red twisted in anger.

"You are going to obey my instructions," he hissed. "Once we're downstairs, you'll apologize to the guards. Then we'll continue with our walk to the dock and catch a *vaporetto* to Dorsoduro." His face started to relax. "We'll sit on the deck, so you can feast your eyes on the magnificent view, which of course, will be your very last time to behold the beauty of Venice."

He threw his arm around her shoulder and squeezed hard. She gasped as what felt like a thousand needles pricking her sore shoulder as his laugh filled her ears.

"I have something to show you." He tossed back the flap of the cross-body bag and showed her the contents.

She caught a glimpse of the white mask nestled inside the satchel and twisted her head away. "Let go of me."

He flexed his arm tighter and steered her toward the exit.

A door flew open, and a ray of light flooded into the room. An animated couple stepped inside clutching their cellphones.

"Jacopo da Parma?" The couple spoke in unison.

He released Beth as the couple moved closer. Bright smiles filled their sunburned faces.

"What a hoot running into you here," the woman said.

"Wonderful, indeed. I'm conducting a tour for a very special customer." Jacopo nodded at Beth, grabbed her hand, and patted it.

She pulled her hand free.

"Well, we would've easily paid extra for such personal treatment," the man said with a chuckle. "You know, we've been meaning to stop by your shop. We want to set up an excursion to Verona."

The man spoke as if not sensing the tension between Beth and Jacopo. That was fine with her. She wished that the couple, who seemed friendly enough, turned out to be the chatty type. She stepped away pretending something had caught her eye, made a beeline through the door leading outside, and stepped onto the balcony above the basilica's portal. A few visitors strode along the long, narrow walkway while others viewed the vast *piazza* below. Relief flooded through her. When Jacopo would rush out after her, she wouldn't be alone. Tapping her chin, she wondered how long it would take him to break away from the American couple. Not much longer, she gathered.

Besides the view, the balcony's other man attraction were the horses keeping watch over Venice. The ones she now stood next to were replicas of those inside the museum. Grouped in twos, the horses touched the top of the basilica's central lunette whose "Last Judgement" mosaic reminded all who entered inside the church the ultimate consequence for a sinful life.

She stepped onto the stone platform right below one of the gilded horse's raised leg, and its hoof brushed the top of her head. From her perch, she spotted Jacopo. She ducked under the horse's belly before crouching between the five-foot-high columns that formed the marble bases supporting the heavy statues.

A couple of people traipsed near her, and though she couldn't understand their words, she easily detected their excited tones. She kept her sight riveted on the stone pavement and cringed when she recognized Jacopo's woven loafers. He paused, stepped off the platform, and continued walking in the opposite direction. A pigeon landed on the loggia's balustrade. Like the bird, she wished that she could propel off the narrow railing and take flight.

Seconds seemed like minutes as she prayed that Jacopo would give up, perhaps believing she'd been able to slip back into the museum. But that hope evaporated when he stopped in front of her and ordered, "Get out or I'll drag you from under there."

Determined not to budge, she pressed further back.

He managed to squat on the edge of the platform and throw his arm in her direction. Not able to seize hold of her, he yanked at the tote's strap that crossed her chest. He pulled so hard that the buckle on the back of the strap cut into her skin. After a few tugs, he'd dragged Beth closer to him.

"Stop."

"Get the hell out of there." He yanked the strap again, and the buckle broke.

Beth wrapped her arms around the bag like a life preserver. She had to act. She closed her eyes waiting for her *fey* to direct her. *Scream. Cause a scene. ScreamScreamScreamScream.* She let out a screech. He jumped up and stepped off the stone platform. Feet moved closer to her hiding space along with the murmur of curious voices.

"Nothing to worry about," Jacopo said. "Just pigeons flying by. They make crazy sounds. Now, if you'd like to move over here just a bit, you'll be able to see the two columns that welcome visitors to Venice from the sea."

Damnation. Now he's playing tour guide.

"The breathtaking view would make a wonderful photograph. The column with the winged lion, of course, represents St. Mark. Now if you look...."

His rambling faded as Beth decided to make a move. She crawled out from beneath the pillars as she clutched the broken tote bag. She was still crouched under the bronzed equine body when Jacopo appeared. A wicked smile jumped to his face.

"There you are, my love." He shouted the words, but nobody seemed to pay attention as they posed for selfies and looked at their cellphone screens.

She jumped down from the platform and headed for the door. He followed right behind, caught up, and blocked the entrance.

"Please, if I could have your attention." Jacopo's voice boomed as he once again took on the role of a *cicerone*. "The loggia is about to close, so please come this way." He opened the door. "My lovely assistant and I wish you a wondrous time in our breath-taking and magical city. If you'd like to book a tour or an excursion to nearby attractions, please stop by La Serenissima Travel Bureau."

Like a herd of sheep, no one questioned Jacopo as they swarmed toward the door and traipsed inside the museum. As the last group, a young couple with a small child slipped through the doorway, Beth pivoted away from Jacopo's side and attempted to scurry inside. She didn't get far. He slammed the door shut then closed his hands around her neck. She tried to yell but couldn't utter a sound as he proceeded to crush her windpipe.

SHANE WALKED ALONGSIDE Marinello as they headed toward the police boat docked at the lagoon. A crowd had gathered in front of the basilica. Not sensing anything amiss since crowds in Venice were as commonplace as the city's throngs of pigeons, he continued walking. But Marinello stopped.

"What's up?" Shane said.

Marinello placed his index finger over his lips.

Shane glanced at the basilica's loggia and noticed a figure waving his arms as if trying to catch their attention. The man was yelling something, but his voice was swallowed up amid the surrounding din.

"Come on," Marinello said. "Something's going on up there. *Polizia*," he barked. The thick crowd opened and allowed the two men to pass through. Picking up speed, they ran to the church entrance. Marinello led the way into the sacred building. Not pausing at the staircase, he ran up the steps with Shane on his heels.

NOT HAVING ANY OTHER choice, Jacopo released Beth. He'd been certain that all the sightseers had exited the loggia. The one that had escaped his attention was now causing a scene, and this made his blood boil. He rushed toward the elderly man who was leaning over the balcony and screaming some foreign-sounding words.

"Shut-up," Jacopo yelled and grabbed him by the collar. The man spun around. Their eyes met, and Jacopo read the fiery determination in the blue orbs that bore into him. The man thrust out his ancient chin as bony fingers closed into a fist, belying his feebleness. He swung. Jacopo ducked. Now enraged, Jacopo lunged forward and plowed his knuckles into the man's jaw. The aged man fell backward, and his head slammed into the stone balustrade.

Jacopo grimaced as he rubbed his hand, but he breathed relief realizing the man was out cold. The trickle of blood pooling on the pavement assured him that the remaining irritant aiming to thwart his mission was no longer a threat. He turned his attention to Beth who was bent over, gasping for air. He stuck his hand into his pocket, freed his knife, and released the safety. The blade shot out from its sheath.

STILL GASPING FOR AIR, Beth sprinted to the door. Jacopo grabbed her shoulders. She winced and a wave of dizziness blurred her vision. She refused to allow pain or fear to stop her. With a fierce motion, she jerked up her knee. It missed Jacopo's groin but landed firmly in his gut. He doubled over. She lunged for the door's handle. Before she could turn it, he'd snatched a handful of her tank-top and yanked her backward. She thrashed, but it only made him jerk harder causing the shirt's thin fabric to rip and Jacopo to lose his balance. Barely touching the stone floor, he stood and flashed the stiletto in front of her face.

As he waved the knife, Beth grasped his wrist trying to shake the knife loose but he only squeezed it tighter. She let go and slammed her elbow into his face. Blood sprayed from his nose. Not deterred, he caught her arm and flung her down. She crashed into the stone platform next to her abandoned tote. She snatched the leather bag and held it in front of her body like a shield. With a quick turn, she aimed at retreating to her hiding spot beneath the pillars, but he grabbed her ankle. She fell hard onto the pavement.

He stood over her. Blood streamed from his nose and dripped onto the stone floor.

"The police will hunt you down."

"Let them. It'll be worth it knowing you're dead." He dropped the knife on the platform's edge, wedged his hands under her armpits, and pulled her upright.

She reached for the knife. Before even touching the mother of pearl handle, Jacopo tackled her. Her head slammed against the railing's balusters. Exhausted, she conceded that he'd won.

"I have you now," he said swiping at the blood with the back of his hand. He lifted the knife and laid it against her neck.

"Okay," she whispered. He pulled the knife away and she struggled onto her knees. "You've won, Jacopo." She reached for the heavy tote bag and managed to stand. On shaky legs, she pressed against the side of the lunette's stone arch. With a renewed surge of energy, she swung the bag in his direction. As the strap slipped through her hands, it caught his left shoulder. He staggered backward. She lunged forward and reached for his arm. Not quick enough, she watched him totter backward against the balustrade. To right himself, he overcompensated and twisted over the railing. He swatted at one of the balustrade's ornamental spheres but missed. For a moment, he hung suspended in mid-air as his arms flayed aimlessly before he plunged downward.

Beth sunk to the pavement and peered between the railing's balusters. In his descent, the *Bauta* had fallen free of Jacopo's cross-body bag. The mask's whiteness glistened in the bright glare of the summer sun and laid next to Jacopo's body. Closing her eyes, she rested her head on the pavement. "I tried to save him."

Chapter Sixty-Two

BETH TOUCHED THE LUMP ON the back of her head and winced. The diagnosis, a slight concussion, had her admitted to the hospital. She sat up in the bed, dressed in the same clothes from the day before. Shane had promised to bring a bag of necessities: fresh clothing, toothbrush and paste, a comb, and most importantly some edible food. She looked around the private room, and a smile touched her lips, remembering how Shane had insisted that she wasn't going to spend the night in the women's ward. Here, she had a private bathroom, a television, and a window that looked out over a canal.

Even so, he'd acted against her wishes. Shane had agreed with the emergency room doctor that she should remain overnight for observation. All because of a wee bump. His sad eyes and doleful expression led her to reluctantly concede. The cheerless, sterile room hadn't lifted her spirits; in fact, it had the opposite effect—sleep had eluded her, while her head ached and her stomach grumbled with revolt—a bowl of sugared milk and a slice of dried toast had hardly sated her hunger. She'd had enough of Santi Giovanni e Paolo Ospedile Civile and wanted nothing more than to return to their little flat where she could snuggle in bed with Shane's protective arms around her.

Before that would happen, she was determined to shut down the haunting images that played repeatedly in her tired brain. Last night, as she waited to be examined, Shane shared the difficulty they'd had trying to apprehend Jacopo. After Marinello and one of the church guards had carried the unconscious elderly man, a true hero, off the balcony and blocked access to the loggia, they'd spread out along the precarious space. Not once, had she'd seen Shane, let alone Marinello or the guards.

323

As he'd watched Jacopo attack Beth, Shane's anger welled to a boiling point, but as he'd explained to her, he had to block out his feelings; otherwise, he'd be useless in his attempt to keep her safe. At one point, Marinello had cocked his gun and aimed, but he lowered the weapon, afraid that he might hit Beth.

In her mind's eye, the struggle had persisted for at least an hour, but in reality, the whole ordeal had lasted only a handful of minutes. The accolades that Shane had showered on her in the ER resounded in her ears—brave, scrappy, determined, brilliant—but most of all, he'd expressed that he was damn proud of his Betty Getty.

She grabbed the pillow from behind her back and fluffed it. Realizing that it probably wouldn't help much, she returned it to its spot against the raised mattress. She shut her eyes and prayed for mercy on Jacopo's soul, whether he deserved it or not.

"What's wrong?"

She flashed her eyes open and met Shane's worried face.

"Nothing, darlin'. But I can't seem to purge my mind of..."

"Give it time." He took her hand and squeezed it. "I promise you; I'm going to do my best to chase away those memories and replace them with new ones. They'll be made from a lifetime of being cherished by the man who adores you." He gently kissed her lips. "And I'm going to start with a redo of our honeymoon. How does a couple of weeks in Ireland sound?"

"Ah, my darlin' boy. I don't need another honeymoon. Being safe within your lovin' arms is all I'll ever want. Or need."

Shane leaned in for another kiss. This one touched her with more passion. When he pulled away, she wished he hadn't.

"Anyway," she said, "I'd like to go home after Deirdre's funeral. Then maybe we can plan a bit of a getaway."

"Sounds like a plan." He lifted her carry-on bag and laid it at the bottom of the bed. "I've brought all the stuff I thought you'd need." He tugged on the bag's zipper. "I've got a dress, shampoo, hairdryer—"

The door opened, and Marinello entered with a colorful bouquet. "I hope I'm not intruding."

"Of course not," Beth said. "My Shane brought some items so I can freshen up a wee bit since I'm ready to be discharged."

Marinello handed her the fragrant arrangement of wildflowers. "So, you're feeling better. Good."

She nodded.

"Please accept my apology. I'm very sorry," Marinello said with a shake of his head. "Jacopo da Parma never made it high on my list of suspects. But, if I'd insisted he take that damn polygraph the other day, things may have played out differently."

"Now, don't be blaming yourself, Commissario Capo."

"Please, call me Daniele. And you're right, of course. No use dwelling on what could've been."

"That's something we can all agree on," Shane said. He took the flowers from Beth and placed them in the small sink across from the bed.

"But I'd be amiss if I didn't congratulate you on your detective skills, Signora. The evidence you discovered closed the case," Marinello said.

"I can't take all the credit, Daniele. It was my *fey,* my sixth sense, that led me to Jacopo's study to recover Jonathan Shelby's passport."

Even though he nodded, a quizzical look crossed Marinello's face. "Well, regardless. Once Lorenzo Caravello was informed of Jacopo's death, the young man broke down and admitted to Shelby's murder. I kind of feel sorry for him... the way Jacopo manipulated him. But, at the end of the day, Lorenzo chose to do his master's bidding."

"Jacopo," Shane said with a shake of his head. "That guy was a piece of work. A braggart and a bully. A fitting end to the Jacopo da Parma dynasty."

"To think," Beth said, "his killing spree all boiled down to gratitude that Jacopo misinterpreted for love." She paused a second. "Though I wasn't particularly fond of her, what's going to happen to Nicole Shelby? I believe, she too, was a victim, but in a different sense, since Jacopo only wanted to use her as a broodmare after murdering her husband."

"I met with Mrs. Shelby earlier today," Marinello said. "I'm confident that she was not involved in Jacopo's reprehensible actions. By now, I imagine, she's boarding a plane back to the States."

"His selfishness caused so much pain. If only a sliver of redeeming value could emerge from this whole awful situation, then perhaps Deirdre's death wouldn't have been completely in vain." Tears filled Beth's eyes as Shane patted her arm.

"Hmmm. I'll let you decide," Marinello said. "Are you up to receiving a couple more visitors?"

"Visitors?" She inched further up in the bed, wiping her eyes with the back of her hand. "I don't see why not."

Marinello moved next to the door and motioned. Lidia and Oriana stepped inside the hospital room.

A wide smile broke across Beth's face. "Lidia. You've been exonerated. I'm so relieved and happy for you. And this beautiful girl must be your daughter."

"Thank you so much, Signora," Lidia said. "We owe you a debt of gratitude. Without you, Jonathan's killer might never have been exposed. Everything seemed to point to me. A jury, I'm sure, would've found me guilty. And then my poor Oriana would not have only lost her father but her mother as well."

The heaviness of grief lifted, and a bubbling up of joy brought happy tears to Beth's eyes. "Will you continue to live in Venice?"

Lidia nodded. "But first, Oriana and I will be visiting Los Angeles. She has so many family members and relatives eager to see her."

"How lovely," Beth said. "A grand reunion."

Oriana nodded. "It's going to be wonderful now that Mamma will be going with me. And Signore Bernardino."

"Ah." Beth shot Lidia a knowing look.

Lidia nodded as a rush of color rose to her cheeks.

"Say, why don't we all get together for dinner in LA?" Shane asked. "We'll be home in a week or so. And I know the perfect place. It's a little hole in the wall, but the food is out of this world. It's called *Mangia*, and it's a very authentic Italian restaurant." He winked as the music of laughter filled the hospital room.

Acknowledgements

The crafting of any book requires the keen eyes of others and especially so with the writing of *Death Unmasked*. For me, writing is an exhilarating experience, but it can also be challenging with the thorough researching of facts and the fine-tuning of awkward sentences and passages. My process was enriched with the encouragement of those who read and offered suggestions on early drafts. I offer my deepest thanks to Shirley Pratt, Debbi Mack, Karen Esibil, Geraldine Smithson, Lois Anderson, and Connie Sanfilippo.

Special thanks also to Sheri Williams and my editor Kimberly Carlisle Coghlan. I don't know where I'd be without the support and direction of my critique group, *Dreamweavers Ink Writers*: P.J. O'Dwyer, Mike Sage, Missy Burke, L.R. Trovillion, and particularly R. Lanier Clemons and Kim Hamilton.

For their unfailing support, I'd especially like to thank my siblings: Roy, Patricia, and Thomas. Thanks also to Pegi Taylor, Karen Brown, Janis Wasser, Geneva Fletcher, Pierre Parker, and Amy Harke-Moore. Above all, I'd like to thank my husband extraordinaire, Chuck Smithson.

CPSIA information can be obtained
at www.ICGtesting.com
Printed in the USA
LVHW021533280821
696353LV00007B/490

9 781952 816529